SCABBY QUEEN

SCABBY QUEEN

KIRSTIN INNES

4th Estate • London

4th Estate
An imprint of HarperCollins*Publishers*
1 London Bridge Street
London SE1 9GF

www.4thEstate.co.uk

First published in Great Britain in 2020 by 4th Estate

1

A catalogue record for this book is available from the British Library

ISBN 978-0-00-834229-6 (hardback)
ISBN 978-0-00-834230-2 (trade paperback)

The writer acknowledges support from the National Lottery
through Creative Scotland towards the writing of this title.

This novel is entirely a work of fiction.
The names, characters and incidents portrayed in it are the
work of the author's imagination. Any resemblance to actual persons,
living or dead, events or localities is entirely coincidental.

Set in Portrait and Frutiger

Printed and bound in Great Britain by CPI Group (UK) Ltd, Croydon

*This one is for Bis,
and will always be for Bis*

Though cruel Fate should bid us part
Far as the Pole and Line,
Her dear idea around my heart
Should tenderly entwine:

Though mountains rise and desarts howl
And oceans roar between;
Yet dearer than my deathless soul
I still would love my Jean.

ROBERT BURNS, 'The Northern Lass'

SOME PEOPLE

Adele Roberts – a nurse

Danny Mansfield – a tour manager, a husband

Donald Bain – a godfather (unofficial)

Eileen Johnstone – a mother

Hamza Hassan – a boyfriend

Ida Edwards – a woman on a train

Jess Blake – a comrade

Malcolm Campbell – a father

Neil Munro – a journalist

Ruth Jones – a friend

Sammi Smith – a girl who lives in a squat

Shiv West – a popular musician

Simon Carruthers – a man at a wedding

Xanthe Christos – a former comrade

Q Magazine, June 1990

Ginger Nut

Pete Moss sets to with pop's newest It Girl

Teatime telly was changed for ever one Thursday evening in March this year. Dads all over the country froze, forkfuls of egg and chips halfway to their mouths. Mothers tutted and turned their heads away, scraped plates jealously. And the kids, pressed up against the screens? Well, they'd never seen anything like it – a young woman defying those stodgy *Top of the Pops* conventions, unbuttoning her waistcoat to display a curve-stretched anti-poll tax slogan T-shirt underneath.

Clio Campbell has an . . . effect on people.

Everyone pauses to look at her as she walks into this bog-standard London boozer at lunchtime, in her lipstick, short skirt and casually scuffed Doc Marten boots. Their eyes are drawn by that shock of red hair and held by the fierce, piercing beauty in her gaze. They know her. They recognize her. They point. And she smiles at them, gently, accepting this new-found level of fame. Her eyes meet mine and she poses the question, unspoken. Are you? I nod; it's me. She folds her legs delicately into the chair opposite me and flashes me a big, bold grin. 'Fancy a pint?' she asks.

Campbell is, demonstrably, Scottish. With her head of scorched curls, her milky skin and her honeyed, lilting accent, she seems to have walked straight off the set of *Highlander*. She likes to keep her origins a mystery ('Och, I grew up in a tiny wee place. You'd never have heard of it,' she says, when I press her), but she will admit to a musical apprenticeship around the folk-music clubs and dance halls of the Scottish Highlands.

When she entered the pop pantheon earlier this year with the insanely catchy anti-poll tax stomp 'Rise Up', there were those questioning whether a 23-year-old girl could possibly have written so musically complex a song herself (answer: yes, she could and did). Her father, she tells me, is a well-known front man on the folk-music scene and it's clear that she must have inherited from him that swaggering charisma that borders on magnetic; her godfather is the session musician Donald Bain, a trusty pair of hands on any album and the man she credits with her musical education. But Clio Campbell belongs firmly in the here and now, not hidden amid the beards and jumpers at the back of a dusty old folk-music club. 'Rise Up' caught the mood of a nation, charting at number two and dancing angrily in and out of the top forty ever since, but Campbell's rise to stardom was not the conventional one. She had written the song to be sung by the masses at anti-poll tax meetings in Glasgow; she began to perform it onstage at rallies, and as her stages got ever bigger she was spotted and brought down to the big smoke.

'Like a tractor beam pulling me here. Like I'm an astronaut – travelling so far from my native habitat I don't know if I'll be the same again when I go back. Maybe I'll just stay here, floating in space, eh?'

She is here for good now, it seems. EMI signed her up for a three-album deal and she's spent the months since Rising Up working on new material. Her next single, 'Can't, Won't', nods towards the still-brewing political debate that made her name, but its lyrics are tamer. Dare I say, I ask, that it lacks 'Rise Up's bite?

'Aye, the record company asked me to slow down a bit! Not my choice, right enough. They said they wanted me to focus on the music for this one. If I keep making the tunes, I'll still have chances like this to make sure the issues I care about are getting heard, anyway.'

She sets down her pint of snakebite, the glass rimmed with red lip-prints, and fixes those eyes on mine. Then, in that chiming, soaring voice, she lists off a series of things that worry her about the way the country is being run – the government chief amongst them – with the truly earnest passion only a young, beautiful woman can get away with. I could listen to her all day. Clio Campbell, it seems, is ready to fight.

'Can't, Won't' by Clio Campbell is out on 1 June.

RUTH
Kilbarchan, 22 January 2018

On her fiftieth birthday, Clio had asked guests – if they *insisted* on presents – to bring her something they'd made themselves. Her friends, she was always fond of saying, were creative people, and mostly they rose to the challenge. Clay pots, hand-knitted scarves, specially bound books containing photographs, earrings, poems. Clio courted her admirers from drama students and young revolutionaries; earnest kids, basically. And then there were the crumpled faces and puffy stomachs of her original fans, the lonely souls who'd loved her at concerts in tiny bars and who still couldn't really talk to her now they were friends with her on Facebook. Creative people. People who were not ordinary.

Twelve days before Clio's fifty-first birthday, Ruth walked into the guest room and found her dead, surrounded by those gifts. Clay pots jammed with now empty tea-light cases, all their wax burned away. Scarves tied between the bedposts like bunting. A mix CD made for her by one of her lovely twenty-something boys ticking in the portable player. The empty packets of painkillers had been neatly stacked, the vodka decanted into a porcelain jug Ruth had inherited from her grandmother. Her kitchen pestle and mortar, a thirtieth birthday present, sat to one side, with a white residue in it. The scene had been stage-managed, set not just for Clio, but for whoever would find her. And she must have known that would be Ruth. Who else would it have been.

'Oh,' Ruth said. 'Clio. Sorry.'

Clio's voice, in her head, 'Oh fucksake, Ruth! You have to stop apologizing!'

When she made herself look at it, she saw that the body was contorted at a strange angle, one hand wrapped around her stomach. Some pale yellow foam had crusted around the left-hand side of her mouth and stuck to the pillow. Her face was wedged into an ugly scream – eyes screwed shut, mouth gaping open. She looked like a wax figure from a horror film, a shonky approximation of a human.

Ruth breathed in. The curtains were drawn and the room smelled sour. Then she steeled herself, placed two fingers on Clio's neck. She wasn't quite sure what she was looking for; the skin was cold, didn't feel like flesh although it had the same texture. She moved her hand around. There was no pulse. Of course there was no pulse.

'Right,' Ruth said, to Clio. 'OK.'

She pushed past the bed, opened the window, scooped up the four empty boxes of supermarket own-brand paracetamol. There was one of those supermarkets round the corner from Clio's flat in Glasgow. None near here. She put them down.

Ruth began to pull at a knitted pink scarf wrapped around the bedpost. Blood bulged in her fingers as the wool tightened on her hand. The scarf started fraying and she thought she might be disturbing a crime scene. She decided to leave the room.

On the line to the emergency services, she'd tried to be factual. 'There's a dead body in my home,' she'd said, when asked which service she wanted to be connected to, because she wasn't sure, suddenly, whether it was police or ambulance you asked for. 'I know I don't want the fire brigade, anyway.' She might have chuckled there. It's what you do when something's awkward, isn't it? You make a joke.

The woman on the other end of the line had a sharp Northern Irish accent. 'OK, ma'am. Ma'am? Is the body someone you know?'

After that was done, she'd looked at the phone still in her hand, and called Alison.

'Hi. What's up? I'm at work—'

'Hello. Clio is in the room upstairs, and she's dead.'

She realized immediately that it had been a mistake, calling her.

'She – what? Oh. Wow. Wow. What? What happened? Oh. Oh. Ruth, are – is everything all right? Well, no, of course everything's not all right. Right. Oh. Wow. Um. Um. Do you – do you want me – I could come. I mean, there's the marketing meeting at four, but I could – yeah, it's not. Right, I'll be there. I'm on my way. It's OK.'

'No, don't worry. Stay where you are.' The thought of Alison huffing about in the quiet of her living room. 'I just needed to tell someone.'

'Have you called an ambulance? Is she definitely dead? She's not just – I mean, what's she done? Er, yeah. Yeah. Suicide, I take it?'

Suicide, I take it. Clio would hate that Alison was the first person to hear about her death. Would have hated. Alison hadn't slept over at all during Clio's stay at the cottage this time, said that she didn't like to think of Clio listening to them having sex. Really it was that Clio couldn't hide her disdain for Ruth's girlfriend. She thought Alison was possessive and stupid, and she'd told Ruth so. Often.

Alison was still sputtering down the phone.

'It's fine. Don't worry about it. I think that's the police, now. Some-one at the door. I'll need to go. Don't worry about me.'

The policewoman was young; thin with order and neatness, a delicate single diamond on a plain band on her left hand. Already. Like a bird, a well-behaved little bird. Ruth felt huge beside her, rangy and child-less. The policewoman pecked at the tea and biscuit. Ruth had felt compelled to provide for them, although they'd told her to sit down.

The man, the senior, stood at the back of the room, hands behind his back, letting the women get on with the business.

The ambulance men were having a lot of trouble getting the stretcher down the staircase. She heard it knocking against the walls, their gentle grunts and mutters to each other. Something thumped, one of them swore.

'So, can you tell me the nature of your relationship with Mrs Campbell?'

Clio never, ever stood for being called 'Mrs'. Ruth let it go. Let's just get all this over with, she thought.

'Your relationship?'

Why did she need to know that, this little bird? She was just being nosy. She saw two older women – well, Ruth was a bit older than her, at least – together and was poking around after scandal. That was what.

'We were friends. She often came to stay with me when she was feeling depressed. She liked it here.'

'And when was the last time you saw Mrs Campbell?'

Scrawny thing. Snuck snuck snuck; her little teeth on the biscuit. The male officer looked up at the ceiling.

'The last time?'

'This morning. I made us breakfast, and she came downstairs to eat it. I told her what I was doing today – I was in a hurry to leave. She seemed fine, but I wasn't paying attention. She'd seemed fine for days. Fairly peaceful. I didn't think she was having one of her episodes.'

'One of her "episodes"?'

Yeah, that's what I said, Ruth thought and didn't say. Be nice. Be civil. Use sentences.

'Mania. She suffered from periods of mania, which would then throw her into quite a hard depression. Undiagnosed, but I looked it up – she fitted all the symptoms. She'd been like that when she arrived, about three weeks ago, but I'd thought she was getting better.

She'd been calmer. Talking about going home again, about getting back to work.'

The policewoman wrote with a translucent hand crossed by delicate blue veins, the pen fatter than her fingers.

'I wasn't expecting this,' Ruth said. These were half-truths – if that – and she wondered whether she was obstructing the course of justice by sort of lying to a police officer. Of course not. There was no justice to obstruct. It just meant they'd get out of her hair more quickly, if she told them these things.

'And is there anything else you think we should know?'

'I – yeah. The vodka.'

'The vodka?'

'I don't like vodka, so I don't buy it. And she couldn't drive, so she must have picked it up somewhere in the village. You should ask. Maybe someone saw her today.'

All those bags she'd arrived with full of her trinkets and faff. Because she wanted to be able to wake up in the morning and see physical evidence that people loved her, she'd said. Easy enough to tuck a bottle and a few packets of pills in a side pocket somewhere.

Those pills.

The policewoman leaned forward.

'Mrs Jones? Are you all right?'

Ruth realized what she was sitting on.

'Would you mind getting off that table, please? It was my grandmother's.'

It wasn't; she'd picked it up for a fiver in a charity shop in town. She wondered why she'd said that even as she could still taste the words. The policewoman scuffled and jumped up, like she'd been caught defiling a relic.

If Clio had brought the pills with her, that would mean she'd known, wouldn't it? That she'd chosen this death, in this place. Chosen Ruth.

Ruth didn't tell the policewoman this. What would that add, to her report in her neat rounded schoolgirl handwriting? A wee bit of extra colour? The outcome was still the same. Ruth couldn't have stopped this happening. And why, really, why would she?

A fairly open-and-shut case, the man police said as they were leaving, as the ambulance pulled out into the street. Seven o'clock now; those people walking up the street to get a chippy for dinner would have seen the stretcher tipped slightly as they cantilevered out of the door, would have hushed their conversation to stare. Goggling nosily at all of their futures, like people can't help but do.

Ruth had always liked the space in her cottage created by people just leaving it, when she could slowly take each room back for herself, get used to where she fitted in amongst her own things again. Today, though, there was silence. Too much of a silence. She stopped still in the hallway and tried to listen. Nothing; there was a large scrape from the stretcher in the new plasterwork at the bottom of the stairs, though. Clio gouging a final proof of her existence onto the wall. The work it would take to cover that up.

Ruth knew without having to go and look that the cat had gone.

Alison had texted to say she'd be there soon. Ruth picked up the half-biscuit the policewoman had left, in a saucer, licked the bitten corner with the very tip of her tongue. She should go for a walk. She should think about food. She should try and look for the cat.

It was the first dead body she'd seen, now she thought of it. It didn't seem to be formed of the same matter as the living Clio, the one who had hunched over a cup of tea and pushed away her toast this morning (those plates had been washed up, though, she noticed, walking into the kitchen). Just something left behind.

People. She should probably tell people. How did you do that, these days? Make phone calls? Post on Facebook? She imagined the cat out there, spooked and jerky, running away from the strange new smell of the house.

It did seem to have taken over, that smell. Like something gone bad in the fridge. She should get out. Look for the cat. Leave by the back door, so there would be no craned necks, no amateur detectives trying to get the story behind the stretcher. She couldn't find the key, so she didn't lock the door behind her, walked straight up the garden, over the little fence and into the woods behind the house. Wet grass already soaking through her slippers, but that didn't matter. Far, far better to be out here.

Clio had arrived at the platform with a battered wheeled suitcase, two tote bags and a sports holdall slung messily across her body. Her hair was frizzing out from a rubber band and her hands weren't still: they twitched and clenched as she glanced about herself.

'Here you are,' Ruth had said, walking towards her with her arms outstretched. 'Hello, my lovely. Let's get you into the car.'

When they got to the cottage, its rough white walls seemed to wrap themselves around Clio, swaddle her down. Ruth had lit a fire in the stove before driving up to the station, and Clio settled herself in the big patchy armchair beside it, pulled out a small embroidered quilt from one of her many bags and arranged it over her knees. The cat had jumped on, straight away. The cat loved Clio.

'There we are,' Ruth said, handing her a cup of herbal tea. 'There we are.'

Ruth had seen this before, more than once. The first sign was always the fluttering, the anxiety of her fingers, followed by an inability to choke a full sentence through her teeth without becoming distracted or rising into a panic. In fact, it tended to be this Clio that she saw, these days. It had become a bad-times-only friendship, somewhere as the years passed. The role she filled in Clio's life now was occasional care-giver and calm-bringer, and she wasn't sure when that had happened. Ruth had always enjoyed being capable; something about her sturdiness put people at ease and she liked it. Clio had reacted to that early on in their professional relationship, when she'd been futzing over lost receipts in the old office, and Ruth had poured her some water, ushered her into a seat and sorted the problem out. It had set the tone for the friendship to come.

The gifts usually came afterwards. A mix CD or a hand-picked bunch of flowers (probably stolen from a council display box) sent to the office. These days, colourful cushions, junk-shop vases and books with fulsome handwritten dedications on the flyleaf would arrive at the cottage the following week, after Clio had taken and recovered from one of her turns. And then she wouldn't be in touch for a while, maybe two, three months. Ruth used to think this was out of embarrassment; these days she recognized the terms of their friendship for what it was.

'Upstairs is all ready for you. How tired are you feeling?'

'Just sore. In my bones.'

'Are you hungry? There's some soup in the fridge, or we could grab a curry from up the road if you wanted.'

'No. I'm all right.'

Clio had her rituals while she was at the cottage, and Ruth would tick them off as the signs of recovery. After a few days, while Ruth was at work, she would lift the creaky oilskin that had belonged to Ruth's gran down from its peg, pull on Ruth's wellies, which were two sizes too big for her, and venture out into the woods behind the garden. Not far at first. Ruth would come in and rub her hand over the oilskin as she hung up her own coat, every day, to check whether its stiffness had been disturbed, whether there was any wetness still on it. She never asked Clio about this; old Frank, who lived next door and had courted Ruth's gran for years, would let her know.

'She just stands there,' he said. 'She's right still, keeping the house in her eyeline, not quite on the path. Sometimes for about an hour. No one but us would be able to see her.'

The singing would come back next. Just a faint humming under her breath at first, notes pitched into nowhere as she moved, or a slight drone floating over from the couch where she was reading. If all was going well, in a couple of days this would turn into murmured words, then two or three lines, then the sound; Clio's lungs waking up as they remembered what they could do. The singing stage was a delicate one, though. She was more vulnerable then than when she slumped in chairs without washing for days, fretting her knuckles together. At this point, Ruth would become solicitous, always made sure the cupboards were well-stocked when she left for work. Once, early on, she'd come home to find that Clio had cut her finger and dripped slashes of blood all over the kitchen trying to make soup. Discarded onion skins littered the counter, the saucepan had burned dry, and Clio was back in bed, her hand wrapped in the sheets, soaking through.

This time, though, the house had filled with song as Clio came downstairs each morning. Gaelic lullabies and old pop songs echoing through the hall as she sat on the toilet. This time it had all seemed to be fixing itself.

Ruth leaned on a tree in the gloom, puckering her lips at no one, making that kissy, squeaky noise that the cat seemed to like when Clio did it. The wet bark was cold on her hand. She thought back three nights. Clio had been smiling when Ruth got home, had ushered her into a kitchen full of fresh vegetables and fancy-looking bread and explained that she'd caught the tiny bus to the next town, to the supermarket.

'And let's go out tonight, Ruth. Just to the pub. John was telling me there's going to be a little gathering, with the instruments. We should go.'

Ruth was always more popular when Clio was in the village. The glamour of having been someone still hanging off her, she'd walk into the pub differently. 'Aye, Clio,' they'd say now, all the old regulars. If they saw Ruth in the street later, by herself, they'd stop her only to ask 'Our Clio not with you the now, then?'

Clio could usually be persuaded to sing, too. It didn't take much. They'd pull her into the circle by the fire, men her age or older buying the drinks 'for you too, lass. There you go,' as Ruth was made part of something.

She would always give them folk songs. Usually a bit of Burns, possibly some ancient ballad about a fiery lass who went her own way and ran off with a canny chiel. Usually, Ruth loved to hear Clio do the traditional stuff; that rough husk at the edges of the notes so different from the forced, trilling sopranos Ruth's teachers had affected at school. Over the years and depending on her mood, Clio had said she'd learned to sing from old women in the Western Isles, from traveller folk who went round the villages, from the vogue in folk song in the 1970s, or from her father. She put spit and soul into her song, and the old regulars would bump their glasses on the tables in appreciation, keeping time for her to weave against.

That last night, though, she'd been pushing herself, forcing out one last song and another last song even though the attention had started to wander, though the regulars wanted back to their pints and the young barman was itching around by the CD player. Her voice had strained, her eyes had gone flinty, intent on pushing a party, but eventually she'd crashed back down onto the bench beside Ruth and John, who drove the buses, seeming drunker than she could possibly be. Something about the way her limbs flew about, almost knocking things over, about the way she showed her teeth to gnash out a laugh at John's little jokes, the feral baring of them, reminded Ruth of her two tiny nieces, the way they went half-savage as they frayed and needed to be steered to bed.

'Come on, lovey. It's been a late one, and we should get going.'

Clio was tucked under John's meaty arm at this point, his moustache beaming down at her.

'No, I think I'm going to stay on for a bit. You go, though.'

Ruth should probably have recognized this as a danger sign, but she was tired and drunk, unaccustomed to beer. And for God's sake, she was not Clio's keeper! They'd woken her as they crashed in, a couple of hours later, an indecent hooting and old wheezing from the living room, muddy footprints crushed into the carpet the next morning. She'd worried that this would be too much, but the singing had continued over the next few days.

Oh, you suspected something, she told herself now. There had been some small alert trying to flicker on in the back of her brain, and she'd dampened it down, thrown a cloth over it, carried on with her life around the big sad fact of Clio at the kitchen table. Be honest with yourself, she muttered, into the trees. You were getting sick of her. You were. You wanted her gone. So you decided not to care.

She had been going through the motions a bit. She had. There would still be toast and tea but only if she was making it for herself too. Well, it had been almost a month. Longer than before. And Clio wasn't really giving anything back. It was all right, she told herself, to feel a little bit of resentment, surely?

The cat wasn't out here. She could tell. The cat hated rain; it would have sucked up to someone warm and dry, someone who didn't have death in their house. Ruth felt so tired. Maybe, she thought, maybe I should just sit down for a while. There was moss and it looked comfy, and through the trees she could still see her kitchen light.

Clio Campbell

Folk singer, activist

SUDDENLY, at a friend's home, 22/01/2018. Best known for her 1991 single 'Rise Up', which reached number four in the singles chart during the height of the poll tax protests, Cliodhna Jean Campbell lived a life of political integrity. Despite her undoubted beauty in her younger years the Ayrshire-born musician was never a comfortable fit with the pop-music establishment, which perhaps fed into her famously acrimonious divorce from music mogul and Big Rock Festival founder Danny Mansfield in the late 1990s. Notably outspoken on a number of causes, Campbell claimed in interviews she was 'married to the fight'. In 2011 she was a high-profile witness for the prosecution in the case against undercover police officer Michael Carrington, accused of infiltrating a group of anti-globalization activists. Campbell claimed to be one of the women he had slept with and deceived under the guise of an environmental activist.

In later life, shunning her initial success as a pop musician, she began travelling Europe and became a regular on the folk-music circuit performing invigorated takes on folk and traditional standards, and was acclaimed for her 2007 album of the songs of Robert Burns, *The Northern Lass*, although many traditional-ists complained about the hip-hop, blues and grime influences in the instrumentation.

Campbell was public on her Twitter account and in interviews about her struggles with depression and regularly played concerts to raise awareness around mental health issues. She had no children and is not survived by family.

NEIL MUNRO

See story, page 8.

NEIL
Glasgow, 22–23 January 2018

Neil sat there in the office, the near-empty vastness of it like a shock blanket around him. He'd tried calling her immediately but the email had been sent almost three hours earlier while he'd been on deadline, and now her phone slipped straight to voicemail. Her dirty laugh and a 'go on then, leave us a message.'

> Neil,
> Goodbye.
> Remember me well. Please.
> Clio x

What else could it be?

What did you do, with something like this? He looked around the office, where the skeleton crew of kids were packing up, heading out, yapping insults at each other as they went. Tell any one of them and they'd jump on it as an easy story, expect him to do the same.

He realized that seven minutes had gone by since he'd put down the phone. Those seven minutes could have made all the difference, and he'd just been staring at his screen. He called 999.

'Police. I think I want police. Or maybe ambulance. Yes, ambulance.'

'Can you tell me the nature of your inquiry, sir?'

'I've just – an old friend has emailed me. She emailed me a few hours ago – I've just seen it. And it's a suicide note, I think. And I don't know what to do. She's not answering her phone. I don't know what to do.'

'All right, sir. Can you give me your friend's address?'

'I – she had a flat in the East End. I can't think of it now. Wait, I'll look for it.'

He struggled to think of the last time he'd spent any proper time with her. Her birthday party – before that? Passing her in the foyer of a concert hall, a quick hug and a promise to catch up.

'Sir? We'll need a name and address.'

'Clio Campbell. Her name is Clio Campbell. And I don't know her address. I'm sorry. You'll know her, though. She'll be on your books, surely. She's somewhere in Glasgow, I think, or she was the last time I saw her.'

'And you believe she's sent you a suicide note? How long have you known Clio Campbell for?'

'I know. I know. I wasn't expecting this – well, you wouldn't, would you. But can you find her? You must have people's addresses registered or something – the electoral register. I'm sure she'll be on that. Please find her. I've tried – she's not answering her phone. That's all I've got.'

The late squad had come on, over in the far corner, were laughing and typing and taking calls, but this barn of a place, with its seventy unoccupied post-redundancy desks, ate up their sound.

Then he was swiping his pass through the security gates, stretching his hands out into the cracked pockets of his brown leather jacket. He hadn't worn this for ages, he realized, rubbing rotted-off lint in between his fingers. Years, even. And he'd picked it up today.

He shoved the pass into his pocket and headed down the hill, over the self-consciously shiny pink flagstones the paper had put in seven years ago, just before they announced the first round of redundancies. It was wet out; he felt it soaking through his jeans.

Clio.

She'd been wearing her red lipstick, that time he'd seen her recently, in the crowd after the Patti Smith gig, had smelled of rotting flowers, gin and something sickly as he'd bent in to kiss her and she'd placed a hand on his shoulder to guide him. She'd been with people. There hadn't been time to talk long, but she'd held his hand and swung it, squeezed it tightly even as she moved on.

He'd done all he could, really. He didn't know where she was. He'd phoned her. He'd phoned the police.

Now he was in the Albannach, with a tired young girl staring at him from behind the bar. Yes, a drink.

'I might be in shock,' he heard himself saying, 'so I think I need a whisky.'

'Are you all right? Have you been hurt?'

'No.' He waved a hand, held it there in the air, looked at it. 'Bad news. No.'

It was a double of the cheapest stuff. Rough on his throat. He coughed through it, sank down onto the bar stool.

The advantage of the Albannach now was that none of his colleagues would go there. This bar, practically pressed up against the office, would have been filled to bursting with reporters just off the beat (and on it) in the old days. Moustaches, shabby suits; later leather jackets, well-worn jeans just like his. All gone. The kids from the online team zoomed further into town, to Wi-Fi hotspots with craft beers, he assumed. The mobile reception in here wasn't good enough for Twitter; there was no jukebox. In his youth he'd hated this place, called it out to other members of his own young guard as emblematic of everything that was wrong with journalism. The macho culture. The refusal to embrace new ideas. The cronyism.

Well, all those cronies had been edged or insulted out by the new regime, the pay cuts, the rounds of voluntary redundancies and the Internet, and now here he was, the old man at the end of the world. He took another sip, nodded at the white-hard auld jake at the other end of the bar and felt all fifty-two years of his age sink through him.

He'd brought Clio in here once. She'd helped herself to one of his cigarettes while he was at the bar.

'Sorry, doll. I've been on rollies for so long that this just looked too good.'

Her accent had changed again, he noticed, a bit more of a lilt and whisper in it than before. That day, she'd wanted to talk to him about land reform. She'd been living up north, working on community buy-out projects, and she wanted him to write a feature.

'I'm going back up in a week and I think you should come with me. We're staying in bothies, because the absentee landlord is letting the tenancies go to ruin, foul feudal bastard he is. But the community there, darlin. You need to feel it. It's proper. I'm in different folks' houses every night for dinner – they're just so happy we're there and helping them. The bothy's basic, but people give you a few logs for the fire, or an extra blanket, you know. Come with me. You could write the article that could become, like, the call to arms for the land reform movement, you know? You'd be the voice – the first person to voice what's really going on to the self-satisfied Central Belt. You could become the expert; you could even write a book! Tell you, some-times, Neil, sometimes I think I might settle up there. Permanently. There's this initiative to encourage people to take up crofting. Tax relief. Keep a couple of pigs, grow vegetables. Does that appeal to you at all, ever? Be a good place to get on with your writing . . .'

She looked at him, full-on, that look she did. He was two pints down on an empty stomach, so it came out as a giggle. 'You? Settle? You're not going to settle down.'

'Excuse me?'

'Sorry. I just meant – well, it doesn't seem likely, given your ... your history. We're – well – I think if you'd wanted to settle you probably would have done. That's all.'

'What are you saying, Neil? If you're not interested in the story, I'll take it to someone else. Plenty of journalists with open minds and the vision to see where this could go.'

Brian McGuire, one of the old school, had chosen that moment to stotter past them to the toilet, the flaps of his grubby raincoat swinging about him.

'A lovers' tiff, eh?' He stood behind Neil, drumming thick hands on his shoulders. 'Just you come and have a chat with me, sweetheart. Just you come. And you will.'

Clio glared at him till he turned and left them to it, wheezing out an oh-ho-ho as he pinballed down the corridor.

'You've been at this rag too long, Neil. It's killing your spirit. What are you going to do – file stories on love-rat local councillors and keep cashing the cheques? I'm disappointed in you.'

She stood up, began gathering her many bags about her.

'Clio. Come on. Look. Sorry. Hey. Where are you staying tonight?'

'I'll crash on someone's sofa.'

'Well, I've got to get back to it, but why don't you take my keys, head back to the flat, have a bath? We can talk about this later.'

'I'll be fine, Neil. I've got plans.'

She always had plans.

By now, someone would have found her, surely. Four hours ago she was alive and sending emails, and he couldn't have been the only person she'd contact. She wouldn't still be living by herself; there would be flatmates, a man, maybe?

Was she dead, then? All that hugeness, that person, that Clio, had it just stopped?

Nine hours later he woke up to an alarm he vaguely remembered setting, under what had been Alan the sports editor's desk on the abandoned second floor. It wasn't the first time: the cleaners only went in weekly now, so he knew he wouldn't be disturbed. He coughed, inhaled stale ethanol from his own breath and felt his gag reflex jerk. Early shift started in five minutes; he had time to stop by his desk and grab the toothbrush he hoped he still had in one of the drawers.

'All right, mate? Need you in here.'

Craig, the new editor – Neil would always think of him as the new editor, even though he'd been there almost two years – spoke in scrubbed-up laddish clichés, an approximation of cheery workplace banter spread thinly over the top of his management style. His clean-skinned head shone out round the office, the faintest trace of sculpted stubble extending from ear to cheekbone. Even now, leading the early shift at 5 a.m., he radiated the smug certainty of someone who had already run a 5K and digested his macrobiotic porridge before coming to work. Neil, at least ten years older than him, was always his 'mate' – all the men in the office were – and never convinced. He'd been brought in by management after the fourth round of voluntary redundancies, after Patrick, who had run the paper for twelve years and worked at it for forty, had finally had enough and walked out. Craig was returned from London, from the red tops, to raise a family with his much younger wife; had met the new owners at a party, been lured back home by house prices and schools. Craig was not one of the team; mind you, now their union rep had gone, nor was anyone really.

Craig glad-handed the guy from ad sales who always sat in on editorial conferences now, as Neil took his seat in the circle, trying to keep a hand casually over his mouth.

'Big news this morning. Z-list celeb suicide. Possible lesbian thing. You know the old pop singer, Clio Campbell?' He puckered his lips, crooned. '"Rise up. People gotta rise up" – her? Yeah? Neil, mate, this is your beat? *Arts*. So I want you on it.'

'There's nothing out there about it yet, Craig,' said one of the girls from the new intake, her phone lighting her face from below.

'I've just had a pretty good tip, darling. This minute. Neil, here's the address the body was found at – you'll need the car, it's a bit of a trek – her dyke girlfriend's house, my source reckoned. Anyway, you'd probably want to talk to the girlfriend, maybe take Mike or whoever's on today with you, be nice to get a teary shot. What else – yeah, Suz?'

'Didn't she used to be married to Danny Mansfield? I could pop down their offices and have a chat with him.'

Neil looked down. He was holding on to the faded fabric over the knees of his jeans with both hands.

'I should do that. I know Danny. I also know Gordon Duke, back from when he and Clio were an item. I'm your man on this one, Craig.'

The boy two seats along was making a show of wincing at Neil's breath, but Craig smiled, a thin baring of teeth.

'Excellent, mate, excellent. Suz, you get out to this village, babes. You do the additional on this. Aidan, we'll want pics from the archive – a couple from when she was young and sexy and the worst one you can find of her from nowadays, eh? I mean, it's a tragic story. We should go big. Neil, mate, how do you feel about a tied-in obit? You're probably pretty good on this one, right? Something appropriately sombre, you know the stuff. The lovers, the headlines, big beats: two hundred and fifty words. It's not like she's Kylie Minogue or anything.'

In the corridor, after, Neil grabbed at Suzanne's shoulder. She glared at him.

'Suzanne. Don't do it like that. Don't doorstep a grieving woman, for God's sake. That's not what we do.'

'OK, thanks,' she said, turning away from him.

'Wait! Wait. Craig was giving you the wrong steer there. She's not a lesbian. I know – knew – her. Have done for years. It's not a dyke thing.'

'OK,' she said again, and walked off to the car park.

He wondered who the woman was – some friend of Clio's, some paranoid, dreadlocked old protester with a kind heart and a spare room, probably. Poor cow. He thought of the name blipping across police radios, picked up by whichever old boy Craig was keeping in expensive whisky. It was comforting to know that some aspects of the fourth estate remained unchanged. The very worst aspects, right enough. The end of the world was coming and, even as the human-built institutions of the past two hundred years rotted away, their cancerous old bones still stood. Anything pure or graceful about this job was long gone, really, wasn't it?

Two hundred and fifty words.

Linwood, 1989

Gogsy Duke's kitchen. A thin open galley with its bare light bulb, rusty hob and a sink jammed with mucky crockery. He'd woken up on the sofa by the doorway, covered in a pink crochet blanket, with a strong baccy scent in his nostrils and very little idea how he'd got there. They'd been in the Welly up at the new community centre, couple of drinks, and Gogsy had called him over, locked him deep into conversation. He remembered a stumble, a realization that he'd left his keys and his mum would kill him; he remembered Gogsy's voice, an arm wrapped round his neck, a whiff of sweat.

She was leaning on the kitchen unit, tapping a rollie into a mug, wrapped up in a rich green dressing gown; a streak of colour that shouldn't have been there, in amongst the brown ordinariness of Gogsy's house. All that red, red hair in a bundle on top of her head. He fumbled about for his glasses, and she swam into focus. Her skin was pink and he was struck by how very young she must be.

'Hullo.'

'Hullo yourself.'

'Mind if I—?'

'Go for it.'

He squeezed past her, careful not to brush up against the dressing gown, tried not to breathe. He was conscious of the sticky film of sleep on his skin, the raw smell of himself, the stain on the leg of the jeans he'd slept in. The tap sputtered and farted water all over his hands, his T-shirt, everywhere but into the mug he'd held underneath it.

'Fuck!'

She laughed. Three notes, bell-clear.

'That thing's walloped. Don't worry. I'll get you a spare one of Gogsy's.'

She was back in a minute with a faded Deacon Blue tour shirt. She smiled at him, revealing a single deep dimple in her left cheek, big enough to stick his finger into.

'I'll give you some privacy.'

She turned her back, faced the cooker, laughed again.

'Thanks.'

'Are you wanting some breakfast?'

He was battling with the T-shirt, trying to pull it over his head quickly, suck in his stomach.

'Yeah . . . yeah, that would be great.'

She hunted around the cupboards, found two eggs and the few end slices of a loaf of Mother's Pride in a waxy bag. He liked the way she moved: quick, certain motion under the classy drape of her dressing gown. The deep green chimed off her eyes. When she stretched up to the shelf he realized that she wasn't wearing a bra.

'So, bit of a late one last night, eh?'

'Eh. You're not wrong.'

'Youse must have stoated in at about two in the morning!'

'Uh. Really?'

Yeah, that's a killer comeback, Neil. Killer.

The eggs hissed as she cracked them into the fat.

'I'm Cliodhna, anyway. Clio.'

'Neil. I'm Neil.'

'Hi, Neil. Do you want to get that bread buttered?'

She gave him that smile again, all the way. A little curl was breaking loose from her topknot, slipping slowly down into her face as she wielded a spatula and the grease jumped and spat. He forced himself not to reach out and stroke it back in for her, concentrated instead on sawing chunks off a fridge-solid block of butter, a constellation of crumbs pushed into its surface.

'So. Neil. Where did you come from?'

He'd wanted to ask her the same question, actually – her accent wasn't local at all. Could be Borders, could be Highland, could be something else entirely. But he didn't get to ask or answer, as the atmosphere changed sharply. Gogsy pushed his way into the kitchen, soft in vest and Y-fronts, crooning Wet Wet Wet's 'Angel Eyes' with transatlantic soul, shoving past Neil to slip his arms round her waist from behind. His smell – Brut, sweat, stale booze – filled the tiny space. Neil retreated to the couch.

'See you've met ma wee honey then, eh?'

He planted a big wet kiss on her neck. She was tall but thin; he was twice the size of her, his big arms. 'Smart as a whip, this yin. Wee genius.'

'There's only two eggs, Gogs, so that'll be breakfast for me and your guest.'

'Aye, aye. No problem, hen.' Gogsy bent down to the fridge, cracked open a can of beer.

'Only one way I'm going to get through this, know what I mean?' He burped, loud, nodded approvingly at the air around his mouth, then grooved over to the LP player and set the Clash spinning through the house, hooting along to the loose background sounds of 'London Calling'.

'Still drunk!' said Clio, smiling that way at Neil again to include him in the joke, bind the two of them back together, as she served him egg and tough bread, lumpen with cold butter.

Gogsy stood behind him as he ate, rubbing his shoulders. Gogsy was always this familiar, liked to touch everyone. Nobody minded; it was just Gogsy. It was just his way, they said. He never forgot a name, either; had started talking to Neil when he'd noticed him standing on the touchline of the pub league Saturday football game with a notepad, then called him over in the street one day.

'It's the reporter boy, isn't it? Neil, aye? Good to see you, pal, good to see you. Listen, got a wee story for you as it happens. Me and the boys here are doing a wee bit of leafleting, all furra good cause, right now. We're trying to raise awareness of whit the housin association are trying to get past on their tenants – it's another rent increase, basically, while the lifts in they high flats have been stuck for almost six months now. There's poor wee old ladies in there can't get their shopping in because they cannae manage with the stairs. I mean, I've got my pals here trying to do messages for them when they can, but do you not think it's a scandal? Thought mibbe a wee article in the local paper might do right by them, light a wee fire under certain backsides if you know what I'm saying?'

Neil, who was new to the job and the beat, had just moved back in with his mum after a couple of years away, assumed at first that Gogsy was a wannabe gangster, trying to make a name for himself. He suspected protection rackets, worried what those old ladies were expected to give back out of their shopping in return for one of Gogsy's 'boys' collecting it for them. He thought this might be the making of him, imagined smashing a profiteering ring, an exclusive, a press award, job invites in Glasgow or even London. His imagination roamed so fast and far that he was almost disappointed when the story revealed itself to be exactly what Gogsy had said it was: the housing association on the make. The photographer got shots of the old ladies, Gogsy grinning with them by their fireplaces. The local council elections were over a year away, but Gogsy was playing the long game.

He'd pulled Neil into his circle; at first, some of the men had been suspicious of him, but Gogsy's word was like a passport. These were factory workers and union men, most of whom had worked at the car factory until it had been closed down. There was no work for anyone in this town any more, and Gogsy had been clear with them; their anger would only serve them if they used it productively. It was the poll tax had given him purpose, though; a clear enemy, a line of fire. He organized one of the earliest Anti-Poll Tax Unions in the country and started reading groups to discuss basic Marxist texts. He got his 'boys' out blockading houses marked for warrant sales so the sheriff's officers had to get back into their car, drive slowly away past jeering immovable walls of people. Then he turned his eye to the estate, to the work the council weren't doing. The hardware store donated a couple of tins of paint, after the owner was mown down by Gogsy's lightning-fast patter, so that the team could get to work tidying up 'they clatty fences along the Glasgow Road'. Grievances were addressed, civic issues put to rights, and the day Gogsy's boys filled in the pothole on the high street that had been left there for years went down in local history. There was never any doubt, when the election came around, that even lifelong Tory voters were going to put their crosses in the box by the local boy. And Neil had been there – a useful tool at first, sure, but very quickly a friend and even a believer – reporting on it all. The *Daily Duke*, some of the boys had started calling the local paper, as Neil's editor didn't really seem to notice the number of times his one reporter came to the same source for quotes. So Gogsy's hands were on his shoulders? It was allowed. And it felt good.

'My man Neil here is the local hotshot reporter, babe. Maybe he could make you a star. Actually, couple of wee geniuses here the both of you. Clio went to the college like you. She was doing music, though. Neily the boy wonder's got a proper diploma in journalism, haven't you, pal? He can do all that shorthand stuff. He knows it.'

Gogsy himself had gone to Glasgow University, but he didn't like people to mention it.

'I never got my diploma,' Clio said. 'Well impressed with you, like. My daddy's a folk singer, and I found out they couldn't teach me anything at the college I didn't already know, so I ended up skiving off to do my own gigs. Bit different when you're actually learning a trade, now.'

The baton was passed back to Neil with a smile he got lost in, and he found he didn't know what to say.

The Welly, a Thursday maybe. Everyone pulling notes out of their giro envelopes, getting rounds, slapping backs. The boys from the Militant were over in one corner, some of their wives and girlfriends sitting bored nearby, sharing a packet of crisps and lighting fags for each other. Clio was amongst them, thinner and taller, her clothes and make-up brighter, her long fingers flexing around a half-pint glass. The jukebox had broken, so that auld wife off the Glenbrae had started singing – 'Ohhh, Danny Boy' – and the older ones across the room were clapping or thumping the bar in time, slurring along. And Clio was suddenly up and over there, as the final chorus ended, quick, small movements, kneeling at the side of the auld wife from the Glenbrae, holding her hand. They did 'These Are My Mountains' together, Clio's voice pulling against and high above the old woman's burr, taking the whole room with her. Neil had never heard the Welly so quiet before, never seen such an explosion of applause afterwards. Gogsy was looking on, pleased; he pulled her in to him as she went back to the table and planted a wet, showy kiss of ownership on her neck, called out, 'That's ma girl! That's ma girl!'

Once you were Gogsy's, you were Gogsy's. Neil watched Clio walk down by the shops, afterwards, the heads turning like she was Madonna let loose on a housing scheme. Perhaps they would have done anyway; Clio didn't look like anyone else round here. She went into the butcher's and he decided his mum could probably do with some bacon.

'Aye, well, it's for Gogsy, intit?' The butcher was winking at her as he went in, shaking his head at the proffered purse. 'At boy sorted my brother out with a wee problem recently.'

'He's like the Godfather, isn't he?' Clio said, as they had a cup of tea together in the chippy. 'I've hitched my wagon to a Mafia don. Go on, Neil, you can tell me.'

Say something, he told himself. You need to actually talk to her.

'Honestly? I thought so too when I first met him. But then I looked into it, and I realized, he's just a very, very community-minded good guy.'

'Yeah,' she said, pulling a face. 'That's what I was afraid of.'

Neil grinned at the sacrilege, began to relax a little.

'I mean, don't get me wrong. He's got his eye on the prize, likes –'

She puffed her cheeks, blew out a gust, warm on his face. 'Tell me about it. He'll be Councillor Duke before the ballot's even counted. Right now I reckon the only problem he's going to have is that nobody will be looking for the name Gordon on the paper . . .'

'Do you mind me asking how you met him? It's just, you seem so—'

He didn't know, in that second, what she seemed. She waited a grace note to see if he would finish.

'Politics, politics. What else would it be? With this one? I went along to a poll tax meeting in Glasgow. He was one of the speakers, and of course, being Gogsy, he blew the rest of them away. I asked him a question afterwards; he asked me for a drink, course he did. I was dropping out of college, staying in a crappy hostel at the time, and he suggested I move in with him after something like two dates. So it goes.'

'So, you're into all this stuff? All the Marxist theory, all the left-wing – it's not . . . you know.'

She did a laugh like something out of the movies. 'You saying that because I'm a girl? Honey, I was born to this stuff. I was singing "The Red Flag" while you were still stumbling over "Baa Baa Black Sheep".'

'That's not – not what I meant.' It had been what he'd meant. She tapped her CAN'T PAY, WON'T PAY badge.

'It's all important, this. And Gogs, he knows why. I wasn't just a wee runaway in need of a home, you know. Well, I was, but still. I could tell Gogs was trying to do something here. He spoke about what he'd been trying to do with all the unemployed men in this community, and I thought, that sounds like the sort of place I could be. He's gonny be a great man, is Gordon Duke. Save a lot of lives. I mean it.'

Warrant-sale protest. The third one they'd known about; the first one Neil's editor had actually suggested he cover. Over the opening of the new bingo hall, too. Clio, formidable, stood in a phalanx of women, all of them smoking and staring, faces hard-set. Clio's fingers were wrapped around those of Neil's own mother, which was as big a shock as he'd ever had. Clio's bright T-shirt and Doc Martens, his mum's good coat.

'We're the first line of defence,' Clio said, brisk and formal into his tape recorder. 'Our theory is that none of these, ah, gentlemen, are going to be able to touch a woman. We reckon their bosses might take it a bit more seriously than if one of the boys back there got hit "accidentally", eh?' She nodded to Gogsy's ring of muscle, massed in front of the front door.

'That's right, hen,' muttered a couple of the women around her. Neil's mum nodded with her chin once, although she looked scared.

Clio followed his eye.

'And I'll look after your mum, Neil. Don't worry. Throw my body in front of her if I have to, isn't that right, Mrs Munro?'

'Ach, it's oor Carol, Neil. She cannae even walk. She isnae trying to make a point of not paying or anything, son – she just cannae get oot the hoose. I'm no lettin those bastards in there.' His mother pulled herself up to her full five foot, smiled at Clio with fire in her face.

The blue sedan everyone now recognized as belonging to the sheriff's officers pulled into the street. Clio nodded and the women linked their arms, began hissing, their spit and smoke thickening the air.

*

She was the only woman on Gogsy's canvassing team, and she preferred to go it alone. Gogsy was standing as the Socialist candidate, and had somehow enlisted what seemed like every resource the national party had to his cause.

'It's because he's the only one with a chance of winning,' Clio had snorted, when Neil mentioned it. He'd made the excuse that he was writing a piece, to come out with her; she had no intention of walking the beat with any of Gogsy's monkeys, she'd whispered. He was trotting alongside her, trying to keep pace; in her high heels she was much taller than him.

'Och, they'd be fine. They'd be fine, but it'd only be because I'm Gogsy's girl. They'd say, "Oh, I'll get this, sweetheart, you just smile," at every door. They'd talk over me if I tried to speak, and they'd maybe pat my bum on the way down a garden path. Just for fun. I know these boys. Every time I go to a meeting I'm supposed to take the notes, and should one of them need a cuppa he flags me down like I'm a waitress. Naw, I'm good on my own, pal.'

She'd picked that up from Gogsy, he'd noticed, the harder edges of the local accent swirling into the fluting hybrid she spoke with. He almost believed her, too, until she chapped on Chae Macfarlane's door, and the Grand Master of the local chapter of the Masons, imperious in socks and moustache, told her that Gogsy was a charlatan, she was a daft wee lassie, and he'd be voting, as he always did, for Mrs Thatcher's Conservative candidate.

'For a party that has completely decimated your local community and continues to hold you in contempt? Really? There are boys hanging around the streets here who will never have another chance at work now that car plant's gone! Your precious Thatcher has used this country, your people, as a testing ground for some of the harshest policies in living memory – your neighbours will be thrown in jail through no fault of their own! She has no love for you, you know!'

It wasn't that her points were wrong, but she had utterly failed to read her audience. As her voice grew shriller his granite slab of a face closed down completely, until he simply shut the door on them.

Still, almost everyone else met them with smiles. Clio had the right name on her rosette, and most of the community had already made up their minds. She wore a black dress, her one pair of high heels and a very bright lipstick at the count, threw her arms around Gogsy who had only begun to relax in his suit over the last couple of days, and Neil's photographer pal rushed forward to get a picture of them, handsome and young and victorious.

DONALD
Achiltibuie, 24 January 2018

It was Morna told him. She came in the kitchen door with the washing basket on her hip, the newspaper rolled in beside the clean sheets, smell of cold on her cheeks. What had he been doing? Ach, it didn't matter.

'Donald,' she'd said, and just with the tone of her voice he'd known something was wrong. Soft voice, lower note, pulling out the second syllable. 'Donald, love.'

'What is it?' His first thought was one of the grandchildren, but then their roles would be reversed. She wouldn't be coming to him, consoling and soft, if one of her Ishbel's kids had—

'Donald, it's that lassie. Malcolm's girl. Cliodhna.'

The main picture the paper had used was an old one, how he liked to think of her. Young, red, on fire. She never smiled in pictures back then. In an inset, the lassie's face older, grey flecking at her hair, tired. DEPRESSION it said underneath. *Campbell had battled the illness for years.*

There was a strange, low noise in the air, like an animal, and it was himself making it. He pushed the paper away from him along the table. Then he reached his arms up and wrapped himself round Morna's waist, resting his head on her big, warm stomach. What would she have been? Forty-five? Fifty, the paper said. A year older than Morna had been when they'd married. A grown woman. A woman with half her life behind her.

Donald blamed Malcolm, but Donald had been blaming Malcolm for over forty years, silently. Malcolm never knew while he was alive, and blaming him hadn't done any good then, had it?

He'd not been there when Malcolm had met Eileen Johnstone. His father had insisted he help out on the boats, never mind that the band had been taking off, so they'd headed off down south without him, picking up some greasy fool from Inverness who'd said he could play but couldn't. Maybe if he'd been there, he would have been a steadier influence, got them to take it a wee bit more slowly. Ach, maybe not.

Malcolm had stepped off the ferry with this small, strange woman, her hair a grabby colour of blue-black Donald had never seen in nature, her mouth a grim slit in a hard face, and introduced her as his wife. All red-gold and glowing, Malcolm was, bending down a whole foot to listen to his tiny bride, and folk nodded, gave them two weeks' grace as a pair of lovesick fools. Malcolm was keen to push that story as he felt it suited him: being in love, marrying in a flight of passion, marrying to do the right and honourable thing by his woman. That was the way he'd always been – working out the story that showed him in the best light, then sticking to it until it became his history, until he'd convinced himself of it.

'It's a good thing for a man to be married,' Malcolm had said in the pub that first night, new wife safely stowed with his sister-in-law. 'It's about bringing the right balance to life. You need to do it, Donald. And she's smart, this one. Thinks about things. She'll be the one to find a living for us.'

But Eileen started showing too quickly, and the scandal began clanking. A number of women, including Malcolm's own sister, suddenly refused to talk to her, not that she'd ever had that much to say to them. As though no one on the island had ever married for a baby before. Eileen seemed to fold their silent anger in on herself; when she was four months gone, they caught the last ferry on a Friday night off the island, didn't come back. Everyone shrugged, because they expected nothing better of Malcolm Campbell, sure they didn't. Donald received the summons three weeks later, a postcard with an Inverness address and the unsigned sentence: *Could use a better fiddle player . . .*

In Inverness, Eileen talked. She talked as she moved around Donald's bed on the floor of their one-room flat, while she got ready for work and Malcolm snored through in the press. She talked while she served up their dinners in the evenings before they went off to play. She talked about how important it was that she got all of the girls on her factory floor to join the union before she left to have the baby. She talked about whatever book she was reading – one of the first things she'd done, after they'd found this place, was become a member of the library – explaining the plot of a whodunnit or a Labour Party pamphlet with the same serious tone and weight. She talked about how dull it had been on the island where no one read anything. Her voice was a harsh caw, nothing musical about it, and even as Donald grew to like her, like their conversations, he wondered again what had attracted Malcolm to her. She talked only to Donald, even when Malcolm was awake; at night, though, waking up, he'd seen them wrapped around each other, a tangle of limbs, faces pressed together and Malcolm's hands strapped over her stomach, as though their sleeping selves were stuck deep in a secret love affair they couldn't let the conscious bodies know about. It calmed him to watch them, sometimes for hours, till dawn broke. One morning he didn't move to feign sleep quickly enough. 'Getting a good eyeful, are you?' she said, but her voice was peaceful.

The length of that pregnancy. The long wait of it. It sometimes seemed more real to him now than the years that came after it, because each day notched itself off on Eileen. Her eyes and neck swallowed in a fatty ball, the hairs sprouting out of her face, those blue-veined and swollen feet that needed to be soaked the second she came in, the stink of her wind. She insisted on 'keeping herself good', though: religious application of pan and lipstick in the tiny glass that hung above his feet; touching up the colourless roots of her hair with that noxious inky liquid, the stained towel draped around her shoulders. It was a blessing, Donald thought, that there were no full-size mirrors in the building.

Malcolm was quiet in that flat, a curious and down-hearted version of himself, as though some spell had been cast: a transaction exchanging Eileen's new-found voice for his own. Really, Donald knew, this was all part of the work: Malcolm's body preparing itself for a night onstage, for its nightly rebirth in the spotlight. While Eileen had found them a flat and a factory job for steady work, Malcolm had charmed his way on to the books of a series of bars and hotels, had organized a programme of regular gigs for what he was then grandly calling the Malcolm Campbell Three (the third was a bodhrán player, Fraser MacAllistair, who they'd toured with a couple of summers ago). Onstage, Malcolm roared and glinted, drew easy laughs from the working men and women in the harder bars, played douce and fluttered at the bus parties of older ladies in the hotels – it was always people that were his talent, more than the music.

In the daytime, he took phone calls in the pub across the street, made things happen. Donald took casual labour in the port, delivered half his wages to Eileen each week until the fortnight before the baby was due, when he moved into a boarding house round the corner.

Although to his knowledge there was never a christening, of course they named him godfather. In the only picture he had of himself with Cliodhna Jean Campbell, she was three days old, balanced on a cushion in his lap and mouthing the rough wool of his jumper in her sleep. Malcolm had bought the Box Brownie especially, seemed always to be snapping her; it was lost or pawned sometime before her third birthday.

Her mother called her both names, Cliodhna Jean, emphasis on the second. Malcolm had a litany of pet names, each more ridiculous than the next and never used twice, and yet the wee girl always seemed to know who he meant, would fix her eyes on him like he was a gorgeous big plaything, gazing at the way his hair glowed as it soaked up the sunlight in the flat. She favoured Malcolm from the start – his easy, rangy limbs in miniature on her, his wide eyes, the wisp of gingery hair. Another blessing, that, Donald would think to himself, feeling disloyal to Eileen as he did. It was Malcolm who sang the baby to sleep, Malcolm who she seemed to cleave to, Malcolm who she'd take a bottle from and settle for more easily. Maybe it was just because he was calmer, Donald thought. Since the birth, on a night when they'd been playing out at the hotel in Garve, hadn't made it back until 2 a.m., Eileen had been tighter, shorter with her praise, her movements brisk. She was retreating back into herself, as Malcolm blossomed in fatherhood. He wondered what she'd gone through in that hospital by herself, far away from her family. It was not a thing you asked a woman.

For the first few years of Cliodhna's life, he had been there almost all the time. He and Malcolm travelled together, sometimes with Fraser, sometimes with another couple of boys, always with what Malcolm referred to proudly as his 'womenfolk'. Musicians and instruments on blankets in the back of the rusty van Malcolm had bought for five bob and fixed up himself; Eileen holding the baby in the front. The years she was one, two, three and four they lived from April through to September in a run-down cottage at the edge of a farm on Skye. They played ceilidh sets every night in the big hotel packed with tourists, Malcolm a strutting rooster as he called the dances, affecting a Yankee twang and a bootlace tie pressed on him by a drunk old Texan over a malt. The baby chased chickens about in the mud, laughing at the splatch of her bare feet; they bathed her in the sink. Malcolm learned Gaelic songs from the old boys round the way and taught them to Cliodhna. Eileen walked out to the bed-and-breakfast a mile away to help them with the cleaning, and all of their faces freckled and toughened, being outside and out of the town again. In the daytime, once they'd woken, Malcolm would strap the baby to his chest in a sheet, or sling her, giggling, onto his shoulders, and they'd walk together across farmland, two men and a tiny girl, till they got to the sea, breathed it in, the salt air scouring their hangovers away. Malcolm searched the horizon for America, tried to orientate himself towards it. 'Just out there, Cliodhna. Just out there. That's where we'll go, my girl.' Then he'd set her down on the beach, strip all of his clothes off and run into the water, a fierce hooting coming off him as the cold hit.

Donald watched him from a distance, the red hair of his chin and crotch bouncing in time, his cock spinning, his pale skinny arse tensing as the waves reached it. His friend was beautiful, a tiny naked offering to the sky god, the sea god, the ancient shrugging mountains watching but not caring. The baby ate handfuls of wet sand, smeared it on her face, vomited down her jumper.

Donald loved Cliodhna's teeth, when they came in. He loved it when she bared them, like a little savage, in her enjoyment of a wrestling match or when he made the fiddle screech and wail like a train, turned wild runaway tunes for her. He loved the elbows and knees of her, always moving if she could, that orange scribble of tight curls still twitching when she was compelled to be still. He loved her furies and rages against the unfairness of the world, because he couldn't think of any adults with that much fire in them.

'You're no lady, Cliodhna Jean Campbell,' Eileen would say, pulling her off by the scruff of her jumper, a snarling kitten overexcited by rough play. 'You apologize to Uncle Donald, and then you sit in there until you've simmered down.' Cliodhna, still carried by the force of herself, would fret and push something, break a cup or kick a chair, and Eileen would calmly slap her on each calf, two loud and terrible cracks resounding through the room.

'Don't you hit the lass,' Malcolm would mutter, sunk in a corner.

'Don't you tell me how to raise my daughter, Malcolm Campbell. Unless you're interested in contributing.' Just a girl, Donald thought to himself now. Nothing but a girl really, Eileen was. Twenty-three? Eileen had never seemed young, though. She was one of those who'd never got to have a youth.

Cliodhna would be locked in the cupboard, the broom looped through the handles, bangs and scuffs as she threw things eventually dying down. After an hour, she'd be retrieved, asleep, dried tear-stains on her cheeks.

'Aye, it's Eileen knows how to handle her really,' Malcolm would say, as someone else put his daughter to bed.

Eileen's anger was cold and brisk and always there. She hated, but she hated with logic and organization. Donald couldn't remember seeing her eat, those last two years; watched her changing shape again as she sloughed off the body her daughter had grown on her, painted her nails red to hide the yellowed tobacco stains on her skinny, pointed fingers. In Inverness, in the winter, Eileen subsisted entirely on tea, cigarettes and disdain. On Skye she was less sharp, her fingers didn't flutter as much, but her sighs would rip round the cottage when she came in from work to see the mess they'd left. On more than one occasion, Donald had caught her staring at Malcolm's back, hands clenched and eyes shooting poison.

Malcolm's rages were something else. They only ever happened when he was drunk, would ratchet up in volume and incoherence, seemed designed to turn heads in the pub or the street, before fizzling off. On Skye, in the summertime, he drank because someone would always buy him one. In Inverness, in the winter, he drank because the pub was not that flat full of Eileen's curdled nicotine hate, or because he wanted to pass out at the place they'd played and have Donald carry him gently back to the van, tuck him up in there next to the kit and post a note through the door to his wife. He'd murmur, 'Come on then, man. Come on,' and heft his friend to his chest, Malcolm's head cooried in to his clavicle. He'd ease him down like you would a baby, pull the blanket they insulated the instruments with over him. Sometimes he'd just look at him for a while. The sweep of long sandy lashes on his cheek, the perfect sheen of his skin in the spilled street light from the window. Once, just once, he reached out and stroked his face; and Malcolm grabbed his finger and pulled hard, eyes open and glaring.

'Keep your fucking hands to yourself, you bloody fairy. Don't think I don't know what you're up to, because I do. I always have.'

Donald was backing away, stumbling on knees in the dark.

'Malcolm, man—'

Malcolm stayed lying down, but the force of his voice hit like a punch thrown. The words were suddenly crisp and clear, no slurring any more.

'What are you doing here, eh? Why are you still here, Donald Bain? There's me and my wife and my child, and there's you. There always seems to be you.'

'Eh. It's just the way it's happened, Malcolm. This is what we do.'

'We. We. How about you just worry about you from now on? How about you just stay out of my business, always hanging about, always there, from when we were boys, just mooning about, aren't you. What is it you want, exactly? You want to fuck my wife? Is that it? You want that sharp-tongued bitch in your bed instead? You want my little girl calling you Daddy? Or do you want to be the woman, Donald Bain? You just going to hope that some day all this sheer persistence will pay off and I'll turn to you instead? Just get away from me, you disgusting fucking fairy. Just get away and I'll not call the police.'

Donald closed the van door, turned and ran down the street, Malcolm's muffled swearing still ringing out, lights in the flats around flicking on. They didn't talk for a month. Donald went to work, went back to the boarding house, tried to find new routes to and fro that avoided Malcolm and Eileen's street, until their next gig, a wedding, both of them just turning up at the venue and avoiding each other's eyes through the sound check. They stood at opposite ends of the bar while they waited for the party to come in from the church, until Malcolm broke it, walked over.

'Last time. I spoke out of turn. Pals?'

Donald took the proffered hand, shook it, said 'Aye' and nothing more, because it seemed right.

The woman, when she came, was an American. Of course she was. She called the flat in Inverness, long distance at nine in the morning, got Eileen. Fraser would chuckle when he heard, said Malcolm was getting sloppy, but Donald suspected it had all been meticulously planned.

Malcolm arrived at Donald's boarding house with a black eye and a cut cheek from where Eileen had thrown shards of smashed plate at him, peeled a red-eyed Cliodhna in only her vest and tights off his shoulder and handed her to Donald.

'I'm going back there to talk sense into that idiot woman. She'll not take my girl away from me, especially not right now. She's not fit to be a mother right now. A child shouldn't have to see that,' he concluded, self-righteous and tall. 'You keep her here, Donald. Don't let anyone take her.'

Cliodhna sat up on the kitchen counter as Mrs McKenzie, Donald's landlady, made soup for the tenants' lunch. He watched the girl watching the action – knives flicking through onions, water sluicing dry lentils, the lid over the huge pot of bones clacking at the boil. She hadn't said a word or moved herself since her father left, and he'd had to carry her downstairs.

'She'll need to go back to her mother, Donald. There's nowhere for her to sleep here tonight.'

'I thought maybe she could bunk in with you?'

'No, I don't see that happening. Do I, lamb?' Gentle and final, handing Cliodhna a slice of cooked potato that she took and held.

'Eat it, lamb. You need to eat.'

'What if I just bed down in the van for the night?'

'And leave an unsupervised child in my house? No, that won't do either.'

Cliodhna sleeping in the same room as her 'Uncle' Donald was not even an option to be considered, so neither of them mentioned it. Donald left her with Mrs McKenzie while he went upstairs to get his things, came back down to find her curled on the floor and howling out a single low note.

'This won't do, Mr Bain. This won't do at all.'

Donald picked the girl up; she folded herself into his chest like her father had done when he was drunk, and the howl bubbled down to a whimper. In the hallway, he threaded her skinny form through the neck and arms of his good green jumper; it came down to her feet like a big wool dress.

'That's a pretty colour on you, little bird. Shall we go for a walk then, eh?'

He carried her down the street under his coat. She was much heavier than she had been the last time he'd held her, some months ago, but any time he tried to put her down her legs would buckle and she'd crumple onto the flagstones. He tried not to think about what she must have seen. He had no shoes for her, anyway, so eventually they worked out a silent compromise: the girl on his back, her arms locked around his neck almost tight enough to choke him, her breath funnelling hot down his spine. He walked through the town towards the river, at a loss so simply pointing out what they could see – a car, a dog – and then he started to sing. Just humming at first, 'Green Grow the Rashes O', the vibrations moving through his back to her, and slowly she pulled her head out of his shoulders. When he got to the chorus

Green grow the rashes o
Green grow the rashes o
The sweetest hours that e'er I spend
Are spent among the lasses o

she began tickling the words into his ear, not much more than a whisper at first. By the time they'd reached the river, though, she was belting out the top notes of Malcolm's harmony with him. He found them a bench, and she curled in under his armpit to watch the river, flowing fast, swollen after a week of rain. He thought about singing her through a set list – Malcolm always liked to start with 'These Are My Mountains', get the crowd warmed up – but decided against it; Cliodhna didn't need to think about her parents just then. So he started at the beginning, Robert Burns, 'A Red, Red Rose', his own mother's favourite. Malcolm was the singer, of course, but Donald could hold a tune, form a useful bassline. When he concluded, they sat in silence for a second, and then Cliodhna whispered, 'Again please, Uncle Donald.' This time she joined in, a sweet note of wordless bird-song, from the third line.

Almost two hours they sat there on that bench, repeating the song over and over. By the time her stomach started rumbling its own rhythm, and he realized they should go back and get some of Mrs McKenzie's soup, she had it by heart.

Guardian Weekend **magazine, August 2010**

The Song I Love . . .

. . . by Jennifer Hayman, Labour MP for Hoxsmith

One song I'd want to have played at my funeral is 'Rise Up' by Clio Campbell. I think it's absolutely genius – a bouncy pop number underpinned by real bite and anger. It hasn't necessarily aged well in that it's got those big synthy chords which were very typical of the late Eighties and early Nineties, but it's actually a really complex piece of music underneath the bubblegum sound. I sometimes can't quite believe she was only in her early twenties when she wrote it!

The lyrics are about the poll tax riots and the idea of communities coming together to resist a specific injustice; however, unfortunately, given the world we live in they ring just as true today and could be applied to any number of contemporary international events.

I remember being a little girl and watching her on *Top of the Pops* [Campbell famously refused to mime the lyrics of her song, instead shouting an anti-poll tax slogan over the backing track until the producers cut her segment] and being blown away, as my dad tutted about her 'uppity behaviour'. What was amazing about that moment for me was that there was this young, pretty woman, absolutely refusing to behave like all the other young, pretty women on *Top of the Pops*. I'm fairly sure she started something in me!

SAMMI
Brixton, 2018

Spider was the only one who even thought to stay in Brixton after it all fell apart, and the only one Sam even sees occasionally now (if she didn't count Fran's byline picture popping up above a column on trans politics in the *Guardian* every now and then). Usually she avoided his eye. Here he was, leading a three-crusty protest outside the arches where the squat had been. She had to pass the arches to take Elliot to football practice on the days she didn't have the car, and usually she kept her head down, eyes on the pavement, and walked quickly past. If you see a thing every day, sometimes you can render it nothing, force it into the background by sheer overexposure.

Elliot, who was refusing to hold her hand, slowed down to watch the protest, a small sneer forming round his mouth. Spider's dreads were frazzled and grey now, his face a worn little nut cracked with years of hard living, and he was waving a sign. RESIST GENTRIFI-CATION, it said, in splotchy neon lettering. KEEP BRIXTON WEIRD.

Brixton was never weird, mate, she thought to herself. Brixton thinks you're weird.

'Ha! Freaks!' muttered Elliot.

'What did you say, mister?'

The boy looked back at her, his face weighing up the options. He doubled down. Poor choice, kid.

'I said – FREAKS.'

His little defiant chin. She grabbed his wrist and pulled him across the road towards the protest, as he squirmed and shouted trying to get out of her grip. She kept him with her as they approached Spider.

'Hello, Spider.'

Spider's face creased in and in on itself in the smile.

'Bloody hell! Sammi! Hello yourself, matey.'

The placard hit the ground as he came in for a hug. Elliot winced.

'Elliot, this is my old friend. You've met him before but you were very little.'

'Gah, this is the baby, eh? Number two? Where does all that time go? Where does it go?'

Elliot scowled. 'Is your name really Spider?'

'It sure is, buddy boy. It sure is.' Spider was apparently one of those people so uncomfortable around children he had to affect an American accent. Still, she felt surprisingly warm to him. Although she had seen him around, the last time they'd met had been in the corridor of that lawyer's office, Spider coming out having given his testimony as she was ushered in. He'd given her elbow a squeeze as he passed, whispered 'Go on, gal' in her ear. She was aware that the others had met up occasionally afterwards but she wanted no part of it, or them.

But Spider was a good soul. She'd always liked Spider. He was smoothing out a crumpled flyer – still hand-drawn and photocopied, in 2018.

'Social and cultural preservation, Sammi. Taking one more stand against the wankers in suits. They've got the whole bit earmarked for demolition and another block of luxury fucking flats.'

He looked down at Elliot's suddenly thrilled grin, caught himself, hacked out a cough in confusion.

'Sorry. Sorry. Tell ya what, tough guy, they've got history, them arches. You should ask your mum sometime. There was a whole sub-culture living in them back in the day. Parties all night, an great big debates in the daytime. We was making the world a better place, eh? Wasn't we, Sammi?'

Knock it down, she thought. Burn the whole fucking lot to the ground. Cover the ashes with your smooth-fronted residential developments that block out the skyline and drive up the property prices, just so I never have to think about it again.

She snapped back to herself. Elliot's eyes were pinballing between the two of them.

'This all true, Mum?'

'This is a smart lad you've got here, Sammi. A smart lad. Anyway, how are you? Still at the old social work?'

'Nah, mate. Not for years now. I – I had to take a bit of time out. After. Wasn't doing so good for a while there. And we had the settle-ment, so I – yeah. You know.'

He knew. He knew too many things, understood too much, in that kindly crumpled face. She was thinking about how to make a quick exit, with Elliot already pulling at her hand, when Spider stopped her.

'Here. Bad business about Clio, eh?'

'Clio?'

'Yeah. The, you know, *kkkch*,' he drew a finger across his throat. 'You know?'

'Is she dead?'

Spider tried to turn his face away from Elliot, who was still follow-ing everything very intently. He mouthed 'Su-i-cide.'

'No!'

'A couple of months ago. It was in the press an that, her being famous an stuff. They mentioned all the –' he squinted at Elliot again and Sam tried to give him the tiniest shake of her head '– well, all that shit again. In passing. Would have thought you'd have seen it because of that.'

Brixton, 1995

It was the first time they'd held a formal party in the squat, and the faultlines peeled open. Gaz and Spider were against the idea that any cleaning whatsoever should be done to prepare the space.

'They take us as they find us,' Gaz said. 'We're not putting on a show of respectability when we ain't.'

Xanthe countered that this was another manifestation of patriarchal individualism over the communal identity they were attempting to foster.

'It doesn't seem to matter what you say your politics are – in here, you're quite happy to have women skivvy for you.'

Fran said she'd never seen any of the men so much as washing a dish while she lived here, and she was sick of dealing with a sink full of dirt. Spider took a can of lager out of the fridge and pointedly sat down on the new armchair they'd pulled out of a skip last week, the one they'd all been fighting over, smacked his lips loudly as the ring pull cracked and fizzed.

'Right! That's me ready for the party, maties. Let the games begin.'

Sammi had been involved at first, but now she was hanging back in the doorway, Mark's thin arm round her waist keeping the two of them apart from it all. His lips moved up her neck, breathing lightly and deliberately, teasing her.

'Wanna fuck?' he whispered, close to her ear.

She tried not to move her mouth too much in reply.

'Not really the time for it, mate.'

'Seems like the perfect time for it to me. Just a quick little fuck, that's all . . .'

Xanthe was holding forth again, her gestures growing ever-bigger with anger, eyes flashing. Gaz burped showily and she wheeled on him. Mark snorted, grabbed Sammi's wrist and ran down the corridor with her to the sleeping area, where their zipped-together sleeping bags were crumpled in a heap on the one double mattress. Sammi had begun to paint faces on the wall around their space – not in a way that would denote ownership, just so that she'd have something to look at in the long mornings while everyone else slept and the sunlight filtered in. Across the way were the beginnings of her mural, its letters already sketched out. Over Mark's shoulder, as he mouthed wet on her nipple, pulled her knickers down, as Xanthe's scrawny baby whimpered in its sleep, she read it to herself again:

FORM TRIBES. TAKE LAND. LIVE FREE.

They lay there for a few minutes after, warmed in a ray of sun from the skylight, tangled up in each other. She could smell woodsmoke on his skin, and earth, something dark and real.

'This is well nice,' she said.

'I agree,' he said, kissing the top of her head.

'We should get back, though.'

'You're a perfect worker bee, you.'

'Yeah well, maybe I am. Come and help me stop this, yeah.'

In the living space, it was still going on. Fran was on her knees, huffily scrubbing the floor with a rag, while Gaz and Spider tried to occupy the maximum amount of space with their bodies, Xanthe shouting into each of their faces in turn. Sammi pushed Mark, in the small of his back, and he grinned at her. There was something cruel about his smile, sometimes.

He walked into the centre of the room with his limbs long and loose, movements easy, arms out, flat palms at angry face-height.

'Now look here. We need to resolve this.'

The reason she'd wanted him to sort this out was because, when he spoke, people listened. She'd known schoolteachers to have that effect; never one of her peers. The stern confidence of him, like it had been bred in somewhere along the way. They all responded to it; the room stilled, settled itself quietly around that lean, golden centre-point.

Mark shook his hair out of his eyes and reached out to each of them in turn. He looked like Jesus, Sammi realized, one of those blond master-race Jesuses from the Sunday School books.

'Spider, mate,' he said, his accent blunting. 'Let's look at this rationally, eh? We're not just trying to recreate the old systems here – we all came to this place because we're committed to making a new way of living, yeah? And we're not going to do that if we fall into these easy traps where the women end up doing all the housework.'

He was careful not to use any of Xanthe's buzzwords, Sammi noted. No 'patriarchy'. Clever. He was clever, that man-not-hers. Every word measured out and perfectly placed.

'And, Xanth, it's important to be mindful that men like Spider bear the scars of their upbringing. Spider wants to overcome his conditioning, don't you, mate? But he needs our support as he goes through that process. I'm not asking you to do his dishes for him; I'm asking you to understand why he leaves them out.'

Had anyone else said this, Xanthe would have ripped them apart. Dizzied by the full beam of Mark's enthusiasm, though, she looked almost pacified.

'So here's the thing, guys. We invited people tonight because we want to show them this new way of being we're creating. The ecology of what we're trying to do here – the free shop, the drop-in centre, the zine – it all depends on the support we can generate on evenings like this. We need to build on the community we've got here and not take anything for granted just because we've made the first step and found this place. And that means all of us, working hard and being con-tinually mindful as we bond this, the first tribe, together. If, for now, that means letting go of an argument, getting on, pulling together to create a space that we know will work for the interests of the greater good, then that is what we need to do in this moment.'

As they unclenched, as the tension hissed slowly out of the room, Mark turned around and winked at her, a split-second shaking off of his sincerity. And Sammi, who had been nodding along, letting his words carry her into visions of their sunlit community growing stronger together, felt sick in her belly. She looked back again; his face was at peace, the mask back on. Maybe she'd been imagining it.

The party was huge. Gaz had got his mates to help him set up a sound system, crackling as it soaked up almost everything in their generator. Bulky cider bottles and towers of paper cups lined the kitchen unit and floor, and the air was fat with weed. Almost too heavy. The fairy lights Spider had nicked from the discount shop flashed off if the bass got too loud. Xanthe held court in the free shop, her baby rolling about on cushions, and a group of young women sitting cross-legged as she explained the exchange system. 'It'll be good for nappies, baby stuff, all of that. We need to support each other on this, you know? Old toys; when they grow out of their shoes, we'll get the local women here and they can drop off their stuff and take what they need. It's not like those bastards are going to do it. You know the saying "It takes a village to raise a child"? Well, this is gonna be Dido's village, isn't it, darling?'

The baby chuckled at the attention and the women smiled at it, through the haze of a shared joint. This had been a tactical move that she, Fran and Xanthe had worked out earlier in the day: keep the free shop as female a space as possible, so that the worst of Gaz's mates would be scared off, wouldn't trash it.

Sammi stumbled about between the rooms, just taking it all in. It was happening. Just like they'd hoped.

Mark was sitting in the middle of the sofa, playing that brilliant trick he always had of being the centre of the conversation whilst not leading it. It flowed through him – he was the joining point, the connector, but he was mostly listening, mediating, making sure everyone was heard. Those teenage girls Sammi had stopped with a flyer in the street had come along – probably more after free weed than having their consciousnesses raised, but the important thing, as she knew from her own experience, was that they were here. That they were exposed to a way of doing things different from their mothers, their school social order. They were sitting around Mark's feet, half-following the chat (a couple of crusty guys from Greenpeace and Mandy from the ALF were in a gentle argument), giggling occasionally and rolling their eyes at each other when it got earnest, passing a joint between themselves and making faces if it had been left wet with saliva. One of them was leaning up against Mark's legs. He caught Sammi's eye and shrugged, stuck out his tongue, absolving himself. Sammi grinned, to let him know it was all right. They were working towards non-monogamous harmony. Jealousy had been hard for both of them at first, but Sammi was pretty sure it was a hang-up from a social order they'd been conditioned to and were rejecting. If that was how it was tonight then that was how it was.

She felt everything loosen as the party opened up for her, began to move her legs with purpose. It was a very white crowd, natch. One of Gaz's dealer mates picked up on what she was sending out, began vibing her. He wasn't bad looking – bigger than Mark – broad chest, hefty arms. The sort of bloke her sister would have brought home. What would it be like to have a man like that in your bed, she wondered, throwing you around? He seemed to read her thoughts. Something flicked on behind his sleepy eyes, and he made his way through the tangle of legs on the floor, the lone crusty dancing wildly to some blurred, fuzzy dub, a slow, easy swagger she'd seen before, hanging around outside the tube station.

'Well then, little sister,' he said, as he reached her. 'What you doing here, baby? With all these lily-white fools?'

'I live here,' she told him. She was bored of him already. Sure, he looked good; sure, she could take him into the sleeping space and fuck him now; but she knew he'd just give her the same attitude as the boys at school had in the same fake patois. Same attitude her brother had had, when she'd been spotted with a white boyfriend.

'You live in this shithole? Nah. This ain't no place for a sister.'

'Yeah? It's the place for this sister, mate.' She walked away from him, down the corridor, where the thump of the bass evened out a bit. Her head was spinning, and she wished for a second everyone would just fuck off and leave her alone with Mark, with his skin on hers. But that wasn't the point. That wasn't the purpose of this party, or of the way they were trying to live. She needed to get better at this, at suppressing these urges for solitude, for chocolate biscuits and a telly that worked, a sofa that hadn't come out of a skip, and a proper bed, a mum to cook her breakfast.

She could hear singing, through and over the bassline. Wild, strange singing, in a language she didn't recognize. She followed it, down the concrete stairs that still smelled of men's piss from when this was a dosshouse, into the room they were going to make into the magazine office, although just now it only contained a big table for layout, and they hadn't rewired it for electricity yet. There was a circle of older crusty types in there, but it was difficult to make out their faces. Two of them had guitars, there was a little fire crackling away in one of the tin bins, and there was a woman singing, using the persistent heartbeat boom from the sound system upstairs to mark her time. Sammi leaned in the doorframe, closed her eyes for a second, and just listened. The woman's voice rasped against the low notes then rose, pure, clear, somewhere above all of their heads. Sammi had never heard anyone sing like that before. The girls at her school who'd thought they had good voices were always trying to do Whitney or Mariah; self-indulgent screeching that took you out of the tune. This woman wasn't showing off – it was like she'd found the melody in the air, was turning it over for them. Sammi gazed at the fire, thought that it seemed so old, full of secrets. The way it danced. Man, she was well stoned.

The song stopped and the air in the room was perfect for a second, before all the old hippies started clapping. Conn, who washed dishes at her work, beckoned Sammi in and murmured her name to the circle – they all raised gentle hands in greeting. She'd be safe in here. The woman who'd been singing patted a spot on the blanket beside her and, as she got closer, Sammi could make out curly hair burning red in the firelight glow, a wide smile.

'How you doing, Sammi? Nice earrings,' she said, her voice weird and soft, lilty.

'What – what language was that you was singing in?' It just came out of her, before she'd had time to remember her manners.

'That was Gaelic. It's the language of the Highlands and island communities in Scotland. It was a traditional folk song. A lullaby. For getting the babies to sleep?'

Sammi must have been gawking at her. She closed her jaw for a second.

'You Scottish, then?'

'I am.'

'Long way from here, innit?'

'It is. I'm here visiting some friends. I ran into Spider on the street and he invited me. I ran away.' The woman looked delighted with herself, looked like she was sharing a massive, brilliant secret.

The hippies continued to sing their old protest songs, sawing away at their guitars. Usually Sammi found them embarrassing, but she didn't mind tonight. The woman, who she could see now she was up close was actually a lot younger than the rest, kept her involved, sharing a silent joke with her when someone sang off key. And she looked familiar.

Sammi nudged her. 'Mate, do I know you from somewhere?'

Her new friend smiled. 'I'll tell you later. Listen, do you wanna get some air?'

'I really do. Have they shown you the roof, yet?'

And they were running, giggling, up the stairs, climbing the shonky metal ladder at the end of the hall, and Sammi led her friend whose name was Clio by the hand, over the slates to the flat bit, and they were talking, and Sammi got out her pouch and rolled a joint, a big one, five-skinner, and smiled at the woman with a bit of a tease, like, oh, you think you can handle it? And then they were sitting together on the woman's coat on the slates, looking down over the city, its smoke, its car horns, its shouts and its lights going out.

'I mean it,' Clio was saying. 'I want to know how you got into this.'

'You mean, what's a little black girl from Brixton doing living in a squat with a bunch of posh crusties?'

'No. Well, yeah. I mean, where did your politics come from? What drove you into this life? I think we've got similar backgrounds, you and me. I'm always interested to hear from people who made the same journey. Because there's always something, or someone, that starts you off, that fires you up and makes it impossible for you to live any other way. You know?'

'It's a long story, mate.'

'They always are. That's what's good about them.'

'You sure? Really? Your funeral.'

'I'll take that risk. Talk.'

It was a command, from a queen, suddenly serious. Sammi sucked long and hard on the joint and passed it over. She wasn't usually a talker, but she wanted Clio to know her, know her politics, be impressed.

'All right. I was coming out of school one day and this woman, a bit older than me, short dreads, wax-backed skirt, like proper in touch with the heritage, like the sort of thing my mum would be ashamed of, she was standing there trying to hand out this magazine to the girls as we were leaving. The white girls were giving her the eye, like, brushing her off, but she looked straight at me and said, "There's something in here for you, little sister." An it was called that. *Sister-Hood*, it was called. The main photo was of this girl a bit older than me, hair wrap like woah and some really awesome lipstick. I'd never seen a magazine with a black woman on the cover before. I was all suspicious, like, what, is it free then, and she just smiled at me. She was like, "We had extra on the print run. I wanted to get it to people who need to read it. No charge for you, little one." And then she turned it over, pulled up the back page and pointed to an address, in tiny print.

She told me if I liked what I read, they was just round the corner, and that I could drop in any time. Then she said, "We could do with smart young voices," and that appealed to me, right, cos I was a cocky-as-fuck teenager, but no one ever wanted to listen to my smart young voice, huh? So maybe I was already predisposed to like it, I dunno. That was Constance. She became more like a mum to me than my real mum. Anyway, I took the magazine, didn't I. And it was like nothing I'd read before. I mean, it was mad. It had, like, hair tips and articles on feminism and racism and interviews with a feminist rapper and, like, some really shitty poetry about wombs. But it was speaking to me, you know, like nobody really does. Nobody really speaks to little black girls as themselves. The school, when they talk to you, they talk to you like you're an old rich white guy. The telly, when it talks to you, and the teenie magazines, they're saying you should be white and blonde and skinny. So I spent the whole night reading this magazine, like, three times, even the crazy poems – I could probably still recite them for you, yeah! The ink rubbing off on my thumbs; couldn't get my hands proper clean the next day. And then after school, I found myself knocking on their door. Fourteen years old, still in my uniform and clutching my copy of *SisterHood* under my arm, all, like, *hellooo* – and it was like a world I'd never been to before. Five women in this big sunny upstairs room, and a couple of them looked well cool, like, cool hoops and trainers. Natural hair, no weaves. Lot of wraps. It was basically my mum's nightmare – she was well into us trying to look as white as possible, and she always turned her face away from anyone who looked like that if she saw them in the street. Muslims and loo-na-tics, she'd call 'em. We're Jamaican, she'd say; we're Jamaican and we're Christian and we're British. But I was into it. If this was where they made *SisterHood*, then this was where I wanted to be. Sorry, mate. God, I'm running right off at the mouth, ain't I?'

Clio took a final drag of the joint and handed it back to her. The roof thumped with bass beneath them.

'Nah. Go on. This is what I'm into. I wanna hear how people got radicalized.' The way she spoke, the 'r' came out like a purr. 'Women especially, eh. How we found it. You're doing magic.'

It seemed to Sammi like a weird thing to say, but her voice was foreign honey; not like the flat London vowels that dragged out of everyone else's mouth. And she was pretty, and Sammi liked her, so she took a drag, held it in for a second, felt the burn, and started talking again.

'Right, well. You sure, yeah? So, I just hung around there at first, and I think a couple of them were like, what is this kid doing here, you know? But Constance, she was always trying to include me. At first I was just, like, making the coffee, putting the copies in the envelopes for subscribers, and then, if any of them had tapes of interviews they wanted typed up, they'd get me to do it. I was better than them as I was doing typing at school, see. And I was superkeen. I did not make a single mistake. I'd spend hours after school listening and re-listening to these interviews – with poets, with politicians, with campaigners. Almost all of them black women. Local women. I'd sit in the office, and there was always someone in there, something happening. It was volunteer-run, obviously, so them usually brought they kids in with them – it was always one person's job to look after the kids in the room next door. And sometimes other women in the area would come in, and have a cup of coffee, and moan about their men, or them not able to pay rent, or something. And I was just sitting there, taking it all in. I got ideas above my station, mate. I went to the careers adviser and told her I wanted to be a painter and, failing that, a journalist.'

'What did she say to that?'

'She said I'd been getting really good scores on my typing, had I thought about secretarial work? Pfff. I told this to Constance and she was, like, fuming. Next day, they're giving me my own column in the magazine. "Little SisterHood". They told me to write about it, and I did, and then I would write about everything like that, every month. The pressures that teenage girls feel, that sort of thing. People loved it.

'It weren't long before I was going on protests with them. Anti-fascist marches. At first they'd just take me to be the photographer, because all of them was getting so swept up they kept forgetting to get pics for the magazine. But I got into it, heavy. Started my own group of the Anti-Fascist League at school; couldn't get that many of the thick fucks I hung around with interested. *SisterHood*, and those women, and like just *waking up*, it changed me for the rest of the world, you know? I got my GCSEs, but school just didn't seem that important. School looked at me and said, oh, people like you drop out at sixteen, end of, so I did that. My mum was shocked that I wasn't going to take a job, that I was going to sign on and write full time for *SisterHood*. We had a row, and I went to live with Constance for a bit. It spoiled me for boys, too, yeah. All the boys my age, they're just nothing, man. Just into tits, not ideas. That's why I've started seeing older men. That's why Mark and me work.'

'Who's Mark, then?'

'You not met him? We moved in here together. He's the posh guy with the blond hair. Mark's my fella – not "mine" in the possessive sense, innit.'

'Open relationship? I take it that was Mark's idea?' Clio looked amused, laughed two notes of smoke out.

'Nah, I know what you're thinking, but it was honestly a mutual decision. I'm not even sure I believe in monogamy. I fancy other blokes sometimes, and I can go off with them for fun if I want. It works for us, mate. Trust me.'

Clio smiled at her, and she didn't think she was being mocked, or maybe only in a good way. 'And where did you meet the lovely Mark?'

'He came into my work. I wait tables and sometimes do the cooking at the café in the 121 Centre up the road – Constance got me it, she knows Antoine, who I guess is my boss? Mark kept on coming in every day for a week cos he was new to the area, didn't know many folk, and we got talking, and then we got fucking, and we never really stopped.

He's all right, is Mark.' Sammi thought again about that smile on his face today, that split second of unease, and brushed over it.

'Anyway, yeah, *SisterHood*, was that what I was saying? It folded, mate, about a year ago. I was gutted. We was all gutted. But they just didn't have the funds to keep affording their rent. They tried to keep doing it from people's houses, but it didn't work. So that's what I thought, when we found the squat, there was a room big enough to start doing this all over again. You see? Me and Xanthe are starting up a new freesheet, a zine. We'll work from here, lay it out, photocopy on the sly at the copy shop and leave piles of it in all the little caffs and community centres and stuff. I'm going to paint the front cover, every time, a different face of someone in the community. It's going to be feminist, political, no effin poetry, yeah? That's the plan, anyway.' Sammi ended quietly, aware she'd been shouting, that the Scottish woman was smiling wide again. 'You're laughing at me.'

'Naw. Well, aye, but it's only because I think you're fucking brilliant, Sammi.'

'You what?'

'I do. You're brilliant. It's been amazing to meet you and just hear you talk. I want to know you better.'

'Really? You mean that?'

Clio had reached an arm out and pulled Sammi along the slates and in to her. She'd stroked her face and kissed her on the lips in a way that was and wasn't sexual all at once, and then they'd cuddled up together, under the street light, sharing the last of the joint and a little silver hip flask of something much, much stronger than cider. Sammi had told her all about the squat, what they planned to do, about her ideas for the mural, about Xanthe's free shop. She talked and talked; the words just kept coming from her, and all the while she felt warmth rising up between their two bodies, side by side, keeping each other from the cold. And Clio turned and smiled at her, and suddenly Sammi had it.

'I do know you! You're proper famous, intya? You had that song, when I was a kid. Rise up! People got to rise up!'

'Aye, that's me. But that was a long time ago now. Not so famous any more. One-hit wonder, eh?'

She grinned and blew a smoke ring, and Sammi gazed at its perfect circle for a second until it broke, drifted.

'Well, what about you, then?'

'What about me?'

'Yeah. You know. You're like a pop star and that. You was in *Smash Hits*. An now you're in a party in a filthy dirty squat. How did you get –' and here she started giggling, because it was fucking funny, everything was fucking funny '– rrrrrradicalized?'

'I'll tell you a story about my daddy, Sammi, some day. My daddy was a great revolutionary. A freedom fighter. He travelled the world helping the oppressed wherever he could. When you've got someone like that in your life, someone who's a constant beacon of what's right, you know; it all just comes naturally. I had no choice in this, in a way. I couldny just settle down and live a normal life when there's fights to be fought for folk who canny do it themselves. You know? You know.'

'Yeah. I know.'

'But really, babe, I'm like you. I left home and school at sixteen too. Never looked back. We teach ourselves, you and me, right? We know we're smart enough, so fuck their fancy university degrees and all that shit. People like us, we live by our moral codes, eh? A finely honed sense of what's right.'

'Yeah,' Sammi said, and she shouted across the rooftops, across the city: 'Fuck your degrees!' They held each other tightly again, laughing as the sun started to rise.

SIMON
Bristol, 2008

It was not a wedding Simon had really expected to find himself at. It wasn't that he'd ever really thought Jess and Greg were going to break up, it was just that the idea of marriage could have any interest for them. And yet, here they were, in a scuffed church hall decorated with paper flowers made by friends, drinking from a bar composed entirely of bottles the guests had brought, but married under the law all the same. At the end of the day, they were still a nice middle-class heterosexual couple, he supposed, raising his glass to the uneasy gathering of well-dressed friends-of-their-parents clustered in the corner of the hall, flecked by the sweat of a dance floor moshing to Chumbawamba.

It came to them all, though. All the straight couples from his little group had parked the sculptural prams bought by their well-off parents far away from the crackling speaker set up by Greg's friend who organized raves; wheeled them home after an hour or two. Their places had been filled by the second-tier guests, colleagues and comrades in their twenties, invited in after 7 p.m. to make the dance floor look busy. No matter how ostentatiously they'd skimped on the trappings of what he remembered Jess once calling 'the self-policing patriarchy of the matrimonial industrial complex', they had observed the protocols. She even wore white, although the back had been cut out to show her tattoos. Within six months, there would be a pregnancy announcement. There always was – the way the marriage certificate seemed to give all these radical feminists permission to ditch their contraception had made him laugh at first. Now it just seemed grimly inevitable.

Oh, it was easy to be mean. He looked about and realized he was pretty much friendless. He recognized a few people from the service earlier, but didn't know them well enough to go and plonk himself down beside them. He wished he'd brought someone. He'd considered Luke, but worried that the pressures of being seen as a couple in that context might trough up all the issues they'd ignored on their last go-around. He'd also thought that Luke's clean-fingernailed perspective on what he'd always jokingly called 'Si's crusty crew' might leave a sour taste in his mouth – and yet here he was, providing the acid-tongued commentary for himself.

Maybe it was time to go home.

Soft heat and a gentle sweat smell, as a woman threw herself down at the table. He recognized Clio Campbell right away – she'd sung 'A Case of You' at the service, as they were signing their names, after he'd rolled his well-taught enunciation around a straight recital of the lyrics to Bob Dylan's 'Wedding Song', but he would have known her anyway. The gorgeous young Asian guy she'd been snogging in the middle of the mosh pit leaned over her for a final kiss, but she was already reaching for the discarded bottle of wine in the middle of the table. He made a toking gesture at her, and she laughed, slapped his bum and sent him on his way. She poured more from the bottle into the nearest glass (Simon thought it had maybe been his at dinner), drained it noisily and smacked her lips at him.

'Oof. That's me done dancing for another year, eh! You not getting up there?'

Had he known she was Scottish? He wondered whether he'd ever actually heard her talk. He remembered seeing her on *Top of the Pops* when he was a kid – she must be at least ten years older than him by that reckoning.

'You're Scottish.' He'd said it out loud – he must be drunker than he'd thought.

'You're not.'

'No, I'm not.'

They smiled at each other, and he realized she was probably as drunk as him. She filled up her glass again.

'Nothing like a warm white wine to really not slake a thirst! I'm Clio.'

'I know. I'm a huge fan.' Huge? It was what you said, wasn't it? He qualified, hastily. 'I mean, your song today. "A Case of You". I've loved it for years and I don't think I've ever heard it done so gorgeously. Maybe not even by Joni herself.'

Too much? Too much.

She waved a hand.

'You know what? I've never worked out what I'm supposed to say to that sort of thing. The polite thing to do, it seems, would be to blush all dainty-like and apologize for my presence. Unless I was a bloke. Then I should just nod, like of course, take what is probably just you being a nice polite guy as my due, graciously allow you into my presence. But a woman doing that, you think, ooh, she's up her-self, don't you? So instead I get all flustered and self-deprecating when what I really want to do is say yeah, today I fucking nailed that, didn't I?' She beamed at him. 'Thank you! Thank you is what I should say. Jesus, manners, you silly bint. It's Simon, isn't it. Si?'

His head was swimming with her.

'So, how do you know the happy couple?'

'Oh God, just uni. We were all in the Green Party student chapter at Bristol. Went to dance parties. Bit more hardcore than this.'

He smirked, being Luke again, tried to tell her about the thrum of bassline, bloated cartoon characters done in UV paint shining on the walls, the smell of Jess's sweat, her cropped top and massive frayed army trousers, a keffir scarf wound round her head; running his hands over Greg's flat teenage stomach and under the waistband hanging off his hips that once. Simon had been a handy sounding board for all those enlightened little straight boys feeling a bit curious, had wrapped palms round each of their cocks at some point or another, received precious little back. A tick-off along the way, a thing to do before you were thirty, before you got the girl.

'And nine years on, here we are. Wearing suits, signing marriage certificates –'

Jess, in the centre of the hall, spun in a circle and rolled herself into Greg's waiting arm, a pastiche of old-time dance-hall moves.

'– watching all your old pals committed and settled down, feeling lost and wondering where your youth went?'

'It's like you're in my head.'

She poured the last of the wine into two glasses, then reached over and grabbed another half-empty bottle from a different table, topped them up red-into-white. He winced, involuntarily, imagining his father's thoughts on the subject, and she caught him at it.

'Sorry. Call it a cocktail. I don't think I'm spoiling any particular vintage, eh no.'

He grinned and she clinked his glass.

'Anyway, here's an unasked-for life lesson from yer Auntie Clio, as she's had a bit to drink and feels like spreading her wisdom. I was you for years, sitting at weddings as the people my age paired off and had their babies and stopped being fun. I realized after a while you just need to find the people who are still at your level. The kids and the gays, basically. No offence, pal. Obviously. Because I don't know about you, but I'm not really interested in the conversation of parents, and I don't think they're interested in me. No matter what they believed in before those wee darlings popped out, no matter how radical they thought they were, there's something that changes about them. All they really want to do is sit on some comfy seats with other parents, comparing notes on exhaustion and bleeding nipples and laughing at cute little flubbed sentences, maybe get competitive about which one walked first. It's evolution, isn't it? Mama Nature ensuring that parents can't think beyond their babies for more than five minutes at a time means those babies don't get eaten by wolves. Good parents make shitty friends, hon, as I'm sure you're finding out.'

'You've never fancied it yourself?'

'A big fat no to that. I'm one of the ones who'd make a shitty parent – fortunately I realized it in time.'

'Maybe you're just too good a friend,' he said, toasting her. Her face wasn't quite readable.

'Kids chain you down. That's not really a new observation, but it's something I saw happening from quite a young age to my pals, and realized I couldny take it myself. Maybe I'm just too selfish, ha. Anyway, I come to the weddings of people I've loved through their twenties and sometimes they ask me to sing, and it's all very nice, but what they don't realize is that in my head, as I'm raising a glass, I'm saying a silent goodbye. I mean, what do you give it before these two are letting us all know about the little bundle of joy on the way?'

'Six months. You *are* inside my head.'

Clink.

'Exactly so. So, you read them your toast, you give them a wee present that you've made yourself and put some love into, and you'll send them something nice again when the first baby's born, if you're not too fucked off that they not only didn't come to your birthday night out but forgot it completely, but you know that really that's all that's left. When they come out the other side, blinking in the light when the kid's about ten or something, you might meet them in the street by chance, and it'll be so friendly; you'll hug, you'll swap numbers, you'll make promises to go for coffee, but you know they're secretly hoping you don't call. You've lived on different planets for too long by that point.'

Simon slumped even further into his seat. 'Shit. I was hoping you'd tell me it was just a phase, and we'd get through it.'

'Babe, I'm forty years old. Loads of people my age have teenagers now. I've had it happen time and time again. They're gone, they just haven't realized it yet.'

'Biology.'

'Biology. See, as a woman and a feminist I'm not supposed to admit that, but it totally, totally is.'

'You really don't look forty, by the way. I'd never have thought—'

'That's very sweet, but I do look forty. This is what forty looks like when you still get eight hours' sleep a night, all your pals are twenty-four, and you don't really have anyone else to worry about beside yourself. See, at – what age are you?'

'Twenty-nine.'

'Yeah. When thirty still feels like a big scary monster on the horizon, forty seems like death. But you take all that biology out of the equation and it's pretty fucking great, actually. I'm not in a race to procreate before my body trips me up; I've been around long enough to know what sort of clothes, drink and pals do and don't suit me; I don't feel the need to apologize for who I am any more. So, you have to say your farewells to the people who got you through the first bit of growing up, and that's the toughest hurdle to face. But if you have a look around, you're actually in the perfect place to meet your next set of friends. Look at all these babbies still dancing away because they don't have anything more pressing to do on a weekend evening. Imagine how wise you'll seem to them, hon! Ten years' time and you'll be looking this fucking fabulous, sitting someone else down to talk their face off just like this. You find your team, your new tribe, in the leftovers after the ceremony's done. The ones hanging on to the bitter end.'

'I just – I really hope you're right.'

Clio's young boyfriend was weaving between the tables, his beautiful amber eyes stoned and shining for her. She rose, put her arms around his neck and he dipped her backwards for a kiss. She winked at Simon over his shoulder as she rose again.

'Hamza, my love, this is Simon with the lovely speaking voice.

We're hanging out with Simon for the rest of the night. He's sad, and he shouldn't be. Have you got a little present for us?'

'You know I have. Come and get it.'

She fished inside his suit jacket and extracted a little polybag of white powder, magician-quick, tucking it into her sleeve, then grabbed at Simon's wrist gently but firmly. Her hand found its way into his, her fingernails painted shiny iridescent purple, glittering in the party lights.

'Come on, babe. Let's go celebrate the momentous occasion of your rebirth, like people with fuck all responsibility should.'

NEIL
Glasgow, 23 January 2018

Gogsy had answered his phone the same way for decades now. Crisp, irritated intonation, 'Gordon Duke.' Every time. Even after he got a mobile phone that showed him the name of the caller on the screen.

'Hi, Gogs. How are you, man?'

'Is that you, Neil?'

Oh, you know fine well it's me, Neil thought. Stop this.

'A wee bit early, is it not? What can I do for you today?'

There was something sad about Gogsy these days. He'd lost his seat in the SNP general election putsch two years ago, to a woman, of all things. He'd been far too easy a target for the vitriol aimed at the Labour Party post-referendum, because he'd bought into the party mindset far too much by this time. Neil saw him on television not long after his defeat talking about the 'post-truth' age the electorate were living in, where truth meant Labour, meant Gordon Duke.

Like Clio, Gogsy would only contact Neil when he wanted a story placed, so they hadn't seen much of each other in the last two years. The suit was as sleek as ever, the hair as thick and silvery, the sovereign rings as prominent, but he'd deflated, somehow, no longer commanded a room just by entering it. Faces did turn, eventually – he was still a former cabinet minister, had been regularly on television for ten years – but once they registered him, turned back.

'Nobody from the paper come here any more, then?'

'There's nobody from the paper left, Gogs.'

'Christ.'

It was ten in the morning. They drank.

'Off the record, Neil, the now. But what a stupid, stupid lassie. To do a thing like that.'

'Aye.'

'Stupid waste.'

'Aye.'

'Tell you about the last time I saw her? We were on this BBC panel discussion up at the university. Run-up to the independence refer-endum, you know, passions were high – but she just *lost* it, eh. Fell to pieces right there in front of all these students, just because I'd challenged her on something – oil or who knows what. The rage, this incoherent emotional nonsense she was talking, making it all about me, about my "moral failings". She stood up and she screamed "Judas" at me. Actually screamed it. I'd not seen her like that, the whole time we were together, but then it takes its toll on women, doesn't it? At that age. The hormones. I mean, you could see something wasn't right. And all these students laughing. I wanted to stop the whole thing, right away, just wrap my coat round her and take her offstage, you know? Make it stop. But I didn't, because it meant we were winning.'

He exhaled noisily, went back to his drink.

'That was always Clio's problem, though, was it not? Never knew when to keep her mouth shut.'

Neil just nodded.

'Do you know what I think it was with that one – and I'm still off the record here, Neil. I'll let you know when we go on, eh. What it was, I think, was she never could just settle down. She had to keep itching away at the next thing and the next, she never really grew up, you know what I'm saying. I mean, when we were together – I actually asked her to marry me, can you imagine. What a close escape that was, eh. She wouldn't have made a politician's wife, would our Clio. She broke my heart at the time, right enough, but when I think of taking her along to, say, dinner with the Prime Minister, or even officiating at a constituents' evening? Oof. I mean, at the time she turned me down, she said, "I'm not the marrying kind, Gogs," and I thought she was being cool, you know, that this was her feminist principles or what-ever. Something to admire about it, even. A younger man then, Neil. A younger man. But then she went and married that music guy and I'll admit it, even though I was very happy with Sharon by that point, there was a part of me that took that as a punch to the stomach. You know what I'm saying, pal. That didn't last, though, did it? I met him, you know, some sort of council bash or something. He was looking at moving his festival to East Ren at the time. I did say to him, after a couple, "I understand we have an old flame in common, pal," you know, and I regret that. You don't refer to a man's wife as an old flame, ex-wife even. There are lines, Neil. There are lines.'

'There are lines, Gogs.'

'Always struck me as a bit of a Flash Harry type, that one. She probably thought she was going up in the world with him. No con-science, do anything for a buck. I mind I thought at the time that they wouldn't have that much in common. You know. You know, pal.'

Neil knew.

Last night, in the pub, he'd spun a vision of himself, one of those legendary *Rolling Stone* journalists matching the band drink for drink, putting everything on expenses, turning in definitive interviews down the line to the copy desk from truck stops and neon-blasted motels, and round the table everyone had nodded, believed him.

Squinting through the hangover now, digging his hands into the disintegrating foam of the Skoda's seat as his stomach lurched with each swerve, he felt embarrassed for himself. Beside him, Deek clenched the wheel, his pink head bumping the car's ceiling. Neil could have been sitting on a nice calm train now, reading the papers, gazing at the scenery; however, both his editor and Danny the tour manager had been keen for this, the much cheaper option.

'Deek'll get you there,' the tour manager had told him yesterday, cocky and smooth through the warped line from some Highland payphone somewhere. 'He's a good boy.'

As the car strained and whined under the bald giant's foot, Neil imagined his own obituary, a tiny paragraph in the back of the paper he had not been working at long enough to merit much more in.

The scheme Neil grew up on had been full of Deeks, lumpy boulders of self-satisfaction, utterly impermeable to reason. Until this point, Neil's tried and tested method of dealing with them had been to keep his head down and duck away: it was perhaps the only great benefit of being small. Nowhere to duck to today, though. Deek fumbled in the tiny glove compartment with fingers the size of sausages, the old ink of a faded eagle seeping into the skin of his wrist, chucked out a road atlas greying and tatty, not quite held together with ring binders and Sellotape.

'Here. We get lost, it's on you, eh.'

'So. Are you working on this tour then?'

'What tour?'

'The singer. Clio Campbell. Touring the Highlands. Are you a roadie on it or something?'

'Fuck naw. I know the boy Danny cos I've done security at a couple of his club nights, eh. He asked me if I'd drive a wee journalist up somewhere. Probably could've charged him more if I'd known you'd keep me waiting around, eh?'

'Aye. Ha ha. So, is that what you do, then? You're a bouncer?'

'Only in the evenings, pal. I do removals. House moves. Ken?'

'Oh aye. So, have you got a van?'

'We can get a van.'

This was painful, Neil thought. Painful and due to continue for another four and a half hours. He kept his eyes on the road ahead, trying to discourage Deek from turning his head to engage him.

'So, you said you knew Danny, aye? What's he like?'

Deek smirked. 'Danny's a good boy.'

'Funny, he said that about you.'

'Did he, aye? Cheeky cunt.'

'Known him long?'

'Bout five year. He keeps the work coming, aye. Good about paying cash in hand, ken. We could aw do with a bit of that.'

'But you've not heard of Clio?'

'Who?'

'The artist. The singer on the tour he's promoting.' The reason we're trapped together in this rusting deathmobile. 'She had a big hit a few years back. "Rise up . . . everybody rise up . . ."?'

'Oh aye, rings a wee bell.'

'Red hair. Lipstick.'

'Bint, aye? Well, Danny'll be getting stuck into it.'

'Sorry?'

'Aye. He'll be right up in about that. Proper fanny-magnet, Danny boy.'

They arrived in Ullapool two hours after they were supposed to, with the gig due to start in forty minutes. Neil had tried calling the number Danny had given him from a payphone at a service station, but the receptionist had said she was sorry, the rooms in the bunkhouse didn't have phones, so she wouldn't be able to get hold of anyone. Another great sign.

Deek pulled in across from the hotel. 'Right. That's where you are. Now I'm going to get something to eat, then I'm away down the road.'

'You not coming to the gig?'

'What? Naw. No into that lassie music pish.'

Neil felt like kissing the pavement. He pulled the holdall out and didn't look back, hearing Deek clanking and banging the car into reverse as he crossed the road. The hotel looked nice; cosy. He imagined sleeping in crisp sheets.

'Sorry, love; we're all full tonight, I'm afraid.'

The receptionist, a warm lady in her fifties, smiled at him.

'No, no, there should be a reservation for me? Neil Munro.'

'I've nothing in that name, I'm afraid.'

Neil looked around himself. The street was empty – Deek had driven off.

'I'm with the Clio Campbell tour party. Danny Mansfield was my contact name – he's maybe booked the room himself?'

'Oh, of course. Sorry, son, I must have given you a wee fright there. They've already got the room key. You're over the road in the bunkhouse. Have you brought your own sleeping bag?'

'Eh, what? Nobody told me ...'

'OK. Well, you can hire a sheet sleeping bag – we need to take a five-pound deposit, I'm afraid. Been losing a few of them this season.'

The sheet didn't fit into his already stuffed holdall, so he draped it through the straps. One corner kept falling loose and dragging along the ground, picking up dirt that would probably count against his deposit. As he walked along the street – mostly chippies, tartan-hemmed pubs and mountaineering-gear shops – he reflected again that it was a strange place for a gig.

'That's the point, though,' Clio had said when she'd phoned, out of the blue, a month ago. 'Thirty dates, none of them in cities. That's what makes it revolutionary. We're challenging the hegemony of the cities; we're bringing the music to the real people of Scotland. Don't you think there's a story in that?'

Admit it, he thought to himself. Admit why you're here. He hadn't seen her in years, not *seen* seen her. Television didn't count, nor did the posters that went up everywhere when the single started to sell, Clio's wild hair smoothed out by some potion or other, her slash of lipstick a red flag, single point of colour against the monochrome. The closest he'd got was at a poll tax rally in George Square, before the song had been signed, when she was welcomed on the stage by Tommy Sheridan, hand at the small of her back, as 'a very talented young lady with a song I think you'll like', but he'd been one in a thousand that day, couldn't even fool himself that she was looking at him. Her voice had been hesitant at first, but she'd found herself quickly, the whole rally joining her on a chorus they'd only just learned.

'Rise Up' had become the anthem of the anti-poll tax movement, Clio standing on stages in Liverpool and Edinburgh and Manchester and London, her hair in a scarf and her denim jacket studded with badges. People began to cheer for her in advance if they knew she was on the bill. Cli-o! Cli-o!

Some opportunist A&R man had seen the potential and snapped her up, and Neil had eaten dinner to the incongruous sight of Gogsy Duke's ex on *Top of the Pops*, refusing to mime along, and stripping off a paisley waistcoat to reveal a CAN'T PAY, WON'T PAY T-shirt, just standing there in front of the soundless mike, staring into the camera, while the recording played out around her and the rent-a-crowd bopped confusedly. There was a fade and cut back to the grim-faced DJ, who tried to smooth it out with blandishments, but you could hear Clio chanting 'We're not gonna pay your . . .' in the background. He had loved her all over again in that minute.

The single had charted at number two, and wobbled in and out of the top twenty for a few weeks before heading back down again. Clio's antics had earned her a bit of rock and roll credibility, though – there were a couple of oozy, swoony interviews with male journalists in music magazines, lovingly documenting every pint of snakebite she ordered, every swear word her red lips formed. The sense Clio was trying to talk, and the cause itself, was in danger of being drowned out by her glamour, so Neil found himself strangely relieved when 'Rise Up' left the top forty and Clio's face stopped following him. She had apparently toured as a warm-up for the Housemartins; her guest vocal soared over the grinding guitars on a Teenage Fanclub B-side, and he'd switched on the Hogmanay programme a year later, after his mum had fallen asleep with her one and only whisky in hand, to see Clio and Eddi Reader singing back-up for the Proclaimers. There had been no follow-up single, though, no album; nothing for at least two years and now this tour, of village halls and pubs, run by a local promoter. Neil suspected the record company had had enough of their anarchist pop star – all very well having a pretty face, but if the words that came out of it weren't the right ones – well, there were plenty more pretty faces out there.

And then the call had come through the switchboard to his desk at the paper. 'Hello, Neil,' and then that husky, gorgeous laugh. 'Remember me?'

Remember her.

He'd sat there listening to her, feeling like he was bathing in sunshine. She remembered *him*; remembered him enough to have tracked his byline, know where he worked. Perhaps she'd been reading his articles at the same time he'd been poring over her profiles, thinking of him and smiling.

That wasn't the reason he was here, though, squinting into the cold light of this tiny Highland town, salt in its air. He was here because he'd heard something else in her voice, something she'd tried to cover up with the in-jokes and the purring. Clio Campbell needed him. All right, she needed him for the column inches he could provide, but that was still something, wasn't it? The more he'd thought about it, this profile she'd basically begged him to write, his tour diary of the first week, could be her last roll of the dice. The thought of her beholden to him . . . well, he wasn't proud of it, but it was a good feeling, a strong one.

The hall had been banged together with cardboard in the Seventies and then just left to rot in the weather. Three sandwich boards outside bore Clio's face, photocopied into pixels, with 8 P.M.

TONIGHT slashed over them in marker pen. Neil walked up a dingy corridor to where a teenage boy sat behind a cash tin.

'Neil Munro – my name should be down?'

'Ah, nope – sorry, buddy.' Americanisms forced out of a plukey Highland mouth.

Again. Had anyone on this tour even remembered he was coming?

'Don't worry, Duncan. This gent's with me.'

The well-oiled Edinburgh public-school tones he recognized as belonging to Danny Mansfield. Neil's first impression was of a satyr. Something about the goatee and the grin, the staccato tap from his Cuban-heeled boots. The hair sprouting from the open shirt-neck. Danny Mansfield wrapped an arm around his shoulders and ushered him into the venue space.

'You finally made it, then! Been waiting around for you for ages. We had to just assume you'd turn up here eventually.'

Neil pushed down the urge to point out that this was because of the motorway maniac Danny himself had assigned him.

'Yeah. Sorry. Deek – well, we got a bit lost on the road.'

'You met big Deek, then? What a character, eh? Top notch. Anyway, here we are. We'll get your stuff back to the room after, if that's OK.'

A few rows of plastic chairs in a dingy room. The stage was just the area of the floor they'd erected a couple of microphones, amps and a drum kit in, old patterned rugs under each of the mikes the only thing drawing the eye. There were about ten people already sitting in there, clutching plastic glasses; a table was set up at the back with cans of beer and jugs of squash, a plate of home baking. Danny Mansfield caught his gaze.

'Provincial entertaining, eh? But that's how she wants it. It's important to Clio that we're reaching people on their own terms.'

'Can I pop, er, backstage? Say hi to her before the gig starts? We're old friends.'

Too eager, he realized, even as he said it. Gave Danny Mansfield too much information to play with.

'Don't think so, fella. She needs a bit of space before she goes on. Just getting her head together, you know. Why don't we sit you down here just now – can I get you a beer? Yeah? Irene! A beer for my good friend over here . . . thanks, my darling. Right, Neil, I'd better get back to it. Enjoy the show and we'll see you after, yeah?'

His hairy hand with its glaringly manicured fingernails patted Neil on the shoulder twice, and then he was off. Click click click.

The hall filled up a bit. Neil counted thirty-four people in total, and himself, and the woman standing behind the drinks table. At two pounds a ticket, that probably wouldn't even pay for their accommodation for the evening (although, he reminded himself, he hadn't actually seen this 'bunkhouse' yet). He slurped warm Tennent's from a can so old it still had a rusting bathing beauty splayed across it, tuned in to the gentle swoops of pre-gig chatter. It was a mixed crowd – a few kids in their late teens up the back, a couple of grey heads scattered about, the rest looking like young parents, dolled up for a rare night off.

Plukey Duncan flicked the light switch in the hall off, and the kids up the back moaned like ghosts. Danny Mansfield stepped into the spotlight, created, Neil saw, by three large anglepoise lamps craned at the stage.

'Ladies and gentlemen, a very warm welcome to the McCandlish Hall in beautiful Ullapool! This evening's show will be just over an hour long, and the bar will be open for half an hour after that. Can we ask those of you who've brought cameras not to use the flash, please? Gets very distracting. Anyway, I think that's quite enough from me. Please join me in giving a very warm McCandlish Hall welcome, for An Evening With . . . the beautiful, the passionate, the effervescent . . . CLIO CAMPBELL!'

The McCandlish Hall welcome was self-conscious, a couple of

notches up from tepid. The stage stayed empty for a few seconds, then suddenly she was there, purring into the mic.

'Oooh, hello there. Good evening, Ullapool! My name's Clio . . . and I'm going to sing a few wee songs for you.' She turned to the side to tune up her guitar, suddenly shy, as two wan boys and a large bearded man filed onstage behind her and picked up their instruments.

He took the opportunity of her distraction to risk a proper glance at her. She looked good. Her hair was chucked up on top of her head, tiny curls escaping down her neck, behind a patterned scarf. Huge earrings in a sort of African tribal pattern, white sleeveless top of some sort of lacy material, pretty much melting into her pale skin. Ripped jeans, Doc Martens. She was thinner than he remembered; he could hardly make out the shape of her breasts as she turned back to the front, and the jeans hung off her hipbones. There was a briskness and competency to her movements that he didn't recognize, as she plugged up the amp, checked the first few notes. It felt strange to be so close to her now, watching her, knowing that she wouldn't be able to see him while the anglepoise shone in her eyes.

Her mouth was at the mic again, counting down. 'A-one two three and—'

One of the wan boys screeched his guitar, and Danny ran forward, bent double, to fiddle with the settings.

'Dearie me!' Clio said, pulling a face, covering up. A couple of mild chuckles rose from the people around him. He wanted to let her know that they were with her, that they were on her side. 'Shall we try that again, boys?'

She counted down again, and this time the guitar was fine, twangy but fine, sliding out chords that sounded faintly familiar to him, although he couldn't work out from where. Then Clio began to sing, the slow rasping warmth of her starting somewhere near his stomach, flooding out and through him till his hair crackled with her, even on that crappy PA system.

'*O, Danny boy, the pipes, the pipes are calling.*'

Under her lashes, she glanced off to the side, where the tour man-ager was standing, winked for a fraction of a second, something like a smile working on her, dimpling the words. Her skin seemed to be beaming in the light.

Proper fanny-magnet, Danny-boy.

She played for the promised just-over-an-hour. Rocked-up versions of the auld songs, folk-tinged covers of some recent hits – 'Joyride', 'Losing My Religion' – and only three of her own tunes. Neither of the two new ones were particularly memorable; slow and acoustic, the other musicians stepping aside to stare at their feet or smoke. *Her voice is like whisky*, he jotted in shorthand, in the dark, reminding him-self to follow up on that later. In between songs, she tried to engage the audience, anger them, as though they were a rally crowd, with lists of the Tory government's crimes and how they themselves, the people of Ullapool and their children, were being affected. The audi-ence was silent, impatient for her to start singing again, like sleepy junkies focused only on the delayed gratification of the next hit. She finished, of course, with 'Rise Up'. The teenagers in the back row started whooping and singing along, and she even managed to get the more sedate audience members up the front clapping their hands for a final a cappella take on the chorus.

As soon as the music stopped, she seemed tiny, confused. She bowed twice, muttered 'Thank you, Ullapool' into the microphone, then ploughed offstage by the door to her right, as the applause died away. Duncan flicked the light back on, and the room emptied quickly.

Clio had been given the community hall's kitchen as her dressing room. It was wincingly bright. Guitar cases were balanced on cabinets; a make-up bag spilled over the small electric hob. The band leaned around, cans in hand; Clio was perched on a flimsy-looking table, feet on the room's sole plastic chair, swigging from a bottle of red wine.

'No. It was shit, it was shit, it was shit,' she was saying, pausing to top herself up. 'Fucksake, what a bunch of fucking stiffs. Giving me nothing, so of course I fucking froze. Neil! Neil Neil Neil – Neil's here!'

She stretched out her arms towards him and he mock-ran towards her, mugging.

'Here you are, *here* you are. I was so worried when you didn't show, but Danny said you'd be fine.'

The hug was tight and real, her arms over his, taking all of him in.

'Argh! It's been so long.'

'Thank you for doing this, my darling. Really. I'm so sorry you had to see the show on such a terrible night. That audience, eh? My God. The other nights have been so much better – tell him, Donald.'

The big bear man with the beard who had played accordion and fiddle nodded towards him, silently, while the sallow drummer piped up, in a thick Scouse accent. 'Yeah – the crowd in – what was that place? Durness? Like nothing I've ever seen before.'

'I think they liked it,' Neil said. 'They were maybe just more naturally reserved – there's a few of them still hanging out there, waiting to meet you.'

'Ah, fuck 'em. Not tonight. Tonight I'm going to stay here in my strip-lit kitchen prison and drink wine with my old pal Neil.' She had grabbed his hand and was swinging it, smiling hugely and slightly drunkly at him.

Danny stepped forward. He'd been so still until that point that Neil hadn't really registered he was in the room.

'Come on, Clio. That's not the deal. That's not what we agreed.'

'Danny—'

'No, you know the score. You made up the score, in fact. The point of this tour is that you get out there and you communicate with people. On their own level. You've got half an hour. Then we can go to the pub and you can catch up with Neil. I'm sure he understands.'

Neil found himself nodding, trying to please teacher.

Clio held up the hand that was not clutching the bottle.

'All right. All right.'

Danny poured some of the wine – a polite amount – into a small paper cup. It had already left a thick purple crust over her lipstick. He ushered her out with a hand on the small of her back, left Neil alone in the kitchen with the band.

'That really was a great show tonight, guys,' he said, into the silence.

'It weren't our best,' said the guitarist, also Scouse.

'It weren't bad, though,' said the drummer. 'She's being hard on 'em is all.'

Of the three, the drummer had the most alert face. Big round eyes in a bouncing head, like a friendly children's puppet. He took a couple of jerky steps over to Neil and held out a hand to shake. 'Lee. Hiya. So, you're a pal of Clio's?'

'This is the journalist,' the other one, the guitarist, said. 'This is the boy that's coming on the road with us.'

'Oh, right! That's you, then. Pretty handy that, that you're a mate of Clio's an all, eh? Neil, is it? That's Sean, there, and the big fella here is Donald. He don't talk much, but he's sound, aren't you, mate?'

Neil just nodded. He honestly couldn't think of anything to say.

'Anyway, you're in with us tonight,' Lee was saying, trying to invite him in. 'Pretty cosy arrangement we've got! Donald here snores a bit – don't you, big lad – but you get used to it.'

Neil thought about Clio out there with the straggling autograph hunters, wondered if she was talking to them about politics, or if they'd got bored and gone home. He thought about how small she'd seemed out there on the stage.

'So. Lee – how did you meet her?'

'Clio? Oh yeah, yeah. Me and Sean are in a band of our own, see, and she was on before us at this massive poll tax rally in Liverpool – that were the night she got signed, weren't it, lad? A&R fella was there. We all went out to the pub after and, ah, a few ales were consumed, shall we say, and we've all been pals since. Amazing gel, int she? Proper, like. We played some more rallies together, and then when

"Rise Up" went all massive she had us come and be her band a couple of times. Did you see *Top of the Pops*? That were us, eh.'

'Closest we'll ever get,' muttered Sean.

'Yeah, she looks after her own, that gel. So she said she wanted to do this tour and would we come; well, me and him were doing fuck all in Liverpool, like, and we've never been to Scotland before, have we? Sean's looking forward to the Isle of Skye and Orkney, aren't you?'

Sean nodded. 'I'm into ancient monuments, like.'

At this, the older man, Donald, got up and left the room, nodding to them all.

'Ah, don't mind him, like,' said Lee, with a conspiratorial smile, and Neil wondered what he'd done to attract the unswerving devotion of this puppy-dog. 'He's just a bit shy with new people is all. Man's magic with a fiddle, like. You hear all those folk arrangements, on the R.E.M. song? That's all Donald. Him and Clio go way back, far as I can make out. Like, she's known him since she was a kid. That sort of thing.'

'Hoi, soft lad,' said Sean. 'Don't go sharing everyone's life story when they're at the bogs, eh?'

'Sorry,' said Lee, his smile getting even wider. 'I love a gossip, me.'

Neil coughed, tried to make his face seem friendly, finally had the breathing space to say the thing he'd been bursting for.

'I might head back through there – see how she's getting on. You boys coming?'

Some of the plastic chairs from the auditorium had been rearranged into a loose circle that Clio somehow managed to be at the head of. As the door creaked she looked up and called to them.

'Come in! Come in! Come and join the body of the kirk!'

The teenagers from the back row were sitting on either side of her, gazing in. An older couple, who had shyly put themselves at a distance, were gradually unfurling under Clio's beam; the woman had kicked off her heels and tucked her feet up under herself. Irene from the bar table was there too; and little spotty Duncan, sitting admiringly by Danny, who had pulled himself slightly out from the group, was watching Clio with a tiny smile.

'So,' she said, beaming up at Neil as he and the Scousers fumbled for extra chairs. 'We're just discussing the first records we all bought. Siobhan here,' she indicated the teenage girl, 'actually says hers was "Rise Up", can you believe it? Her taste in music has got way better since then, though, hasn't it, Siobhan? What about you, Dorothy? It is Dorothy, isn't it? I thought it was. Just wanted to make sure. What was the first record you ever bought?'

Round the circle she went, glitter in her smile, everyone blooming. He noticed that the lipstick situation had been sorted, and also that no one else got to talk for too long. Clio was the conductor. Donald moved silently around behind them, packing up the instruments, reeling in the wiring. At one point he ambled over and touched Danny on the shoulder, and the promoter got up to help him. Clio continued to talk, about nothing much, bursting into that peal of a laugh often, steering well clear of the brimstone of her stage chat, and the room danced.

Danny broke the spell. 'Right, that's us all packed, and we really need to be letting poor Irene here get locked up and away to her bed.'

Irene tried to protest ('Och no, I don't mind, son'), but Neil had a feeling that Danny Mansfield always got his own way.

'Shall we head up to the Argylle Bar, Clio? And anyone who wants to can join us – provided they're old enough, of course.'

Neil lay in the top bunk, under his sheet sleeping bag and big Donald's long wool coat, with a bladder over-full of beer and no idea what to do about it. It had taken him a suitcase balanced on a table and a leg-up from a swaying, friendly Lee to get into the bed in the first place, as there were no ladders provided in this bunkhouse, apparently, and the bunks were not designed for short people. There were actually two bottom bunks free, but one had everyone's luggage heaped on it, and the other one, he was told, was Danny's. Well, he'd been in bed for almost three hours now, marking the passage of time by Donald's gentle snoring and Lee's occasional whimpers, and Danny had not decided to make use of his bunk yet.

Fuck it. He would go to the toilet, take that bottom bunk on his return, and if Danny came in he could get himself up into Neil's bed somehow. He cantilevered himself off the side, his feet scrabbling air for the safety of the bunk below. For one horrendous second he thought he was going to fall, but then his toe caught the mattress, the strap of a rucksack.

The floor in the corridor was freezing, but it was too dark in the room to look for socks. He hadn't thought to bring pyjamas, either, so faced the long walk in his T-shirt and pants, hoping it was late enough that no one would see. He passed Clio's door, number 28. She was the only person on the tour to get a room to herself, it seemed. Tiny sounds from back there: a woman whispering, a man laughing, a soft moan.

Well, what were you expecting, he thought to himself, breathing in cheap, sharp disinfectant that didn't mask the smell of someone else's shit, as he clenched his bare feet in front of the urinal. You knew what she wanted you here for, and it wasn't ever going to be that. She's a beautiful woman. Beautiful women take lovers. He'd just never worked out why the lovers they took had to be such total arseholes.

In the bar earlier, Danny had oiled the conversation, buying rounds of drinks for everyone out of the tiny jar of takings from that night, kept everyone up, egged them on, determined, it seemed – he definitely wasn't imagining it – to keep Neil from getting any sort of meaningful time with Clio. Was he jealous? A man like that, the satyr, the fanny-magnet, jealous of someone like Neil? Perhaps he sensed Neil's connection with Clio – perhaps that was getting to him. He couldn't imagine there was much going on between them besides shagging. Danny didn't seem the socialist sort to him, didn't seem like he had any convictions at all beyond the getting of money. Greasy prick. Oh, he'd do well in life, Neil had no doubt.

In his anger, Neil had forgotten to shake himself, had to climb the stairs and hobble his way back along the corridor with his hands cupped over the slow-blooming stain on his crotch. He was about to turn the corner, but a shaft of light cut through his vision and he froze against the wall. A female figure, silhouetted, some loose thin thing flowing over her upper body, doubling and pulling back. The pointed goatee. The hooves. Neil was sure he could see cloven feet. The small sound of a kiss, the click of a door as the light shut off. Danny was lying in the lower bunk by the time Neil got down the corridor, apparently asleep.

Their days on tour, in a beaten-up old minibus that had been the property of a community centre, had a particular rhythm. The two Scouse boys lolled along the back seat, lost together, talking their own codes, passing a joint back and forth. Between that and the sharp smell of last night's whisky from everyone's breath, the air in there was overbearing. Neil cracked a window whenever he could, but the wind was too much if they were on the motorway. The boys would get restless if they hadn't had a drink by two, so pubs and off-licences needed to be sought out regularly. They raided garages for crisps and sweets, all of them eating like children let loose on a tuck shop.

As they drove, Clio consumed newsprint like food, stocking the bus with five papers every day, occasionally ripping out stories, tutting and exclaiming, fizzing with anger. Nobody really spoke. Neil and Clio had had a bit of a gossip, sure, the first time she was sitting in the back with him – she'd asked after Gogsy 'or the Right Honourable Member, as I hear we're now to call him. Labour Party, eh? Who'd have guessed?' (*wink*) and his new wife – but they were both too conscious of the silence, the four other people right there, listening in, to say much.

*

For two days, whenever they arrived at their next location, Clio would take her musicians straight to the venue. Neil thought it would be interesting for his article to sit in there, but Danny had suggested it might make Clio nervous.

'At some point,' Neil told Danny, on the morning of the third day, 'I'm going to need some time just the two of us. Me and her. This piece is nothing without the interview – I can't just turn in an extended gig review, you know. And I'm only here till Sunday.'

Danny's body language was big, expansive. His hands patted the air between them, soothed it.

'It's cool, it's cool, amigo. I know that. Let me have a word with her and see what we can sort out, eh?'

Onstage, though. When she was onstage, he felt like he was working. It was the only time his mind could focus on the article, push ideas around. It was fascinating, watching her night after night, the way she tried to take the temperature of the audience and adjust herself around them; the way she didn't always succeed.

The night after Ullapool had been Oban. The big upstairs function suite of a pub, bar and clientele both built in. Danny took the stage, asked for a very warm Ochil Bar welcome for An Evening With the beautiful, the mind-blowingly talented . . . and she stepped in front of the mic and just stood there. No shy smile, no hello Oban. The band around her totally still, and then Donald began knocking out a slow, sturdy heartbeat, bare knuckles on the wood of his fiddle.

Her voice, then. More ragged than usual – the after-effects of the long, slow toke she'd taken of the boys' joint in the bus, maybe, her eyes daring Neil to comment.

'Is there for honest Poverty
That hings his head, an' a' that;
The coward slave – we pass him by,
We dare be poor for a' that!'

Sean joined her on the chorus, a honey tenor harmony.

'For a' that, an' a' that.
Our toils obscure an' a' that,
The rank is but the guinea's stamp,
The Man's the gowd for a' that.'

A couple of bearded older blokes in the row in front of Neil picked up the beat and it spread slowly through the crowd, their feet moving as one. The room crackled. Lee met the thump with the bass drum, allowing Donald to raise his arms, draw single notes off the fiddle into the air.

'For a' that, and a' that,
Their tinsel show, an' a' that;
The honest man, tho' e'er sae poor,
Is king o' men for a' that.'

Donald sang the next verse with her, a husky bass rasp that echoed under Clio's sweet-and-sour. From the back row came a wavering note of soprano, growing stronger as the people around her smiled encouragement. Clio stretched out an open hand. And then they were all singing together, the whole room, even those who didn't know the words joining in at the refrain.

'For a' that, an' a' that,
It's comin yet for a' that,
That man to man the warld o'er
Shall brithers be for a' that.'

Neil would hear Burns, and that song in particular, performed many times over the years. In 1992, though, it was still unfashionable. Tartan tat, the stuff of shortbread tins and fat conservative men at

Rotary Club suppers. He still thought the spirit in that room had never been equalled.

As the storm of applause didn't seem to be dying down, Clio spoke over them.

'Robert Burns, Oban. A true radical. A revolutionary. And born just half an hour up the road from where I grew up, in Ayrshire. Hello, Oban. I'm Clio Campbell. And I've got something to say.'

Back in the bed-and-breakfast, Neil put a pillow over his head to muffle the noise of Clio and Danny's celebration in the room next door.

The next night, though, a working men's club in Fort William, their hangovers still pulsing, the room cold from a draughty window and only a quarter full because the football was on, no one stamped, no one sang, and Clio drank and swore and tainted the air around them in the pub afterwards. The cut seemed all the deeper for what had gone before, and Neil eyed his travelling companions round the table unsure of how on earth they'd get her out of it.

'Look,' he said, eventually. 'You've still got last night, right? It doesn't matter that this one wasn't your best. You'll always have Oban!' It was intended as a joke, but the reaction was seismic.

'It wasn't my best, was it. Oh God. I should have engaged them more – that sort of cold open is sometimes a mistake; I should have been able to see that they needed warming up. God, I call myself a professional at this, but I'm so fucking inexperienced really. Ah, man, why did I ever think this was possible? A month-long tour! A fucking month! I want to go home.'

The other men at the table were frowning, looking away from him. Lee had reached over to stroke her shoulder.

'Hey, la. You listen up. You were bloody great tonight, all right? This is some shit you're talking now. You had a small crowd freezing their bollocks off, and you gave them a show. You gave them a helluva show. Their own lookout if they couldn't appreciate it, eh?'

'This boy knows what he's talking about,' said Danny, thumping the table. 'No more of this sort of chat, now. They're lucky to have you.'

'Aye, you were damn good tonight, sweetheart,' said big Donald, mumbling through his beard.

At the bar, a little later, Danny tapped Neil on the elbow, smiled at him.

'Listen, man, don't worry about earlier. It's just an artist thing, you know? When they come offstage they're like great gaping wounds, basically – need to be treated very carefully. You know? Always better just to tell her she was wonderful, yeah?'

He was smiling. He was perfectly, totally reasonable. But Neil understood that he was being told off, that a flag had been raised.

'Yeah, yeah. Got it. Sorry, man. Yeah.'

'Good boy. Let me get this round, eh?'

All that night, back in his single room in the hotel, much nicer than anywhere else they'd stayed, Neil had fumed. They had begged him – begged him – to come on this tour. She had. She wanted this article. Made him wrangle with his editor, pitch harder than he'd ever pitched a piece before. Brought him here, away from work for the best part of a week. And what did she expect him to write, exactly? Two thousand glowing words about the landscape and the timbre of her voice? 'Drinking Dens of Highland Towns: A Comparative Study'?

The next morning, he'd hung around in the breakfast room until Danny had come in, then taken a seat opposite him. Made his demands: interview. Now. Danny had patted the air again, looked genuinely worried, and Neil had climbed back upstairs to pack his holdall, feeling that the scale had finally been reset in his favour.

*

Clio and the boys were in the lobby, lounging about on sofas too well-upholstered for them when he came to check out, surrounded by their luggage and instruments. Her Doc Martens rested on a coffee table, and it was impossible to tell whether she was awake or not through her sunglasses; Sean was glaring at the world through a particularly greasy fringe, and Lee appeared to be skinning up on the back of a glossy magazine.

'Morning, lad. There's a bit of a hold-up, eh – Donald and Danny had to go and take the little bus to the bus hospital,' he said, still cheery. 'I'd go get yourself a cuppa if I was you – if you're going over could you grab me a Bloody Mary, too?'

Neil smiled. 'I'm all right just now, pal, but thanks for the concern.'

Lee beamed at him. 'God loves a trier, mate. Actually, it's good you're here. With four of us we can get a proper game going.' He shoved the pile of ripped-up Rizlas to one side and pulled a grubby deck of cards from the pocket of his cagoule.

'Card games,' said Clio, from behind the shades.

'Very well observed, that woman. What does everyone fancy? Quick round of rummy?' Lee's skinny fingers rippled and shanked the cards.

'Watch him. He's a shark,' muttered Sean.

'Texas poker? Scabby Queen? Blackjack?'

Clio pulled her shades off, turned to face him.

'What did you say?'

'Blackjack?'

'Before that.'

'Scabby Queen?'

'Yeah.'

'You never played it? It's a good one, that. You play with an almost full deck, except there's only one queen in it, and she's hidden in there somewhere. Everyone gets a full hand – that's why you need at least four, see, otherwise there's too many cards – and you take it in turns in drawing from each person's pile. Every time you get a pair, they're coupled off and taken out of play. The queen goes round and round, and the object is to get rid of her – pass her on to the next one as quickly as you can. Person left with the queenie at the end loses, you see. Poor girl, int she. And the guy left holding her – he gets hit over the knuckles with the full deck. Papercuts and all. Can get a bit scabby, like.'

Clio laughed. It sounded a bit forced.

'I'm from a mining town, hon. That means something pretty different back home, that does. Or maybe not.' She breathed out. 'Anyway, I hate to spoil your bridge party, but me and Mr Munro here are going to use this time to conduct our all-star celebrity interview. Away from your nosy face.'

She pinged one of Lee's ears with affection.

'Fancy holing up in the bar, Neilio? I'm sure the sun's over the yard arm somewhere. All that talk of Bloody Mary has me thirsty. Bloody Clio time.'

She stood up, offered Neil her hand and turned that megawatt smile on him. He felt warm again.

Daily Mail, October 2016

AND FINALLY, Nineties has-been poll tax one-hit wonder **Clio Campbell** took to Twitter yesterday for a spectacularly unhinged rant about Brexit. The ageing former star, who has in recent years made more noise with her outspoken political rantings than her music, condemned all Leave voters as 'ignorant racists' and sent a string of offensive messages to UKIP leader **Nigel Farage**.

The once sexy redhead should perhaps pay more attention to her own lyrics – people gotta rise up indeed!

JOHN BIDDIE

HAMZA
London, 24 January 2018

All he had was flashes. Six years and he don't know how he spent it. They were off their tits a lot, being fair. But this felt bigger than comedown-smashed brain cells, like he'd deliberately blanked it out.

'It's weird, right,' he said to Calvin, 'like you live through something then your brain just tidies it away, like na mate, you don't need to see that again, I'll just drop that into the charity shop for you. Know what I mean?'

Calvin knew.

'I mean, here's this woman who I fucking grew up with basically. She was there all through me coming into myself. Becoming a man. Yeah? And she had a lot to do with that. I'm not saying she made me who I am but it can't have been far off, right? I mean, we got together when I was twenty-fucking-two. I was nothing. But see, because it ended so fucking terrible I can't remember anything but what a pain in the arse she was then. An it's pissing me off, mate. It's like it's poisoned the whole rest of the experience, so I can't remember any of the good stuff. And there must have been good stuff, yeah? We was together for a long time. Know what I'm saying?'

He doesn't even remember, like, stuff she said, so much. He thinks of Clio and he just remembers wanting out, how needy she got by the end, how she kept on slumping and crashing and trying to bring him down with her. The smell of her unwashed body after he'd been on tour for a week. He remembers that. Her flat full of snotty crumpled toilet paper and the seep of old alcohol coming out of her pores. The tears, caused by nothing, just existing to make him angry. These things he'd told Gemma about over and over, so he'd made them a bit more concrete, maybe. He couldn't tell Gemma the good stuff, because you didn't do that, and because he definitely wasn't feeling it when they first got together, so maybe it had all just evaporated. What was the point of having good times, then, if they just pissed off?

It was fucking toxic at the end was what it was, he says to Calvin, and Calvin, who wasn't there and never met her, says, 'Yeah. Sounds it, mate, yeah.'

Flash. The massive fight they'd had in a B&B before some wedding. No idea what it was about, just Clio's face screaming up at him, her finger-nails near his eyes. They'd needed half the coke they'd brought with them to get through that one; he remembers twitching in his seat, the only non-white face in the whole congregation with all these rich old fuckers edging away from him, not knowing anyone, her stood up at the altar or whatever it was called and her voice ringing out, her trying to meet his eyes, singing the words just for him. Some Joni Mitchell thing he'd never heard before she started practising it. By unspoken mutual agreement, they'd kept themselves drunk and high all day, even dancing and snogging, not talking about it. Their first real break-up had happened the week after and that song had followed him about for two months, on the radio, on telly, people singing it in the fucking street until he'd found himself shitfaced and ringing her doorbell well after midnight.

Two days after Clio died, Gemma came back from work early and sat him down on the sofa, held both his hands.

'I think you're struggling with this more than you're letting on, aren't you?'

'With what?'

'You know what I'm talking about. I think you need time and space to grieve, and I'm sorry if I haven't really acknowledged that.'

She was doing that thing again where she talked like a self-help book, and he knew she'd been workshopping these lines with her mates on group chat.

'It's hard for me, because of my role in it all, to be objective. But here's someone who was hugely important to you, and you're dealing with the knowledge that she wasn't at peace when she died. That's huge. I'm sorry if I've been, like, flippant about it or whatever.'

'Na, na. Gem, come here. You're solid. Don't worry. You've been fine.'

'But, we should talk about it. We should talk about Clio and what she meant to you. I mean, otherwise you're just bottling all that up – it's not like you can tell anyone else, is it?'

'I'm good, babe. I'm dealing with it in my own way. I'm gonna be honest, I'm not really remembering much. You know? Like those years happened to someone else, or it was a dream I had a while ago. It's not – this is my life, now. This house and you and the dog. All right?'

She flopped into him and he stroked her hair a bit. He and Gemma very rarely talked about Clio now. At first, there had been a lot of talking, because they'd been trying to justify their behaviour. ('What a strain for you! I mean, you were basically her carer. While trying to make your own work. That's too much for anyone to bear.' Vindicated, he'd nuzzled his face back into her naked stomach.) But when it stopped, it stopped dead. He'd overheard her once, backstage at a festival. 'You know what? Za's ex-girlfriend is a folk singer. They collaborated on some cross-genre stuff really early on in his career; you should totally look it up.' The words had shocked him into some other life, just for a second, then he'd shaken it off and got on with the tech prep for his set.

*

Flash. Clio in a bar, holding forth, red mouth a blur and her hands jabbing the air as she dominated the conversation, the other people with them gasping, laughing, nodding in respectful silence. He remembers being proud of her then, proud of his woman and her brain. There, that's a good one.

It had got under Gemma's skin, though. Next morning she was itching into it again. Woman could never let something just lie.

'I'm sorry, hon, I can't not talk to you about this. I'm feeling my own role in this, like, really strongly; I mean, did we basically push a woman to her death? I know it was years ago, but these things have a knock-on effect, don't they? I mean, there's no mention of any other relationships in any of the stuff online.'

He wasn't awake enough to deal with this yet and told her so.

'I just don't understand how this isn't affecting you. I mean, it's making me think, what if I died. Is this how you'd react to me, all these years later?'

He buried his face in the pillow and a noise came out. It was loud and angry and he could tell she'd flinched. Fucking good. He felt for a second like the wolf man again. He rolled over to see her looking at him with those big eyes, sheets tucked under her armpits like some girl in a movie hiding her tits.

'Fucking HELL. It's affecting me. I don't know how and I don't want to talk about it, but it's affecting me. OK?'

It was too warm in the bathroom with the door locked. He climbed into the empty tub and reached round the trailing plants to open the window, let the London morning in, horns and voices. Then he just sat there, in the bath, one toe under the tap catching the drips, looking at nothing.

Gemma was dressed by the time he came out, hair scraped back on a hard face, forcing mascara round her red eyes. He stepped behind her, wrapped his arms around her waist and she tensed up.

'Cummere, babe. I'm sorry I shouted. This is – this is really fucking hard for me. I ain't worked out what I think yet, but I promise you if I need to talk about it I'm gonna come to you. All right?'

She relaxed a little.

'And I need you to know this ain't got nothing to do with you, right? Clio was sad. She had problems way before I met her. You and me's been together for a long time, now. There were loads of other stuff going on with Clio. OK?'

'OK.' She was going to say something else. He could see it coming.

'Listen, hon. I wonder if maybe you should go public about this. Like, everyone is paying tribute to her. Maybe you should do, like, an Instagram story or something. Announce it all – just say that, like, your record company didn't want anyone to know you had a much older girlfriend or something. Can't possibly hurt you – it's like every-one's discovering her for the first time, her politics and stuff. Poor cow. She's suddenly well cool but she had to die to get there.'

'Na, dunno, babe. That's not me. I don't even like people knowing about *us*; why'm I going to put something that personal out there like that?'

'See, I also thought it might help you with whatever you're going through. Try and put it into words, sharing it with people. Could become a new track, maybe?'

She was good, Gemma, he had to give her that. While he'd been switched off in the empty tub she'd come up with a whole plan to get him to deal with his feelings, boost his profile and maybe shake him out of the creative block he'd been stuck in. He wondered again whether he would have even had a career if they hadn't met. Not like this one.

'I don't – she fucking killed herself, Gem. I don't want to be, like, profiting out of that.'

'I'm not saying that at all. Is that what you think of me? God. I'm talking about paying tribute to someone you loved. You did love her, Za. You knew her in ways nobody else did, maybe better than anybody else. You should do this. Right, I'm off. Gimme a kiss. You call me if you need me, OK?'

Hamza lay back on the bed, flicking at his phone. The Gram; couple of private messages from that little babe at the Bristol gig last month to delete. He typed in her name as a hashtag: #cliocampbell. The search function suggested #cliocampbellrip.

There she was. Her face in tiny squares, mostly much younger than he'd ever known her. Holding her guitar. Onstage at a rally, with her fist in the air. Videos of what he knew was her stoned grin as she flashed her T-shirt on *Top of the Pops*, those five seconds before the camera cut repeating for ever. A drunken candid shot posted by some indiscreet cunt, jaw squint, blurry hair and a cigarette falling out of her hand. There was one they were using a lot – Clio at a microphone, in close-up, black and white. Her eyes were shut and lined in black, her mouth was open and dark. She was singing and she was lost in it. It was impossible to tell how old she was, whether that was before or after him. Or during. Sometimes these anonymous people, out there on Instagram, put washes or filters over it, or graphics with their own comments: #peoplegottariseup, over and over again.

He scrolled into the cloud, began zooming through the years of pictures stored there – him and Gemma in Ibiza, him and Gemma the day they got Snoop, taking selfies with the puppy. He wasn't even sure he'd migrated all his photos over from the old laptop. Even the earliest ones were all of Gemma, started in 2013.

Had he known Clio better than anyone else? For a time, maybe. To be that person, though, that was a big responsibility, and here he was having fucked it. A nice fucking send-off, he thought, if the person who knew you best in the world, for a time, couldn't remember you properly.

He mooched about in the garden with a joint for a bit, started wondering half-paranoid whether there was some conspiracy going on, if even the computer was in on it. What kind of man you think you is anyway, he asked himself, out loud, if you need pictures and videos and the fucking cloud to keep your memories for you? Of a relationship that ended less than ten years ago? Fucking machines are winning, he muttered to Gemma's three-hundred-quid garden chair. Fucking machines are coming for us.

Flash. Clio in the bath in the shared bathroom of the bedsit, knees pulled up in front of her chest, smiling at him, reaching out to wrap a wet hand round his neck. There were never any words, though. Her mouth was moving but he couldn't hear her voice.

He hadn't bothered to open the blinds in the office and the effect, when he stepped back, looked a bit serial killer, he had to admit. There were boxes all over the floor, tipped on their side and their contents emptied out, the drawers in the desk hanging open, the shelves bare and shoved around. It was like she'd been scrubbed out of his life. No letters, no mementos, nothing. Had he done this? Had Gemma?

He'd found his old laptop finally at the back of a cupboard. It was dented and covered in stickers, and he couldn't believe how heavy that thing was. It wheezed and whined and took ten full minutes to boot, during which time Hamza had rolled himself another joint and sparked up. You're grieving, intcha, he told himself. It's fine to have a puff in the day when you're grieving. And if there was ever a time Gemma was going to let him off smoking in the house this was it. He chuckled to himself.

Pictures. Finally. Only a few, from back before camera phones made decent pictures, but it was enough. He sat cross-legged on the floor, hunched himself over the screen, one finger clicking. Their holiday to Berlin. That weekend in Brighton, when the couple who'd run the bed-and-breakfast had been racist as fuck and Clio had screamed them out and thrown the fry-up on the floor. A picture that was of him but that he knew she'd taken – him doing a shaky thumbs-up just before he went onstage to support Tinie the first time. That

Christmas Day when they'd gone for a Chinese and sat at the table by the window giving the finger to anyone who passed. One night at a club, their eyes red from the flash, peeking out from under all her hair as she snuggled into his shoulder. A grainy shot of them in bed, taken on the first phone he'd had with a camera, bare shoulders and mock-surprised faces. There were some nudes too, he could see, but he didn't want to go in close. It wouldn't have been right. Not now. He kept clicking, and waiting, and there it was – his first time in a recording studio, the day he'd come in with her to lay down a track on her album.

Flash. The dry-skin warmth of her hands on his eyelids and the gentle pressure of her at his back, pushing him along. Her usual smell – shampoo and face powder. She was on tiptoe to keep her arms up at his face and kept tripping. They rounded a corner and he heard some scuffling as she tried to open a door, then she nudged him into a room and the light flooded in as she moved her hands. It was a tiny space, a bit shabby, not really what he'd thought a studio would look like, but there was a mic in the corner, headphones hanging from a hook beside it and a huge yellow plastic bow tied round the stand. 'Tah-dah!' she'd said, laughing, jumping up to kiss his jaw as he'd hugged her tight just because she was so happy.

The little egg timer froze as the pictures were loading to his mobile hard drive, and a window popped up to tell him there was only ten per cent of battery remaining. Shit. Shit. His ransacking session had not unearthed a charger and, now he thought about it, it was prob- ably in that pile of wires they'd chucked out a couple of years ago. He knew what else he thought was on there – the rough-cut files from that studio session. He wanted to hear their voices singing together. He wanted to hear her talking, stopping takes, giving him instruc- tions that he remembers being pissed off about at the time. Having made sure the photos were safe, he shoved the laptop in a bag and made for the door, chucking a hoody on over his pyjama bottoms as he went.

Flash. Scrubbing lipstick off coffee cups every time it was his turn to do the dishes. Can't you just wait till after breakfast before you put your slap on, he'd asked. Dinnae come between a woman and her lippy, darling, she'd said, getting all Scottish on him, and left the room. He only ever saw her without the make-up on last thing at night, during her meticulous cleansing and moisturising routine, as she was always up before him in the morning. That's how he'd known when she was getting bad again, towards the end, her face blanched of all colour, blending in with that ratted ashy dressing gown. After a while he just left the pink tannins on and sipped around the stains. Nobody else really came to visit them anyway.

The Uber had dropped him off at a really grotty-looking shop, a sign on faded neon card in the manky window: WE FIX COMPUTER'S.

Still, this must be the place. Calvin said he swore by the guy, and Calvin was nerd enough to know. The fat little man behind the counter sucked in his breath over his teeth and Hamza winced.

'Yeah, I can do it. Cost ya, though.'

'You've got a charger for it?'

'Yeah. Well, I'll be able to source one.'

'And you can just put it all on a hard drive for me? The lot?'

'Yeah. Take a bit of time, though.'

'What you reckoning, price-wise?'

'Yeah, see with the vintage models it's difficult to tell, innit? Could be anything over four hundred if I got to get new parts. Could be up to seven hundred.'

Hamza thought for a second. There was a pretty big chance he was getting ripped off massively, but he realized he didn't care. He wasn't paying the man for his work. He was paying to get control on his emotions back. If he had all his Clio stuff on one hard drive, and he knew where it was, he could access whenever he needed it and not feel like bits of his brain were falling out. And he was pretty sure this guy, at least, had no idea who he was.

'Just do what you gotta do, mate. I'm good for it.'

Seven hundred pounds would have been two months' rent on Clio's bedsit in Homerton. They'd walk back for over an hour after nights out at the Bar or the Eski, where she'd be self-conscious about being the oldest one there and he'd just be fucking proud to be seen with her. When she entered a room she slayed, didn't she, and the way she held herself, that face – all those little girls with their flat arses had scowled at her because she was so much more than they'd ever be. Walking home, he'd push her up against a wall on a deserted street, or drag her down alleyways, both of them laughing like kids. She'd pull her tights and knickers aside, shove her skirt up, and he'd come inside her, roaring as she sang out long high notes into his ear, hands clawing at dirty brickwork. Those 4 a.m. orgasms with the night-time cold on his skin.

Stepping out into the street, the fresh air a relief from the stuffy, sweaty nerd lair, Hamza felt the sun on his face for the first time in days. He pushed his hood down, enjoyed the warmth on his shaved scalp. His phone was in his hand and he'd already thumbed to the Uber app without realizing, but he let it slide back into his pocket. He wasn't exactly sure where he was, but some sort of force larger than his own will was telling him he needed to go for a walk, and he always made a point of listening when the universe sent him signs like that.

It hadn't been just sex, though, had it. She was always fizzing with something, always talking. Something else to be angry about. Something else that they could do. Somewhere new they could try. Clio had kept moving, at least during the first few years, and when they'd fought, they'd fought high and hard, but he'd been young, and he'd fucking loved it.

*

Four blocks down and he began to recognize the streets. He broke into a run, people jumping out of his way in alarm as he went. This was meant to be, today.

Homerton, London, 2005

He couldn't remember the first time he'd seen her, as she'd been coming into his uncle's restaurant every month on giro day for a couple of years, maybe even before he'd started working there. She'd been a fantasy for most of the waiters, as by far the best looking of their regulars (and the Shish had no customers that weren't regulars), and they often fought to serve her table. The nights she was in were a rare highlight. The job was shit, the food stank and his uncle could be a right prick, especially to Hamza, acting out every last beef he'd ever had with Hamza's dad while pretending it was all because he couldn't be seen to show favouritism to his nephew. At weekends Hamza would work eight-hour shifts without a break then bust it to get out of there and make the night bus to the open free-style nights in Bow, changing his white shirt and pressed trousers for a hoody and jeans on the top deck, downing a can of Red Bull on the walk and a second one just before his slot came up, shifting his weight from foot to foot in the crowd, a little tick-tick-tick pulsing in his ear while he assessed the other acts. He'd fall into bed at four or five then sleep till twelve, muck around with samples and beats in his bedroom for a couple of hours, shower, be back and ready for the opening-up shift at three. That energy you only had when you were twenty-two.

Thursdays, though, Thursdays he wasn't running anywhere. And the first Thursdays of the month were Clio days, although none of them knew her name as she never paid by card. She was usually alone with a book, would always have the same order – jalfrezi and a glass of red wine, aloo saag on the side, requested in a soft Scottish voice that made his stomach flip. Her little treat to herself, he liked to think. If his wank of an uncle was in, he'd barrel his way out on to the floor, doing the rounds of the tables and greeting the customers, hovering like a fly around Clio as Hamza was trying to take her order, jumping in with an oily 'and anything else?' while Hamza was still writing down the main.

He'd tried to start conversations with her before, but it was always difficult when he was being watched. Plus he always felt stupid. What's the book, he'd ask, and she'd show him the title without saying a word. Any good, he'd follow up, and she'd nod, smile, not take it any further.

Sometimes she brought a friend, although it was almost never the same friend. Earnest-looking women with bad shoes and no make-up, one arrogant dickhead who kept clicking his fingers, hippies who would always order the one vegetarian option, and once another absolutely stunning Scottish girl who Aftan was sure was a pop star and who Hamza would years later be introduced to as Clio's very-dear-friend-Shiv-you-know-Shiv-*West* (he wasn't big on rock so it took him a while to work out that she was proper famous). They were often Scottish, her friends, so he'd figured she brought anyone she had visiting her to the Shish. Why she chose that restaurant when she had the whole of London available to her, even if she was local, always mystified Hamza at the time – later he'd realize how much she needed, in fact clung to her favourite places and routines, a tiny bit of order in the barnstorm chaos she created about her. Like that greasy spoon she always made them go to for breakfast on Sundays, even after a really nice-looking café opened up just across the street from the bedsit.

The night it happened, she'd been with this white guy, balding, thin face. He seemed a bit posh and awkward, a weird choice for her, and he was definitely uncomfortable. He'd arrived before her and sat right at the back as though he didn't want to be seen, although all the waiters had clocked his unfamiliar face. Hamza had been in the kitchen when she'd come in, had jostled in front of Aftan to take the order when he saw her there.

'Never gonna happen, mate. She's too classy for the likes of you,' Aftan had hissed, passing by as Hamza stood at the table with his pad out. Aftan was wrong on both counts, wasn't he.

'Do you know what, Hamza, I'd like whatever the chef recommends for me tonight,' she said, those huge eyes and a big beautiful smile turned on him. She turned back to the man across the table. 'Telling you. Best curry this side of Brick Lane, and without the tourist mark-up. Properly authentic.'

Hamza was reeling from her knowing his name, hadn't really taken in the rest of it. He focused in on her. There was no real chef, just a rotating calendar of three men whose job it was to grill meat and heat up the six pots of sauce, make more according to the laminated cards his uncle had hung all over the kitchen whenever they ran out. However, he could tell she was putting on a show tonight, and she needed him on side.

'That will not be a problem, ma'am.' It came out like he thought he was Prince Charles or something. He wasn't sure where the 'ma'am' had come from, either. He wrote down 'Chkn jalf, AlS', and took their wine order.

His uncle wasn't in tonight so the floor was clear, and he could walk in wide circles looping in and out of their conversation with no one else bothering him. It was a weird vibe, for sure – the man looked uncomfortable all night and any time he came near, she would give him that huge smile again, rest her chin on her hand and gaze towards him, like him asking whether everything was all right with their starters (he'd brought her pakora on the house) was some sort of beautiful compliment, like he and she were in it together.

He decided their water needed refilling.

'Robert Burns?' the man was saying, pulling a face.

'Contemporary versions, though. Maybe collaborating with pop or techno artists. Hip hop. The poetry angle. Sort of Martyn Bennett style. Isn't it genius? That's why I need someone from back home on board. I can line up the connections down here but it's the sort of thing that will need a good grounding in the Scottish market first, will hopefully travel outwards from there. I mean, it hits the nostalgia crowd, the tartan crowd, gets in the papers because it's a bit controversial, maybe the sort of thing that schools could use. Ready-made sales, Danny.'

'No offence, Clio, but it's been a while since you were up on the Scottish market, you know . . .'

Hamza lurked near the kitchen door for a while, unable to hear the conversation but clocking the signs of an argument building. Her fists clenched round her napkin and her face distorted – and Aftan sailed past him carrying their main courses. They both stopped, put their faces down, lifted forks in silence. Aftan slunk back, whispered in his ear, 'Mate, you're being fucking useless today. Sort it out.'

Ten minutes seemed like a decent amount of time to regain his cool. He began walking towards them again, checking the forks were laid correctly on the empty tables en route. He heard her laugh, loud and false.

'Make Poverty History? Oh of-fucking-course you did. That's got your fingerprints all over, doesn't it? All those self-obsessed whelps on the first and second rungs of the property ladder, making a difference to precisely no one by wearing a white rubber wristband and going "Wooo!" at some bloated corporate rock in a park. A vaguely feelgood message, no further thought or understanding required, and everyone toddles back to their cubicles and continues to prop up the same systems of structural inequality as were ever there, feeling like they Did Something. That wasn't political. It was the opposite of political. It was a distraction. You basically all got together with Tony fucking Blair over a glass of bubbly at Number Ten and said, "Hey, all those people who marched against Iraq? Wouldn't it be cool if we could get them to chill out a bit? And maybe access them as a market at the same time?" Did it make your poverty history, Danny? Nice little earner there for you, I would have thought.'

Hamza would tell her afterwards that that was the moment he realized he was in love. At the time, he had to smother a laugh as the Danny spork turned to him and requested the bill.

'It always goes this way, doesn't it, Clio? You can't just be civil for half an hour over a shitty curry. I give you one little bit of feedback you don't like and you get personal. Well, I've got to go. I'll get this. You probably can't afford it.'

Hamza walked him down to the till at the door and took his card without a word. He didn't tip, or make eye contact, nodded at the floor and left.

She was slumped back in her chair, staring at nothing. He crouched down beside her.

'Hey. You all right? Need a glass of wine? On the house.'

'Yeah. Yeah, thanks. That would be nice.'

When he came back, she was rummaging in her bag for something. He set the glass down and tried to catch her attention.

'Well. He was a bit of a dick, right?'

She burst out laughing.

'So, like, a mate or something? Old boyfriend?'

'That was my ex-husband, would you believe. Dunno if you could tell, but it wasn't a – what's the word – amicable divorce.'

'Was you a child bride or something? He seems way too old for you.'

'Ha ha ha! Keep it coming, pal. You're the sweetest.'

She touched his arm and looked at him, and he thought, oh, hello.

When she left, she reached up to his ear on tiptoe, and whispered that she would be in the pub at the end of the street until closing. He rushed through the next hour, whisking away plates the second the last mouthful had gone in, and traded till duty for two nights of doing the bins with Aftan. She was sitting up at the bar facing the door, dandling a straw in her drink, her legs crossed towards him, an invitation. From the pub to her bedsit round the corner was just mouths and hands and the noise of her breath in his ear and the bloodrush of knowing that it was happening so, so soon.

Long hot nights, lying on that cheapy foam mattress, sticky and stoned from sex, unwilling to sleep while the other one was still there. Her fingers dancing slow circles round his flaccid cock as she told him about Robert Burns, the Scottish poet, the radical, jumped up to play him snatches of folk songs and they both laughed at the women with their strange, too-serious fluty voices. He lent her his iPod, tucked the buds into her ears, played her Dizzee and Wiley and tried to make her realize what he wanted to do with himself.

It was a while before Clio took him seriously, he knew that. The second time they slept together, and he told her how old he was, she shrilled out one high note of a laugh and balled her fist into her mouth.

'Darlin. I am fifteen years older than you. Fifteen. If someone had got me knocked up at school I could be your mammy. I actually went to school with a girl who's got a kid your age. Jesus.'

'Yeah, but int there a thing about sexual prime, though? Like, I read it somewhere that the ideal age for men and women to fuck is twenty-two and thirty-seven. Those are the prime ages. Best possible models of who they could be sexually.'

'Oh really. You read that, did you? Those very ages?'

'Yeah. Well I mean I don't remember the exact specifics. Evidence seems to stack up, though, know what I'm saying?'

And he rolled her over and they lost themselves in skin and sweat again. All he had to do was keep coming back, turning up at the door after his shifts, staying the night, making her breakfast, and eventu-ally she got used to him. In that first year, he would catch her on the occasional low point; they'd be getting ready to go out and he'd see her fretting her fingers together, her movements becoming jerkier as she paced in front of the mirror.

'Oh, what are we doing. What am I doing. This is stupid. Hamza, wouldn't you rather be out with someone your own age? Maybe with a smooth forehead and perky tits? Some little skinny babelet?'

No, he'd tell her, holding her, kissing her, he wouldn't. And at that point, it was the truth.

The first time she came to watch him do his thing was the first time they fought. He had been made up to see her in the crowd when the light caught her hair, even though she'd promised him she was coming. And everything had been lit. He'd hit each beat perfectly, the track hadn't skipped and the DJ hadn't blurred down the last notes, had let them soar out. And his flow had been beautiful. Each word clear, nothing fudged, each breath timed. The crowd had been right there with him, jumping, shouting for each new sample, even his little Easter egg kiss blown to Clio (although he was pretty sure none of them would have heard her before). He came off the stage feeling like he'd arrived, the prince, the boy, ready to claim his prize and hear her realization of his talent.

She was quiet, smiling with her mouth only while they stood at the bar, other guys bouncing up to punch him in the arm or grab him in a headlock, tell him he was on fucking fire, mate, on fire. There was something about her reaction that was bothering him, but there was too much else going on to work it through. Instinctively, something told him he didn't want to push it right then. He waited till they'd left, till they were sharing a joint at the bus stop, a strange silence between them.

'So. What did ya. You know. Whatcha think?'

She exhaled, turned away, folded her arms; signs he'd come to know all too well. A funny thing he'd notice about Clio over the years, eventually, was that despite the fact she was hyper-sensitive to criticism herself, she never pulled any punches about dishing it out, did she?

'I just – it was good. It was really good. Obviously technically perfect. I just—'

'What.'

'I just think – ach, you're a clever guy, Hamza. You could make something so much more interesting.'

It hit like a gut-punch.

'I mean, what was that about, really? About going to the club, and the bouncer didn't let you in but now he lets you in because of all the designer gear you're wearing, and then you pop the champagne, then just list off all the drugs you've taken? Who cares? You're not some big-shot rapper in the States. You're a young Pakistani guy waiting tables in his uncle's restaurant in Homerton. You should be making music about where you're from. About the stuff that's happening to you right now.'

Well, that was a fucking load of shit. After he'd put that bit of her stupid song in there for her too.

'Wow. OK. Well, that's your view. Maybe you just don get what I was doing. You maybe just don understand the music.'

'Maybe I don't. But I think you're selling yourself short. Fucksake, Hamza. We walk down the street and people shout that you're a terrorist, tell you to go back to the Taliban. You see the fear in white people's eyes when you get on the fucking Tube these days. That's the stuff you should be getting up there and spreading. People should have to hear it. There were loads of other guys in there doing harder-hitting material – that little girl with the braids, too. You should make them listen to your voice.'

'Na. Na na, lady. Don't try to tell me you know what it's like being Asian. You don't know. See, that all makes sense to you, nice white person, sure. You know who want to hear a Pakistani boy being angry right now? Nobody, mate. Nobody want to hear it. Didya maybe notice that I was the only brown kid up there? It's black music. You

got to fit in, and do what everyone know. That's how you get the fucking record deal, innit. You wanna know how to get people shouting
"Taliban" at you? You be a Muslim kid with a big mouth. Aight? So na,
you don't get it. At all.'

'This is exactly the stuff you should be doing. Exactly. Use it. Anger
is an energy. I think the Sex Pistols said that.'

'Sure. Yeah yeah. Skinheads, is it? More white people who ain't
going to have a bomb scare called on them if they just get on public
transport. Them's exactly who I should be listening to. Really help-
ful, that is. Listen, you mean well, just like all them teachers I had
meant well, but you ain't got a fucking clue, Clio. You's maybe just
too old or something. An you should just butt out where you don't
know what you talking about. You not even mentioned that I put
your song in there for you, either. People gotta fucking rise up. Ripped
it off LimeWire an everything as a surprise for you. Na, this is bullshit,
man. Bullshit.'

'You feel that way, you'd probably better run off back to your
mum's tonight, then. That song isn't about a bunch of kids in a club
coming up, by the way. It's about real anger. Real anger bringing
people together to make something change, not just moaning about
the door policy at their local club. Go on. Scram. Off you go. I'll get
myself home.'

He kicked the side of the bus shelter as he left, felt it shudder
beneath him.

'Wow. Such maturity,' she called after him.

'Fuck you too,' he screamed at the sky.

They didn't talk for two weeks. Then he turned up at her flat early
on a Sunday morning, having stayed up all night to make a new track.
She answered the door wrapped in a towel, her hair falling down her
back. He opened the towel and pushed her back on to the bed without saying a word. Afterwards, he pulled out the iPod again.

'I'm not saying you was right, OK? Shouting your mouth off still
fucking dangerous if you look like me. But I had a think about what

you said, and I tried to do something that might make you believe in me a bit more. Just, also, making it funny. Know what I'm saying?'

The track he played her was the rough version of 'Hearing Me (Rising Up)', which was the first single he managed to get on Rinse FM.

XANTHE
Santorini, 2012

Xanthe's fingers fumbled at the stone, easing it out of its sheath. The wind rushed her, throwing up her skirts and spraying a tangle of hair into her mouth. It tasted stale, grubby: she would need a proper wash soon. Something sharp on the rock face tore at her forefinger and she let the gust take her curses.

All this for a cigarette.

For the last couple of years she had always kept a packet hidden in this crevice, midway up the staircase hacked out of the cliff between the beach and the studio. Actual cigarettes, in a plastic-wrapped box, with a neat, machine-folded foil wrapper, the ugly Cyrillic health warnings. The pleasure of their order in the carton, their uniformity; when lit, the chemical sweetness of the first pull. That gorgeous toxicity. She inhaled, heard the crackling draw burn down, watched the glowing tip and then exhaled out into the huge blue Aegean in front of her.

It usually took her about a year to get through a packet, because the circumstances had to be right. Nikolas had to be safely away, for at least a couple of hours. There could be no guests staying in the apartments, in case they wandered down to the beach, saw her and brought it up in front of Nikolas; just casually asked for a light or something. Finally, she had to be angry enough with

Nikolas to want to reject everything about his ethos and the way of life they'd built together, just for the length of time it took to smoke.

The wind was too sharp today to sit up on the steps. One-handed, she wrapped the cigs back up in their plastic carrier, placed them deep into the crevice, and wedged the rock in, tight enough that no hippy's horned toenail could unlodge it, even at a run. Then she carried her lit cigarette with solemnity down to the beach. The tide was coming in with a ferocity she appreciated, battering at the rocks. Slap. Slap. She slipped her sandals off and stood on the sun-scorched black sand for as long as her skin could take it. She inhaled again, imagined weed-killer and asbestos filling up her lungs. Above her, on the cliffs, the sun hit the glass wall of the yoga studio, made white-hot patterns on her retinas.

Nikolas and the van would be halfway to the airport by now, she guessed, creaking up hills, an awkward silence between them all, patchouli cloying the air as none of the windows worked. She hadn't gone out to say goodbye, for the first time ever, but she'd checked from the window that Clio had actually got in the van and gone, and there she was, squashed in the back seat, staring pointedly the other way. Off to the ferry port with you. Sit on a hard plastic seat alongside a hundred stinking backpackers till your arse blisters, breathe in the horrible smells from the cheap cantina. Get seasick. Throw it all up over the side. Go on. Do you some good.

It wasn't that Nikolas had a problem with smoking per se. They didn't do it quite so often any more, but there was usually a bag of grass lurking around their residence space, a pouch of tobacco. It was the chemicals and the corporation that got him: a billboard advertising cigarettes would pitch him into a fury very much at odds with his character. Cigarettes were one of the only topics that he spoke quickly about, listing off the thousand poisons that were hidden in there, the callousness with which corporations developed murderous addictions. Weedkiller, asbestos.

The politics of smoking. From her early radical days, the most enthusiastic smokers Xanthe knew had been lefties, all of them so sure that their rollies, their pouches and their papers were another way of sticking it to corporate culture. The old creed of blindness, ignoring that no fewer tobacco plantation workers were exploited and lungs could still grow tumours even through you rolled your own. These cigarettes, slender things with their rolled-gold ring of sophistication, meant another life entirely to Xanthe. Meant boarding school, three bums shoved together out of a window; meant London members' clubs and dark wood, cocktails, intoxication, bright, penetrating laughter and society pages. They meant everything she'd rejected at the age of twenty, steadily built herself into another person in an effort to get away from, and yet here she was, hiding them in a crevice in the cliff face for emergencies.

Once the cigarette was smoked down to the butt (the beef, they'd called it in the squat, passing the soggy ends of joints around), she would stub it out on a stone that she would then throw into the sea, to rinse away the sooty scar. Then she would cradle it in her palm and walk it along the beach, find a good spot to bury it. The final part of the ritual was to slowly strip down to her bikini, wrapping her various layers together and weighting them with stones on the beach, and inch into the sea. It was difficult under foot at first, with the violence of the waves and the pebbles slapping in riot, but once she'd made it to chest-height, she launched herself in, turned in a circle and lay on her back, cricking her neck slowly down, relaxing into it. She imagined the cold salt water licking away at the smell of the smoke, at the chemical residue on her skin. She lay back, spread her arms and legs like a cross, allowed the waves to take her hair. She squinted at the sky. This was the part where she unclenched, allowed her real life to

ebb back in. All the choices that she had made – good, positive choices
– to get her to this point, to this place, filling her slow, easy life with
health and sunshine and love and peace –

– and Clio's face, that twisted tiny half-smile tensing at the jaw,
came back into her head and blocked out the sun.

'Got it all right here, haven't you? Mind you, you were never exactly
struggling.'

They'd reconnected on Facebook, which was something Xanthe
was ambivalent about anyway but kept up as her main line to Dido.
She was surprised, mostly because her crusty former pals were gener-
ally too suspicious of online surveillance to use it, and Clio had always
erred on the side of paranoid, even in that company. The click had
come through just after the hullabaloo surrounding the Carrington
case had wound down – a little red notification from the past. Expecting another burst of hostility, she had braced. But nothing, for three
years.

Xanthe had kept her distance from the case, but she still ordered
the English-language newspapers in from the nearest tourist town
and followed the online coverage. CLIO ACCUSES TOP COP OF
UNDERCOVER SEX SHENANIGANS.

The headlines made it ridiculous, of course. They had wanted her
to testify, but she and Nikolas had talked through this. It wasn't that
she was denying her past, more that she was at peace with it, and
whatever other people had done during it.

'Bourgeois bitch, intcha,' Gaz spat at her, over Skype. 'Always looking out for your own interests, you was.' A long swim in the sea, her
body suspended in the water, just a tiny floating thing in the mass of
the blue, got rid of that one.

Xanthe had built up an armour of anger in her twenties, filled up the
chinks in it with other people's ideologies. The squat, the Utopia they'd
naively thought they were building there, the demonstrations and the

building of the movement, all that idiotic hope; that was the first of
many solutions she thought she'd found that turned to rot. With a
baby girl to protect, she had run, again and again, from the negative
elements in her life: her former friends and lovers, even Dido's father.
Especially him. She began listening to what other women had to say;
burned harder and hotter with anger than she'd thought possible. She
worked in women's shelters and shaved her head, tried half-heartedly
to be a lesbian, kept Dido in dungarees and pudding-bowl haircuts
until she cried that other children were bullying her, and felt no more
peace for any of it.

Eight years ago, still looking for something, she had taken Dido
on a pilgrimage. They had flown to Athens with their clothes tangled
together in one long rucksack, Xanthe clutching Dido's thin white
limbs to her in the line of tall, tanned twenty-somethings queuing
at the ferry port. Dido, who had never been out of London, seemed
to shrink at first in the face of so much strangeness, retreating into
Xanthe's hips like she hadn't done since she was a toddler. Xanthe
had thought of herself at that age, the leggy boarding-school brat
already well accustomed to flying solo, with a built-in understanding
of her place in the world, flicking her fingers at the stewardesses in
business class. Much better to be this scared little mouse, gripping her
mother's hand tight.

If it had been a true pilgrimage, Xanthe would have simply toured
Dido round the glossy Athens apartment buildings they'd shuttled
between as children. But she wasn't interested in reconnecting with
her parents or the life they'd given her. This was about Greece itself,
and what it meant. Dido's skin tanned gradually, in days puttering in
rock pools or on the decks of ferries, chasing tiny lizards over stone;
Xanthe bought a kohl pencil in a Kos chemist, long heavy earrings
and a flowing white dress from a shop targeting hippy backpackers.
She lined her eyes and held her head higher. They curled up together
under white sheets in budget rooms with shared toilets, the too-sweet
smell of sewage rising in the heat of the night. They took a joint

decision to renounce vegetarianism, just for the time they were there, and ate calamari, octopus and lamb in tavernas, swooning at each other over the richness of the tastes. Dido picked up a basic vocabulary: yes and no, please and thank you, enough to make elderly waiters clutch their hearts and beam.

In Santorini, in a white village carved out of a cliff face, they walked into the cool of a basement bookshop, where the air was thick with incense, to avoid the crush of tourists ploughing to the most westerly point for the legendary sunset. There was an English section, and Dido gravitated towards it; specifically to the word 'sexy' that had been painted on the side of a shelf. Xanthe found herself thumbing through contemporary Greek poetry, still struggling to translate back in her head as she was so out of practice. She had never had much time for poetry: she'd always been too hard for it, in one way or another. But now, here, she felt something uncurling in herself. It was related to the quality of the sunlight, maybe, or the expanse of sea and sky they stared into every day. It had to do with not being in a city, and with speaking Greek again. The poet was a woman, Katerina Elogiat, her eyes brown and liquid in the picture on the jacket. She wrote tiny scraps of things, only a few words, about light on the sea, about the need to stop, be still and breathe. With the tears still in her eyes, Xanthe took it to the till, even though they were on a tight budget for the rest of the trip. The man behind the counter had a beautiful, serene face: he looked older than he was because his long hair was white under the scarf, but his tanned skin had very few wrinkles, and his beard was black.

This was Nikolas, and he took the book from her and smiled, without ever asking why she was crying. Two nights later they were eating fava beans on an old wooden table set up under a grapevine outside his tiny house. Fava beans, Nikolas explained to them in his slow, gentle voice, had to be cooked with love, because it took many hours of stirring to get them to the right consistency. That night he taught Dido how to play Greek tunes Xanthe had never heard on a small wooden flute, and they drew mandalas in the sand on the beach near his house after dark. They stayed on the island for the rest of their vacation, Dido and Xanthe curled into Nikolas's bedroom while he slept under sheets on the floor next door, or out under the stars. On the last night, Xanthe crept out there to join him. They held hands and told their lives: hers as a revolutionary and an activist (she never mentioned her upbringing any more), his as a recovered addict. He had discovered meditation, he said, and it had saved him. Xanthe thought, finally, hopefully, that she knew how he felt. She initiated the sex, stared deep into his eyes in the dark.

He drove them to the ferry the next morning in his crappy old car that smelled of patchouli, and solemnly presented Dido with the flute. She beamed and hugged him, and Xanthe realized that Dido had never had a man in her life.

'I think I need to come back,' she muttered, into his ear, as she reached up to embrace his wiry strength. 'Yes, you do,' he said.

Dido and Xanthe, back in London, were shells. Xanthe went to work and Dido went to school, because that was what they had to do. It rained. Neither of them really made conversation except with each other. Xanthe did not email Nikolas, because there was nothing to be done. She felt calmer; she wasn't as angry, not any more. One wet Sunday, Dido came into the living room and curled up in a ball at Xanthe's feet on the sofa that doubled as her bed.

'Mum, we're sad here. We weren't sad in Greece. Why don't we go back?'

'I'd love to, baba, but we have no money left for another holiday. We won't be able to afford something like that for at least three years. And you have school.'

'I could go to school in Greece, though. I could go to school on the island.'

Slowly it came out that Dido was hating her new secondary school, just as much as she'd hated primary. In fits and sobs, she confessed that she'd made no friends, and that some of the bigger boys had started calling her 'Dildo'. Xanthe cursed again her own stupid 23-year-old self for thinking the name was romantic.

The meeting with her father had been brief. A table in his name at the Café Royal; he'd asked her to come to his office, and she'd said no, you can buy me lunch.

'I want what's owed to me as your daughter. I haven't asked you for anything for fifteen years; I won't ask you for anything again. I want to go home; I want to make a life for your grandchild there, and leave this miserable country behind. Nothing good has happened since you brought us here.'

The old bastard had been surprisingly compliant, agreeable even. She had anticipated more of a fight. He motioned to the waiter to top up their wine, and then wrote her a cheque, which he held in front of her.

'One condition. We want to meet this grandchild.'

She flinched but, having suspected something like this, she already had her answer.

'Mum can meet her. Not you. You know why.'

He looked away from her as he passed the cheque over. 'Very well,' he said. It was the closest he'd ever got to an acknowledgement.

They left just before Christmas, flying all the way this time, shedding layers of thick winter clothes in airport toilets as they did. Xanthe read Katerina Elogiat on the plane, smelled the incense on each page. She walked back into the bookshop and he didn't look up; she pressed herself close to a bookcase, pretended to browse. When she turned around he was smiling at her. He touched his finger to his forehead, to what she would learn to call his third eye.

'I knew,' he said.

The money paid for rent on an apartment, an old car, and a tutor to help Dido with her Greek. Eventually, it also paid for the deposit on the studio on the clifftop, and for a local handyman to come and help them remove the main wall overlooking the sea, replacing it with windows; for them to buy the derelict building carved into the rock and refurbish it into six small apartments, and for a professional company in Athens to create their website. They lived on the last of it until the end of the first season, by which time word had spread and they were running eight yoga retreats a year.

The name had given her pause, when the email came through with the booking, grabbing the last place at the last minute for the beginners' week. It actually took her a second to place it. It couldn't be a coincidence, could it? No, of course, Clio would know that she ran this retreat. They'd used a picture of her and Nikolas, smiling, on the welcome page of the website. But why just book? Why no friendly little message on Facebook, no personal email? Well, Xanthe wasn't going to be the first one to start things up. She counted down the four weeks until Clio's arrival with steadily building dread.

The red hair. Xanthe could see it through the window of the van as it pulled into the driveway. Was it darker? Henna over the grey these days? Still the slash of lipstick, too. As the guests unfolded themselves from the back, she was amused to note that Clio fitted in with them very well. Just another slightly flustered forty-something, flyaway hair and trailing scarves. Xanthe pulled herself straight and tall and strode out to meet them, calling out a general welcome before turning to Clio, arms open but fixed beside her at the elbow.

'And welcome to you, old friend.'

Clio had broadened, fattened up around the haunches. At first, Xanthe wondered whether she'd allowed the beginnings of middle age to subsume her, but watching Clio warily from a distance at that first communal lunch, she realized that old electricity was still there, asserting itself. Their guests, almost all well-to-do women with grown children, spoke a shared language of Spanish holidays and vineyard breaks, upmarket brand names and daughters' gap years that she'd assumed would exclude Clio, but at least two of them seemed to have recognized her from her pop-star days, and she grew bigger and brighter under their attention.

'She'll be tricky in class, my love. Difficult to teach.'

'So suspicious about this one,' Nikolas said, catching her round the waist. 'You may be right, but it's just as important to allow her the space to learn and take what she can from our little sanctuary here.'

'I will be right. But OK.'

Clio finally got her after the first evening's gentle flow session, in which Xanthe usually assisted, acting as interpreter in case any of the guests struggled with Nikolas's accent initially. A hand on her arm, both slightly sweaty. All warmth, all sunshine.

'You. You look amazing. But you know that. It clearly suits you, being here. And what a place. What a view! Ach, I hope you don't mind me being here, Xanth. It just seemed like such a perfect coincidence, that you had a place left. I've been meaning to get into yoga, for a couple of years now – I think it's something I could really benefit from, you know? And I was out here –' she spread a casual arm, indicating, presumably, the whole of Greece '– working with the anti-austerity folk in Athens, helping the potato farmers – some bloody amazing stuff happening there, but you'll know all about that of course. It's been a rough couple of years, and I just thought, why not be good to myself.'

Xanthe had begun questioning herself, under the sunlamp rush of words and smiles – why did she assume that everyone from her past was out to get her?

'I needed to get away. Bad break-up, some health problems, and the stress of that court case. My God. I needed to be here and talk to someone who really knows. Went through it too. The whole thing with Mark.'

And there it was, thought Xanthe.

Clio was beaming at her.

'It just seemed perfect,' she repeated.

'Well, everyone who comes here is trying to heal something.'

Nikolas was being irritatingly reasonable again.

'I just – I've made my peace with it, love. I don't want to be poring over it endlessly. This thing that happened; it's still not the worst thing that has happened to me.'

'But your friend, she hasn't managed to achieve this peace. She's looking to you for help to do that. And that's what we do here, do we not? We help people find their peace. Just as we have.'

'We're a yoga retreat, not a therapist's office. She needs to do some of the work herself.'

'It is a long time since I've seen you this tense,' he said, curling his limbs around her, nuzzling and rubbing at her shoulders. 'Perhaps it is good for you too, to open up again to someone from your past, someone who knows that part of you? It suddenly seems as though you're holding on to too much to be truly at peace – it must be buried somewhere there, no?'

She flinched away from him.

'You're being very patronizing, Niko. How would you like it if one of your junkie friends came here, expecting you to still be the same person you were then, wanting and wanting from you? Trying to pull it all back again?'

He moved off the bed, walked out of the room.

'Most of my "junkie" friends are dead,' he said, over his shoulder.

A low blow. Not like him; not like them. And Xanthe knew who she blamed for it.

The next night, after evening asanas and the closing of the circle, Clio put her head round the door. 'Knock knock,' she said, in that sheepish, ingratiating way British women always had which felt increasingly foreign to Xanthe now. She was holding a bottle of wine that she must have brought with her and two paper cups from the water fountain in the studio.

'I thought we could have a little catch-up . . . ?' she said. Nikolas stood at the end of the hall, nodding and smiling – evidently they'd planned this together. The pricks.

'I don't like to be ganged up on. I've told you that,' Xanthe muttered to Nikolas when she went to retrieve her wrap, not really caring whether Clio heard her or not. He did that loose little dip of the shoulders he always did when he was retreating from a fight, his arms gone stringy. Weed, she thought, a weed come to life, as she always did when he retreated from her. It would pass. It always did.

As they started down the path to the beach, Clio reached for her arm and Xanthe let her grope for a second, awkwardly, before they made a loose link. She had linked arms with friends before, in her schooldays, and remembered that there was a right and a wrong way to do it. The right way, your bodies locked together like you were originally built as one; the wrong way there was just the sore jostling of elbow bone.

Clio began to talk. 'I'm glad we got the chance to do this. I just thought it would be a wee shame if I'd come all this way and we didn't get a little bit of time just us. You must be so busy, too. I mean, an operation like this doesn't run itself, does it? No matter how relaxed Nikolas might be as the public face of it all. We all see the work you put in, by the way,' and here she grabbed over for Xanthe's other hand, patted it.

Does this woman want both of my hands, Xanthe thought. Let go. Let go now.

'All the cooking, all the admin; it's you taking all the bookings and doing the website and stuff, isn't it? Behind every great man is a woman rolling her eyes, eh?'

'That's not quite the way it works, with Nikolas and I,' Xanthe said.

'Do you get lonely?' Clio asked, seemingly out of nowhere, as though the previous intrusion was merely conversational preamble for the real meat. 'Just the two of you now, with Dido away. I mean, sure, you have these customers—'

'We never think of our guests as customers, Clio.'

'No, but there they are, paying you for a service nonetheless. So, you cater to these guests for about half the year, but then the rest of the time, you're just here? Away from the world?'

She gestured to a space on the sand, smoothed it with a hand. Xanthe, who had somehow ended up holding the bottle and the cups, sat down and began to pour.

'There is always something to be done. We are booking the guests, we are deepening our own practice, we are finding new ways just to be in the world. Just being is enough sometimes. It was a great discovery, that. Here. Cheers.'

'*Slàinte*. I suppose I wouldn't really understand that. It's not how I work. I've got to say, I'm fascinated by you. I mean, here we are, the same age –

It would be unfeminist, thought Xanthe, to point out how much younger I am.

'– and we've come from the same position, the same sort of place – I don't mean originally, obviously, but the same point of activism, the same engagement with the way the world is ordered. We've lived in the same squat, fucked the same undercover police officer—'

Here it comes, thought Xanthe.

'How do you just go back on that? How do you wake up, look at the world, the way it is, and not be angry?'

'Did you come here to accuse me, Clio? Did you buy me a bottle of wine and take me away from my evening plans just to tell me my failings? Did you get on a ferry and pay for four days practising a discipline you're not very interested in just to have it all out with me?'

'I'm sorry. I'm sorry. That wasn't what I meant. You know what? I might be jealous, pal. I'm seeing you here, in a place where you're so obviously meant to be. Seeing the peace inside you. I've never had that. I've never had a time in my life where I've felt as much part of something as you seem to be, just looking at you against this landscape right here.'

And for a while, their conversation wound itself around the island

– around the day-to-day beat of Xanthe's life, around Dido's studies in Athens and Xanthe's hopes and fears for her; around Clio's recent heartbreak, a younger man who had left her to be a pop star, or so it seemed. The usual ways a conversation between old acquaintances would flow. But the hidden odour kept drifting to the surface. Clio wanted to talk about the case. Of course she did.

'I mean, we all fucked him, didn't we. You did. I know Fran did even though she likes girls. I mean, that's why – I absolutely understand that the crime against Sammi was the greatest, but I still felt a real sense of violation, which is why I thought I'd really push that way. You know, I could do more, with my profile. I was able to protect Sammi a bit. Take the heat off her, if they all focused on me. That's what I thought. But still, all of us, we need to process this, don't we. I mean, the guys were betrayed too, don't get me wrong, but he was only using them on the one level, know what I mean. It's rape. We were all raped, because none of us consented to have sex with that man, and I wish we'd been smarter about it, you know – I wish we'd had a bit more something on our side. You know, one of those big amped-up lawyers. The expensive ones. We could have got him that way. It's a shame – there was nobody with any real buying power on our side.'

Oh whatever could you be getting at, thought Xanthe.

'I would have thought one of the newspapers even, but no, they liked the sex-scandal aspect, but didn't want to actually take sides against the establishment at the end of the day. Better one dirty copper than bring the whole fucking system crumbling down, eh. And it stays with you, doesn't it? This violation? I mean, I've got to respect the way you chose to deal with it. I don't think that every woman should have to confront their rapist and go through it all again. Me, for me that was the only way, right enough.'

In her very early twenties, when Xanthe ran away for the first time, a succession of dreadlocked men-children had queued up to tell her of the failings of her upbringing, of her bourgeois programming, of her privilege; had tried to dismantle it by dismantling her. The cure they had all recommended, funnily enough, had been a good hard dose of proletarian cock. Xanthe had fucked them and blamed herself, her moneyed-bitch former self, each time the sex got too rough, the language accusatory. She began blunting her accent, her clarion foghorn accent, with a glottal stop, allowing only that her parents were 'Greek immigrants' if anyone asked. Mark Carr, Michael Carrington, whatever his name was, had been different. The more she read about him as the coverage of the case reached fever-pitch, she realized that difference was actually a similarity, one they'd both been trying to hide in the squat. He had nothing to take out on her body; he recognized her because they shared that world. He wasn't a gentle fuck, but he'd been wonderfully disinterested, as though the whole thing had been an academic exercise. She supposed it was, really.

Talking to Clio, now, she just said, 'I think about it differently, but privately. It's not something I want to go into. I worked through it all a long time ago, and it's gone.'

'Gone. This is it. This is why I'm here. Teach me how you do it, Xanthe. Teach me to stop feeling. I wake up every day with his betrayal, with the idea that the state sanctioned my rape, intruded upon everything I thought I knew.'

Rape, rape, Xanthe thought. You fucked a few times, because he was the most beautiful boy in there and you wanted him, and then felt hideously guilty about the girlfriend you were supposedly so close to. Although maybe Mark had been different with Clio and with Fran – maybe there hadn't been that recognition, maybe it had been a contemptuous thing. It is not feminist, she warned herself, to mock another woman's experience as she speaks it.

She really wanted a cigarette.

'I'm just not angry any more, Clio. I cut it all off, walked away. I know, I know, I have the luxury of being able to do that, of finding a place where that behaviour makes sense and a partner who'll help me to do it. I honestly don't feel much connection with that time of my life, I really don't. My whole time in London was misery. Things only started to make sense again when Dido and I landed here. All of it – the squat, all the activism we were doing, that whole communal-living thing. Then afterwards – the women's groups, local politics, the anger. All that anger, all the time, Clio. I wasn't meant to be there, in that scrubby, furious little country. Nor was my girl. It's easier to be peaceful here.'

'Peaceful! Your country is on the verge of socialist revolution. I mean, you wouldn't believe the people I've been working with in Athens. A nationwide movement. They're overthrowing capitalism from the ground up. It's charged, here – like, like in Genoa in 2001. It's an inspiring place, this, no? How can you exist here and not want to be a part of it?'

'It doesn't really touch us. We live on the side of a cliff, for heaven's sake. The very point of this place is to provide people with an alternative to all of that.'

'All of – of politics? The life of the world? It's an escape, then. For people who can afford to look away? Living off the tourist dollar.'

'That's what's usually meant by the word retreat, yes.'

'I just don't see how it's possible. When you've experienced what I've experienced – what you have. How do you stop being angry?'

'Maybe you need to go home. That's what I did. A place can help, the right environment. Find yourself.'

'I don't really know what home is, Xanthe, I'm not like you. I don't have an identity like that.'

'Scottish, aren't you? So go there. They have good scenery, I hear. Go and sit in a misty glen or take the high road or something like that. Go and find yourself a big silent lumberjack in a kilt – someone your own age, someone who's had their own share of it, to warm your bed. It doesn't need to be the place you grew up in. I mean, there's not much inner peace to be found in gated fucking communities full of millionaires in Athens!'

Mistake, she realized as soon as she'd said it. Mistake to remind a comrade, any of them, what you came from. Clio had taken it in, she saw.

'Yeah, I could do that. I could go to the Highlands or something, get a council house somewhere rural. I haven't got the financial security to be able to do something like this, obviously. Buy a yoga retreat for my fancyman. My lumberjack.'

The wine was moving in Xanthe now – they didn't drink much, she and Nikolas, and certainly not during guest season.

'Right, this is what I mean. This whole grudge thing you've got going with me because I had a more privileged upbringing. Don't think I'm not aware of it. None of the old "comrades" ever let me forget it, darling, and you won't ever either, will you now. You can't ever look past that to see the person I am, you're always thinking of me as a symbol. No getting over those bloody great chips on your shoulders that I'm not supposed to mention, am I? Know what? I know you've all had a much harder life than me. I know that. But it doesn't diminish my ability to feel hurt, or pain, or to need to retreat from them in order to preserve my own sanity, that of my daughter—'

Clio's eyes went sly, cunning, sleek at the corners. She was very drunk, Xanthe realized, must have been drinking in her room before coming over.

'Right. It doesn't diminish your ability to feel your own pain. But other people, you'd just rather not think about their pain any more? Is that right?'

'I did my battling. I put in my time. I just – it's exhausting, Clio. What you're describing, waking up angry every day at the state of the world, wanting to fight – nobody can go on and on doing that, indefinitely. Don't you ever get tired of it? Don't you ever think, right, that's it, enough, I'm done now?'

'No. Because if everyone did that, there wouldn't be any point in keeping on going. The world would harden. The bastards would have won.'

Clio stood up – she was clearly going to be the one who got to walk off. Let her, let her, Xanthe thought.

'I see how you've done it, Xanthe. Thank you. You've taught me your ways and I don't want them – couldn't afford them even if I did. Those of us who were born in the fight can't ever close our eyes to it, you know. You go on with yourself, my fine lady. Be unbothered. Be switched off. It's not for the likes of me.'

Xanthe watched her go, struggling across the sand, then picked herself up and went to bed, ignoring Nikolas. At 3 a.m., a quad bike from town roared down the road, stopping and growling outside the apartments, and someone made noisy theatre of stomping back up the stairs, slamming their door.

At five, Nikolas woke to begin the preparations for sun salutation. Xanthe berated him from the bed.

'Don't ever do that to me again, Niko. Don't take it upon yourself to decide that I need to engage with someone, to have a friendship. Ask me things. You don't get to take decisions for me. If I want not to talk to someone from my past, you respect that and let me be, OK.'

That wimpy shrug. She threw a sandal from the floor across the room and it hit the door as he closed it.

She noticed Clio didn't make it to morning asanas. The rest of the guests were waiting there in the driveway, dangling their feet over the wall down to the sea, catching a last tiny bit of sun before the drive to the ferry, and the pitch began to get restless, anxious, as time ticked on. Nikolas went off to bang on Clio's door, and she stumbled down the stairs ten minutes later, avoiding all eyes. That cigarette, she thought, as the fat behind shoved itself into the van. That cigarette was coming soon.

DONALD
1974–84

Donald had shoved his friend's hungover limbs into the van and settled in for the drive to Ayrshire, Malcolm snoring in the passenger seat. Eileen's village, with its grey bricks and bluster, not a colour about the place, did not welcome their arrival. The primary school was poured concrete, all steep drops and hard corners for soft little bodies to catch themselves. They sat outside it, perched on the bonnet of the van, looking uncomfortably suspicious – but these were Eileen's instructions, delivered down the phone to Donald: 'You'll need to pick her up from the school yourselves, and drop her to the house after-wards. I'm not for seeing him.'

'She surely doesn't mean us to get arrested?' Donald muttered, as the flood of parents filed past, eyeing the two strangers and their van. Malcolm merely laughed again, from behind a pair of dark glasses. After twenty minutes and no sign of her, Donald pushed him into the building. They were met halfway across the playground by a hawk of a woman, the sort Donald could imagine thumping out the hymns on the piano; clearly they had been watched.

'Can I help you.' Not a question.

'Malcolm,' Donald muttered. Malcolm woke up, turned on the lights.

'Hello, Mrs—? McGrouther? Mrs McGrouther. I'm here to

collect my daughter, Cliodhna. She's in the first –' he stopped and checked with Donald, who rolled his eyes '– the second class. Her mother told us to pick her up from school. It's her birthday treat, you see.'

The woman was too close, could probably smell yesterday's whisky leaching out of him.

'We have no pupils with that name here. I suggest you leave the premises immediately.'

'Sorry, what? Look here, woman, my ex-wife told me she was here. This is an arrangement. I am here to get my daughter and take her away for her birthday. I've come all the way from Skye and I'm not going to have you stop me, you h—'

'Mrs McGrouther,' said Donald, stepping in. 'Cliodhna Campbell it is we're looking for. Her middle name is Jean. Do you have a Jean Campbell here, who hasn't been picked up yet? And she might be registered under her mother's maiden name, Johnstone? Her mother is Eileen Campbell, Eileen Johnstone that was. Her father and her Uncle Donald are here. She'll know us, don't worry.'

It was not usual for Donald to be the one to spin the charm spell, to make things happen. Small Jean Johnstone was brought out to the front door, and asked if she recognized these men, but she was already flinging herself happily at her father's knees. Their reunion set the tone for the next three birthdays: a van ride to Girvan, the wee wriggling body squashed in between them in the front seat talking non-stop about school, dropping names of other children, giving them high-pitched renditions of all the dreary Presbyterian hymns Mrs McGrouther apparently did thump out. And if it was Donald who would chase her down the beach more often, roaring and pretending to be a monster as she squealed in delight; if Malcolm swayed and stumbled while they walked on the sand, or had a funny smell on his breath, his daughter didn't notice. She would stare admiringly as he made the waitresses in the ice-cream parlour giggle and blush. Every time she'd run straight for Malcolm's legs, the hair rising in a fuzzy orange halo no matter how short Eileen clipped it, screaming, 'My daddy! My daddy!'

That first time, after the last of the fish and chips had been eaten and a second round of ice cream bought even though they were all full to bursting, as the sun began to go down and Donald nudged them back towards the van, something that had been bubbling up in Malcolm burst open.

'Cliodhna. Why has your mother got them calling you Jean at the school?'

She looked at him for a little while, trying to remember.

'Mum saaaaid – that nobody would be able to say it proper. She said it was too silly for school and for here. It's a bit confusing trying to remember it's me when they say Jean!'

'But your name is Cliodhna. Not Jean.'

'Jean's my second name. Cliodhna Jean. Jean's my name for when I'm with Mummy and Cliodhna for when I'm with Da— with you. It's my secret name. Nobody else has got a secret name.'

They pulled up outside the pebbledash terrace Eileen had directed him to, a change of address in the last few months. A quick check that Cliodhna had got all her things – schoolbag, jumper, the wooden xylophone her father had been prompted to buy her during a stop-off in Ayr before they arrived – and there were hugs. A big sweep-up into the air and giggly descent for Uncle Donald, a tight kneeling hold from her father. As Malcolm released her, Donald saw his eyes were wet.

'Cliodhna, I'd like you to ask your mother to come out here, please.'

'Come on, Malcolm,' said Donald. 'You know the terms. She doesn't wa—'

'Your mother, Cliodhna. Now, you sleep well tonight, *m'ghaol*. And always remember you've got a daddy who loves you.'

Cliodhna skipped down the path and let herself into the house.

It was beginning to get cold, so they got back into the car to wait for Eileen. Malcolm was silent, fuming, and Donald knew better than to risk him.

After about ten minutes, he reached over Donald and held his fist down on the horn.

'Malcolm.'

'I'll speak to my wife, Donald Bain, and thank you to keep out of it.'

Nothing. He hit the horn again, this time making two, three, four blasts. A couple of lights went on in the nearby houses – it was a small, close street. A man appeared in the doorway Cliodhna had disappeared into. Malcolm was out of the van straight away, Donald following close behind.

'Might have known. Might. Have. Known.'

'What do you want?' He was big, this one, some ten or fifteen years older than Donald and Malcolm, hard from a lifetime of it.

'And who the hell are you?'

'I could ask you the same question, sunshine. What you doing making a noise outside my house?'

'Oh, you know who I am. Your house? Ah, she's good. Isn't she good, Donald? Anyway, I'd very much like to speak with my wife, please. Eileen Campbell, as she still is called and always will be.'

'She's not interested, pal. She's not coming out.'

'I have an important matter that I need to discuss with her relating to the education of my child, Cliodhna Jean Campbell, as it says on her birth certificate. I don't see what business this is of yours.'

The man bristled like one of those muscly dogs preparing to fight. Donald was not sure they'd make it, even two on one.

'Let me teach you right now what business it is of mine.'

As he began advancing, though, the door flew open, and Eileen was standing there, thinner still, fully made up as ever.

'Leave him, Alec. Let me deal with him.'

She wove her tiny body in between them, catching her man by the face, stroking his cheek. He stopped still, breathed out through his nostrils. Then he turned to Donald.

'All right. You tell this alky joker that if I catch him anywhere near my house again I'll kill him outright and won't mind the sentence. And you get him to sign those divorce papers. OK, boy?'

The front door slammed. Malcolm and Eileen were staring each other down, more engaged now, in their hatred, than they'd ever been when living together.

'Why the hell have you decided to change her name?'

She hissed out a noise to silence him.

'You'll do this quietly, Malcolm Campbell, or I'll bring Alec back out and I won't stand in his way again. Maybe I'll even let the girl watch.'

He snarled at her, but he dropped to an exaggerated whisper.

'Our daughter has a name, Eileen. She has a name, and that name is now the one thing tying her to me and to my family history and language, and traditions. I'll thank you to inform the school that she is to be called by it.'

'Your traditions. It's an Irish name. It's not from the islands. I can't have her going to school with an Irish name. Do you know what people are like round here? Do you know how deep it all runs? Don't be stupid. Besides, nobody could bloody well spell it.'

'And the Johnstone? You are still a married woman, are you not, and it distinctly says on her birth certificate Campbell. Campbell!'

'Johnstone is the same name as her cousins. It makes her part of the family. It means the school know who she is and where she comes from.'

'I'm going to be phoning that school. I'm going to be writing them letters to insist that her name is changed back on all official records. You want me to sign the divorce papers, these are my conditions. And you. You are to call her by her proper, given name.'

'You are no one to tell me what I do or don't call my own daughter. You are no one. Do you understand that?'

Malcolm fizzed, bent double, flailed with his hand outstretched. For one second, Donald thought he might be having a fit.

'You're trying to erase me, Eileen! You're trying to rub me out of my – our child's life!'

Eileen stepped back to her doorstep, pulled her cardigan around herself.

'Och no, Malcolm. I imagine you'll do that bit all by yourself.'

Donald was never told what conversation had occurred between them in the weeks that followed, but somehow, miraculously after his behaviour outside the house, Malcolm was allowed to carry on visiting. Donald would drive him down to make sure he got there, red-eyed and mostly silent, twice or three times a year, watch him sitting douce on his knees on the carpet as she unwrapped his present on Boxing Day, not making eye contact with Eileen or Alec propped stiffly on the sofa with their sherries. He would always buy her musical presents – books of sheet music, a chanter, a tin whistle; on her ninth birthday a tiny fiddle he'd had made for her – but the gifts existed in isolation. He'd never ask how she was getting on with them, never contact Eileen about the girl's music, never offer to pay for the lessons she'd need. And Cliodhna would take the instruments and smile, and set them gently aside.

In the van, driving back and forth from the seaside, they would sing, favourite tunes from their own youth and Burns, always Burns. Malcolm created simple harmonies for Cliodhna's sweet soprano to pull against the more prosaic of Rabbie's songs she'd learned by rote at school. They taught her Gaelic lullabies, reminded her of the songs they'd sung when she was a baby. It was important work, Donald felt; it was keeping the island part of her alive.

On their last trip, she was only mouthing the words, her voice barely catching the notes. 'You need to sing up, Cliodhna,' Donald said, giving Malcolm a look over her head. Her father picked up on it.

'I want to hear you sing, *m'eun bhig*, my little bird. I miss your lovely voice when I'm not with you.'

'Nobody else wants to hear it, though,' the girl muttered, turning herself away to face out the window.

'Who would not want to hear you? Everybody wants to listen to you.'

'Mrs McGrouther said I was singing too loudly and putting the other children off. And Mum told me to stop. She said I was giving her a headache.'

Three years earlier, this would have driven Malcolm into a frenzy. Now he just sagged, went silent. Donald pulled the van to a stop at the side of the road.

'Hey now. Cliodhna. Look at me.'

She turned around, sulking. Between them her father stared straight ahead, blank.

'You have got the most beautiful voice, and you must never stop singing, no matter what people say. Do you remember when you lived with your daddy and me, and we were in a band? Do you remember the island we lived on, Skye?'

She made a half-committal face. Perhaps she didn't, he thought. Could kids forget their lives of five years earlier?

'Well. We thought you were such a good singer that sometimes we would bring you onstage at the hotel where we played. And your daddy would say into the microphone, "Now for the most special guest of the night," and you would hold the great big microphone, with long ribbons in your hair, and you'd sing them "Auld Lang Syne", just like we were doing earlier. And the audience would go wild, really they would. They would cheer and stand up and clap so hard their hands hurt, because that's how good you were. And I remember thinking right there, even though you were only four, this girl has something special about her so she does. And that's why it's important that you sing. I took a photograph and I've still got it somewhere, of you on that stage. I'll mail it to you right away, as soon as we're back home, I will.'

He spent four hours trying to find that photograph when they got back, then put it into an envelope and marched straight up to the post office, banging on the door until old Jacksie came to open it, complaining at him. It was urgent, he said. It had to go in the first morning's post. He was never quite sure why, but it seemed like a very important thing to do.

When the girl was eleven, Malcolm left for America. He'd fallen in love with a bluegrass singer they'd met at the Kenmore Folk Festival: Anouli was forty, with a fantastic rasping voice; she seemed to love the drink as well as Malcolm did. Donald watched them crashing slowly together over a number of nights, their raucous harmonies at the end of one jam session an almost obscene display. Malcolm seemed alive again, offstage as well as on, that pilot light behind his eyes visible once more, so Donald approved and left them to it, assuming that it would fade away when she went home at the end of the week.

Two months later he was showing off his plane ticket.

'Jesus, man, anyone would think you were the wife and it was you I was leaving.'

'Well you are, in a way. You're leaving me and Fraser and the band. But that's not what I'm getting at and you know it. I'm talking about your responsibilities, Malcolm. To that wee girl.'

'Ach, the girl will be fine. She is fine. She's somebody else's daughter now, don't you know. The big man made of meat. And she'll carry on going to her meaty school, and her mother will get her the right kind of job, and then she'll get herself hitched to another big meaty miner. That's what's going to happen to wee Jeanie Johnstone, Donald. And maybe it's for the best that I'm not around to see it, as I've been able to do bugger all to stop it happening so far.'

'Havers. Cowardice, that's what that is. You're cowardly and lazy, Malcolm Campbell, too lazy to make the effort, to be any sort of presence at all in that girl's life. Too cowardly to be there for her. That's all you are.'

Malcolm pulled himself up. The other men in the bar were trying not to look at them.

'I divorced the last person who spoke to me like that. Maybe I should divorce you too, Donald. It seems like it might be time.'

And he got up and walked out.

He did sound like Eileen, Donald realized. Well, maybe Eileen had had the measure of Malcolm all along.

He watched Malcolm leave from the hilltop above the ferry, scooping up his various bags, the only foot passenger that day. And the first thing he thought to do was write to the girl and let her know.

With Malcolm gone, Eileen didn't reply to his letters as often. Cliodhna's birthday was coming up and he suggested organizing the usual seaside trip; no response came until six weeks after the date, that she was sorry, it had been a busy one this year. He saw the girl once more, when she was twelve, when Eileen agreed to let him come down – not take her out for a trip, that wouldn't be right – but just come and hand over a birthday present, sit there awkwardly in the living room till Eileen said gently that they were going over to Alec's mum's for their tea and he'd probably need to be getting back on the road, no? Cliodhna had hugged him tight before he left, but they'd both been aware of the absence he brought in with him, and he reckoned she was probably happier once he'd gone.

He continued to write to her, though, keeping her updated, at least four times a year. He wanted to make sure there was a regular, steady thing in her life, and he thought as her godfather it was probably his job, now. A picture of his new cottage, on the mainland. A programme from a music festival he was playing at, a postcard from Orkney or London or wherever his new life as a session musician took him. 'I play in other people's bands,' he wrote to her, trying to explain it. 'It's a free life, a good life. There's always music around.'

She never replied, over the years, but he thought that was OK.

None of the letters had been returned to him, addressee unknown, so he thought they were probably getting through. In a way it began to free him up, to write things he wouldn't tell anyone face to face.

I thought I'd never really be able to do it, without your dad. He was always the one who was good at finding us work, as a band. But I seem to be doing just fine. Somebody's always looking for a fiddler.

This one on a postcard from Paris, with pretty dancing girls on the front. He'd slipped it in an envelope with a little model of the Eiffel Tower on a key ring. Just in case.

And time passed, and life was good, and he was forty. He was forty, and he was washing up the dishes at half past eight. He heard the late bus coming down the hill like it always did, was confused when it pulled on its brakes. The headlights streamed through the cottage windows and he went outside to see if Roddy the bus needed a hand. Roddy was helping a woman down off the stair, a woman with high-heeled shoes and lots of hair. He was carrying a big bag for her, and they were coming down the path to Donald's bothy.

'What's all this, then, Roddy man?' he called out, at the same time as Roddy was saying, 'Here you go, Donald. Brought her safe to you.' And he realized as she got nearer that she wasn't really a woman at all, she was a girl, with Malcolm's huge, mellow eyes under all that make-up, and she was saying, 'Hello, Uncle Donald.'

He made her tea and offered her a blanket, because her clothes were thin and the fire hadn't properly heated the room yet. All she'd said so far was that she wanted to surprise him; he waited till she'd warmed up and calmed down before asking her properly.

'So, now. What's going on, then? It's great to see you, obviously, but it's been five years, lass. People don't just show up on a whim after five years, Cliodhna. Sorry – Jean, is it now? What's really going on?'

'It's Cliodhna,' she said. 'It was always Cliodhna. Clio, at school. She couldn't make me change my own name.'

'She would be your mother, there.'

'Yes, her.'

'Have the two of you had an argument, is that what this is?'

'Aye, you could say that. I don't want to talk about it, Uncle Donald. I can't go back, and I didn't know where else to go.'

Her eyes filled up, and he got worried. He was never quite sure what to do with women when they cried, and while this might be the same child he had picked up out of muddy puddles and hugged when she dropped an ice cream, she now had the added complication of a woman's body, a body he had registered and put immediately, guiltily, to the back of his mind. He patted her a couple of times on the shoulder.

'Come on now, love. Come on. It's going to be all right.'

'Can I stay with you here?'

He looked around. He had the two chairs, a bed through in the other room. There was a sink that he washed at, topless, in the mornings; the chemical toilet he'd put in last year.

'I honestly haven't got the room, Cliodhna. Look at this place. It's just about big enough for one.'

She started crying harder. He thought back to that last fight with Malcolm, when he'd been angry with him for giving up, for cowardice. Was he just the same, once you scratched the skin?

'All right, all right. There, lass. I can sleep in the chair for a few days, and we'll sort something out. Don't worry. Fash na. Everything will be all right now.'

Had she still been the child he'd last seen, he would have pulled her in, clasped her head close by, wound those curls round his fingers.

He left her tucked up in his bed, tramped the half-mile up the hill to the phone box. Eileen answered on the first ring, like she'd been sitting there.

'It's Donald, Eileen. She's here. She's with me.'

Eileen let out a tiny moan. 'I wondered. I did wonder.'

'I can put her up for a couple of nights at least—'

'She can't come home, Donald. She can't come back.' She said it in exactly the same way as her daughter had.

'Eileen, she's seventeen. She still needs her mammy. She was terrified.'

'I'm sorry, but she can't. There's no way.' Eileen sounded like she'd been crying, could start again soon.

And that was that. Neither of them would tell him what had happened, only that there was no solving it. He found out the next morning that Cliodhna had been in the middle of her exams, and immediately wanted to make arrangements to get her in at the nearest high school. But she'd been adamant.

'I'm done with school,' she'd said. 'It's all part of my old life. I need to grow up now.'

He fried them eggs for breakfast, then they walked out around the bay that the bothy sat on, looking out across the Summer Isles, the sea, beyond.

'It's so beautiful here,' she said. 'I don't think I've ever been anywhere this beautiful. It feels like a good place to be.'

'Aye, it does me well enough,' he said, trying to dodge the implication he thought he detected. 'Do you not remember the Isle of Skye, though, Cliodhna? The time we spent there, every summer? No, you were just a baby really.'

'I remember being on a beach like this one, with you and my dad. I remember the sea being big. But that could be Girvan, couldn't it? When I was a kid?'

'It could. But you don't see as much of the sea in Girvan. Not like this. Do you remember any of the songs we used to sing to you?'

He started out, hesitantly.

'There's nought but care on every hand
In every hour that passes, o –

'Like this one?

'What signifies the worth o' man
And 'twas na for the lasses, o.'

Donald had never been the singer, really. He knew fine his voice wasn't the strongest, couldn't sustain the longer notes, worried too much about where to take the breaths. He hid his face from the girl, sank his eyes on the horizon, moved plainly through the tune.

Her voice was husky, like she hadn't used it much in a while, but she came in on the fourth verse, note perfect, both of them gradually growing louder.

Q Magazine, **September 2007**

The Northern Lass

Clio Campbell

VEY RECORDS

★★☆☆☆

Things the world was not waiting for: an album of obscure Scottish folk songs by a washed-up Nineties pop star, replete with guest appearances by various nonentities and hangers-on scraped from the very edges of the grime scene. As weirdly jarring as it is deeply uncool, this cross-genre experiment by one-time 'Rise Up' popstrel Clio Campbell, getting back in touch with her Scottish roots, crashes and burns painfully.

It's a shame because, unlike other female singers from the past, who tend to drop a few octaves after they've passed forty, Campbell's voice still demonstrates that clear, soaring beauty that thrilled those of us who loved her guest vocals with the likes of Primal Scream and Belle and Sebastian back in the day. The stripped-down power of the almost a cappella 'Ae Fond Kiss', the randy Scottish bard's love poem, becomes a powerfully sexy lesbian torch song in Campbell's throat, lust and regret conveyed in each beautiful nuance. Perhaps her record company should have steered her towards a straightforward folk album – at the very least it would have saved this rock reviewer from having to wade through all those kitschy screeching Scottish fiddles. **PETE MOSS**

RUTH
Glasgow, 23 January 2018

It was like skiving, like playing hooky. A whole day snatched out of time.

As soon as she'd thought this, Ruth felt foolish. Which would you rather have – a day off work, or your friend alive?

Don't answer that.

Alison had been great, really she had. Ruth had misjudged her. She'd appeared there, in the woods, gently pulled Ruth back inside and wrapped a towel around her wet hair. She'd said the cat would come home when she was hungry. She'd refused to let Ruth sleep in her house that night, packing her up and folding her softly into the front seat of her car. The next morning, Ruth woke to hear Alison on the phone, forceful like she'd never been.

'Well, her best friend just killed herself. In her house. No, Ruth's house. She's the one who found the body. You'll give her the week off work, Greg.'

Before she'd left for work, which had happened under extreme protest, Alison had suggested, in this new weak-tea voice she was using, that Ruth would need to let people know.

'Her family. Friends. That sort of thing. People should know. And she was famous, a bit, wasn't she? What happens when famous people die? Anyway, just when you feel up to it, obviously.'

The taxi fare from Alison's to Clio's flat in Glasgow was twenty-six pounds, and Ruth paid it with a giggle, because the numbers suddenly meant nothing. The stairwell smelled of cheap disinfectant, underneath it something sharp and noxious like man's pee. The older women in the close all took their turns to clean it; the mop and bucket would be left, pointedly, outside Clio's door once a month.

Ruth should go in, really. She should open Clio's garish turquoise door, its slapdash home paint-job still streaky, with blobs on the skirting and facing walls. When Alison had suggested she use today to make contact with Clio's friends and family, she'd probably imagined her doing that from the freshly laundered sheets of her own bed. But Ruth had scrolled through her phone and come up with very few people who knew Clio, and she didn't think it was appropriate that any of them were the first to hear about it. She needed to go through family if she could.

Alison had not been able to find Clio's phone last night. It was almost as though she didn't want them to find it, she'd said, refusing to let Ruth go back into the house to look. The most sensible course of action would have been to go back and look herself, but Ruth was here in the city instead. It's like I'm drunk, she thought, and grinned, wide and loony. I'm making the decisions a drunk person would make. Actually, she felt a little bit drunk. Her senses were all a bit off. 'A bit skew-whiff!' she said out loud, calling it up the flight of stairs to Clio's neighbour. 'Ha!'

The door, the door. She fumbled for the key (thinking momentarily that it would be *hilarious* if she'd come all this way, paid all that money and not brought the key) and opened it. She pushed it with the palm of her hand, had it bounce back on her twice, before she stepped into the dark hallway.

Her nose adjusted before her eyes did – something was sweet and rotten in here. It would be fruit, bought before the trip to Ruth's house, or mould growing in a coffee cup somewhere. It occurred to Ruth that she was probably the person whose job it was to clean this all up, now.

She'd never been sure where the light switch was. The cramped hall was dark and full of danger; shelves overflowing with books, mysterious stacked objects, what looked like a roll of carpet. There was an old glass lamp, mock art deco, perched on some sort of dresser, and she reached along its flex for a switch. Kitchen, bathroom, bedroom and living room swam into focus through their variously open doors. Tiny ornaments balanced precariously along each doorframe, against the dirty glass up there; little coloured bottles in coordinated rainbows, small carved figurines. The smell seemed to be coming from every room.

What did you do with all these things? All the bits that a person had pulled around themself over the years? Things that wouldn't mean anything to anyone else. Ruth didn't want them in her house, that much she knew. Maybe there were people you could pay, who would come in and remove everything, and clean the place too? That seemed like a good use of money. She tripped over a stack of what turned out to be sheet music, which spilled and fanned itself over the rug. She swore out loud, filling the fetid air with it.

People would want to come here, of course. All the people who had loved Clio would want to come and take a small thing, one of those little bottles, a lamp, a fusty cushion. She couldn't just refer them to whichever charity shop she picked first from the phone-book.

Although, if they were people who loved Clio, why weren't they here right now, doing this, instead of her?

All the curtains were drawn, she realized, which was a bit odd – Clio had presumably left here round about lunchtime, almost three weeks ago. She'd gone into the living room first, assuming that anything important would be at Clio's desk in there. She'd never seen the place like this. It had always been cluttered, sure, but when Clio was entertaining – all those uncomfortable, badly cooked dinners where Ruth would be seated beside someone earnest, political and humourless and

Clio would laugh too loudly and drain the last bottle – there had been a chicness about this old junk-shop stuff that Ruth had envied. Now it looked dusty and chaotic, the room taking on its owner's state of mind, and Ruth wanted to be away from it all. A threadbare tartan blanket in the slumped easy chair still held the shape of the person who'd last wrapped it around herself. Perhaps she'd sat here as she'd made the phone call.

'Can I come out and stay with you for a while, Ruth? I need to. There's just crows here. I can see seventeen of them right now, on the aerial and chimney pot across the street. I need you to ground me, Ruth. Every time the wind blows they turn their heads and look at me and caw. Oh, they're in the air now. Like a swarm of bloody – flies! I know I'm not being rational about this. I know I sound mad. I need help again, Ruth. I can't be here.'

Now, in the darkness of the living room, its walls painted a sloppy old blood colour, Ruth folded the blanket up in the chair, then pushed open the heavy curtains and threw the window sash up. The room badly needed air. There were no birds outside that she could see.

Clio's desk was an old bureau. Ruth had been with her when she'd bought it from a charity shop four years ago, the two of them heaving it up three flights of stairs. It was hanging open, papers spilling from the various slots. There were two of the expected fungal coffee cups; Ruth moved them gently over to the other side of the room – she was in no state to cope with whatever was in the kitchen just now. She stuffed her big body awkwardly into the chair by the desk, trying not to knock anything. Clio's computer wasn't here, but the papers, daunting as they looked, actually began to calm her. Most of them were invoices or receipts, sent from some of the organizations Clio worked with. Official noteheads, with phone numbers and names of contacts – colleagues of a sort, people who might have known Clio not intimately, but enough to miss her. People who could provide a good sturdy base from which the news could be spread; people who might take some of this work away from Ruth. There was nothing resembling an address book. Of course there wasn't. The idea of Clio maintaining an address book was ridiculous.

Who was supposed to do all this, Clio? The words sat around her head for a second, and Ruth realized she'd spoken them aloud, to the room, its mess, to the shed snakeskin. She carried on.

Who was going to come in here and clean up after you? Who was supposed to do this? It wasn't mad, she realized, to talk out loud to someone dead. Not just now. Not when you were clearly suffering from the sort of shock that made you feel drunk and there were things that needed to be said. She wheeled round and addressed the empty easy chair, the now-folded blanket.

'You know what? I haven't cried yet. It's been more than twelve hours since I found you and I haven't cried yet. Oh, I'm sure I will at some point. There will be crying, because you're my friend and you're dead; because at some point it'll hit me, this great big stupid waste you've committed. But I can't cry because I'm so, so bloody angry at you. Why would you put all this on me? Why would you leave me here, in this room, with your mouldy fucking cups? And even if none of this occurred to you, you still chose my house to kill yourself in, didn't you? You still knew it would be me that would have to find you.'

The waxy face, the silent scream.

'Are you still here? Are you, you . . . fucking . . . cow?'

The room, its emptiness, made her feel foolish, and she wished she could take the last words back even though no one had heard them.

The first number she dialled was underneath a triangular logo, stamped in cheap ink on a thin piece of paper. Glasgow Refugee Support Network. There was music playing in the background as a woman answered, laughing at something unheard.

'Hello. I'm looking for Nancy Okonkwo.'

'That's me, my love. How can I help you?' The new Scots vowels stretching over African timbre, the beginnings of a whole new accent growing in that voice.

'I'm calling about Clio Campbell. I think you—' You what? She couldn't say 'knew', couldn't give the game away right there with the past tense, could she?

Start again. 'I'm a friend. Clio was staying with me for a while. There's a—' She had no idea where these words were going; she really hadn't expected this to be so hard. In her silence, the woman began to panic.

'What's – what's happened to her? Is everything all right? What's going on?'

'She's dead. I'm sorry – I'm sorry you're hearing this from me. I found her yesterday evening. Dead.'

And then it didn't matter that Ruth couldn't cry, because this woman was crying. This woman had enough grief in her for both of them.

'No no no no. No no, don't tell me. Don't be saying that. No no. Oh Clio, oh don't.'

There was some scuffling, and someone else, another woman, was on the phone.

'Hello, can you tell me what's going on?'

In the background Nancy was moaning. 'No no no, Clio. My girl, my friend. No no no.'

'I'm calling about Clio Campbell. I believe she did some work for you. She died yesterday. I'm her friend. I'm trying to let people know.'

'I'm so sorry to hear that.' This woman was formal, businesslike. Much easier to deal with. 'Do you mind if I ask what happened?'

'She killed herself,' Ruth said. Then she blurted out, 'With pills. In my house – she was in my house.'

'My friend, my friend,' wailed Nancy, her sobs louder than the other woman's voice, so Ruth assumed they were still sitting at the phone together.

'I wanted to let people know – please could you tell anyone else she was close with? I'm sorry you had to find out this way.'

'And I'm sorry for your loss,' said the other woman. Someone else was comforting Nancy now; Ruth could hear yet another voice in there.

'Look, please – don't spread it about. About how she died. I shouldn't have said anything. I don't think we're intending to release that information. Not yet. You know?'

Where that had come from she wasn't sure. It seemed to be the sort of thing that people said. But really, who would care, if the manner of death got out there?

It had been a stupid mistake to start with that one. Ruth had met a Nancy, now she thought about it, at a dinner in this very room about two years ago. She remembered a big woman with a mesmerizingly glossy weave, in her mid-twenties; Nancy who couldn't stop laughing at Clio's jokes, who followed her round the room adoringly, helped carry the plates in, helped clear the table; Nancy, who later whispered to Ruth that Clio had volunteered to take in her auntie, to help her asylum claim. Clio never mentioned it herself. Too shy, Nancy had said. She don't want people to know all the good things she doing.

Too shy. Ruth had covered a snigger with a cough when she realized Nancy wasn't joking. She'd never really thought much about Clio's refugee work – my Nigerian girls, she'd call them if she brought it up – but she knew she'd been running a music group for the women and kids living in soon-to-be-demolished schemes in North Glasgow while their asylum claims had been debated, and that occasionally she went to court with them. But Clio didn't really talk about these things with Ruth. That wasn't the point of Ruth, any more.

She pulled all the papers out, trying to stack them in what felt like an order – invoices on one side, bills and writs from the housing association on the other. She didn't want to risk any other seemingly innocuous-looking letterheads, any more unexpected outpourings. She wondered how a person could exist in the world with such minimal family. Didn't everyone have a cloud of blood relatives who would bustle in and know intrinsically what to do, how to go about this? She imagined her own sister managing her death, imagined the paperwork being processed, her mother consoled, every important person on her Facebook notified swiftly and beautifully, within the hour. But Clio had seemed to shed connections as she'd got older, really. There had been friends who *adored* her and were always there and spoken about, and then they were never heard of again. Over by the fireplace, a couple of photo albums had been stacked, and Ruth pounced upon them, sat down cross-legged on the floor. Only the first few pages had been stuck down, of course, the rest over-full of loose photos which slipped out as she tilted the album towards her. A very much younger Clio than Ruth had ever known, surrounded by faces she'd never seen before, grainy shots, half-remembered. There was no way of tracing these people and why would they even care? Because they once sat in a bar and put their arm round this woman's neck while someone shone a flash at them? Just write down some fucking phone numbers, Clio, Ruth shouted to the emptiness, then realized that she was holding a wedding picture.

Glasgow, 2007

It was one of those things that made Ruth feel old, even at twenty-eight. The name had been announced at Ben's Monday meeting and there had been a stark divide in the open-plan office space; the people her own age or older who had nodded in acknowledgement or even looked excited, versus the two or three blank-faced younger ones.

'Who's that, then?' Keeley hissed over the desk, pulling a face.

'Scottish pop star from the early Nineties,' Ruth said, and Keeley nodded, went back to her screen, leaving Ruth feeling like she should have explained better.

Ben continued on, enthusing just as much as he always did about the new signing. 'Something really bold and new that's going to open up multiple markets for us: the folk dimension, people attracted in by her name, and hopefully also a much younger audience – I mean, she's talking about bringing in grime artists on this. That's going to have huge youth appeal. We could cross-promote it to schools as a teaching aid. It all just seems like a really good idea.'

Ruth had always loved this in him, the sweet excitement over every new project, the way he could always be totally convinced by an artist with a bit of passion to hoof off into a commitment that numerous other record companies would have already passed on. It usually meant a nightmarish web of his printed-off emails to untangle in order to make the thing actually happen, but that was her job, and she was good at it. She'd always enjoyed bringing order to chaos and Ben Vey's shambling folk-music label had been a swamp of dust when she'd taken over the admin side of things a few years ago. He was waiting for her at his desk after the meeting, loose sheets stuffed haphazardly into the poly pockets she'd patiently taught him to use if he had to keep a paper trail for everything.

'So, Clio Campbell then?' she'd asked as she perched on his desk, trying to sound casual. She'd felt a little prickling of excitement when she'd first seen the name down in his diary but hadn't wanted to enquire too obviously. She liked to let Ben do his thing out there. It was why they worked well together.

'Were you aware of her before this? You would have been a child, no? A teenager? Sorry. I'm never sure what sort of reach people have to the younger generation.'

'I was twelve, when she was famous. And yeah, I was a bit of a fan.'

Aware of her. Seven years ago, when she'd come out to Becca, one of her oldest friends from school, Becca had laughed over her pint and said, 'Well, yeah. There was that Clio Campbell thing, wasn't there. I mean, you were obsessed. I think I knew from round about then, really.'

The single had been everywhere right at the time when Ruth was starting to be aware of music, and seeing Clio being so young and red-coloured and brilliantly disobedient on *Top of the Pops* – something Ruth hadn't even realized it was possible to disobey until then – had really cemented it. She wrote it on the insides of jotters – PEOPLE GOTTA RISE UP! – daubed it on her schoolbag in Tippex where other girls were drawing the Bros logo. In amongst the stuff her mum had handed over when they'd moved out of the old house was a box containing every magazine interview Clio had ever done, from *Smash Hits* to *Q*, meticulously clipped with the kitchen scissors, hidden under her bed and layers of dust for at least a decade. Each one had seemed so shockingly familiar, the design, the placement of the pictures on the page sparking off little pulses in Ruth's brain. She realized she still knew some of them off by heart; she'd copied Clio's quotes about wanting to be an astronaut out into a little notebook she found at the bottom of the box, remembered pacing about her bedroom with her T-shirt knotted up over her belly button reciting it, a hand moving expansively through the air as she tried to imagine how Clio Campbell would have looked when she'd said it.

Ruth had wondered, going into that first meeting with Ben and Linda, how she'd feel. Would meeting the person who had been her first crush, who she'd gravitated to before she'd even realized that she liked girls, unlock something in her, as that box of magazine cuttings had done for a while? Would she get the shakes, or blush, or be unable to stop the attraction coming back? She felt dizzy with the anticipation as she paused at the door of the meeting room, knowing who was in there, but it was just a woman. A woman with a very familiar face, but just a woman. As with every other artist she dealt with, she often found herself talking maternally, calmly, down the phone, and the thrill of that voice being on the other end, saying 'Ruth! Ruth, it's Clio. There's been a bit of a fuck-up . . .' had faded by the third or fourth time it had happened.

Ruth had gone down to London to make sure everything ran smoothly on recording sessions for *The Northern Lass*; she'd done all the sums and the cost of transporting and housing Clio and the number of London-based musicians she'd wanted to bring in on the album up to Glasgow far outweighed the more expensive studio rental. Donald Bain, who Clio had referred to as 'Uncle Donald even though he's not really my uncle', was staying across the hall from her in the cheapy hovel she'd mistakenly chosen for them on Clapham Common; they'd worked together in the past as he was often in demand as a backing musician on other Vey Records albums, but their interactions had only ever been over the phone. She enjoyed his usually quiet but always pleasant company over breakfast time, where they learned early on not to order the watery, sloppy scrambled eggs. They were also very similar in their ways of dealing with Clio, her threats and strops, the high emotions of her. Ruth noticed early on into the recording that Clio craved reassurance from one or the other of them at any little jolt or snag in the process, almost like a child careening between parents. If something wasn't quite right with the music, some aspect of the sound, Clio would fret herself anxiously around Donald who would speak calming words to her, rub her shoulder, go off to intervene with the album producer on her behalf; for everything else in her life there was Ruth. It seemed very strange behaviour for a woman of almost forty, particularly one who spoke often about how she'd always really been a lone wolf, providing for herself.

That fretful, twitchy side of Clio was completely hidden when-ever the guest musicians came into the studio, though; the shoulders would pull themselves back, the dimple in her left cheek would wink away at all comers, and she'd be tactile, adult, fully in control, her persona grown to fill the room and charm the newcomers. These were usually young men, cockney, loud and flustered, unsure of what to do, and Ruth and Donald watched their girl ease them into the situation with the same arm-patting and stroking they'd been using on her maybe half an hour earlier.

Decorating the wall of the studio for the duration of their stay there was a huge A1 poster, Robert Burns's face repeated in smudgy pop-art neons, occasionally wearing Ray-Bans. Ruth had spotted the image on a book cover, presented the cardboard tube to Clio on the first day of recording.

'A little gift from all of us at Vey,' she'd said (even though it was really just a little gift from her) and watched the delight in Clio's face, her beaming insistence that it had to hang on the wall, and felt totally fulfilled in that second. She'd noticed Donald watching her, with what she thought was a tiny smile of approval or something like it, on his face.

The reviews, when they'd come in, had been more or less brutal. Ben had called Ruth through to the meeting room on the second one.

'It all seems a bit extreme, doesn't it? I genuinely don't think it's as bad an album as all that. I mean, of course, there are places where the experiment doesn't, maybe, work, but this –' he held up a copy of the *Scotsman* '– this is pure vitriol here.'

It's because she's a woman, Ruth wanted to point out to his big, well-meaning, confused face. Clio would call up every time a new blow hit now, needing Ruth to tell her the same thing over and over.

'They can't handle this much divergence from the norm, Clio. That's all it is. The Scottish ones are taking it personally because they think their precious Burns is sacred, the English ones are making fun of it because they find any sort of Scottish culture funny these days. That's all it is. You're caught in the middle, but I have faith that once we get you on the road, get people actually hearing it, things will pick up. Your average member of the public hasn't got time for this sort of tribalism. They just want to hear good music and—'

Ruth had the speech down rote. 'Just stop taking the calls. She'll learn to deal,' Linda said. Ruth didn't feel she could. It did seem unjust.

Sure, the album was rough around the edges in places, but this, this seemed to be a needless, jeering pile-on. The tour was proving even harder to organize; not only trying to arrange times for the various guest musicians to make it up, but even just booking slots and finding venues seemed to be difficult. Clio caught the overnight bus up from London for interviews, stayed on Ruth's sofa (after Linda suggested their original marketing fund for the album might be better distributed towards covering the various guest fees), and Ruth ran through the various refusals she'd had while they finished a takeaway and a second bottle of wine.

'The Big Rock Festival – that one was a surprise; actually all the Mansfield Music venues as well.'

Clio laughed, harshly, showily.

'That's not a surprise at all, darlin. Ha. You know who runs the Big Rock Festival? Mr Mansfield Music himself? My ex-husband. Yeah. He's not going to do anything so kind as give me a break, the petty vindictive fuck. Some men just can't cope with being dumped, can they? Not even – God, what was it? Fifteen years ago.'

'Fucksake!' said Ruth, topping up Clio's glass sympathetically. 'What an arsehole. I did think it was a bit weird – we usually do manage to get most of our acts on at the folk stage at Big Rock, at least.'

Clio put on an American accent, a bruised, bold Lauren Bacall.

'That's men for you, sweetheart.' And she took a long drink, smacked her lips.

Glasgow, 23 January 2018

Donald Bain. Of course he should know. Ruth scrolled back through her email, found something in there from 2009, with a landline phone number, lengthy Highland area code. Then she sat and looked at it for a while. Then she decided to open all the windows – the living room, the tiny, grimy bathroom, the overstuffed bedroom with its faint tang of unwashed sheets and female sweat; the hot dead fruit of the kitchen where she registered the plates and cutlery stacked in the drying rack by an empty sink thankfully, then stopped herself. You're giving thanks, she thought, that in the middle of this horrible thing this woman has visited on you, you don't also have to do her dirty dishes? You flaccid great doormat.

She wanted to leave, get another expensive taxi back to Alison's and sleep and sleep, but had a nagging feeling that she needed to do something more. She crashed back into the armchair, suddenly exhausted, and noticed that wedding photo, lying on the floor. Clio pale and young and lovely, tiny against the background of that big cathedral in Edinburgh; the husband seeming much larger, more present, with a very Nineties goatee beard and datedly baggy suit. There we go.

'Hello, Mansfield Music, Francesca speaking.'

'Hello, my name's Ruth Jones. I need to speak to Mr Mansfield on a very urgent personal matter. It concerns his ex-wife, Clio Campbell. I have some bad news. I understand this is irregular, but do you think you could put me through straight away?'

She hadn't expected that to work; had assumed there would be a finely honed machine of secretarial protocol preventing access to The Man. But here he was on the end of the phone, sounding irritated and busy and possibly a bit scared.

'Dan Mansfield speaking.'

'Mr Mansfield – you possibly don't remember me. I'm a friend of Clio's – I used to work for Vey Records, but I'm not sure if we ever – no, just email probably. Sorry.'

Pull it together, Ruth.

'Uh-huh. Go on.'

'Well. Clio – Clio's dead. Suicide. Yesterday, while I was at work. She was staying with me. She hasn't left an address book or anything, and I wasn't sure whether – well, I know the two of you didn't have the best relationship but it just seemed as though – I just thought you should know. Sorry. Sorry that you have to find out like this.'

He was breathing down the line, in, out, very controlled.

'Right. Right. OK. Thank you – thank you for letting me know. Does anyone else know yet – I mean, the media, have they got hold of it?'

'Um. I don't think so? I don't see how – it's just me and the police who've been involved so far.'

A dry half-laugh.

'So it won't be long till the press are on it. I'll get the girls in the office ready. Sorry. And you – did you find her? The body.'

She took a couple of those breaths herself, swallowed the collapse back down. 'I did.'

'That must have been very hard for you. I'm sorry. Listen, someone will need to let her mother know.'

'Her mother?'

Ruth was blindsided. She'd never formally asked, but she had heard Clio refer to herself as an orphan on a number of different occasions. Sometimes with mocking laughter in the bright light of a pub, sometimes maudlin at the end of a night. Knowing of the father's death, the way it had fed into *The Northern Lass* and some of the press had tried to focus on it, she'd made assumptions.

'I just – I thought—'

'Well, they're estranged. Don't talk much. Didn't. Before – Eileen was diagnosed with vascular dementia, about four, five years ago. Shockingly early, she's really not that old. But, no other family left, and Clio is of course barely able to support herself, so she came to me. Eileen's in a care home in Ayr – it's nowhere fancy, but I wasn't going to leave her to rot. I always had a soft spot for Eileen. She explains a lot about who Clio is. Who she was. Jesus.'

Ruth's head swam with the information, with the almost-too-personal things this man, who she'd only ever encountered as a symbol, a power within her own industry, was telling her.

'Anyway. I'll get you the details. I'm not – I'm not going to go there myself. I think it would be too confusing for Eileen. I've been once; she jumps about in time, she's come unstuck. She'd need to hear this from a stranger, I think.'

DANNY
Cumbria, 1993

He couldn't get over how conscious he was of her. It was like the first wild days of attraction on tour all over again, the leaning into each other, trying to find ways to touch, always aware of where she was in the room even when he couldn't see her. Not sexual this time; something just as primal rising in him. He found himself scanning the street that they were walking down for potential hazards

'Are you OK? Do you want my coat?' he asked again, as the wind hit his face, and he tried to position himself in front of her, like a shield. 'This is too cold out – look, let's just get you inside, shall we?'

She moved her head, nodded as he ushered her into the pub they'd spotted from the car. She'd been quiet for the whole walk, he realized, just listening to him talk through the issue with that arsehole Adam and the bookings for Edwyn's tour, until she'd asked if they could turn around and go back, and he'd felt immediately guilty that he was making her go out and exert herself when she should have her feet up. They'd been badly prepared for the walk anyway; both in their Converse, picking around the puddles and shivering. He'd thought it would be a good wholesome thing to do: drive to the Lakes, see some countryside, really spend some time together. Making plans, dreaming up the future, not in a city.

Wherever they went at home, people knew them, whether it was idiots who recognized Clio 'from off the telly, aren't you' or scenester kids in bands anxious to get Danny to book them. In the city, they were too visible. It was always something he'd loved, the way heads would turn as they walked into a bar, the way shy girls in band T-shirts or Beatle-haired boys would approach Clio, supplicant, while he stood just behind her, stroking secret messages into the small of her back. His wife was not ordinary.

She kept her hair huge and curly even though the fashion was for short and boyish, decked herself in sparkling Lurex and old fur scavenged from second-hand shops while every other girl zipped her chest into tatty Adidas. She painted her eyelids and fingernails silver, and the shimmery powders coated their bedroom carpet, the bath-room, the walls, never quite washed out. She managed to pull focus to herself even in the crowd at someone else's gig; in a dimly lit nightclub a spotlight could always locate her, a bold streak of scarlet in a world increasingly brown. But since they'd found out, he'd found himself irritated at other people's insistence on sharing her.

'Our first ever family day,' he'd said as they set off, kissed her hand. She'd made a small, soft noise and curled up in her seat, slept for almost the whole journey. He'd stopped the car at one point, very gently, and tucked his scarf in between her belly and the seatbelt, just to be sure.

Sure enough, heads turned as he shepherded her past a sad-looking Christmas tree and across to a table by the fire, but the two of them were always going to stand out in a place like this, a pub full of sensible hiking gear and a wall-mounted newspaper rack stuffed with copies of the *Daily Mail*.

'There,' he said, 'there. Is that – wait, are you going to be too warm sitting right beside it? Tell you what – you get warmed up and then we'll swap places when it gets too hot for you. Make sure you let me know, OK? Right. I'll get menus. I bet you're starving. What do you fancy? Lasagne? Burger? Something with iron in. Not much choice here, but you know – can't beat pub grub.'

'I'll just have chips.'

'Just chips? You should eat more. Go on. My treat.'

'It's always your treat, isn't it?'

Oh God, was she going to be like this again? Since the royalties from her song had all but dried up, at more or less the same time as the bookings, Clio had been snappy about money. She never really listened when he explained that they were married now, a unit, that it made him happy to spend his money on his wife; anyway, it wasn't like she was doing anything about it either. She hadn't even picked up a guitar since their wedding. He'd gone out of his way to get her session work at first, pressured those bands who owed him favours from the early days to bring her in as a backing singer, but that only made her more miserable. And he understood that. It was an artist thing – she didn't like taking second place. He knew the feeling all too well himself. If she wasn't going to be making music, though, he was sure she needed something else in her life. He'd been amazed when she'd agreed, further amazed that it had happened so quickly, jumped from an idea to a blue line on a stick in only a month. So today he swallowed down the same old argument they'd always had, moved round to sit on the bench beside her, pulled her in to him and kissed her head.

'Just think of it as my way of saying thank you. For all the work you're doing. I never want you to feel unappreciated.' He intoned the words into her hair, breathing in the high floral pulse of her shampoo.

She just flopped into him, and he let her, held her there in silence for a while. He felt huge, muscled and male wrapped around her. His cock throbbed. This was what he was supposed to be doing. It all felt right.

The barmaid ambled over. She smiled at the two of them, put a hand on her heart.

'So cute! What can I get you, then?'

'I think I'll go cottage pie actually. Did you decide, babe? What are you having?'

He liked the way the girl smiled at his accent.

Clio muttered, 'Chips,' into his shoulder, didn't look up.

'She's not feeling too well,' he mouthed, to cover for her. 'Maybe a burger and chips? Cheeseburger? Make sure it's cooked all the way through, though – please tell the chef that my lovely wife here is pregnant, so to take whatever precautions he normally would with the food. And nothing with eggs, like mayonnaise or anything.'

Clio's body tensed beneath him.

'Oh congratulations! That is going to be one good-looking baby, if you don't mind me saying.'

'No, we don't mind that at all, my darling! So, cottage pie and cheeseburger.'

Clio wrenched herself out from under his arm, wheeled round to face him, still ignoring the waitress.

'I said I just want chips.'

'You'll change your mind, though. When you see mine. Tell you what – I'll eat the burger if you can't face it, all right?' He winked at the barmaid. 'Lucky she brought her back-up stomach, eh?'

The girl retreated.

'Come on, babe. I know you're not quite right today. But let's not spoil it, eh? That was a wee bit – well, the girl was just being nice.'

She sat for a few seconds, turning her hands over, picking at a fingernail.

'I know. Sorry. I'm sorry.'

'It's OK, honey. You must be exhausted. And hungry. Come here.'

This time the hug only went on a few seconds, before she broke away.

'Why did you tell her?'

He could feel the smile pulling at his cheeks.

'Well. It's nice to be able to tell someone. She doesn't know us. I want to tell people! I want people to know.'

She looked down.

'Got to pee. Back in a sec.'

Almost as an afterthought she turned back, picked up his hand and kissed it.

She'd taken her bag with her, he noticed, so he settled in for the long haul; grabbed a tabloid from the bar. It was progress, he thought, that he could challenge her on behaviour like that and it hadn't flared up into a row. They were learning each other, gradually, learning how to live together. Nobody said marriage was easy, after all, and perhaps they'd been naive when they got together, assuming that trying to blend their separate lives would come as naturally to them as shagging had. But then maybe this was the pregnancy working on her, just as it had on him. Perhaps it was natural that her hormones would compel her to get on with him, to agree with him even, to keep her protector close. Biology, that sort of thing.

She was in there for at least ten minutes. He buried himself in the paper to deflect the awkward glances from the other punters, tuned in to the Christmas pop songs blaring away on the bad PA system. The barmaid leaned over at one point and said, 'Is she all right? Do you want me to pop in and check on her?'

Danny sucked back a smile at the thought of Clio's reaction to that invasion of privacy.

'No, no, she'll be fine. Don't worry. It happens a lot at the moment. She just needs a bit of space sometimes. She'll be doing her make-up, you know. Putting her face back on. And thank you, doll. Eh?'

And suddenly, there she was, sitting in front of him, her face freshly painted into sharp lines and her head up high. Her hands were tensed, fretting and clawing at the air above the tabletop.

'Are you feeling OK, love? Do you want a wee sip of my beer? Little treat?'

She took a long, controlled breath in through her nose and closed her eyes for a second.

'Right. Right. Look. There are two ways this story goes, darling. Danny-boy my love. Let's talk them through – here's the deal, right – let me tell you two stories, give me space, and if you don't agree with me then you tell me your story. So. Here it goes. I have this baby. You probably stop fancying me the second the weight piles on, but eh, you know, I'm young. Ish. It'll come off again soon, nah?'

Her fingers twitched, twitched, twitched.

'So I'm fat, and I don't want to have sex even after it's out because I'm all cut up and sore with it. That's what they do, you know. That's OK, though, because you've got this baby. It's probably a boy, he's your son, and you think he looks just like you, apart from when he looks like me. And for a wee while, that'll do us. Even though he's screaming all the time and we're not getting any sleep, and the house – oh, your mum has helped us get a house, by the way, because even though she still doesny like me – no, sssh – she's no having her grandchild, grand-*son*, the heir, grow up in some damp wee tenement just cos you want to carry on playing bohemian with your muck-common ginger singer wife. It's a nice one in the Grange, near hers; she's not cheap, your mum. It's got a back garden with grass and flowers and everything. Anyway, it's a shithole because I don't clean it, because I'm spending all my days looking after the baby and crying. But when you come back from tour, and you roll a joint and toke up in the garden before coming in and sitting on the stairs – cos this isn't none of your base-ment flats, this house, it's got an upstairs – and you sit there on the stairs and you listen to me singing your son to sleep, singing Gaelic lullabies, you think it's beautiful and we'll work through it. You think that because you're an optimist, but every day you stay in that lovely shithole, with those great high ceilings, big windows letting in all that light so you can see the dust piling up on the mantelpiece, you start to feel trapped. Maybe there's a stain on the sofa where I pissed myself because giving birth to the son, the boy, ripped my fanny open and now I can't feel the muscles down there, and you notice it every time you walk into the living room, remember how you just noticed it dripping down out of my leggings as I sat there feeding the baby, how I burst out crying (again) and swore at you when you pointed it out, how you had to scrub your own wife's pee out of that lovely sofa your mum bought. That happens. I've heard that from more than one person. No. Stop. I'm talking. I'm talking. Anyway, you think about that piss stain every time you go into work and see Sadie or Francesca sitting there behind the desk; she's not your secretary, pal, I'll give you credit for originality, but she works in admin or something. Let's be frank, you're not making the whole shagging-an-artist mistake again, are ye? She was maybe in first year at your school the year you were leaving. She remembers you playing guitar in the final-year assembly and is disappointed that you aren't still making music, but she totally gets that you're doing what makes money, and my God, Danny, she really admires you for it. Or maybe she's a Home Counties girl, fresh out of uni and just sometimes it crosses your mind that *she* probably wouldn't be swearing at your mum or refusing to come to family parties, which we both know is what I will have dissolved into by that point, eh? When you're *in* the house, and those gig nights are getting later and later, but when you're finally there, and you're trying to help, what you don't realize is I'm swearing at you behind your back. Seriously, you go downstairs to our scummy-as-fuck designer kitchen and you're thinking that you're helping, you're actually telling yourself, what a great guy I am for helping, and if you turned back for one second you'd be terrified. You'd turn round to the woman holding your baby, your son, the heir to the Mansfield fortune, and you'd see her face creased into this ugly thing, all spite and hate and fire. You'd see the words she mouths at you, you cunt, you fuck, you useless shit. It would scare you. Your bones would be properly chilled, pal, especially as you'd watch your baby pat her face and laugh at first at the funny shapes it makes, while she pushes all those hard words out. But he'd learn them after a while. Your baby would learn that these words were normal, that they were how human beings communicate. He'd make those faces himself, going through life, to the other boys and girls in the class, to his teenage girlfriend, to whichever luckless cow he manages to convince to marry him. You fuck. You useless shitty cunt.'

Of course, the barmaid chose that moment to bring their food over, realizing too late what she'd walked into.

'The, uh, cottage pie?'

'That was me, my darling. Thanks. Thank you so much.' He felt he had to be extra smooth to make up for it all.

'And the cheeseburger. Well done. No mayo. With chips.'

Clio grunted. The girl looked at the floor.

'OK, can I get you anything else now?'

'No, we're fine thanks, angel. Thank you.' He slapped on a smile till she'd edged out of sight, then leaned over his plate and held his wife's hand.

'Listen, babe, I know you're scared. I know you are. I'm scared too. I know it's not going to be a walk in the park. But you're going to be an amazing mum, and we'll get through all the tough times. We're a team, hey? It's you and me.'

Her hand wriggled out from his, grabbed at the air again.

'You are not hearing a thing I'm saying, are you? It's not – God, Danny. Just, just shut up for a few minutes, would you?'

She pushed the plate with the burger across the table, away from her.

'Here's what I'm trying to get at, right. Do you remember that conversation we had, my boyo, my love? When we decided to have a baby in the first place? I mean, I don't want to say you got me at a low point, but we both know that you did. You talked to me about being twenty-six and time ticking on, and it not being the end of my career, just the right time to take stock. It's not a failure, you said, it's maybe just the world letting you know you need to make a change. Just do something differently, just for a while. And it's like my mum always told me: never be beholden to a man for money or it'll work on you. I didn't listen because I never listened to my mum, but she was right, and it's worked on me. I can't deny either of those things. But that's not the point. Imagine me, right. I take the kid out to local mums and tots groups or whatsit to try and make pals, but the other mums all look down on me right away, because we live in a posh area and I give my baby crisps or I'm doing something wrong that seemed perfectly normal to me where I came from like, fucksake, putting whisky on its dummy to make it sleep or whatever, I don't know. And it's just me and this kid all day, and I love it, of course I do because it's my kid and that's what you do, but I don't know, maybe I hate it too because I'm thinking where's me, or whatever. You hear that, don't you? Women just dying for a wee bit of adult conversation. Oh, you probably don't, babe. Where would you hear that? You don't talk to women who aren't your wife, or lovely young musicians, or Francesca in the office with the perky tits.'

'Clio. Babe. There's nobody in my office called Francesca—'

'Oh, there will be. And then it starts to nag away at me, the eight millionth time that I've got baby shit under my nails and haven't put my lipstick on for weeks. *Didn't you used to be someone? Wasn't that you, causing a storm on* Top of the Pops? *Didn't music magazines queue up to interview you, all these geeky boys in band T-shirts basically Morse-coding I LOVE YOU into their notepads? Didn't you used to care about things beyond the PTA or the baby's shoe size or whatever mummy shit fucking mummies have to care about? Didn't you used to fight things and stand up for folk and try and make something happen, some change in the world?* See, cos I've got nobody else to think this through with. It's just me in the house, all those days, all those nights. This is what I keep playing over and over and NO. SHUT— sssh. Let me talk. Please. While the walls are closing in on me, your world is going to be getting bigger and bigger. Because we both know you're going places, aren't you, my darling. Danny Mansfield is on the up. The famous people you'll be meeting. The parties you'll be going to. Sometimes the parties are at our house, by the way, because it's nicer than everyone else's, and our wee boy sits there at the top of the stairs listening to the basslines and the laughter floating up. You think to yourself when you catch him, scoop him up in his jammies and take him back to bed, this is great. Isn't he lucky to have this sort of experience? You think that when you cuddle him for half an hour before bed, or pat him on the head before you go out to work in the morning. You think that when he clings to your legs when you come in the door every evening, not realizing that he's trying to tell you *Don't leave me again, Daddy, don't leave me with this woman, this wretched bitter witch who stares at me all day.'*

He decided to stop it all, all the words.

'Babe. Babe. This is silly. This is just so you. We take some sort of step, any sort of step at all towards something new and you dig your heels in, the panic sets in, and you come up with a million different reasons why it's not going to work straight away.'

She sniffed. A big, deliberate sniff. The sort of sniff he knew too well.

'Wait, what is this right now? Like a cokehead rant happening here. Are you on something? Are you seriously pregnant with my child and on something?'

She leaned back.

'No and yes.'

'What? What the hell is that supposed to mean?'

He didn't care who in this shitty little country pub could hear them now. She had a funny half-smile on her face, and she looked him straight in the eye as she unbuckled her belt, shoved a hand down her trousers. What the hell? What the hell was she doing?

She pulled her hand out, displayed a bloodstained finger to him, showed it round to the rest of the pub.

'No, it doesn't look like I'm pregnant with your child, does it? And yes, I've taken a little bit of speed. I had it in my bag for emergencies, and this seems like an emergency, this state of affairs.' She waved her bloody hand about like royalty greeting the masses, laughed.

She's crazy, he thought. She's actually crazy, and I married her. And on speed. On speed. There was a high, electrical note shrilling in his brain. The blood was very, very red. And then, suddenly, the dull thud of it hit him.

'What, what is that? Is it – are you having a miscarriage?'

'I don't know. It might just be my period. I've been feeling it coming on all day.'

'But – you were pregnant. The test.'

'Well, now I'm not. And I'm – I can't – I don't want to be.'

He sank back into the bench, stared down at his plate, still full of food, as the air left the room. Over. It was over.

She came round the table to him, scooted her bum along the bench, stretched out towards him, stroked his shoulder.

'I'm sorry, my love. My boy. I'm sorry. It's just felt wrong, the whole time. I felt myself disappearing. I haven't been able to breathe all week. Then I went to the toilet, and there it was, and the world suddenly made sense again. It's not for me. This isn't what I was supposed to be. And it is definitely what you were supposed to be, isn't it? I mean, you've been – you've been the one fucking glowing, Danny.'

Her arms were around him, and she was ferreting inside his jacket for his wallet. She pulled out a couple of notes and placed them down on the table between the burger and the pie, and then she guided him into a standing position, wrapped his scarf round his neck, surprising him with her tenderness.

'Did you do something?' he heard himself saying. 'Did you do something to the baby?' He wasn't even aware he'd made that connection until he said it.

She laughed again, that hard little laugh he didn't recognize. 'Not unless it's possible to think something away. Maybe it worked out I was going to be a shit mother and decided to get the fuck out of here.'

'Are you totally sure? It could just be a bit of blood.'

Cold air hit his face and he understood that she'd walked him out of the pub, on to the street.

'I just know. I know in my body. It was like a switch this morning – something had just flicked off – but I couldn't work out why.'

They were leaning against the wall of the pub. He was crumbling limestone under his fingers. She reached inside his jacket again, this time for his cigarettes, lit two and put one in his mouth. It seemed like something a girl in a film would do.

'Do you think you can drive, Danny? Are you going to be OK?'

Oh, who knew. Who knew. He nodded, a very small movement, but his head felt so heavy it might fall off.

'Let's just get back to the car, OK?'

She took his arm to walk him down the street.

'I mean, I can't drive us. I couldn't anyway without a licence but I think they'd pick up pretty quickly about my brain right now, ching ching? Eh?'

She was trying to make a joke, and he let her have a tiny flick of a smile.

They sat inside the car, and Clio leaned over him to turn the key in the engine, put the radiator on. It was getting dark already. He didn't want to sit in this box with this woman for the next two hours. He didn't want to go back to their flat and begin the process of splitting up their things, watch her pack away her clothes and books. He didn't know what else they could do.

'What was the other story?'

'Sorry?'

'You said there were two stories. That heap of shit you were spinning yourself into a frenzy about, that was the first story. What was the other one?'

'I don't know. I was hoping you'd tell me. I think there probably isn't one.'

She stroked his face. He pushed her hand away, forcibly.

SAMMI
Brixton, 2009

It will start with a friend request flashing up there on the corner of the screen. Sam will click on it, and it will take her a second to connect the name and the tiny thumbnail picture, red hair, red lipstick. There will be a – something – there. A faint unease, somewhere at her temple. She'll think it through. Nothing had ever been proved, she'll think. It had all been speculation, insinuation. The way a group can turn on nothing, a person can become a scapegoat.

Accept. Why not.

Half a minute later, there will be a peaceful chime; a red message icon. No hello. No acknowledgement of the years passed, of blood, bad or otherwise.

SAMMI MY FIREND TOOK THIS ON HIS PHONE IS THIS MARK CARR????!!!!

A picture of a middle-aged man, grainy, profiled, taken in bad light. A moustache, a tuxedo, a champagne flute.

Brixton, 1996

Sammi crouched low to the pavement and put her shoulder under the shutter. It stuck at the point it always stuck at, it needed a shout to force it, a 'ya!' that rang out along the empty street. She stepped in, groped in the dark for one of the torches they kept on a side-ledge, then hauled the shutter back down again behind her.

'Does it ever strike you as funny,' Mark had said, when they'd been going through the ritual at 4 a.m. after a night out in Camden and a long, sexy walk home, 'that a group of squatters who believe property is theft should take security measures to keep the rest of the world out of their living space?'

'Well, it's not like it's actually locked, is it?' she'd said.

'So why keep it closed at all? Why don't you – don't we – just unroll the shutters and invite the world to come in and join us? Wouldn't that be the ultimate extension of our philosophy?'

Sammi had faced him, there in the cramped porch space, his face only half visible in the torchlight. He'd been looking straight at her, his mouth twitching and amused, like a teacher pitching on-the-spot maths problems.

'Mate, you wanna leave that shutter open? You want to wake up spooning some of the junkies we got round here? Pretty white boy like you? Go for it. I'm sure they'd love you.'

As usual, she saw his point. But he was doing it again, floating his brain above them, pointing out wrinkles and discrepancies, handing down solutions from on high like he wasn't even affected. The shutter was the perfect compromise – to get it open you had to know the knack and be strong enough to shove at precisely the right bit (Spider often had trouble during his bad weeks; that's how they knew), and to find your way up the stairs into the living space you'd need to know where the torches were. You'd have to be proper determined. It was a system they'd put together themselves, without ever discussing it.

The hallway stank of must and damp. Fran had tried burning oils in the space for a while, but Gaz had been caught out using the burner as an ashtray, and it had caused another fight. Nevertheless, Sammi sat herself down on the bottom step and just breathed it in, all its foul notes, for a while. Imagine bringing her mother here. The rusted shutter would confirm all her fears; the smell would finish her off.

It had been a rough one, tonight's Tuesday dinner at her mum's. At first, when she left home, her mum had tried to insist she come back every Sunday, for church and lunch. Sammi's refusal had been gentle but absolute.

'I'm not gonna pretend, Mum. Not even for you. Besides, I need my Sundays, don't I? Got stuff on. Stuff to do.'

Tuesday dinner had become the compromise, and Sammi stuck to it. Most of the others didn't get it, but then none of them were squatting twenty minutes away from the street they'd grown up on. Tonight, Avril had pulled out all the stops. The aunties had all been there, Sammi's brother and his fiancée, and she'd even had the bloody vicar stop by for a guest appearance. Sammi was usually quiet at Tuesday dinner. She usually tried to keep her head down, make pleasant chat, not give her mum too much to wail over. Given an audience, though, Avril just couldn't help herself, had pick-pick-picked away at Sammi's table manners and clothes, her face squirming in displeasure every time her daughter had spoken. Sammi had left earlier than usual, when Avril was slamming dishes in the kitchen, after the vicar had sensed the tension and made his own excuses.

The squat was quiet when she got up there, no lights on (which didn't always mean nobody was in). Sammi squinted and could make out Xanthe, curled up on her mattress in the sleep space with Dido's tiny tousled head nestled into her neck – her eyes glinted in the wan street light coming through the window, and she smiled and put a finger to her lips. Sammi nodded, blew her a kiss and stepped back out. There was nobody in the living area, so she plugged in a side lamp and climbed into the big armchair.

Mark had been trying to organize them on manoeuvres recently, trying to get everyone into the animal rights group he and Fran were pretty much running these days. Sammi had been with them on a couple of recces of a lab Fran swore she'd heard on good authority were testing on animals. She squashed into the clanking old van with Mark's gloved hand in hers, breathing in Spider's dope and sweat stench. They'd parked some way away, snuck up to the facility from a distance and checked it out, the three of them. Mark had a surprisingly swish camera, had managed to get some pretty clear shots of the things he spotted – a weak point in a fence, a broken security camera – when he wasn't acting like bloody James Bond or something, practically commando rolling on the concrete. Sammi had been reminded of that little boy on her mum's street when she was growing up, playing spies by himself in the back alley, flattening himself to the wall with his fingers pointing a pistol, muttering.

Sammi went in the van runs to support Mark, but not because she cared particularly. There had never been animals around when she was growing up – her mother hated the hair, the shedding, and she'd learned to shy away from cats or over-friendly dogs in the street, to keep her clothes good – maybe that was it. Maybe coming from the inner city she just didn't get it. She'd noticed Mark had recently convinced their pals from the animal liberation group to meet on Tuesday nights, when he knew she couldn't be there, and she assumed he must be disappointed in her for it.

Xanthe cited Dido as an excuse, as she always did, but most of her other energies were going into feminism these days. If Xanthe wasn't in, she would be at the library, ordering books, carting them home to read on the roof space or by torchlight beside the sleeping child. 'Xanthe's politics only really happen in her head,' Clio had said, and Sammi could see she was right. Clio herself, on the days she was staying, was not only critical but the most hostile towards the animal project.

'Look, Fran pal. I get it. I do. I can see this means a huge deal to you, and I understand where you're coming from. It's an injustice, it totally is, and more power to you for trying to do something about it. But me, what makes me get up and fight, is oppression. Oppression of people,' she added quickly, over Fran's open mouth. 'I've just no got the energy to spare on bunny rabbits till we've made sure that all of our own are all right. There's people kept in conditions similar to those animals at the behest of this fucking government, I'll tell you that. It's the global capitalist machine, babe. Once we get that ironed out, things are going to improve for everyone. Including your hamsters. Meantime there's enough people getting screwed by this system I'd like to help first. But you keep doing your thing. I can see it means a lot.'

Nobody could deny that life was just a bit more exciting during the weeks when Clio shared their crash space – she made the air electric, was always active, always doing things and full of ideas. But she and poor awkward Fran, a rebellious vicar's daughter from the Home Counties, were the far poles of the group. Clio's glamour and sparkle rubbed up against Fran's seriousness and purpose. Fran couldn't take a joke, and Clio took too many (although never at her own expense). And Clio also made them feel a bit more connected to the world immediately outside the squat. Apart from Sammi, and Spider, who had moved to Brixton aged eleven with his mum, most of the others just put their heads down and speed-walked to the Centre, the Roxy or the tube station any time they had to venture out. Clio had only been with them a few months when she and Sammi went walking down Electric Avenue, and Clio had smiled at or stopped to chat or nod at six people in as many minutes.

'Fucking hell, mate,' Sammi had said. 'You already know more people than me, dontcha? And I grew up here.'

'Ach, I just talk to people. I grew up in tiny wee places, villages, where you dinnae get the chance of ignoring folk on the street; they'll whisper behind your back that you think you're no better than you should be.'

'You what?'

'That you think your shit doesnae stink.'

'Gotcha.'

'It was one of the things that really freaked me out when I first came down to London. All those faces just staring ahead. I like it round here, though. Folk talk, don't they?'

'Ha! They talk too bloody much, mate. Moira over there with the veg stall, she don't never shut up. She used to live next door to my nan and she's always telling me I need to call my mama. Maybe I could do with some fuckers just staring ahead sometime.'

'Aw, I love Moira. Moira! Hiya, Moira! Anyway, do you need to call your mama?'

'I just got dinner at hers last night, dint I?'

'Well, you're definitely doing better than me on that score. Carry on, pal. As you were.'

She tucked an arm into Sammi's, pulled her in until their heads were touching, and they walked on together, skip-hopping down the street, not caring who saw.

The boys, Sammi and Xanthe had often whispered to each other, were all secretly in love with Clio (Gaz, Sammi would always point out, was just as much into Xanthe). The unspoken vagaries of Sammi and Mark's arrangement meant that, while she was pretty sure he'd had it off with most of their female room-mates at some point, none of the boys would even approach Sammi. She remembered a David Attenborough documentary she'd watched during Tuesday dinner with her brother recently, something about a stag fighting off all the other stags to declare himself the alpha male of the pack, with none of them daring to go near his doe, and thought, yeah, that seems about right. Avril had bustled back in and been scandalized at the animals rutting on her television screen, smacked Joseph, who was holding the remote, around the head and called him dirty.

'You got us by immaculate conception then, did you?' Sammi had asked, in a rare bit of cheek, and her mother had wheeled on her.

'And you! Samantha Geraldine Smith! Living in that hovel with them unwashed freaks! Who's this blond man you been seen with then, my girl? Oh yes, everybody talking to me about you. Everybody talking! Bringing so much shame on your poor mother! Flaunting it in front of the whole neighbourhood like you was the whore of Babylon!'

Sammi had got up and left at that, but she'd come back to Tuesday dinner the week after.

Xanthe wandered into the room and flopped into the other chair, kicking a pair of heeled boots Sammi recognized as Clio's out of the way as she did.

'Oof. She's unsettled right now.'

'Who is, mate?'

'Dido. Dido is. Who else would I be – never mind. She wouldn't sleep. And you know what? I'm not surprised. It's never the same for her two days in a row, is it? She doesn't know who's going to be there when she wakes up in the morning. Jesus, Sammi. What am I doing here? What sort of shitty mother am I that I'm bringing up a tiny kid in a house full of exposed wires and crusty fucking speedfreaks?'

Sammi, having privately thought this many times, decided to stay quiet.

'I mean, I came here to make a new way of life and I spend my time doing the dishes for a revolving door of ungrateful pigs – mostly male, the irony's not lost on me – whose understanding of "communal living" is pretty fucking capitalist if you ask me – oh, never mind. Never mind.'

Sammi was too tired for this again. She nodded at the boots.

'Clio back then? Where is she?'

Xanthe's face clouded a bit.

'On the roof, I think. I'd just leave her, babe.'

'She OK? I haven't seen her in ages. I could just pop up.'

Xanthe reached under the sofa and pulled out the ancient box of Scrabble someone had found in a chazzer.

'Stay here. Have a game with me instead. She'll be down soon.'

Clio came down half an hour later, her cheeks and nose a little red, bringing in the smell of cold air and something else. Mark entered the room five minutes after that, same smell, same expression. Sammi shot Xanthe a look, as if to say, mate, don't baby me, I'm fine with this, unfurled herself from the chair and went to kiss him on the face. Clio was quiet in the corner, went to bed shortly. Sammi was fine with it, of course she was fine with it, but she began to avoid going up onto the roof.

Although they tried not to rub her face in it, Sammi soon came to realize that Clio and Mark seemed to fuck more than any of the others. And it was something that always confused Sammi, because in all of their other interactions they were ice-cold to the point of dislike; their mutual need to control every situation tending to interfere with even the simplest conversation. Sammi would watch them dance around angrily, and think again of the noise those stags made as their antlers smashed into each other. These were the times when she really felt so much younger than everyone else there, as though they were all talking in a code she hadn't been taught yet.

The only place where Clio, Fran and Mark found common ground was in the protest against the new McDonald's on the high street.

The café was busy. Sammi had a song stuck in her head (no time to work out what it was) and she moved and flexed to her own rhythm as she bumped down bowls of dahl and snatched up used cups. Step step step, ba dum ba dum spin. What's that, darlin? Yeah, no probs, coming right up. Oi, Jimmy, two falafel plates for number three please. Ba dum ba dum woo!

She might moan about it, and it's true that the job didn't pay well (Antoine claimed to have ambivalent feelings about being an employer and to dislike the concept of 'wages') and unless it was busy and she could work up a sweat the whole building was bitter cold, even on sunny days, but discovering the Centre had brought so much joy to her life. She'd heard talks that had redefined her politics, danced till the next morning at sound-system parties, and it was here she'd met Fran, and Xanthe, and Mark. Today, Giancarlo and Utti were curled up in a corner under the pig-policeman mural, arms and legs entwined but heads turned away, one reading a rolled paperback, the other a zine. The Italians had met Spider at a party over a month ago, were the latest of his lost lambs. Spider and his big heart kept on bringing people with nowhere else to go back to the squat; usually they were introduced as 'comrades' or 'fellow travellers' and half the time they'd end up nicking clothes or shoes.

The Italians were very serious. They only ever wanted to talk anarchism and revolution, were uninterested in the day-to-day running of squat life (leaving Xanthe to mutter at their backs that once again she was acting as an unpaid cleaner). But they both stood up with huge smiles and gave Clio noisy, kissy embraces as she arrived and pulled up a stool, a great big slash of red against their funeral clothes. They were joined a few minutes later by a group of people including Fran and Spider, with Mark ambling up after that, and as extra seats were added to the table and Sammi took their coffee orders, she wondered who had decided on this meeting time and place, and why none of these six people, all of whom she had seen in their shared living quarters in the last twenty-four hours, had thought to mention it to her.

The café was too busy for her to give the group her full attention, but it seemed to be a pretty official meeting, not just a gathering of friends. Clio, Mark and Fran all took their turns to talk and, as she dipped in to drop off plates, she picked up phrases like 'creating a visible, public show of force' and 'direct action'. At one point Mark, scoffing and interrupting Fran, said, 'I think this calls for something bigger than a letter-writing campaign'; led the table in laughter against her. Clio had been talking passionately for some time – Sammi had heard 'poll tax' and 'getting our point across in a public display that properly involves the community', and Utti had stood up and applauded whatever it was she'd been saying while the others cringed,

Englishly, looked at the floor. But by the time the lunchtime rush had ebbed back down and Sammi was due a break, the meeting, whatever it was, seemed to have broken up. Mark still sat there, smiling at her. She flopped down beside him.

'That seemed well intense.'

'Yeah, yeah. Making plans. Big plans.'

'Big plans that you didn't think to mention to me?'

'Hey, hey gorgeous. It's not like that. Just didn't think it was something you'd be into.'

'Could've bloody tried me, mate. What was it – not the animal rights again? I know Clio,' she tried too hard to keep her voice neutral as she said the name, 'don't give two craps about all that.'

'Something bigger, I hope. Something with the potential to get really involved.'

'Well, I got five minutes and no more patience for your mysteries. Seriously, what's the score here? You deliberately trying to keep me out of the stuff you're planning?'

'Oh, sweetheart. No, no, no. We just – I just thought – it could get risky, this one. I don't want you getting hurt. Or picked up by the police.'

She heard that 'we' – the realization that the whole thing had probably been planned post-coitally after a little rooftop shag sesh – like a cold dash of water down her back.

'Aight. This is coming across pretty disrespectful if you ask me. If I'm old enough for you to fuck, I'm old enough to get involved. Spill. Now.'

The plan was to target the building site on the high street, already decorated with McDonald's vinyl branding, with an ongoing series of posters, leading up to direct action which would hopefully get the local community on side. Sammi was less sure about that.

'Lot of the young ones love their Maccy D's, mate. Dunno how many bods you'll get on side round these streets.' She was reminded of the riots last year, of the way the panic had risen inside the squat even though they'd all initially supported the rioters against the police. The overflowing currents of whiteness and poshness cutting her off from the rest of them as the noise and violence in the streets had got louder. She was cynical about any of them being able to engage 'the community', even Spider. Mark, who showed no interest whatsoever in the wider world of Brixton, had merely shrugged when she'd raised this point.

Once she'd been allowed to attend the follow-up meeting, Sammi could see why Mark had assembled the team he had: Fran and her friends obviously objected to the company on animal rights grounds; Utti stood against all and any big global corporations and Giancarlo, Sammi suspected, just liked a fight; Spider and Clio were riled up by the pushing out and knocking down of three local businesses to make way for the new development, by the soul of Brixton being taken over, by the reports they'd heard of unfair wages for staff. Mark himself, though – she wasn't sure. Just as she'd never quite been able to see what motivated him to get involved with the animal rights stuff. He seemed alive with it, though, his eyes sparking about like they hadn't done in a while, his hands never done pulling her into the sleeping space, his thrusting faster and more urgent. Much like Giancarlo, he seemed to be energized by the fight, but she was sure there was something else going on there, something that she couldn't place.

'So, who was you going to get to do your posters, then? Need someone with a bit of skill to do that, dontcha?'

Clio looked shamefaced, Sammi was pleased to note. She wasn't in a mood to let them off with it.

'Should've come to me earlier, that's all I'm saying.'

'Of course! We got a proper artist right here, int we? Can't believe you was all thinking about just doing it with some marker pens. Sammi, you actually got time to get on board with this? Make it look right for us?' She loved Spider in that moment, could've kissed his stinking dreads, flashed the room a big cheeky smile.

'Might be too busy with all my other high-art commissions now. I'll speak to my people, see what we can do for you.'

They were getting dinner ready – Gaz and Xanthe chopping and stirring what smelled like a curry while everyone else sat about, helped when told, Sammi rolling a ball to little Dido sitting on the floor. An unusually full house that evening, which she always enjoyed – it made it easier to feel that sense of community she thought they'd all been looking for when they came up with the idea in the first place. Clio was kneeling, meticulously applying her make-up for a night out with some musician friends or other, the small green bag spilling products out across the seat of the big armchair in front of her. Fran bent down and scooped up the bag, squinted in at it.

'Clio, you know that most of these products are tested on animals, right?'

Clio rolled her eyes for the effect, before looking up.

'Yeah, and they're mostly factory seconds, charity shop or left-overs, pal. I cannae afford to buy them new, so nobody's getting the profits, all right?'

'I still wouldn't be able to put those products on my face, knowing the conditions they'd been created in. I mean, this stuff –' Fran waved a tiny tube of something pink and shimmery '– they poured that into rabbits' eye sockets to check that it wasn't going to hurt humans.'

'I just wouldn't put any of it on my face,' Xanthe called, over her shoulder from the kitchen space. 'You don't need it, Clio. You're beautiful enough. I've told you this before. You're modifying your face to please the masters; conforming to patriarchal beauty standards motivated by insecurities programmed into us by capitalism.'

Clio looked riled. Xanthe had often called her out for her make-up use, it was true – the way other women looked was her current bugbear and she was also always on at Sammi to let her Afro out of its braids – but never on quite such a public stage as this, with seven other people in the room. Rising to her feet, finding her spotlight, Clio turned, took a breath in, addressed her audience.

'Listen, let me tell youse something. In the town where I grew up, the women were glamorous. I'd watch my mum getting ready for a night out at the Labour Club, the same place she went to every Saturday night, sat in the same seats in the lounge, drank the same gin out of the same glass, probably. And she treated it like, I don't know, the Oscars or something, mate. I'd watch her piling blue eyeshadow up to her brows, doing that Liz Taylor sweep with a pencil all the way round. She'd have the rollers in for four hours before she went out, she'd spot-clean her best suit or her old dress and have it hanging up in the kitchen by the kettle. She made her face up like it was an art, and my stepdad, he'd put his suit on, and a fresh tie, offer her his arm, and they'd step out into the street with all the neighbours they saw every day for work or at the shops, all of them *done*. All of them with that Saturday-night sparkle on, like it would be a dishonour to step out without it, like it was church or something. And the Labour Club, that same old building with its tired walls and the haze of fag smoke, that would become somewhere else, just with one wee tinsel curtain hanging over the stage, the sparkly bow tie on the old boy who sang Sinatra well into his seventies.

'I'd be allowed to go along and stay up too late, bag of crisps and a bottle of ginger, forming a gang who crawled under the tables with all the other weans. I'd sit there, watching the women's faces, the laughs they put on, the shimmering rainbows around their eyes, mysterious streaks of dark stuff cutting through their round cheeks, and I'd understand they were all casting a spell. They were all, by the power of these potions, by mutual agreement, transforming this place, where people worked hard jobs for never enough money, where every choice was difficult, where everything was functional and ugly, into Hollywood, or Las Vegas, some projection of what they'd seen in the movies. Where the same old spouse you woke to every morning was suddenly Lee Majors or Farrah Fawcett, where you lived next door to Burton and Taylor, where auld Archie from up the loan really was a member of the Rat Pack; where money didnae have to matter, just this once.

And it could only be sustained if everyone kept buying into it together. Oh my God, when there was a wedding! Doreen who did the hair was booked out from six a.m., and there was always some fancy ones who'd get the train through to Ayr for it, make the journey back with these beehives and sculptures poking out over the tops of their coats.'

They all watched her as she paused for breath, no one jumping in. Clio never spoke about her family, so this flood of words, the silty Scottish accent she usually toned down around them – it was something else.

'What my mother taught me was that you always looked your best. It was a matter of honour with her – you let it all go you might as well shout to the world that things are sliding, that you're not coping; it lets the rest of the team down, when they're dealing with things just as hard and worse. She never let anyone outside of me and my stepdad see her in her housecoat; I hardly ever saw her without her make-up the whole time I was growing up with her.

'It's a working-class thing, this. Youse don't get to tell a working-class woman that her lipstick isny feminist, because it's a signal of solidarity. This is a great big slash of solidarity I'm wearing across my face right now. And you can leave Sammi alone about her hair, too. I bet your mum was something like this, am I right, darlin?'

Sammi grinned shyly, embarrassed to have the spotlight back on her, and not sure how she felt about siding with Clio at the moment anyway. 'Yeah, my mum never let us leave the house looking less than perfect. They put this in you when you're young. I mean, it leaves you judging other women who ain't made the effort pretty heavy, you know—'

'Well, that's what I'm saying,' Xanthe said. 'It's another example of conditioning used to divide and conquer. Another tool for the patriarchy to use to have us tear each other apart, enforce a code which we use to contain each other.'

'Nah, you're not hearing me,' Clio said, no trace of the patient voice they were supposed to use when conflict occurred, like Fran's book had suggested. 'You ask a working-class woman who was brought up in a certain way at a certain time to ditch her make-up in order to raise her consciousness, you're asking her to break a bond she's made with her working-class sisters. No offence, doll, but going make-up free is a luxury for bougie women because they can always afford to buy more; it can be just a temporary state, a bit of play-acting between times. You don't need it to convince the world you're more than it thinks you are. You're asking them to take away the one wee bit of sparkle, of glamour, in what are, let me assure you, some fucking appalling lives. Black women, poor white women – we need to look good when we face out into the world, because the odds in life are already stacked so hard against us and people are already prejudging us on sight.'

'Yes, so we need to dismantle that system, get everything on an even playing field—'

'Aye, aye, sure, sure. But you're not going to do that by turning your own judgement on the women stuck in it – which you do, every time you suggest to Sammi she should let her Afro grow out natural, or me that I'd be better off without my lipstick. You're setting up one of your false di-whatjamies there, doll.'

Sammi looked about her. Over at the kitchenette, keeping his head down, Gaz was crumbling something into a frying pan of vegetables and lentils, flooding the air with spices. The room felt cosy even though they were all wearing extra jumpers, the fairy lights keeping the cold night outside at bay even though they still didn't have any curtains. Spider was rummaging through a pile of tapes by the cassette player, tickling Dido under her chin as she wandered over to him. Xanthe and Clio were all warm colours and anger, and they might be disagreeing but they were disagreeing about the way to make the world a better place. This was important stuff they were doing, she thought, in their own little corner, and she felt again so sure she was in the right place, was glad for it. It was maybe the last time she felt that connection between them all in a positive light.

*

Her posters, which Spider and Mark snuck out to pin up on the site after dark, were methodically ripped down every morning, meaning only late-night bodies wandering outside the Ritzy would see them. Sammi began using the copy room they'd never quite managed to get the magazine going in to crank out smaller versions, then leaflets, the text dictated by Fran and Mark, both leaning over her as she stencilled. The revised plan was to stand outside the site in daytime, directly engaging the people. Sammi took a walk down there on the third day, after work, stood at the other side of the road and watched Fran and her friend being sneered at and ignored in their earnestness.

'Fran mate, you gonna need to let me do this,' she said casually over dinner duties that night. 'You ain't from here – you ain't able to reach people. It's just a matter of knowing how to talk to them, know what I'm saying? Let me do the flyers tomorrow.'

'We were getting along just fine, thanks,' Fran said, shutting down like she always did. 'We had a lot of good conversations with people actually.'

'What's all this?' Mark had pricked up his ears, moved across from the side of the room.

'I was just saying maybe I should get involved with the action on the streets a bit more. People might listen if it was coming from someone from the area.'

'Mm, not sure that's such a good idea, sweetheart. You're already doing so much designing the leaflets – don't want to put too much on you.'

'What? Come on. I want to get involved in this. Use me.'

'I'll do it with Sammi,' said Clio. 'We could bring a bit of common touch to this, nah?'

Fran bristled at the sink, went silent. Sammi's eyes went to Mark, who was sitting back on his heels, taking it all in.

Clio and Sammi fared much better on the street outside the building site – people were at least taking their leaflets, and both of them managed a couple of conversations, even though Clio, emboldened, tried to get a group of young guys about Sammi's age involved and had one of them yell at her to fuck off and leave Maccy D's alone. Sammi tried hard to keep herself busy, so she wouldn't have to talk to Clio – she could tell that Clio really wanted to get serious with her – could see the orange head always turned towards her out of the corner of her eye when there was nobody there, kept her face trained along the road towards the next passer-by.

After a couple of hours, Clio said that that was quite enough for now and suggested they get some lunch. Sammi couldn't think of an excuse quickly, and so they ended up opposite each other on hard chairs, unwrapping plastic off a pair of egg sandwiches, looking down at the table. Clio stirred three sugars into a Styrofoam cup and coughed, and coughed again, and Sammi couldn't bear it any more.

'Is there something you wanted to say to me, Clio?'

She jumped, spilled her coffee. 'Yes – no. Well. It's just – it feels strange to me. And I suppose we should talk about it.'

'You want to talk about you fucking my boyfriend a lot. That it?'

'That's it.'

'Well, I don't really want to talk about it with you, so how about that?'

'I don't really know what to say anyway.'

'I mean, I don't like it. But it's not like I got grounds for official complaint. Maybe I thought we was better friends than we are for you to be doing – that – this much. Maybe I'd like you to stop. But I can't ask that. See?'

'I see. I'll stop, Sammi. It'll stop.'

'Whatever. I got leaflets to hand out. Shall we get back to it?'

'I mean it.'

'Sure.'

Another Tuesday dinner, her first in three weeks. This one wasn't so bad. Just her and Avril, alone for the first time in over a year, and her brother had obviously had a word with their mum. There wasn't much conversation, but there was no confrontation, just a nice companionable silence. It was neither Sammi's nor Avril's way to pick at a scab unnecessarily. They watched telly for much longer than they normally would, and Sammi did the washing-up, and they did not mention their fight. In the bathroom, just before she got her coat, Sammi paused for a little ritual she'd always liked since leaving home – sitting cross-legged on the floor in front of Avril's fastidiously arranged bathroom cabinet, its rows of plastic-wrapped guest soaps shaped like roses, its clean stores of toothpaste, moisturizers and sanitary towels. Avril liked to plan ahead, never ran out of anything. Then Sammi looked again at the sanitary towels and realized she hadn't had a period for about three months.

She didn't really notice herself getting back to the squat, she'd been so preoccupied. As soon as she'd allowed herself to think of the possibility, she knew it to be true. Yes, her body seemed to be saying. That's right. Caught on at last, have you?

She wondered what Mark would say, whether there was any point in telling him without a test to back herself up. She needed to share the weight of it, that was for sure. But the squat seemed empty when she got there – no lights on, no sign of Xanthe and Dido in the sleeping space. She braved it to take herself up to the roof, found Gaz sitting there by himself in a cloud of smoke, red-eyed.

'You all right? This place is like a ghost town tonight.'

'Aight, Sammi. They've all gone down to the Maccy D's site, ain't they. Giancarlo and Mark's idea. They're breaking in – Giancarlo getting all excited about destruction of something or other. I just told them I ain't up for it, and him and Mark got right up in my face, pair of fucks.'

'Bloody hell. Why they always pull this shit on a Tuesday? It's like they deliberately don't want me involved or something.'

'Dunno. Take it up with your boy. They've been planning this one for a while far as I know.'

'And where's Xanthe and the kid? They've not taken Dido down there?'

'Nah. Nah, mate. Xanthe's gone, int she. When she heard what they was planning she said she'd had enough, wasn't going to risk getting involved in it all by proxy. I think she's had this in mind for a while, to be honest. She popped out to the phone box, then a woman with a van came and picked the two of them up about six. Didn't even say much of a goodbye.'

Sammi had been aware of Gaz's crush on Xanthe but didn't really feel able to offer any comfort right then, so she patted him on the shoulder a couple of times and went to bed. She'd been curled up in her sleeping bag for a couple of hours, her brain spinning out with the worry of it all, her blood pulsing fast around her stomach and thighs, when a loud metallic clanging reverberated through the house. It didn't stop, took her a while to realize it was the shutter.

Downstairs, barefoot, with a torch, bumping into an equally confused and very stoned Gaz in the corridor, the two of them reached the entrance space, the noise making them wince. Gaz nudged her, indicated that she should be the one to speak.

'Who is it?' she yelled, over the din.

'Spider. And Utti. Can't get this thing open. Sammi, matey, you've got to let us in.'

Over cups of tea, Utti and Spider managed to piece together a story. They'd broken into the McDonald's site with the intention of occupying the space and disrupting the building work the next day, but Mark and Giancarlo had got into an argument about who could go further, both of them apparently daring the other one on to do something more. Clio had tried to stop them, pointing out that there were flats above the space, but Giancarlo, after Mark had goaded him, had set something alight. Clio had walked out at that point, leaving the rest of them unsure what to do, and the police had shown up almost immediately.

'Like they was waiting for us or something,' Spider said, and Utti nodded. '*Si, si,* this is not a coincidence, this one.'

Utti and Spider, having been furthest back, had been able to sneak out without being seen, but they were definitely sure that Fran, Giancarlo and Mark had all been arrested, had watched from round the corner as they were put into vans.

Sammi and Gaz just sat there, watching them, neither of them in a fit state to cope with any of this information.

Clio showed up after eleven the next day, as Sammi was getting ready to leave for work, having managed maybe an hour of crappy sleep, worried about Mark. Smell of drink off her, make-up smudged.

'What happened to you last night?'

'Went to a bar. Met a nice young man. Didn't feel like coming home.' The smirk was lazy, done for show.

'Well, looks like you got out right on time, dintcha?'

'What do you mean?'

'Your little stunt last night. Down at the building site. They all got themselves arrested right after you left.'

'What?'

Sammi would play this expression back to herself over and over again in the coming weeks. She might not be Clio's biggest fan, but she was pretty sure the shock was genuine. However, as Fran and Mark reminded her when they arrived back on bail the next day, Sammi had not been there.

'Listen, Frances,' Sammi heard Clio saying, as their voices reached breaking point through the wall, 'why the fuck would I call the cops on you? On anyone? This was as much my project as yours – why would I want you to get in trouble for it?'

'Because you don't like me!' Fran burst out. 'You're always finding ways to put me down. Maybe you wanted to see me punished because of my background – because you secretly hate anyone who wasn't born all working-fucking-class salt-of-the-earth?'

Clio's laugh sounded contemptuous. 'Not liking one person is not a reason to sell a group of friends out in the middle of a project you believe in. Take stock of yourself, woman. Get a fucking grip.'

'I think Fran's just maybe pointing out that it's a bit convenient, Clio, the police showing up just after you'd left the site.' This was Mark, seemingly all rational.

'What? By that logic you should blame fucking Xanthe! She actually left the squat for good that day!'

'Xanthe's my *friend*!' wailed Fran. 'Xanthe would never do anything to hurt me!'

'Come on, mateys. I don't think Clio gonna call the pigs.' This was Spider now. 'Not for anything, but certainly not on her comrades. Int that right? Why don't we all calm down here a bit, eh?'

Sammi rolled onto her side, pulled a pillow over her head and pressed it down on her ear, tuned in to the fast, fast pace of her pulse, and kept her secret for another day.

NEIL
Glasgow, 23 January 2018

'Tributes have been pouring in for the musician Clio Campbell, who died yesterday . . .'

Tributes always poured, Neil thought.

The First Minister, douce and sad, said that Clio had been a great talent and was a huge loss to the country.

Shiv West, hair pulled back, no make-up, apparently on her own doorstep, said she was a great friend and a lifelong inspiration.

Jools Holland, looking harried outside a BBC building, said that he was shaken, that she had been one of the truly great voices in folk music, and that she would be missed by everyone on his show.

'The well-known concert promoter Danny Mansfield, founder of the Big Rock Festival, who was married to Ms Campbell from 1993 to 1995, sent us the following statement: "I'm devastated. I've lost a great friend and the world has lost a great talent." Mr Mansfield went on to ask that the media respect his family's need for privacy at this difficult time.'

His secretary had emailed Neil the same thing, and they'd run it in the piece. He was surprised anyone except himself remembered the marriage. He was surprised Danny Mansfield did. He suspected the secretary had copied and pasted the statement from someone else's death, someone else's tribute.

It seemed like an awful lot of coverage for someone who'd only had one hit single and a couple of critically panned albums. The benefits of living in a small country, he supposed.

Neil flicked the telly off, picked up his phone and refreshed the newspaper website again. It was up. He copied the link and tweeted: *My obituary for Clio Campbell. A great friend and an even greater singer.*

Then he searched for her name. For some reason it seemed like an awful lot of young women were talking about her and linking to videos of 'Rise Up' on YouTube. Nobody else had published an obituary yet, so they were ahead of the curve there at least.

Great.

He wondered how you would translate that word each time.

She was a singer who I vaguely remember liking in the Nineties, and she once sang at a function I was invited to.

I met her three times in ten years and never had that much to say to her.

She had a lovely voice and was a massive pain in the arse.

She was a maddening, impulsive, humourless force of nature, who changed her mind every five minutes, never stuck to plans, and would pick people up and drop them again as and when she needed them. And I fucking well loved her.

He'd shouted that last bit, he realized. His flat was silent in response. The traffic outside the window hooted appreciatively.

Then he was on his hands and knees, raking through the CD storage case he kept in the cupboard. There it was. *The Northern Lass*, signed in black marker around her face, the letters tangled in her hair.

For Neil.
C X

He hadn't used the CD player on his old stereo in a few years, was surprised it still gulped the disc obediently. Lying on the sofa as the strings led him into 'Ae Fond Kiss', as Clio smoked and shimmered around the room, he found he'd reached for his phone and was thumbing. Twenty-six notifications already. He switched the fucking thing off, shut his eyes, let his ears do the breathing for a while.

Had we never loved sae kindly,
Had we never loved sae blindly,
Never met – or never parted,
We would ne'er be broken-hearted.

It was perfectly dark when he opened his eyes, a creeping neck pain doing the work of waking for him. The only light in the room was the green LED display on the stereo. He fumbled for his phone and turned it on, almost an automatic reaction, before he'd eased himself up. His body scolded him with each twinge for two concurrent nights of bad sleep out of his bed, to no purpose. 4.18 a.m. Christ. It had been early evening when he'd gone down. The phone buzzed and twitched itself to life, messages and notifications filing in – no, pouring in.

His obituary had been retweeted over eight hundred times.

There was a voicemail from Craig, because of course Craig was the sort of person who would still leave a voicemail.

'Neil. Mate. This Clio Campbell thing – getting more hits than anything else this week. Great stuff, great stuff. Really blowing up. Think we're going to go for a big feature in the Saturday mag. Want you to lead on it. Can you call me asap?'

He'd actually said 'ass-ap'.

Fare-thee-weel, ma first and fairest.

Edinburgh, 2003

They rounded the corner onto Princes Street, trudging obediently, a polite phalanx of navy-blue cagoules and expensive all-weather coats.

There were not very many placards and no banners; a few people had been handed now-soggy Socialist Worker posters to wave, their slogans unrelated to the issue of the day, but mostly they just trudged. It was a very well-behaved protest, despite the best efforts of the students up ahead who kept trying to stoke a half-hearted chant into something more.

'*Who let the bombs out?*'

'*BUSH! BUSH AND BLAIR!*'

They'd bark and howl into the drizzle, then shut themselves down again. At every burst of noise, Neil would check the tape recorder, even though he'd drawn the short straw in the office and come out with a clunky shoebox of a thing, at least fifteen years old, with no way of measuring the sound levels. The wheels were still turning, at least. He felt like a right eejit holding it up at the great man's mouth as they walked along: Neil was also considerably shorter than him and his arm was getting tired; he had to try and keep his elbow slightly bent so it didn't look like he was marching along giving a Nazi salute. He wished they could just sit down, go to a café, but his editor had wanted colour, a sense of the life of the protest, the big man's politics in motion, he'd said. So this. Stupid, stupid. Neil was sure he'd play it back and have hardly anything usable.

A couple of girls in their twenties, fake fur and umbrellas, glittery eye shadow, had clocked the writer – he wasn't necessarily a household face, but they might have recognized him from the book jackets, the odd TV interview he'd done. They were nudging each other and giggling.

'Be cool. Just be cool,' the dark-haired one said. The writer turned and smiled at them, a smile that said, yes, it's me.

'Do you get that a lot?' said Neil, nodding at their backs and trying an all-boys-together sort of grin.

The writer shrugged. 'It's not the worst bit of the job, is it.' He'd spent the whole interview at a frustrating reserve, careful not to say anything incriminating on tape, even though Neil had tried hard to reassure him that he was a huge fan, that the readership would agree with his anti-Iraq War stance because basically everyone did, now, and they'd get in loads of plugs for the new book. Advance word says it's the great post-9/11 Scottish novel – how do you feel about that, Neil had asked, and the writer had leaned into the tape recorder and enunciated clearly.

'Oh, that's for other people to decide. I just write the things.'

'George BUSH!

You're a WANKER!

Fuck off with your OIL TANKER!'

Beside them, two old ladies in tweed coats drew to a halt.

'Well, I think that's me now, Morag.'

'Absolutely. No need for that. Let's go and have a cup of tea.'

Neil worried that he'd gone wrong somewhere. The big man was well known as an interviewer's dream, so friendly you felt you'd always known him. Perhaps he was just as embarrassed as Neil was by the awkwardness of the set-up, the march, the tape recorder. Maybe I shouldn't have brought the recorder, Neil thought. Maybe I should have just taken notes.

He'd tuned out.

'. . . and I think that's reflected in the demographic we're seeing here today. After an apathetic, prosperous decade, the middle classes are waking up, and standing up for issues that don't directly affect their lives.'

'Yeah, yeah. Exactly. I know what you mean,' said Neil, covering frantically.

The march filed quietly down the damp slope into Princes Street Gardens for the rally at the bandstand. Neil thought about the footage he'd seen of the London protests, all that vigour and anger and youth. He remembered marching on George Square in Glasgow, screaming and spitting, one small drop in a wave of fury, consumed with the righteousness of what they were doing. Maybe the difference was the city, maybe the difference was him. He had turned thirty-eight the week before, had gone to see the Fall with some friends, drowned in a leather-jacketed sea of men his own age and older, all holding pints. He'd watched Mark E Smith writhe and swear and wondered that someone could still find the energy to feel that much.

The writer was going to be speaking at the rally; unusually for a protest he'd been announced in advance, a press release sent out.

'No, it's not something I'd normally do,' he said to the tape recorder, as they huddled at the back of the bandstand, glad of the roof. 'Not anything I've ever done before. But we're living in exceptional times, aren't we? Where over a million people can march on the capital city making their wishes known and the government just ignores it? Where we wage war on countries under completely flimsy pretexts to get at their oil? If people like my books and want to listen to me, and I can use that to get more and more of them to realize what's going on – well, it becomes a duty, doesn't it?'

Neil nodded eagerly, took a second to notice he was motioning to stop the tape recorder.

'Listen, I think – I mean, do feel free to come backstage here with me, but you'd probably better switch the machine off. None of these people have agreed to be part of the interview, or recorded. You know?'

Neil kept on nodding – it was something to do with his face. He takes me for a fool, this man, he thought. He thinks I'm a rank amateur, some wee freelancer who struck it lucky and is on his first big celebrity interview. It's the tape recorder. The fucking tape recorder.

'Good man. Good man.'

Backstage, Neil tried to stay out of everyone's way. There were a few musicians dotted about, tuning up, a socialist MSP he recognized from the telly. Fifteen years ago, he reflected, this would have been Gogsy Duke in his element, networking and charming, making everyone feel warm and enthused, part of the same project. But the Right Honourable member for Glasgow Possil toed the party line now, would not allow himself to be even tenuously associated with an event created to be critical of his boss. Gogsy had voted to invade Iraq. Neil had overheard one of the subs in the office chuckling about it when they got the list of MP votes through, about how the mighty had fallen, something like that. People always found it funny when principled men betrayed themselves. Neil had got drunk that night, by himself, in the Albannach, avoiding his colleagues' eyes and not talking. Drinking by himself.

And then, like a ghost, as though the thought of Gogsy had summoned her, there was Clio. A light touch on his arm, a waft of something female and flowery. Of course she was there. It made perfect sense.

'Long time, stranger.'

She was there, and she was talking like a dame from an old movie. They hugged and she held tightly on to his neck, let him keep his arms on her waist, one, two, three.

'You doing a wee turn at this, then?'

'I am. All very last minute. Special guest yet to be announced, that's me. Play the hit.'

'I thought you were living in London.'

'I still am. Sometimes. Been in Europe a bit. Up north some more. I go where it takes me. But today I'm here.'

'Flying visit?'

'Megabus back down tomorrow morning. You look well, Neil. It's good to see you. Listen, I'm going to go and get warmed up now, but how about we get a drink or something later? Have you got any plans?'

He did not. She retreated back into the darkness and the crowd started clapping, a few whistles, the loudest they'd been all day, as the writer took the stage. He was passionate, he was well spoken, he drew laughs and stoked outrage, expertly. He made them feel good about themselves and their involvement in this cause, fed their anger, inspired them to think of doing more, if only in that moment. And

Neil could not record a single bit of it, because his tape had run out. He let himself ease closer and closer to the wings, drawing a couple of looks from the organizers, trying at least to memorize some of the lines that got the biggest responses, whispering them over to himself so he missed the next sentence, lost track of what was being said.

The writer left the stage on the opposite side, a fanfare of stomps and cheers heralding him off, and Clio was standing beside him again, guitar strapped across her, staring straight ahead. He knew better than to disturb her right before she went on, even just to give her a thumbs-up. The MC or host or whatever you called someone at a rally was talking too close to the microphone, sound booming everywhere.

'Well, wasn't that something, folks? I think it's a testament to how serious this issue is that we're getting this calibre of speaker out. We're sending a message – Mr Blair, your warmongering American friends are NOT WELCOME here!'

More cheers.

'And now, let's keep that spirit going, my friends! I'm delighted to announce a very special guest indeed, a surprise addition to the bill. We can't quite believe we've got her, so let's have some music. People got to rise up! Put your hands together for Clio Campbell!'

She couldn't have inherited a more receptive crowd. Clio stood centre stage, silent and half-smiling as the stage hand plugged her guitar to the amp. She was wearing purple-toned leather cowboy boots and a dress too thin for the weather, shivered visibly as she reached for the mic stand.

'Afternoon, Edinburgh.'

A few well-mannered helloes.

'Yeah, that seems about right. Let me tell you something. I was there, when we marched in London. Over a million people in the streets. It wasn't anything like this. People were there because they were angry. Now, I know it's raining today, but I was in that march earlier, and I wasn't really picking up on that much anger from you.'

Stick to the songs, Neil was thinking, trying to push the words through the air to her. Just sing. You're not so good at this.

'And do you know what, Edinburgh, you should be angry. Not just about a warmongering oil baron who happens to be the most powerful man in the world getting a fancy tea with the Queen on your taxes, but because you're all being taken for fools. Every day. And you just don't seem to care, do you? Even those of you here today, you're not doing much about it. You're really not making very much noise. Can you make some noise, Edinburgh?'

'Fuck off!' shouted a young male voice. Laughter.

'No I will not. I will not fuck off. Don't you – I've been actually doing something with my time to make a difference, not just tiptoeing along a wee march on the local high street. Don't you talk to me like that. You don't get to—'

She stopped, pulled back for a second, her lips moving and nothing coming out.

'Anyway, here's a song. You probably know it. It's called "Rise Up".'

A few people clapped, a couple of whistles, but she'd lost them. A clamour of conversation rose above the noise of the PA, and people at the back started peeling back off up the hill. Her voice was ragged over the first verse and she didn't manage to reach the high note of the chorus, ended it a verse early. Downbeat applause, a muttered thanks, and she scuttled off the stage, across the other side.

The pub they ended up in was supposed to be spooky. Bell jars covering plastic specimens, coated in sprayed-on dust, cluttered up nooks and tables; skeletons hung from the ceiling and a tape played the 'Monster Mash' on repeat in the toilets, which were accessed through a door covered in fake books.

'Do you think those are real skeletons?' Neil asked, as he brought the drinks back to the table where she was hunched, hadn't even taken off her coat. It was something to say. 'I mean, actual people. That was once a living person. Maybe.'

He shunted the pint across to her. 'Right, get that down you, and tell me what you've been doing for ten years. I ordered us some chips and onion rings and that. Don't know about you, but I always work up a hunger after a day's marching!'

He'd said that too loudly, and they both winced in the silence that followed. Slowly, though, she began to uncurl. She bent towards him, stretching her purple cowboy boots out along the leather bench she was perched on, her dress rucked up over her thighs.

'I like the boots. A wee nod to the Texas President?'

She grinned. 'Yeah. Bit on the nose, you reckon? Much like my set.'

'You were fine. You were great. Come on now.'

'I lost it up there. I'm – ach, Neil, I don't see what the point is sometimes. I mean, back in the day, when we were taking direct action – our protests counted for something. You know? We could form a human shield around a house. We could show up in our hundreds of thousands to George Square or mob the buses down to London and feel like we were making a difference. We got the fucking poll tax binned! That, today. I just didn't feel like there was any energy. And why would there be? Nobody cared about what we did there. It was just a group of people getting together to murmur their displeasure. Ach. Ach ach ach. When did protest become a hobby for rich people? Did you see some of those fuckers out there? I mean, it's like mass gatherings have become marketable or something.'

'There's still a place for anger,' he said, gently. 'Maybe even more so now.'

'But how? How does it get out? It's maybe the age I am, but I'm sitting here with my guitar after a failed gig and a failed march, wondering what the hell I'm doing with my life. I can't go on like I have been doing. I can't. It just doesn't work. Nobody wants my music and nobody wants my voice. I've never not been helping before. You know?'

She gulped lager, stared down at her legs, began talking again before he'd worked out quite what to say.

'They were a present, the boots. Just got given them yesterday. I'm maybe not convinced they work.'

'I like them.'

'I wouldn't have chosen them. Just trying something. Ach, sorry you had to see that, Neil. I'm not really doing much with the music any more. It's been a long time since I performed anything, and I've forgotten how to interact with a crowd.'

'Well, that's a shame. You should always be singing, Clio.'

She looked straight at him and he felt that pilot light go on. It would take them four more pints and an untouched bowl of onion rings, but when he bent across to kiss her, after steadying her when she'd almost fallen off the seat, he did it with confidence, knowing she was going to kiss right back. Cold beery mouth on his and her hands intense, the shock of contact for both of them. He pulled away and cupped her flushed face in a hand, rubbed the lipstick off her chin with his thumb.

'So. What are we going to do about this, then? Have you got – did they give you – offer to put you up anywhere?'

She shook her head, and he tried to slosh through a mental calculation. It would take time to get her on the train to Glasgow and back to his flat, and he didn't think he could risk her sobering up along the way, under harsh ScotRail lighting, crowds of football fans and the wait to buy a ticket. Fuck it. Time for a grand gesture.

'Would you like to crash at mine?'

A nod, as if she didn't want to put words out there. Perhaps she needed him to take charge, just for today. He picked up her coat and helped her into it, one arm, two, steered a hand at the small of her back, and stepped her out into the street. The click, click of her boots on concrete. She was muttering something. He pulled her close so he could hear.

'Lot of disappointments, Neil. Lot of disappointments in the last couple of days.'

He didn't know what to say to that. Fortunately his eye caught the welcome orange light, and he flagged it down, and it stopped.

'Thanks, mate. Big trip for you, this one. How much to get us to Glasgow, the West End.'

'Ooh, that's a steep one, pal. Flat fare is eighty pounds.'

'No bother.'

'Neil, you – we're going to Glasgow? What?'

'Don't worry about it. It's on the paper,' he said, and pressed his mouth to her neck.

They snogged for the whole taxi ride, almost an hour. He didn't want her to come up for air, didn't want to give her time to think, remember who he was and what he wasn't, change her mind. Slow. Pace yourself. His fingers found the low neckline of her dress, danced gently at the warm skin under there with increasing pressure; by the time they passed Falkirk he had his whole hand inside her bra, was rubbing her nipple between finger and thumb. There was heat coming off her, from between her legs, and his other hand needed to be up there. He guided her hand down and felt dizzy when, after a couple of seconds, she fumbled obediently at his belt buckle, slipped in there, held him in her fist, not stroking but pulsing faintly with her hand, slowing to a halt as his fingers reached her knickers and she breathed in-in-in. Out of the window, Glasgow approached, just as he was considering whether he could in fact be the sort of person who could fuck in a taxi with the driver right there, through a half-open pane of Plexiglas. He drummed his fingers lightly over the cotton, the softness beneath it, pulsed again against her hand just at the idea of slipping under the elastic edge, pulled back as he felt the cab slowing, heard the driver clear his throat.

'All right, pal, thanks very much. Here you go, keep the change.'

'You not wanting a receipt?'

She was slumped forward slightly, staring at her boots.

'Nope, nope, all good. Night, pal. Night.'

She was stepping out, the cold night air hitting her face.

'Aye well. Have a good night. Thanks for the show.'

'What did he say?' Clio asked, waking up, wheeling about on the pavement.

'Arsehole. Don't listen to him.'

He steered her through the gate, pushed her up against the door with one hand and kept kissing her while he groped in each pocket of his jacket. Got them. Got them. Door unlocked, he held her hand and practically pulled her up the stairs, three flights, her arms feeling thin and her body swaying dangerously over the concrete drop behind.

'Christ, Neil, that's some workout.'

'Uh-huh. Come in.'

He could offer to get her a drink or something, but leaving her alone in his drab wee hallway would probably be counterproductive right now, so he steered her straight to the bed, walking behind her, holding her hip and her breast, pressing his erection into her arse.

'You seem to be a bit overdressed, my lady. Shall we get you out of this?'

Again, she said nothing, and he pulled her dress over her head. She wasn't looking at him, reached around behind herself to undo her bra, and he brought his face down to her breasts, appreciating them close up. They had always been small; she looked much younger than she was there, in the half-dark, in nothing but her knickers and a pair of cowboy boots.

'God, you're beautiful, you're so fucking beautiful.'

No response, so he pushed her down flat onto the mattress, positioned himself on top of her, held her legs open and scooped her knickers to the side. Red hair, bright even in the gloom. He breathed her in, put his face right there, his mouth.

'Let me worship you tonight,' he told her, just trying to alleviate the sadness. Tonight, he thought, she needed to feel wanted. And he could provide. When he finally got inside her, he groaned, loud. How long since he'd had sex? His last relationship – if you could call those three months of awkwardness with Louise a relationship – had ended well over a year ago.

'Fifteen years in the making!' he said, smiling down at her.

'Sssh,' she told him.

Afterwards he brought her wine and crisps from the kitchen, and they consumed them together under the sheets, in companionable silence. He stroked her arm.

'Dunno about you, but I've wanted to do that for a long time.'

She sipped. 'It was nice.'

'How would you feel if I held you tonight?'

'Yeah, OK.'

He kept the warmth of her close to him, skin on skin, lining her. She was angular, bony even, and he was aware that the slump of his beer belly was pushing at her back, tried sucking it in till he was sure she was asleep.

Clio Campbell, in his bed.

He woke first, spent a little bit of time just looking at her, thankful for once that his cheap curtains let in too much daylight. Freckles on her cheekbones, delicate blue veins under that thin milky skin, wrinkles at her eyes and deep lines pulling her mouth into a frown. Well, she was still younger than him, he reminded himself, and definitely in better shape. Her eyes opened.

'Hello there, sleepy.' He smiled at her.

'Hi, Neil. Morning. Time is it?' She didn't take even a second to come to; he wondered briefly if she'd maybe been awake for a while.

'Almost eight. Go back to sleep if you want. I could make you some breakfast? Seeing as I worked later yesterday I can take a bit of TOIL this morning.'

'No, I should go. Need to – shit, we're in Glasgow, aren't we? I'm going to have to go. My bus leaves from Edinburgh. Where's your bathroom?'

He heard her run down the hall, a hurried splashing in there; pulled on boxers and T-shirt to cover himself. The cowboy boots stood to attention at the foot of the bed, waiting. She came back in buttoning her dress up. Her feet, he noticed, were red and covered in scabs and blisters.

'Can't I even make you a fried egg sandwich? For old times?'

'Eh? Sorry, but I can't afford to miss this bus. I have to be back home today – need to sign on first thing tomorrow. Sorry to run off on you. Sorry.'

He stood, picked up his dressing gown from the floor.

'Do you know where you are? Need directions?'

'We're not far from the Subway, are we? Look, Neil, I hate to do this, but I don't suppose I could borrow a tenner for the train? I'm sort of broke right now, and I didn't really intend to wake up in Glasgow, if you know what I mean.'

His leather jacket was hanging off the doorknob. He reached in for his wallet and realized he'd given the driver a hundred pounds last night.

'Shit. I've got about seven quid in shrapnel – that do you? Sorry. Sorry about this.'

She gave him a brief hug at the door, seemed to relent from something at the last minute and relax herself back into his body.

'It was good to see you again. Thank you, thanks for the drinks and the crash space. Listen, if – if I come across a story, anything you might be interested in, could I give you a call? Just get you at the paper? In your office?'

'Of course. Any time,' he said, trying to sound grown up, disinterested. Trying to stop the screaming he could hear in his head.

The door closed and she was gone. He didn't want to go back into the bedroom and see the sheets, smell last night. He made himself a coffee, stirring the granules in with the milk while the kettle boiled. A few years ago he'd gone out with a woman who had hated that he drank instant coffee, had taken him shopping for a cafetière and tried to get him accustomed to it, and when they'd broken up he'd gone back to his jar of Nescafé as an act of rebellion, a point of working-class pride. This morning he realized that it really did just taste like shit.

He sat there at the kitchen worktop, staring at nothing, whipping himself with every humiliation he'd endured since stepping out the morning before – the tape recorder, the writer's disdain, Clio's silence and sadness, her leaving him. Gradually the warm, shitty coffee began to do its job, and he began to feel himself awake, getting angry. Had she done this just to get somewhere to crash? Where the hell had she been intending to stay, as she clearly didn't have money for a hotel?

Right. He'd go into the office, type up his transcription, make a start on the puff piece, maybe get a pie or something on the way in. At least he'd had a shag. At least he'd shagged *her*.

It was only once he'd dressed and showered and was ready to leave that he realized that the bloody fucking tape recorder had fallen out of his bag.

BBC Radio Scotland, 24 January 2018

It's two thirty-five, and you're listening to the Afternoon Show on BBC Radio Scotland with me, Janice Forsyth. Now, in the wake of the tragic and too-soon death of the musician Clio Campbell, aged only fifty-one, this week, I dug into the archives and found a session and interview our very own Jim Arbuthnott did with her on his folk show back in 2007, when her superlative album, *The Northern Lass*, a reimagining of the songs of Robert Burns, came out. Here's Clio Campbell in her own, very distinctive, style.

JA: So, Clio, welcome to the show.

CC: Thanks for having me.

JA: Now, it's been a while since we've heard from you round these parts.

CC: Well, yes. I've been living in London for a while now.

JA: And very nice it is to have you back up here! But I meant it's been a while since the single most of our listeners will know you from – 'Rise Up' – which charted in, what was it, 1991?

CC: Well, I've been doing a lot since then.

JA: Of course, of course. But sixteen years between releases – there are some people who'd call that a bit of a block.

CC: I don't feel as though it's been a block, Jim. People do different things with their lives. Music isn't the only part of me.

JA: Of course not. But it's something you've come back to recently, would that be fair to say?

CC: Yes. I came up with the idea a few years ago now to do sort of radical reinventions of the songs of Robert Burns. It's something I'd done on tour for a while, back in the day: my band and I would do these gigs up in tiny villages in the Highlands and we'd always try and bring them something they knew, but in a new way, you know? So we'd do new takes on 'A Man's a Man', that sort of thing.

JA: Because you grew up with these songs, didn't you?

CC: I did. I was raised in Ayrshire, where he's basically a local god. So of course we sung those songs at school throughout the year, not just on Burns Night. It's the sort of thing that'll get you drummed out of town – um. Well. Not knowing those songs. In Ayrshire. Yeah. So. On top of that, my father was a folk musician—

JA: That's right, Malcolm Campbell. He passed away a few years ago, didn't he. Was he with you in spirit while you were making this?

CC: Not really.

JA: Was it perhaps your way of paying tribute to him?

CC: No.

JA: But he sang these songs?

CC: Yes, he sang these songs.

JA: So. Anyway. You mentioned that you would do slightly different versions of them on tour – was this back in the Nineties?

CC: It was. Yes. And I thought about just recording an album in that style, but then I realized that the most important work I could do would be to find what Robert Burns had to say about today. Because, you know, he was a deeply political artist—

JA: He was, and—

CC: And the messages he was preaching – egalitarianism, equality – they're messages that we need to hear today. But he was also working class, so I thought, well, where are the artists of today who are doing what he did. And it occurred to me to look at what the younger rappers and grime artists coming out of South London were making, and to involve some of them on some of the tracks, both rapping Burns's lines and laying down some of their own thoughts.

JA: Right, so this is where the album might be considered to be controversial—

CC: Do you know, I've heard that a lot since I came back up to Scotland and I really don't see why.

JA: Well, lyrically, there's a lot of violence – and unsavoury subject matter, shall we say – in what some of these young men talk about, and you can understand some traditionalists might be upset—

CC: Jim, if you ask me, that's some coded racist nonsense. If people up here are upset because some black and Asian musicians are offering their own interpretations of a long-dead poet, rather than finding it positive that his work is still reaching people, then I think that's really their lookout. I mean, are you familiar with the work of any of the musicians I've got guesting on this album?

JA: Ha ha. Well, you've got Donald Bain on there, who long-term listeners might know as a very fine fiddler indeed – he's contributed to any number of excellent albums in recent time and his presence will probably be a point of reassurance for some. And I understand he's your uncle, is he?

CC: He's my godfather. But why would people need reassurance, Jim? Surely we're not that precious about the work of a man who died two hundred years ago that we can't let a woman and some non-white men sing his songs?

JA: Ha ha. Of course not. And on that note, let's hear one of the songs from *A Northern Lass* – Clio Campbell, singing Robert Burns's 'Ae Fond Kiss'.

DONALD
Edinburgh, 1993

Donald hated wearing a suit. It was increasingly necessary now, or at least the waistcoat and shirt were, seemed to be expected at certain gigs, but he couldn't thole it. Just felt the whole time that he was buttoned up wrong, over-fettered. A silly damn muddle.

She'd actually said at first, 'And don't you bother wearing a suit or anything. Just come as you please. A great big jumper with holes in the elbows, and your fiddle. That's how I remember my Uncle Donald.' The girl knew how to work him, he'd give her that. No contact for months then a sudden rush of affection down the phone. But that had always been her way. Almost as though she'd rediscovered him, unearthed him in her memory.

'Well of course it'll be you to walk me down the aisle. Who else would I ask, eh? And maybe you'd play for us too? Just at the signing? It seems right to me.'

The next call was from Mansfield himself, explaining that his parents would probably expect a certain level of attire. 'I mean, it's not a big wedding. Not at all. Just family. But they are taking us all out for dinner somewhere nice afterwards. And you know, the pictures. So. All right, pal. Yeah?' A dry cough. The sternness of a tour manager.

So. A suit it was. He swore at the idiot collar buttons in the tiny bed-and-breakfast mirror, noticed a shaving cut had leaked blood onto the starched point, pulled the damn thing off and started all over again.

Just family. He was directed to the smallest room of the registry office, with the names Mansfield/Campbell on a printed-out sheet, pinned to the door. There were eight people in the two rows at the front on the right, two small children ducking and weaving in and out of the chairs. Mansfield and a young man who could only be his brother were laughing by a table at the top. On the left, only one head, barely visible over the chair back. Black hair gleaming blue in the afternoon sun, a bright pink feathery growth over half her head. Well, they were outnumbered, but at least she was here.

Mansfield caught his eye and strode towards the door, hands outstretched.

'Ah, Donald! Great you could make it. Clio will be along shortly, I hope.' He paused for a laugh, pulled a face, crossed his fingers, and Donald, who was never a violent man, wanted to punch him. 'So if you want to stand outside, she'll meet you there.'

Eileen had turned her plumaged head around with some difficulty to follow her future son-in-law. Her lips were painted the same colour as the hat thing, a visual shock in the motley brown room. She gave him a tiny smile and he raised a hand. She looked very close to tears. He pointed to the door and mouthed 'later', stashed his fiddle two rows back as he left.

He'd expected she'd keep them all waiting, but Cliodhna was not late. She bounded up the stairs and threw herself into his arms before he'd quite realized what was happening.

'Oh, thank you for this. Thank you thank you. Shall we do it, then?'

'Just a second there, lass! Let me look at you first, eh?'

Donald didn't know anything about women's clothes; he registered that she was wearing something creamy, the colour of her own skin, with almost bare shoulders and a flower in her hair, but she was lovely, and he told her so, because Malcolm should have been there to say that.

'Is it just you, Clio-girl? You don't have a whatjamacallum – bridesmaid or anything?'

It seemed to be the first time it had occurred to her. 'No. I suppose I don't.' She laughed. 'I could pop in there and borrow one of Danny's many sisters, I guess. Ach, let's just get this done. Bring on the marriaging.'

'Cliodhna, you know your mother's in there, do you?'

The grin dipped and she froze.

'She came?'

'Aye, she came. She's by herself.'

'OK. OK. Well, that's good to know. I'm glad you told me that before I went in there. She didn't say – we didn't hear from her. So I'd just assumed—'

He gave her a hug, a small one. She was too delicate and he didn't want to crush her; and he was all too aware that he'd started to sweat.

'Is it time now?'

'Aye. Let's go.'

Once he'd escorted her the ten or so steps to her winking fool of a groom, he turned and sat himself down by Eileen. Protocol seemed to demand it. Her jaw was locked in place, her hands fretting at the hem of her pink jacket.

'It's good you came,' he whispered, corner of his mouth, as the registrar droned through some sort of legal requirement.

'It's my daughter's wedding, Donald Bain. I'd not miss that, thank you very much.'

Cliodhna did not turn her head to them once during the brief ceremony, which he was glad of, as Eileen sat there with an expression that suggested she smelled something terrible. Maybe she did and it was himself. Anytime someone wasn't speaking, he could hear the plasticky fabric rubbing between her fingers, little *wheech wheech* noises.

And it was done, and they kissed, and everyone applauded, even Eileen. Clio beckoned him up as they took their seats for the official bit. He wasn't sure where to stand, and the registrar wasn't much use, seemed to have tuned out. Eventually he wandered off to the side, turned half away so he couldn't see Eileen's black-crayoned scowl, and struck up the tune Clio had asked him for, gentle and soft and slow. 'The Northern Lass'. It went on a little longer than it took them to sign their names, and he was conscious that they were all sitting there waiting for him to finish, Mansfield smirking a bit at his audience, so he stopped after the second verse.

'And thank you, Donald,' the new groom said, his vowels flatter and posher than they had been with the lads on the tour. 'Now, everyone, my wife and I –' again, that pause for recognition; one of his sisters let out an obliging *whoop!* '– would like you all to join us in the square outside for the photos. We've got a couple of photographers with us – Ernie, who's doing the shots for us, and a snapper from the *Scotsman*'s society pages. So, best smiles on and all that!'

Donald marvelled at the man again. Here he was, talking to a small gathering of relatives, and his voice still had that soft greasy tone like he was introducing a singer in a club. The couple set off down the aisle, grinning at each other, and the room emptied quickly. He hung back, seeing Eileen just standing there, let the Mansfield family file out before he went to her.

'Well then, Eileen. Shall we go downstairs?'

He offered her his arm, for some reason, and she took it, although she barely came up past his elbow herself. Her grip was tight, and they stood very still together for a second until the registrar coughed importantly at their backs.

'Society pages,' Eileen said, quietly, as they walked down the stairs.

'Aye,' said Donald. 'He's a bit like that, your son-in-law.'

As he watched Mansfield directing the action around the two clearly cheesed-off photographers, insisting that hands be placed just so, that they pose up the steps to the ornate entrance, he picked up on a sort of vibration coming from Eileen. She had that face on her again, and he realized she was probably feeling too many things all at once. She was a lone streak of pink in the stone courtyard, and even a babe in the woods like Donald could tell that her clothes were too bright and tight – Mansfield's mother and sisters were flitting around in elegant jackets and dresses of beige and light green, the other men all wore grey, and apart from her flash of hair Cliodhna was a pale sickle moon, almost translucent in the sun. Despite being at the centre of every picture, she seemed to be holding herself apart from it all, smiling whenever she was told to, but off in a dream. The two women still hadn't acknowledged each other.

'Why don't we get the bride's parents up here then?' One of the photographers was striding towards them, apparently attempting to wrest back some control. 'Mum and dad! You're up!'

Donald half-tried to explain, as the little man put a hand on each of their backs and shoved them towards the staircase. Eileen was silent.

'Right. Ladies in the middle, and how about we have the groom by his new mother-in-law and Daddy by his little girl, eh?'

Eileen and Cliodhna stood side by side, obedient to a higher power.

'Is that dress a – a nightgown?' he heard Eileen whisper.

'Lovely to see you too, Mum.'

'OK, that's nice, that's nice. Now, ladies, can you turn in towards each other?'

A tiny curl had fallen over Cliodhna's forehead. Eileen put a hand up to it while her daughter looked at the camera, then changed her mind and retreated.

'Dad, Dad, can you look over here please? Dad?'

Donald suddenly realized this meant him.

'He's my uncle, not my dad,' Cliodhna called out.

'He's not your uncle,' Eileen muttered.

'OK, OK, have we got enough of that one? Yeah? Great. I think that's a wrap, eh gents?' For once Donald was glad of Mansfield's interference. He pulled Eileen to one side as they all made their way through crowds of tourists to the restaurant just down the hill.

'Eileen. You've not seen the lassie for how long? Ten years? It's her wedding day, and it means a lot to her that you're here. I know it must be strange for you, I know you must be feeling – a lot of things. But you've not come all the way across the country for the day just to pick a fight, surely?'

'I'm not picking a fight, Donald Bain. If anyone's picking a fight—'

'It's her wedding day, Eileen. Her daddy's not here. She'll want her mammy. Please.'

'And exactly who are you to tell me what to do with my own daughter?'

He stopped her, held onto her arm, the two of them an island in a fast-flow of bodies.

'You know who I am. You know what I've done. And I'm saying there will be no more of this today. I'm saying that as your old friend and Cliodhna's godfather. All right?'

Eileen stared down at her pink, pink shoes, a chastened child in its mother's make-up.

'If that little madam would just look at me—'

'Eileen.'

'And she's wearing a bloody nightgown! With no bra that I can see! It doesn't even look new! And that woman, his mother, looking at me thinking was she not even brought up right to know how to dress?'

'Eileen.'

'I just—'

'Have you got it all out?'

Eileen inhaled, her nostrils standing to attention.

'I just need a bloody fag. But I don't want them looking down on me even more for it.'

He fumbled in his pocket for the cigarettes, and her shoulders sagged.

'Here you go. We'll join them in a couple of minutes, eh?'

'Thanks.'

A pause as they both blew out smoke, making space for each other.

'It's good to see you, Donald Bain.'

There was some faffing around when they finally arrived – 'Got a bit lost!' Donald had muttered, to cover them – as the restaurant had had to add an extra chair for Eileen, jammed in at the corner of the table.

'So sorry about this, Eileen,' Mansfield's mother was saying, standing up to usher them in. 'I'm afraid the postman must have lost your RSVP. My own fault for not adjusting the booking earlier.'

Donald understood she was being gracious, trying to mask the mistake; he also saw that Eileen was taking it as a slight.

'But the mother of the bride shouldn't be all the way over there in the corner! Susie, Adam, would you two scooch round, please? Eileen, you must come up here and sit with me. It's so wonderful to meet you finally. I've heard so much about you.'

Donald gripped Eileen's hand for a second, felt her nails dig his palm, imprinting on him even after she'd been bustled away. Sitting up there with her silly hat still pinned on, nodding at Mrs Mansfield, staring at the table, she looked like she was drowning, her usual hard-as-nails armour failing her. He felt overwhelmed himself, as he squeezed into the tacked-on corner seat. The menu was in French with an English translation in tiny print, and there was far too much cutlery in front of him. Cliodhna still seemed to be in her own wee world, sharing jokes with her husband and smiling politely at his father to her left, but mostly absent. It wasn't that she looked unhappy to be married, exactly, more as though it was happening to somebody else and she was watching it all from a comfortable seat in a cinema. It was an expression he'd become familiar with over the years, had seen it on her even as a child in her quieter moments. The unknowability of Miss Cliodhna Campbell. Well, the girl was what she was, and who could blame her if she wanted to hold a bit of herself back?

He ordered soup and beef when the waiter came around, had no idea what would show up. A girl put a hard bread roll on his plate with tongs and he picked it up and bit into it, caught Mansfield's brother looking at him across the table with a smirk that must run in the family. He put the roll back down. The sister at his side turned to him.

'That was really lovely, that piece you played at the ceremony. Was it something you wrote?'

There were crumbs in his beard, he was sure of it.

'Oh, eh. No, no. That's a Burns song that one. No, I couldn't write something like that.'

'But you are a musician, aren't you? Professionally, I mean.'

'I am. I am that. Yup.'

'Runs in the family then?'

'Well, yes. Yes. Cliodhna's daddy is a singer too.'

'Lovely. And that's quite some accent you've got there. Is it from the Highlands?'

She was talking to him like a child, this woman thirty years or so younger than him. He tried to stay pleasant, but he wasn't sure he'd ever been more uncomfortable.

'Western Isles, yes, yes, that's right.'

'Such a beautiful part of the country.' She had a very smooth voice. He couldn't place it. There was a pause, and he realized he was supposed to be continuing this conversation, possibly for as long as the meal lasted, and they hadn't even had their first course yet.

'So, you're Danny's sister, then?'

'One of them, that's right. The baby of the family!'

'Ah.'

'And you're an uncle? On her mother's or father's side? No, wait, sorry – you mentioned her father, didn't you. He's not here?'

The girl scanned the table, perhaps looking for some father she'd simply missed.

'He's not here. He lives in America now.'

'Ooh, a long journey. And really, such short notice – I'm not surprised he couldn't make it!'

Her laugh was ugly, a breathy har-har-har with no mirth behind it.

'Yes, they really did take us all by surprise with this one. I mean, only my mother had even met Clio before last week. I suppose you don't really know Danny, either?'

'I was on the tour with both of them last year. A few months ago now.'

'Ah yes, where they fell in *loooove*.' It occurred to him that the girl might possibly be drunk; her wine glass was empty.

'So are you in her band, then? That's nice. Nice to keep it in the family. Does the mother play music too?'

The mother. He stood up gently.

'If you'll excuse me just for a moment . . .'

The girl nodded, relieved. Across the table, Eileen tried to command him to stay with panicked eyes.

It was cool and quiet in the corridor to the toilets, and he just paused there for a while, allowed himself to stretch out to his full height.

'Did you run away too?'

'Hello, Cliodhna girl. How is married life?'

She seemed almost sleepy.

'I think it suits me fine so far.'

'Have you left your mother in there by herself?'

'She's fine. Danny is being all charming and shit. He's talking her ear off and she's loving it. Rather him than me.'

'At least she came, love.'

'At least she came.'

'She's just nervous. You know how she gets. It's a strange situation for anyone.'

'I'll drink to that.' She raised a glass she'd brought with her.

He decided to steer the topic off for a while. 'So, the society pages, eh?'

'I knew you'd have something to say about that. Danny's idea. He thought it would be good for my profile, keep me in the public eye and whatnot till I'm ready to do some new material.'

'Aye.'

'Ach, what harm, Uncle Donald? I look pretty today. Let people see me.'

'Aye.'

'Anyway, will I let you get back to it? Back to Danny's lovely sister?'

'Cliodhna. She's a child. Listen, lass. Your mother. Are you going to talk to her before she goes?'

'Not if she's just going to nitpick—'

'She won't. I promise you. And she's come all this way.'

'OK, OK. But only for you.'

Back in the dining room, Eileen was, as Clio had promised, prinking and even giggling under Mansfield's determined attention. His own dinner companion was locked into conversation with whoever was at her right, and, relieved, he settled down to eat his soup. Clio was out of the room for a long time, and for a while he thought he was the only one who had noticed. The new groom finally cast a glance round, patted his mother-in-law gently on the wrist and excused himself. Mother Mansfield picked up the conversation, which Donald couldn't quite make out, but Eileen's face closed right down again, her mouth tight and tiny, choking out monosyllables. He suddenly felt exhausted, by all of them. The happy couple returned to the room, her arms fidgeting around his shoulders, his hand on her waist, steering her back into her seat. She was giggling; he was neutral. Donald looked down and tried to concentrate on his beef. For all its fanciness, the food was tasty enough, he'd give it that.

A chinking of teaspoon on glass and they all hushed, looking to the centre obediently, except Eileen, who was jerking her head round to see what had happened. Mansfield rose up out of his seat, jacket off, sleeves rolled and a wine-flush across his cheeks.

'Hello. You all know me – I'm a man of few words.'

No one around the table reacted as though this was in any way true. The brother actually sniggered.

'So I'm going to keep this short and sweet. Speaking for myself and my beautiful wife, I'm delighted that you've all managed to come here today, whether you travelled half an hour up the road or have made it an overnight stay.' Here he bowed, quickly, to both Donald and Eileen. 'It's wonderful to be surrounded by so much love on this, our very special day.'

The whole thing had been rehearsed and memorized, even just for a performance in front of family, Donald realized, as Danny choked slightly over that odd 'very'. It was a speech written for a much larger audience.

'I'd also just like to say a huge thank you to the other most special woman in my life, my little mum, who has organized a beautiful and intimate wedding for us at record speed.' Polite applause.

'On that note – I'm aware that a lot of you were, ah, rather surprised at how quickly this has all happened. It's true that Clio and I haven't been a couple for long. And I just want to take this opportunity to reassure all of you right now that there's no baby on the way –' Clio began to raise her glass '– yet!' The Mansfields round the table brayed and cheered. Eileen was looking at Clio, who had put her glass back down and resumed her vague stare up at her husband.

'But when it's right, it's right. You just know. And I've known since the first time I heard this woman sing. I thought – Danny, pal. That's the girl for you. You need to move fast and lock this one down. And not just as a tour promoter!'

He paused, and they applauded.

'Now, I believe we've got a wedding cake to cut?'

Mrs Mansfield was making furious arm gestures at someone just outside the door; two blushing waitresses quickly wheeled in an enormous white tiered cake, a splat of black musical notes creeping up from the base to sit on a stave, wobbling, two bars sticking it into the littlest cake on top. The Mansfields whistled, the one at Donald's side calling out, 'That is some cake, Mum!'

Danny and Clio bumbled out of their seats until they were standing beside the thing. It completely dwarfed Clio – like the speech, it was a cake in search of a bigger wedding. He wrapped his arms round her as the waitress handed him a huge carving knife, and he folded both their hands over it. They tried to smile as three pocket cameras pointed at them across the table at once, as the knife sank in and the stave teetered and pitched off the top, as Danny's mother lunged forward into the shot to save it.

Danny pulled everything back with a professional chortle.

'The best-laid plans, eh? Anyway, if I could invite you all to join us for a cocktail on the lovely terrace space upstairs, which I think we've got reserved for ourselves for the next couple of hours, I'm sure that cake will be along to help us digest this wonderful meal shortly.'

Cliodhna was just looking at him, silent and faintly amused.

Up on the terrace, Eileen stuck herself to Donald like glue, muttering to him without really moving her mouth.

'I'm going to have to catch my train soon. Do you think – is it going to look rude? What will they think of me?'

'I think you need to talk to Cliodhna is what, Eileen.'

'Och, there's not time now. I'll send her a card or something.'

Gently, but with intent, he pulled Eileen across to the corner of the balcony, where Cliodhna was leaning back into the late-afternoon air, her elbows looped under the banister, nodding sweetly at one of the sisters with her eyes half-closed.

'I'm so sorry – Susie, was it? Would you mind if we had a little family time? Thanks so much.'

Mother and daughter faced each other, both standing silently. He wanted to bump their heads together.

'Well, this is a bit silly of you both,' Donald said, being sure to speak quietly and keep his face pleasant, so they couldn't be inter-cepted. 'I have no idea what it was the two of you fought about, but it was almost ten years ago now. Today seems like a pretty good day for some peace. Cliodhna, your mother will have to go and catch her train soon.'

Cliodhna breathed in and out a couple of times, her eyes never leaving Eileen's face. Then she blinked, her body suddenly unclenching.

'You're right, Uncle Donald. I'm really touched that you came, Mum.'

Eileen was still staring her out, flicking her glance up and down from the dress to the hair.

'Eileen?' Donald said, putting a hand on her arm.

'It was a lovely wedding. Beautiful.' She mumbled the last syllable into her fingers as though she'd given too much away.

Cliodhna laughed. 'Oh, that was all Danny and his mum. All I did was find a dress in a second-hand shop, and turn up!'

Eileen looked for a second as though she was about to faint, steeled herself.

'It's a very unusual dress. Very – individual.'

Cliodhna's arms wrapped round herself, covering up.

'You look very – nice today. Yes. And that's a good man you've got there.'

'Yes, Danny's a good man.'

'He's a hard worker, isn't he? You can tell.'

'Oh yeah. He's always got a few pots on the bubble, does Danny.'

'Well, that's the best way. That's the way it should be. Busy man, brings the wages in regularly, doesn't drink them all. Aye, lass. You've done well. You picked better than me, at least. The first time.'

Cliodhna seemed to absorb the slight with her whole body, just for a split second. Then she pulled back up, nodded it past.

'Yes, and how is Alec? Please give him my—'

Eileen shook her head quickly. Cliodhna finished her sentence in a cough.

'Alec's as well as can be. He's doing a lot of volunteering now. With the youth groups and the Labour Club. Keeping busy. Keeping busy.'

'That's good. Good to know.'

'And you're a singer now. We saw you. On the telly.'

'You did? Yes, yes. A wee while ago, that was. Still, hoping to have a new album out. Working on new material. That sort of thing.'

'You want to make sure you're not a drain on that man of yours. You know I've always said a woman should be able to bring in a wage too. You know I've always said that.'

'I know. You have. And it's your birthday coming up soon, Mum. Any plans?'

'Och, just the usual. Wee night down the Labour Club with Alec. Some pals. Wee vodka.'

'Nice. Nice. Maybe – maybe Danny and I could get in the car and pop through?'

Donald looked up at Clio's tone. She was leaning forward to her mother. He wanted to wrap her up in his coat, right there.

Eileen's granite-locked war-face had descended.

'No, no, that's— No. It's a— it's too far for you to come. No no. Don't do that. It wouldn't be a good idea.'

Clio flopped, her shoulders sank, as though she'd been slapped. For the second time that day, Eileen reached out a hand towards her then thought the better of it.

'I mean, we could maybe meet somewhere else. Just you and me and Danny. Maybe I could hop on the train to Ayr or something. Glasgow, even. Meet you there. Wee day trip.'

Cliodhna's face was all gratitude. Eileen began fumbling in her handbag.

'Here. Here. I brought you a wee thing. Just a wee thing. I didn't know what to get youse for a wedding present, see.'

She held out a little box.

'It was my mother's. I always felt bad she'd never really got the chance to know you, when you were little. I mean, it's no much, but I thought it would be nice for you to have it.'

Cliodhna was blinking back tears as she lifted the sparkling brooch up to the fading light.

'And I'd thought you could've maybe worn it as your something old but, ach, it's too late for that now.'

Eileen looked away. Her daughter's voice was very controlled as she responded.

'Thank you. I'll take good care of it. Don't you worry.'

'Well. It's not worth anything, probably. Tin and paste. But, you know. Nice to have.'

Across the terrace, Donald noticed Mrs Mansfield with her arm around one of her daughters, laughing and stroking back hair from her face. Finally, Eileen reached out a hand, delivered a tiny pat on Cliodhna's arm.

'So I'll see you then, Cliodhna Jean.'

'Aye, Mum. Aye.'

On their way down the stairs, Donald and Eileen had to flatten themselves against the wall as the young waitress puffed up carrying a massive plate laden with carved-up black and white cake.

'I'll walk you to the station?' he asked when they finally got out of there, handing her one of the two cigarettes he'd just lit.

'Och no, Donald Bain. You get back in there and enjoy the party. She ought to have someone there for her, eh now.'

'Aye. Here, that was a nice thing you did up there, Eileen. It meant a lot to her, I could tell. A lovely wee gift to start her married life with.'

'Well. We'll see. We'll see how long all that lasts, shall we. She's marrying up and no mistake there.'

'Now. Cliodhna's a good lassie.'

'Oh, she's bonny enough to get a catch like him, I'll give you that. But keeping him – well, that's a horse of a different colour. She's messy, that girl. Chaotic. She'll do something to muck all this up, you mark my words, Donald Bain.'

'I think you're too hard on the lass, Eileen, but we'll agree to leave it there, eh.'

They puffed in silence for a second.

'So. Alec didn't fancy the trip today?'

'Alec doesn't know I'm here. He wouldn't approve.'

'Of you going to your own daughter's wedding?'

'Aye. And he's got his reasons that I don't need to go into with you, thank you.'

'You don't, that's true.'

'I almost didn't come myself.'

'But you did, though.'

'I did.'

He watched her huff her tiny bulk up the Royal Mile, a bright pink streak against the workaday suits, and wondered whether that would be the last time he'd see her.

MALCOLM
Edinburgh, 2003

She wasn't coming.

Eight minutes past.

Twelve minutes past.

She wasn't coming.

He'd spent the journey down reading. He'd bought three news-papers from a pile in the supermarket in Inverness, but he realized he didn't know how to fold the damn things, and one of them was full of tits. But he persevered, scared of the places his head could go on a long bus trip – on *this* long bus trip – with only the scenery for com-pany. The tiny lettering was making him feel a bit sick, so he ended up poring over the one large-print, stapled TV guide that had come with one of them, reading every listing in depth, his lips moving, chal-lenging himself to memorize them.

Sitting here, now, in the restaurant, having thrown a bundle of paper in the bin at the bus station, he was finding it much harder to block those thoughts out.

The waiter refilled his water again – deliberately, he thought, to make him feel uncomfortable – and he scratched at his beard under the neck of Donald's one good shirt, that Morna had pinned on him. The music was too damn loud in here, too damn loud and shouty, twanging cockney accents yelling nothing. He'd wanted to just take her to that pub, one of the ones he knew and where people might know him, where musicians gathered, had even dared a stupid dream that the two of them might jam together. Donald had talked him out of that, suggested somewhere more neutral first, somewhere they might not be interrupted.

So here he was, in this place upstairs from the bus station, the closest one Morna had been able to find in her guidebook. He'd already checked in to the room she'd booked him, in a hotel next door. A fine trip to Edinburgh indeed, when all he was going to see was three buildings on the one street.

'Remember and get some rest. Just an hour, after the journey. You've got time,' she'd said.

'I'm thinking I should go with you, Malcolm. I'm still not sure,' Donald had chimed in.

'Stop fussing at me, man! I'll be fine to get a bus. Nice warm things, buses. You just sit down, have a wee sleep for a few hours and you're there. Ridden a lot of Greyhounds in my day.'

Donald had done enough.

Donald was thinking of it like the old days, the sentimental bastard, when Malcolm had brought him down for visits to Cliodhna in Ayrshire, for a bit of backup. To keep him straight. Well, this was not Uncle Donnie's time, not now. Malcolm didn't want him here. Not today.

Would you admit that, Malcolm Campbell? Would you admit that you're actually jealous of – no. No he would not.

Oh, why was he even bothering. Stupid idea. Stupid.

Eighteen minutes past.

How long did you wait? This must be like going on a date, he supposed. Being stood up. He was feeling fuzzy, could hear the blood rushing around his ears. He finished his water, poured more from the jug.

Twenty-two minutes past and there she was. Red and golden in the afternoon sunlight from the window. She was like him; much more than she had been in the pictures he'd seen. His features, slimmer and womanly, but undoubtedly his. His lashes, the curve of his cheek, nothing at all of her mother there.

He pushed his chair back and stood up, gripped the table to support himself and hide the shake at his knees and wrist. He was embarrassed to realize his eyes were wet.

'Cliodhna.'

'Malcolm.'

He went to hug her but had forgotten about the table, knocked his glass of water over.

'Oh bugger it. Bugger it.'

She moved very quickly while he was still taking it all in, dived for the napkins to mop up the spill. He felt ridiculous, standing there staring at the top of her head, her hand's swift motion over the table.

'There we go,' she said.

'Right,' he said. 'So. Do you – can I give you a hug, then?'

He hardly felt her touch on him before she pulled away and sat herself down, so he followed her, and she looked at him. Steady and sure. He couldn't read her face.

'It was a long trip for you, if you're staying up with Uncle Donald.'

'It was. Aye. A long trip for you too. London, is it?'

'For years now. Back and forth all over the place, but London's home.'

He nodded. He'd never been to London; had nothing to contribute.

'Busy place, isn't it?'

'It is. Not where I live, so much.'

He could hear the English in her voice, now – a sort of stretching of her o-sound. He'd been conscious of his own accent returning since he'd been home after years around Anouli. Funny things, voices. The way they would adjust themselves without your knowledge in different company.

'Never really took to a city myself. Prefer the open road. Big spaces.'

'Yeah.'

Cliodhna was staring at her fingers. He'd hoped she'd be a chatty one, the sort of woman who could keep a conversation running, but she seemed to want him to do all the work. His foot spasmed out and kicked the box he'd been storing under the table.

'Oh! Here! Here! I have a present for you. Very special. Here!'

He bent down to pull it out, felt the dizzy pins swishing in his head and had to pause, folded in half like a fool. The box was so big he had to get out of the chair again to hand it to her.

'So. So. I bought these for you years ago. They were supposed to be a twenty-first present – well, better late than never, eh? But I kept them with me all that time. I mean, some of the time they were in your stepmother's house, but I made sure she handed them over when I left. What do you think?'

She'd pulled one of them out, was holding it up.

'Cowboy boots?'

'Aye. Well, for women. Cowgirl boots, maybe? But they're good ones. Handmade – lot of really intricate stitching in there. I had them made specially for you, too. One of the finest craftsmen in Austin. In Texas. While we were playing a festival there. And I thought the purple was sort of unusual. I mean, I didn't know your size so I just told them to go for a sort of women's medium. If they don't fit I – well, I can't really take them back now, can I?'

She smiled. 'They're nice. Thanks.'

'Why not try them on. Let's see if they fit.'

'Here?'

'Sure! Why not here? Nobody's looking.'

She fumbled at her feet, untied the laces on the shoes she was wearing. The waiter came over and Malcolm wanted to wave him away, but Cliodhna seemed to jump at the chance, curling her stocking soles under the table.

'I'll just have some chips, please.'

'No, no – have more than that. You need to eat more. How about the steak? Eh? That looks good! Two steaks.'

'I'm a vegetarian, Malcolm. Just the chips, please.'

'Well, let me get you a big good drink, instead. You know what? This is a celebration, isn't it! A family reunion. We'll have a bottle of champagne!'

'No. Come on.'

'Nonsense, nonsense. A bottle of champagne, buddy.'

'And the steak, sir?'

'Well, no. No. I'll just – aye, I'll just have some chips too. Chips and champagne! That's a song title right there for you!'

'And a jug of water please. Tap water.'

The waiter drifted off.

'Look, Malcolm. You don't need to do that – you don't need to feel that you have to spend a lot of money or anything. If you've not got it.'

He waved her off, embarrassed, wished she'd stop.

'I'm fine. I'm fine. Got it covered.' He winked, tried to slap the charm on her. 'Come on, beautiful. Let's see those boots on you, eh?'

It came out wrong and they both winced, but she pulled the boots on under the table, stuck a leg through the drapes for him to see.

'How do they feel?'

'Roomy, but that's OK. I'll wear them with big socks.'

'You will wear them?'

'I will.'

'Because it was quite a travail bringing them over, let me tell you. I'd hate to think they were just going to gather dust.'

'I'll wear them. I'll wear them onstage tomorrow.'

'Tomorrow?'

'Aye. I'm playing a couple of tunes tomorrow at Princes Street Gardens. The big bandstand.'

'Really! Oh, I need to see that. Maybe I could get a different bus, stay a bit.'

'It's late on in the afternoon. Might be about five. You'd never get all the way back up north after. Don't worry. It's not a big deal.'

'Princes Street Gardens, though. That sounds like a big deal to me. I'd like to be there, Cliodhna. As your da— father. I've only ever seen you singing on the Internet.'

'Really. I don't want to make you hang around here for two extra nights. Not in a hotel. Not for five minutes or whatever. It's just two songs. No, no.'

'Well, you could maybe show me around a bit? Didn't Donald tell me you used to live here?'

'Briefly. Back when I was married. A long time ago. But I'm staying with friends, Malcolm. I've got quite a lot to do before the gig tomorrow – I wouldn't want you to feel out of place. We'll just – this is our time, right here.'

Well, he was a man who could see a no. He'd always prided himself on that. Not pushing something like a daft laddie, embarrassing himself. The girl didn't want him to come and that was clear. No point trying. The champagne arrived, was popped undemonstratively under a tea towel. Malcolm said 'Wahey!' anyway, felt immediately foolish for it. The bottle was seated between them, in its own little silver high chair, ice clanking every time one of them moved.

Their glasses filled, he bent his head to his daughter.

'Well. *Slàinte mhath*, my dear. Your very good health.'

'And yours,' she said, then looked down. She knows, he thought, suddenly. She's only here because she knows. And she'll only know because Donald will have told her. A guilt trip, maybe, go and see your old dad before he pops it. Donald. Her 'Uncle' Donald. As interfering as a bloody woman. Always there where he wasn't wanted.

He pulled himself up tall, took a big sip. Perfumed vinegar. Wersh. Those stupid bubbles. He'd never really liked champagne, or any sort of wine, but he wasn't going to show that now, in this fancy place, with this fancy woman already half-pitying him.

'Aaah. That's the stuff. And good stuff, too. So, this gig. Tomorrow. Why is it only two songs you're doing?'

'Well, it's a rally. After a march. There's going to be a big demonstration tomorrow, against the war. Then they get loads of speakers and musicians on after.'

'The war?'

'In Iraq. George Bush is visiting London, so.'

'Oh.'

'It's important. Making a big public stand. I saw they were doing it while I was up visiting you anyway; I know the organizers from a while back – we used to march against the poll tax together, back when I lived up here.'

'Aye. Donald did mention you did a bit of that, but I'd thought you'd maybe grown out of it.'

'Grown out of what?'

'All this – marching. Marching. Stupid business. That's your mother you've got that from, so it is. I mean, what's it going to do? It's not like your whatsisname Tony Blair or whatever is actually going to be there, is he? He's not in Edinburgh. You can't stop these bastards from doing what they want to do and hang the ordinary people. It never changes, lass, believe your old father here. You know that. You're hardly a wee girl now, are you? All the likes of you and me can hope to do is cheer them up with a couple of tunes. That's why we were put on this earth. That's our purpose, you and me. You've got a God-given gift in that throat of yours, lass – you use that rather than your feet. Sing a song for people and at least you give them some hope.'

She took a drink, a big greedy drink. Attagirl, he thought.

'Is that not worse, though? Giving them hope? If in your opinion nothing is going to change?'

He laughed.

'We're all going to die, my lovely. I don't know about you but I'd rather skip off to the gallows with a smile on my face than spend the walk worrying about rope burn.'

She was quiet, just taking it in. He felt a warmth spread over him. The lassie had been confused, had needed some guidance, some proper fatherly advice, and while he might have missed a few years, he'd been able to come through for her when it counted. They had this in common, the gift they had, the life they'd chosen, and he realized that he could help steer her through it.

'I mean, don't get me wrong, it's hard, this life of ours. The music. She's a cruel mistress, eh? There's the days when you don't know where your next meal is coming from and the weeks when you just can't bring yourself to play a note. I've been sick of her, so sick I've wanted to pack the whole thing in. Many times. But the joys, *m'ghaol*. You'll know this. That feeling of setting a whole room dancing, taking them with you, getting them all to hooch and cheer and feel alive again. There's nothing like that, now. Nothing else like that in the world. And once you've done it, once you've had that, there's no way you could ever properly do anything else, could you now? I mean, where else would I go?'

'So you were playing regularly in the States, then?'

'Och, every night, lass. Still would if I could. Me and your stepmother would hit the road – she was a big star back in her day, was Anouli, could still pack 'em in – shove the instruments and a bag of clothes into our van and we'd be off for months, making music every night. Country joints and watering holes, some of them with stages the size of this table, some of them huge, hundreds of people; bottle of bourbon and our guitars under the stars on the nights we slept in the van. Your old man played in every single one of the forty-eight, so he did. Can you imagine? I'll tell you what, my love, I could put you in touch with the right people if you ever wanted to tour the States. I know everyone on that scene, and they'd lap you up, with the hair and the accent. Your looks. Just say the word and you could be there.'

'I don't think it's as easy as that. I'd probably struggle to get a visa, for a start.'

He didn't really know what she meant but was conscious he had to keep the talk flowing.

'Aye, aye, visas are tricky things, so they are. But just you say the word. Just you say the word.'

'It's not really where I'm at just now, you know. I haven't written a new song for years.'

'Writing? You don't need to write a song. There's enough songs out there in the world already. If I've learned anything, it's that people really only want to hear songs they've known before. I mean, don't get me wrong, that was catchy, that wee hit of yours. But the punters, they go to a gig for one reason.'

'For joy? Or for hope?'

He couldn't quite place the look on her face. He sensed she might be being cheeky.

'Aye, well, that too, that too. But the reason people go there is to hear those songs that mean things to them, to add in more layers on top of that. Songs that their mammies used to sing to them, songs that they remember being sung at parties growing up, maybe, songs for funerals, their dead daddy's favourite number – they want to get that feeling again, they want to touch it and make it mean something else. Och, what's that word – nostalgia. That's why people want to hear music. I mean, I bought your wee album. I did. I ordered it specially over from the States and everything. I was – it was very good. I was proud. That's some voice you've got there, you know? But the best song on it was that version of "Green Grow the Rashes" at the end. Beautiful. Beautiful. I played it to your stepmother, and she wept. Your voice. You're a singer, love, and that's good. You're an instrument. You don't need to be a songwriter, eh no? You've already got a beautiful talent to help light up people's lives.'

The chips had arrived, steam rising off them, drawing their eyes and focus. Two tiny bowls, great big skinned potatoes chopped into two or three. Not crispy. She fell silent again, dipping potato into a tiny silver pot of something white. He watched the way she ate, delicate, with small movements. Like someone who wasn't hungry.

'Now that's a chip, eh? Wedges, I'd call these. Not seen the like of this since I left the auld country. In the States, they're called fries. Fries. And they're skinny.'

She looked up, nodded, that half-smile, looked down. Christ, this was hard.

'So then. Cliodhna. Divorced, eh? Welcome to the club!'

'Well, it was about ten years ago.' She shook the hand he'd proffered, though.

'You want to see if you can make it twice, like your old man here. Got husband number two lined up?'

Why didn't she smile, properly? Just these little thin things. He was funny. He'd always known it. Everyone said he was a funny guy. Scotty, they'd say to him, those big burly roadies at the after parties, in Austin and Nashville, you're a funny guy.

'No, there's nobody else at the moment. I'm at a stage in my life where I'm just happy with me.'

'Fair enough. Fair enough. Your stepmother was like that. Till she met me, of course! Nothing wrong with that for a woman. No need for all that flapping about with babies or whatever when you've got a voice like that. It's your gift to the world, isn't it?'

Those thin lips.

'So. What are you planning on doing with yourself, Dad? Now you're back here.'

She hadn't noticed the slip, and he didn't want to spoil things by pointing it out to her, but he felt the blood flow through him a little faster. He busied himself topping up their glasses, trying to hide his smile, feeling the need to celebrate this one. She could 'Malcolm' him all she liked, but somewhere in there behind the skinny smile he was still her dad, and he always would be.

'Oh, you know. I'm going to get myself back out there. Do some gigging again. Actually, while we're here – there's a great auld folk pub you might know? The Sandy Bell's? Your un– Donald says it's still going strong. Anyway, I thought I'd swing by there this evening; brought the bodhrán down especially, see if there's a wee jam happening. Fit myself back into the old networks again, get a few things in the pipeline. See if anyone's needing a session guy. Well, you know how it works. In fact –' and he was careful to make it look like the idea was just then dawning on him '– why don't we finish this bottle and head there together? I bet you'd go down a storm – they'd all know who you are, and we could do a wee daddy–daughter number! I mean, I bet there's folk there don't even know we're related. "Auld Lang Syne", it used to be when you were tiny, you and me at the end of a gig. All the tourists in tears. The tips were amazing on those nights.'

Something in her face closed even further down. He wasn't sure what the hell had happened.

'I'm not really a folk singer. It's not my scene so much.'

'Ach, come on. You know the songs. They'd eat you up out there.'

'Well, I put my guitar and my bags in a left-luggage locker at the station there. I can only really afford three hours of it.'

'Bring the guitar! All the better!'

'Not my bags too, though. And my friends are expecting me.'

'They could come along. Be nice for them to see, no? You could use it as a wee trailer for tomorrow, for your big Princes Street Gardens gig.'

'It's not – no, Malcolm. Not this time. It's not going to be possible.'

'Maybe another time then?'

'Maybe.'

'Tell you what, I'll get along there today and suss out the lie of the land. Drop some hints, see if we could get a couple of gigs on the go, eh? Mention your name. You give me – have you got one of those mobile-phone thingies? Lost mine at the border but if I take your number I can give you a call from a box.'

He grabbed a napkin, pushed it over to her, fumbled in his coat for a pen. A waiter was passing and he snapped his fingers.

'Here! Here! Excuse me! Hello. Could you let me use your pen there? Just for a second. Just to get the girl writing down her number for her old dad. Eh? Thank you.'

She bent over the napkin, and he flushed, warm again with the success of it. This was going pretty well, after all.

SAMMI
Brixton, 2009

A picture of a middle-aged man, grainy, profiled, taken in bad light. A moustache, a tuxedo, a champagne flute.

SAMMI MY FIREND TOOK THIS ON HIS PHONE IS THIS MARK CARR????!!!!

She'd waited a bit, before replying. Thought it through.

Brixton, 1996

Mark had woken her and pulled her out of bed in the middle of the night, taken her up to the roof, even though she'd protested that she didn't want to climb the ladder (her pregnant brain had made her risk-averse and paranoid). He wrapped a blanket round her and held her there, in the street light. His breath smelled rough and he had tears in his eyes.

'This is – I can't – it's not—'

'What's wrong, baby? What is it?' She'd stroked his arm, sleepily.

'It's not what I want, Sammi. This is not what I want to happen.'

'What's not?'

'I've got to go away, princess. I've got to leave here right away. I'm running. Tonight.'

'You're what?'

'Running. An old – an old comrade from back in the day just tipped me off. I've been made. For some stuff I did a long while back. A long while before you, sweetheart. So don't worry. You're not implicated or anything. They're coming for me, though, so I've got to go. I think I might actually have to get out of the country.'

She wondered vaguely if she was still dreaming.

'OK. Should we pack just now, or will it wait till the morning?'

'No no no, princess. Not you. You've got to stay here and look after the baby. It's just me. I don't want to risk anything happening to you, or you getting tarred by association with me.'

'You're – leaving?' She felt helpless and stupid and female saying it.

'Just for a bit. Just for a little while, eh? I'll go somewhere and lie low. No, no, what I'll do, I'll go and get some casual work somewhere – pick fruit, I could pick fruit, yes – and wire you the money.'

He was never usually so scattered, so jerky. He never usually spoke without thinking it through first.

'Mark, I think you're drunk. This is all seeming a bit weird. Maybe you just need a sleep?'

'There's no time, beautiful girl. No time for sleep just now. I shouldn't even have come back here tonight but I couldn't leave you without letting you know.'

'But – the baby. We're having a baby together. In, like, four months. Are you going to be back for that?'

He attempted to put a long kiss on her, holding her jaw in his hand and laying his wet mouth over hers, then tried to turn it into a series of smaller kisses as she wrenched away.

'Answer the fucking question, Mark. Are you going to be here for the birth?'

'Princess. I will do' – kiss – 'everything in my power' – kiss – 'to be back by your side before this' – kiss – 'baby is born.' Kiss. 'Back by your side is where I'm supposed to be. It's where Mark Carr belongs. And I'll write to you. I'll write letters anonymously but I'll find a way of making sure you know it's me. I'll send you ways of getting in touch with me along the road. And the second it all blows over, which I'm sure it will, you'll have your man, this baby's father, right back home again.'

There were tears on his face, glassy in the street light.

'I have no choice. I need you to hear me on that. I have to run, right now, or they'll get me. You know that, don't you, Sammi? You hear me.'

She hadn't known what to do. She'd clung to him, cried, shouted, insisted on coming with him, all the while feeling him peel her off him, sensing that he wanted to leave immediately. She'd suggested they go downstairs and he talk it through with her properly; this had proved a mistake, as it allowed him to make a physical break. He'd placed her, heaving sobs and all, in a chair while he crept into the sleeping space and grabbed a couple of belongings. He'd hugged her again, he'd pulled up her top and kissed the bump, and he'd left.

And that had been it. She'd spent her days patrolling the squat's sour walls, terrified to leave in case a messenger came and she missed it, barely talking to anyone else, marking time in aches and kicks. Her relationship with Mark, she began to realize, had cushioned her from the rest of them, kept her separate; meant now that, since Xanthe had left and Clio was barely there any more, she had almost nothing to say to these people. She hadn't really even bothered to get to know Fran's new animal rights pals who were holing up in the copy room. It was Spider, gentle, grubby Spider, who heard her crying in bed one day and sat down beside her mattress.

'What's wrong here, matey?'

'I'm fine. I just need to sleep.'

'Are you sure about that then? Because I don't think you're doing fine, Sam.'

'I would be. I would be if I could just sleep on a proper fucking bed with legs, and clean sheets! Clean sheets. Just for once.'

'Matey. Matey. I don't think you should be here. I've been wanting to say this for a while now. You need to get yourself back to your mum's. We're not going to be able to give you the help you need here.'

'I have to stay here, Spider. He said I had to, to get the letters. To know how to contact him.'

'This is Mark, yeh? He said you had to stay here, in this squat? This fucking rat trap? When you's what, six month pregnant? With his kid?'

She nodded and collapsed in on his open arms, let her snot ooze on to his shoulder. He rubbed her back.

'Here. Here. Right, matey. I'm going to tell you something you need to hear. What Mark did to you was . . . well, it wasn't good, was it. He's left you pretty much unsupported, in a place that ain't right for no baby to be born in. I never said it to Xanthe, matey, but this ain't no place for a kid. Right now you needs you mum, I reckon.'

'I can't do that. I can't go back there. She'll – she'll—'

'She'll probably give you a right telling off, innit. And you'll have to take that, darlin. But then she'll also keep you clean and warm and well and she'll love that baby. Ain't no mother going to turn her lickle girl away with a baby in her.'

'But Mark—'

'Well now, I don't know what's going on with Mark. But I'm gonna tell you this, matey. If he comes back, he's getting a punch in the nose from me for this little disappearing stunt. This ain't no way to treat your missus, know what I'm saying? It's gonna be hard to hear this, love, but I think for now you've got to be going about your life like he ain't coming back. Even if he does. Right now, you need to look after yourself and your baby. An I'm gonna be right here, so if he comes back I'll tell him where you are. Once I've bopped him one.'

Avril, to her credit and Sam's everlasting surprise, had opened the door late in the night to a pregnant, crying, prodigal daughter, and asked no questions beyond the due date and the last time she had eaten. While Sammi wept and raged against the man who'd left her,

Avril made food and stroked her hair. When Sammi screamed that she couldn't do it, Avril held her wrists and told her to stop fooling, because she was going to do it and she wouldn't be alone. Her mother had met her with so much fierce love and protection that she'd felt ashamed of the mean caricature she'd made of Avril in her head. And in time Deborah had pushed her way into the world, pissed-off and lanky, with aristocratically high cheekbones; just another baby with a missing father and a mother who didn't want to talk about him.

Brixton, 2009

Was that Mark, in the picture Clio had sent? Sam only had one photo of him, and he was in the background, squinting. Like many of her acquaintances from that time, he was paranoid about cameras; she'd seen him go so far as to rip up a portrait shot Fran had taken unawares and developed in her makeshift darkroom in the other toilet. She'd tried to recreate him over the years, mainly from occasional fleeting expressions on Debbie's face that had shocked her into momentary recognition. Then she'd tried to bury it down again.

'Your daddy couldn't be with us, baby. So that's why I've got to love you extra hard for the both of us. You hear me?'

What would he look like aged fifty or so? Carrying extra weight under his chin, balding, wearing a suit rather than a ratty sweatshirt?

Hi Clio,

Good to hear from you! It's been a long time. Hope everything's well with you.

It's certainly a shock to see this picture. It's been years and I don't have anything to really compare it to, but on balance, yes, I think that could be Mark. Or at least his long-lost twin brother.

What have you been doing with yourself, anyway?

Samantha

The response was almost instant, even though she'd written at half-one in the morning.

SAMMI THIS IS A POLICEMAN. HE'S CALLED
DECTECTIVE INSPECTOR MICHAEL CARRINGTON.
IF ITS MARK THEN HE WAS SPYING ON ALL OF US!!!!!!

Sam hadn't known what to do with that. After half an hour of staring at the screen, she climbed back into bed beside Dale's snoring bulk and stared at the shadows on the ceiling. Paranoid, she kept muttering to herself. They'd all been paranoid in the squat, and it was something she was sure got worse with age. Look at Clio's message. The caps lock. The unhinged rush of words. She hadn't even been sure it was Mark.

It was Mark, wasn't it.

She threw the covers off, wrapped her fluffy dressing gown back round her bump and walked back into the kitchen. She loaded up the photo and zoomed in as far as she could go.

It was Mark.

She didn't reply to Clio for two days. She was quiet in the house, tried not to look into Debbie's beautiful face and have anything at all confirmed, watched her run off to school with that gangling lope she certainly hadn't got from anyone in Sam's family and ached for her girl and for the time when it was just them, no one else in the world.

SAMMI WE NEED TO TALK R U STILL IN BRIXTON???

What did it mean, if Mark had been a policeman? She tried to think back thirteen years to the experience of being with him. She remembered the warmth of him in bed and the smell of the sleeping space, the tone of his raised voice in a crowded room. It felt hazy; it could have been something she'd dreamed or a film she'd caught on telly years ago.

She remembered the feeling of watching a man talk, of him not knowing you were watching him, of catching your breath at how beautiful he was. Wanting to see him so badly on the days and sometimes weeks he was away, visiting his mother. She remembered being nineteen and twenty and sick to her stomach with the strength of a feeling. It was one of the hardest, strongest emotions she'd ever had at that point. But the person who'd made her feel that was – what? An actor? A shadow? Not ever really there?

She'd been sitting in front of the same open case file, not moving, for a very long time. The phone on her desk rang. It was Bev at reception. 'Sam, there's a woman here to see you. Won't give her name but says you're old friends. Red hair.'

Clio was in the café across the road Sam had asked her to go to, hunched over a cup of tea. She looked up and smiled.

'Hello, pal. Long time, eh?'

The words she'd been storing in two days' silence fell out of Sam's mouth.

'Clio. You can't just show up at someone's work. You can't. How did you even find me? I've got – I've got a busy day today. You need to ask these things in advance. People *work*. Normal people work.'

'You put your job on Facebook. You want to be careful about what you're putting out there, love. Don't trust the Internet, you know.'

'Well, you've got ten minutes then I've got to get back. And I'm clock-watching.'

'OK. Here you go. How do we nail this bastard?'

Sam eased her pregnant bulk into the chair opposite and studied Clio's face as it moved.

Clio did not seem to have changed much, although Sam wasn't sure if she would still call her beautiful. She had lost something girlish and delicate; she looked harder and flushed. Something frazzled about her. The nail polish on her fingers was chipped. Still magnificent, though. Still queening it up over this skanky little caff.

'I'm not letting him get away with this,' she was saying. 'It's rape, what he did to you, Sammi. What *they* did to you. State-approved rape. I mean, you had his fucking kid, didn't you? It's obscene. This isn't fucking Russia or somewhere! We allegedly live in a democracy and yet the government can send its operatives in to rape women because they don't trust their political beliefs? No. Not fucking standing for it, darlin.'

Their table, Sam noticed, had two salt shakers. Not a salt and pepper. She stared down the pair of pinprick S's. Better to look there.

'What do you think? We need to channel this anger, right? Take it to the press. I've got contacts. We are going to raise a STINK. I'm talking massive compensation, all that. Sammi. You all right, love?'

Sam was crying. She knew that because her cheeks were hot and wet. She could hear Clio talking from somewhere far away.

'Hey. Hey. Come on now. Sorry, this was a lot to spring on you, wasn't it? I shouldn't have come here. I'm sorry.'

Warm, rough guitar-player's fingers wrapped round her fist.

'OK,' she heard herself say. 'Let's get him. Let's get them all.'

Dale was late to the clinic, came bursting into the room as she was hoiking her skirt down and the sonographer was warming the jelly.

'Sorry! Sorry. Here now. Carl was just being a dick and I—'

Sam held up her hand to him, and he nodded, sat himself down by her side and grabbed it. She felt the warm pressure of his thumbnail in the fleshy bit of her palm. The second calloused hand to have held hers today. The sonographer was pressing quite hard and she found herself catching her breath.

'Oh, and there we go. That's a little foot. Right there. Can you see?'

Dale cried out. 'Sam. Sam, oh my God.'

'Now, I'm just going to go on a little trip right round the area, and we'll check this little baba out from all angles, shall we? There's the heart, beating away there, can you see it?'

There was a tiny flicker on the screen. Sam felt a high-pitched noise rising in her eardrums, a rushing of blood.

'And those are the lungs, there, and here we've got vertebrae, all looking very good. Oh! The baby's waving at us!'

'Hello, darling!' Dale's voice was a croak, and his eyes were teary.

'What a little beauty. Everything's looking wonderful here. Now, did you want to find out the sex?'

Why were neither of them bothered by that noise? It was a scream, a weird, mechanical scream, getting louder and louder.

'Samantha?'

'Sam? Sam, babe, you all right?'

And just like that, it cut off.

'Oh, it's stopped,' she said. They were looking at her.

'Samantha, would you like to find out the baby's sex?'

'Can I have a glass of water please?'

'Are you all right, baby? What's going on? Talk to me.' His big reassuring face, close to hers. He'd treated her like porcelain from the minute that test had been positive.

She'd never had any of this, the last time. With Debbie, it had been Avril to hold her hand, and Avril had just thanked God the baby was healthy. Poor Debbie had never had anyone but Sam to marvel at her tiny toes in utero.

The nurse helped her sit up slightly and handed her a plastic cup of water, the screen going blank as the sonogram wand scrolled off.

'I imagine you'll burst if you have any more to drink!' said the sonographer, trying to make them all smile. 'Ready to continue, yes?'

Sam wriggled down and the wand went back on. Dale's head was flicking between her and the screen almost comically fast, with a very worried look.

'Yes, we'd like to find out the sex, please,' she said.

'I thought you said you wasn't sure?' Dale asked.

'I'm sure. I need to know this.'

'Ooh, there we go. Hello there. Ho ho! No doubt about that one, is there? Meat and veg! You're having a lovely baby boy.'

'Thank fuck,' said Sam.

She told Dale, later on that night as they cleared the kitchen, while Debbie did her homework and blasted Rinse FM from her room.

'Listen. Here's what's been up with me. You know how I got pregnant with Debbie while I was living in a squat?'

'Yeah, I know, my lickle crusty gal—' She couldn't bear the smile on his face. She almost wanted to slap it off, that beautiful, happy smile full of love and trust, for what was going to happen to it.

'Well, here's the thing, love. It's about Debbie's dad.'

And she laid it out there, in only a few words.

Dale had big hands, and she watched them snap a wooden spoon he was drying in half without even realizing it. The stalk splintered through the dishcloth and pierced his finger; blood began to seep through the tartan pattern. They stopped everything for a few minutes while he sucked his finger and swore and she dabbed at it, applied a plaster. Then he pulled her to him, tight to his chest, and bent his head over hers.

'Gross,' said Debbie, wandering into the kitchen and sticking her head into the fridge.

And then they all came spilling back into her life. Fran, disappearing from view like a fading picture, somehow even more insubstantial and wispy now. Gaz, now also a dad, shaven-headed and into mountain biking. Spider, wizened in a ratty hoody. Xanthe hadn't answered anyone's messages, was presumably still in Greece. They met in Clio's flat in Homerton, each of them advised to stagger their arrivals, although Fran, Spider and Sam ended up getting there at the same time. A very young South Asian guy let them in with a nod; he was distractingly, heart-stoppingly beautiful and she realized she'd been staring at his eyelashes for longer than was polite.

'This is Hamza,' Clio said, coming up behind him and wrapping an arm round his neck in a show of ownership. 'He's going now.'

'Bye, ladies, gents.' He winked as he left.

There was nowhere really to sit: a couple of beanbags on the floor or a low bed. There was no way she'd be able to get herself up from either of them again. Samantha did maths in her head and realized that Clio must be about forty now; even in the squat they'd had skip-stolen armchairs. She leaned awkwardly against the wall for a bit until Gaz noticed her, and stopped the general catch-up chat to pull her in a bar stool from the tiny kitchen.

'How many weeks are you?' he murmured, rubbing her back a little as he helped her into place. 'Bout twenty, yeah? Halfway there. My missus was big with it too. Bit achy, innit? This seat OK for you?'

She hadn't thought about Gaz at all in the last thirteen years, but if she had, he would have been the last person in this group she would have expected kindness from. Elevated above them, she swung her legs and listened to the conversation without really joining in. Which was just like it had always been.

Clio officiated, waving a mug of coffee, not offering anyone else a drink. She brought them to order, her voice rising impatiently over the general babble.

'So. Everyone knows why we're here, yeah? To discuss the highly intrusive and illegal state surveillance on our lives during the years 1995 and 1996, by the person we knew as Mark Carr.'

'Right right right. We need to backtrack a bit, Clio.' Gaz was holding up a hand. 'We ain't got proof yet. You've sent us all that one photo, and we've all agreed it looks a bit like him—'

'Bloody spitting image, matey. Come on,' muttered Spider.

'But we can't just – what? What you thinking? We all just roll up at his police HQ or whatever and start pointing the finger? I mean, what if it's just a coincidence? Posh blokes all look a bit alike, don't they? Now, it's all right for most of you here, but me and Sammi, we got responsibilities, int we? We got families to think of. We can't afford to get hit with some sort of defamation lawsuit or whatever they're called. We need to be sure about this.'

'I don't see what your ability to reproduce or not has to do with anything,' Fran said, drawing herself up tall from the beanbag slump. 'There are risks for all of us in this. For me, and Spider maybe the most. Mark actually witnessed us committing crimes.'

'And yet have any of you done time for them? No.'

'Well, Fran was arrested, matey,' Spider said, his voice a gentle wheeze. 'The McDonald's thing. And a lot of them lot that really led the Greater London ALF was picked up just before he disappeared.'

'Exactly,' said Clio. 'We weren't necessarily his direct targets, but he was using us as cover. Excellent cover. We lived with him, we vouched for him to other activists, we brought him into our networks and made him look real. Not least his relationship with Sammi here.'

All eyes swivelled up to the bar stool. Sam grinned at them all and waved a sheepish hand.

'Y'all right?'

Having illustrated her point, Clio carried on. 'I mean, this is what we're really going to get him on. It was rape. He raped this woman when she was nineteen bloody years old – he raped me, Xanthe; also you I think, Fran? Did any of us consent to having sex with a man called Michael Carrington? With a police officer? No, we did not. He got Sammi pregnant, and he fucked off. Back to where? The Home Counties and the expensive-looking Tory wife I saw him with at that Burns Night party? Listen, he clocked me from the stage. I'd thought it was him when I came in, but we were seated at different ends of the hall. I got my pal to take a picture because I didn't want him to see me just in case there was something dodgy going on – didn't even realize at the time he was police, did I? I just thought, oh, that'll be Mark, wonder what the hell happened to him. But then I was announced and got up on the stage and he jumped straight out his bloody seat, I'll tell you. He avoided my eye during my set, kept his head right down, and then him and the blonde had slipped out while I was getting the guitar unplugged. That's when I asked the organizer, oh, who was that. Detective Inspector Michael Carrington, says she. The Met. He buys a table every year. He was taken unwell, I think. Unwell my fucking arse. You weren't there. It was him. If I wasn't sure when I saw him, I reckon his behaviour confirms it. That's not an innocent man there, is it? I was a last-minute cover for a friend who'd dropped out. If he'd known I was on the bill, he wouldn't have bought that fucking table, I'll tell you that.'

It was funny how separate from it all Sam felt. Inside her the boy kicked and spun, secure in his paternity, and his mother wondered whether Mark had been married at the time he was fucking her and fathering Debbie. How would that wife feel? Would she just write it off as work? Not really him? At what point did the policeman stop? When he put his cock in? Whose was the sperm that had fathered her child? Was that erection, that constant need to get her knickers off, all part of the performance?

They were talking about her as though she wasn't there again. She watched them all, as the hands gesticulated towards her, helpfully pregnant a second time to demonstrate the extent of the crime. She'd been so much younger than these people when she'd known them that she'd shut up and listened when they talked and talked, impressed by their words and their passion. She saw them now, frayed, middle-aged and flustered, people who'd never held down a job, raised a kid, had managed to coast through to their forties and even fifties on outrage and vim, untroubled by any real responsibility. Mark – Michael – whatever his name was, had recognized them for the squabbling children they were at the time. That's why he'd found it so easy. Of course he was a police officer. Of course he was. She saw it clearly now.

They all flapped their hands about as they talked, the voices rising shrill, changing nothing, and she felt so very, very tired. Couldn't she just find him, go up to him and punch him in the face? Would that be enough? Could she turn up on his doorstep with pictures of Debbie and hand them to his wife? Something like a bomb, a grenade, some sort of violence on his home? Something exploding in the middle of his life? What would make her stop feeling like this?

She would need to see it, she realized that. To feel normal again she would need to watch his face. She wanted to see it dawning that his life had been ruined, and that she had done it. She wanted to be holding his face in her hands while it happened, pushing her nails into his skin.

She'd had enough of them. She slipped her huge self off the bar stool and stood there for a second, in the middle of their circle, holding up a hand until their talk and talk and talk dried up.

'OK. We're going to be methodical about this. You all need to calm down and we're going to draw up a plan of action. First thing we need to do: get proof. Nah, not hearing it, Gaz.'

She raised her hand higher and he stopped. This was good. This felt like having control again. 'Think about Mark. Really think about him. You know he was police. Of course you do. So, we just need to get proof. After that, you're going to get straight on to your journalist mates, Clio. They won't publish anything without checking with their legal team, but they'll be able to get something in motion. And we're going to need a lawyer.'

They all looked flummoxed, again.

'Lucky I know someone who might do it pro bono, then. Good bloke; I've done some work with him. I'll set up a meeting, but one of you is going to have to do the heavy lifting because this baby is my priority, not some mucky revenge plan. But here, let me tell you this – none of you are going to fuck this up, OK? I'm not having you putting me under any more stress. I want you all to remember who he hurt the most with all of this, and who you could hurt the most if you start acting the goat. Me, and my little girl. His daughter. Debbie is thirteen years old and she's the one with the most at stake here. I don't want anybody disclosing our identity. I don't want any of you getting loose-lipped one stoned night and spilling out any information. I am going to need assurance from every single one of you that you are going to act properly and responsibly, hear me? Smallest sign of mucking about and I'm walking and taking your case with you. This is life or death. Take it more seriously than anything you ever have in your life. All right? All right.'

They nodded at her, silent and huge-eyed, like her problem-kids group did when she'd had to lose it at them. Even though Clio opened her mouth, she closed it again.

That night, in bed, she wept into the pillow until Dale woke up, rolled round and curled into her.

'Hey. Come on now, Sam. Hey.'

'The fuck am I doing, baby? Am I putting my own need to see that bastard punished before my daughter's welfare? I mean, what the hell is Debbie going to get out of all this?'

'Do you want to stop it? Cos we can stop it, love. You just walk away right now and it ends here.'

She thought about that.

'I can't. It doesn't. It won't, though, will it? It's not going to let me go now.'

From then on the days bore into her; she felt each one physically. She grew hefty, her hips and feet forced outwards, duck-like, as she walked the pavement, the weight of everything almost too much if she thought about it.

This pregnancy was different. Her belly had popped early and she found herself relishing wearing bright, skin-tight clothes where as a pregnant twenty-year-old she'd slunk under men's shirts nicked off the boys in the squat or bought three for a pound from charity shops. She walked belly-first, hands always cradling her boy from the world, making sure they all knew, realizing for the first time the herd instinct, pushing through centuries of London isolationism, which made strangers automatically protective of her body. It was not how she was used to being treated in a crowd. On the Tube, people stood for her. In the street, they made way, the women smiled, even white women; grandfatherly bus drivers asked how she was doing as she paid her fare. People talked to her, asking how long to go, telling her she looked well. Society had never reacted to her like this before and it had taken her a while to get used to it; her body and space invaded from inside and out.

'Of course, you'll have done all this before,' said the midwife, trying to distract her from the stab and ache of blood-letting. 'How old's your first?'

The two pregnancies conflated, created a wormhole between two very different people, made it all impossible to forget. Thirteen years, the same womb. She'd wake up at night, her veins throbbing, unsure whether she was Sam Burke or scared little Sammi Smith, carrying a wanted and planned-for baby or a piece of collateral damage.

And she ached most for Debbie; for the retroactive shame and humiliation she felt about that birth. She'd never had a problem showing her daughter love but couldn't go near her now without the churning of complication. Their interactions grew more and more clipped, Debbie's voice rising higher and higher, and as Sam's due date approached she shipped her lovely girl off to Avril's every weekend, terrified lest she say something she shouldn't in the heat of an argument. She spent the three weeks of her maternity leave before Elliot's birth nursing hatred, pure, clean and focused, for the man she didn't know how to name, an idea of his blondness always in the corner of her eye, light and lordly, clouding and ruining everything it touched.

She hated at the mechanics of a system that had decided it had the right to use her, she hated at Clio for unearthing it all, and she hated herself. In the red height of labour she dug her nails into Dale's arm and chanted Debbie's name repeatedly, increasingly frantic.

Loaded, February 1996

Hot Scots!

As Trainspotting *becomes the most successful Britflick in yeeeears,* **Pete Moss** *turns his eyes (and his, er, jockstrap) to the frozen north for this week's* **Shaggable Six**. *Och aye the YES!*

1. Kelly Macdonald
Don't worry, chaps! Renton's schoolgirl squeeze is totally legal in real life! And as she plays a jailbait hooker in new film *Stella Does Tricks*, we hope to be seeing a *lot* more of her, er, talents.

2. Shiv West
The pint-sized teenage frontwoman of up-and-comers Costello has a fuckton of attitude zipped into that catsuit, and with a platinum album ringing in the moola, she seems like the sort of girl who'd give *you* a Good Time.

3. Manda Rin
Reckon you could make this Bis cutie squeal even louder? Maybe if you showed her your Kandy Pop . . .

4. Laura Fraser
Form an orderly queue please! The talented teen actress broke hearts in Glasgow gangster flick *Small Faces*, and with a gorgeous small . . . *face* like that, she's probably used to men fighting over her.

5. Clio Campbell
It's been a few years since this sexy ginger encouraged gentlemen the world over to Rise Up, but while she prefers to guest on other people's songs these days, there are those of us who remain firmly, er, arisen . . .

6. Shirley Manson

Another gorgeous ginge (it's like they breed 'em up there . . .), this Stupid Girl is Only Happy When It Rains. Reckon a few *Loaded* readers would be glad to rain on her parade, eh?

SHIV
Glasgow, 4 February 2017

She was relatively early, but the (admittedly small) room was already packed and, having not expected to be one of the oldest people at a fiftieth birthday party, she felt instantly on edge. Clio was dressed in something sparkling, with a centrifugal whirl of youth and energy around her. Siobhan pulled herself up straighter and steadied her heels, relaxed as the heads turned.

'Shiv! Shiv! SHIV!' Clio shouted, stretching her arms out, parting an obedient Red Sea of bodies to create safe passage. Siobhan stretched her arms out too as she approached, mirroring absurdly, aware everyone was watching them, conscious of the whispers as she passed. Yes, yes, it's me. It had been so long since she'd been out that she'd almost forgotten the rush of validation a home crowd would always give her, even when she wasn't playing.

'Happy birthday,' she yelled in Clio's ear as they wrapped around each other. 'Look at us, eh? Two old tarts!'

She pulled back to study Clio, held her by the elbow. Golden glow, shimmer, and the hair at its curliest, huge glass of wine swilling around in her fist.

'You look fucking great.'

'Aww. So do you,' Clio said, although Siobhan heard the dull clank of an automatic response.

'Feh. I look like a middle-aged mother. You're some sort of ageless fucking Botticelli disco ball. How the hell you can afford to look this expensive beats me.'

Clio waved a hand, fingernails painted green like Sally Bowles. 'I felt I owed it to myself tonight. At this age, you can't throw a big party for yourself then trudge out in front of everyone letting all the . . . *fiftyness* drag your tits down. Well, you'll learn all about it when you get there! I might not be able to afford food until springtime, right enough. Where's Paul?'

'Babysitter fell through. I'm here, though – got the guitar, and I'll do the song solo if you want. Or perhaps you could get up and join me?'

'Ha! You shouldn't have asked me in advance. I'll have time to think of an excuse now.'

A beat, in which neither of them believed her.

'Oh, let me think about it. Right, you need a drink. And – Ruth? Ruth? Shiv, this is my dear, dear friend Ruth, who, bless her wee button boots, has agreed to stage-manage the whole shebang for me tonight. Ruth, Shiv is – well, she's *Shiv* – and performing, obviously – could you grab her something on the bar tab?'

Ruth was a sturdy, capable-looking woman, make-up already mostly sweated off a round red-cheeked face. She seemed quite distracted, and Siobhan found it a little awkward that a 'dear, dear friend' was pulling waitress duty. Sensing Clio's attention wandering, she created her exit.

'I will absolutely get my own drink. See you shortly. Ruth, do you need me to soundcheck, or isn't that possible?'

Clio's golden back turned and she embraced the next newcomer, screamed their name.

The businesslike Ruth was saying something quietly about adjusting the levels live.

'It's – well, we did organize a soundcheck for everyone who's playing at five p.m. Before everything started. I think you got the email?'

Siobhan felt the accusation and ground against it. She was doing this for free, for fuck's sake, as a favour.

'Yeah – I couldn't do that. School run, kids need their dinner. You know.'

Ruth nodded. Maybe she didn't know.

'It'll be fine to fiddle with the levels when I'm up there. It's just a birthday party! We're not playing the Albert Hall.' Ruth gave a small terse nod. 'Actually, I think I would like that drink, if OK? I'll take a glass of red just now. Big one. No, wait, make it a double G&T. Not the house – anything boutique, small distillery, that sort of thing. With slimline. Lovely. Ta.'

Siobhan flattened her back against the wall as Ruth's inscrutable face sailed out to combat the bar queue. The crowd shifted into focus; she recognized people. It would be all right. She'd felt quite anxious, going somewhere without Paul, which was ridiculous. They'd been doing professional appearances separately since Daisy was born and had only ever gigged as the band three times in the past decade, so perhaps it was the social aspect of the evening that was worrying her. To be on show at an event like this, with the fierce, constant hug of elastic under her dress making her all too aware of the new flesh she'd never lose, without Paul to tag in and out of their well-rehearsed stories and rescue her from the inevitable parade of humourless former goths who'd loved her when they were teenagers – she had really had to push herself out of the door.

Camden, 1995

The bar that everyone went to was deliberately run-down, made a point of its scruffiness. It was December and Shiv was nineteen, out with two music journalists and one of the record-company guys, all of whom, she was pleasantly aware, were trying to sleep with her. She had been ushered through the bar crowd to a raised, ripped banquette by the broken-legged pool table where everyone could see her through the drifts of cigarette smoke. She'd been down a few times and was talking about moving there, but London still had Shiv enchanted then; the spells it had cast were newness, hugeness, difference from home. That grotty pub glowed and pulsed to her, a kingdom hers for the taking. The album had only just come out and, despite her face being on the cover of the current issue of *Select* magazine under the headline THIS YEAR'S GIRL (with the male parts of the band small and glowering in the very distant background behind her shoulder), she didn't know anyone. The record-company guy kept passing her wraps of chaz with too knowing a wink and unnecessarily complicated hand gestures. Slipping through a mob of rich kids in stained thrifted T-shirts, everyone squinting out through unwashed fringes hoping for a Damon or a Justine, Shiv experienced for the first time the sensation of being famous, of hearing people whisper her name as she passed, and it felt fucking great. She was here. It was happening around her and to her and it wanted her. It's maybe why she would always remember the night so clearly.

There was only one cubicle in the ladies', and barely enough space by the tiny, grimy basin for one person to wait. Shiv squeezed in close to the other body in there, registered the smell of hairspray, the cluster of badges on the jacket, the mass of red hair and the sheer loveliness of that face.

'Oh my fucking God! You're Clio Campbell!'

Her voice rang off the tiles. Clio looked embarrassed.

'Hi. Yeah. That's me.'

'But I LOVE you. I mean, you pretty much made me who I am! You probably won't remember me of course, but my God, you changed my life. Watching you on *Top of the Pops* – that was what made me decide to be a musician. I mean, fucking hell, pal! Clio Campbell! And you're here! I'm Shiv – Siobhan – and I'm, like, your biggest fan ever.'

Clio smiled down at her.

'I know who you are, darlin'.'

'No, no, but we've met! We've met before! I went to see you on tour a couple of years ago when you played my town. Ullapool. Fucking Ullapool. We got to speak to you for ages afterwards and I just – oh my God. You were the only act worthwhile who ever came to us. Oh my God, it meant so much.'

'I do remember. Of course I remember that. Wee Siobhan. And now you're Shiv West? I didn't make the connection. Look at you!'

Snorting and snuffling from the cubicle.

'It's like, what are you doing in here anyway? Oh my God, you have to come and sit with us! You're the only person in here I know. I need to hear a voice from home. Come here, come here, we'll have a bit of this—' She waggled the origami wrap in Clio's face, then banged on the cubicle door. 'Hiya, pal! Could you get out of there please? Other people need to use the facilities!'

Clio would only have been twenty-eight at the time, but just then, even squatting to do a line off a toilet seat with her curls thrown back to one side, she seemed to Siobhan to be some sort of ancient being, a sentinel, her very presence there a sign from the old gods. Her hand, when Siobhan reached for it to guide her to their table, wondering momentarily if she was allowed to touch her, was cold and smooth.

'Guys guys guys, you will not believe this! This is Clio – she's, like, the reason we started the band. She did this amazing song, "Rise Up", a load of years ago, when I was tiny, and it was like the first single I ever bought, and then she played a gig in our town and you've got to understand, this was a tiny town. I mean, nobody ever came to our town. Nobody who wasn't a fucking folkie in a beard, yeah? And I heard her play that night and that's when I realized it properly, like I started the band the next week. So she's going to join us for the night. Budge up! Budge up, boys! Make way for an actual living legend, eh?'

She pushed at the air around the men impatiently until they'd shifted. Clio had glanced at one of the journalists, who was staring straight at his pint.

'Evening, Pete. Long time, eh?'

'Clio.'

'Oh wow, do you know each other? I mean, I bet everyone knows each other down here, don't they? You all seem to. In this pub, at least. It's like living in a wee village, but you're in this pure massive city.' Shiv's accent thickened in her gullet in the presence of another Scot.

Clio cleared her throat.

'Mm. Pete brought me here to this very bar, years ago, when my single came out. For an article. Same table, I think. Good optics, you said – right, Pete? "Let's sit here where everyone can see us."'

Pete coughed. The other men seemed to be looking away.

'So this is Shiv here's tour of victory, eh? Because you're Roger from the *NME*, aren't you?' She pointed across the table at the other journalist. 'And you must be from the record company. I mean, sorry darling, but you stand out a mile. It's nice to see that the traditions are still being preserved. Taking the new pop princess out for a public crowning, getting her nice and drunk and malleable, writing the pieces up afterwards. Yeah, I think I'll sit in for this one, boys, if you don't mind. We go way back, me and this girl here, so I fancy keeping a wee eye on her tonight.'

Shiv felt her stomach turn. It was as though her mother had turned up at the school gates and tried to wash her face with a spat-on hanky. You had to show these guys you were cool and this wasn't cool at all. And God, she could handle herself just fine. But, still, this was *Clio Campbell*.

'Nah nah, Clio, pal. Everything's fine. This is all just friends hanging out, isn't it, guys? They're great, these guys. Here, Ed—' She flicked a hand at the record-company guy, feeling in command. 'Ed will get us a couple more pints of snakebite, won't you? And you can tell me what you're doing here, in this pub of all places!'

The two journalists pressed themselves into the wall of the booth, kept their eyes on the table.

'I was just meeting a guy – do you know Norman from the

Fannies, yeah? – friend of his, new band, he wants someone to do some backing vocals. But he's late. I don't usually come here – bit scenestery for me these days.'

'So you live down here? I'm thinking of moving – we all are, the band. I mean, what the fuck is there back home? We're staying in Glasgow in the dump near the college we stopped going to, but we're hardly there. What's the point, eh? I want a flat on Camden fucking High Street, right in the middle of this!'

'I'm actually staying in Brixton. In a squat, would you believe? With a brilliant bunch of people. I like it much better round there. You're actually living in a real area with a real, diverse mix of folk, not just white music-industry blobs in their twenties. No offence, gents – although I don't think you're even technically in your thirties any more, are you, Pete?'

Roger from the *NME* snorted. 'Brixton? Good fucking luck, sweetheart. You wouldn't catch me in that shithole without a Kevlar vest.'

'I know, Roger. One of the area's many attractions.'

Clio raised the pint that had been set at her elbow in his direction. Shiv wasn't sure what to do. There was some sort of undercurrent pulsing out from the older woman, a weird fizzing electricity, even though her smile was quite pleasant. She could tell it was making the men uncomfortable but she couldn't name it.

'The folk I'm living with are working in the underground,' Clio said. 'Campaigners. People who've really dropped out of the rat race and aren't just slumming it for a couple of years. Trying to make a difference. It all just feels a lot more important than – this. I don't know if it could possibly make sense to you just now, Shiv, when all this –' she gestured around the bar, its shabby walls and peeling paint '– is amazing and new. I know how you feel, I really do. But I suspect some day you'll understand what I'm getting at.'

'So, those who can't go to Brixton, eh?' Pete seemed to be speaking to the ceiling, but everyone heard him.

Shiv thought the best thing to do was probably change the

subject. She had no idea what was going on but they were all beginning to spoil her buzz, and she was pretty sure she needed these guys
on side. She kind of wished Clio would just go, but she was sipping her
drink very slowly.

'You're still making music, though? If you're doing backing vocals?
Oh my God, we should totally work together. Ed, Ed, can you set that
up? I mean, you have no idea what a beautiful voice Clio has.'

'Yeah, he probably can't remember back that long ago,' Pete said.

'I mean, if I could sing one-tenth as well as Clio, I'd just – God, we
could have really used a voice like yours in the studio.'

'Hey, don't you be hard on yourself, babe,' Roger from the *NME*
muttered, pressing his leg into hers as he rubbed her back. 'You've
got star power. The real thing. Don't underestimate yourself, or other
people's jealousy of that.'

'All seriousness though, Clio,' Pete said, 'I've been really enjoying
the guest spots you've been doing. That Primal Scream one. Made the
song. Made the EP. Took them somewhere else entirely. Using your
talents sparingly but well, eh?'

'Thanks.' It snipped out of the corner of Clio's mouth, but she
seemed mollified. Shiv was grateful to him, decided to run with it.

'Yeah, I mean, you don't have to be releasing new work all the
time, do you? It would get exhausting. I mean, I want to take a great
big break after we finish this tour. You know, maybe a year. Maybe
more.'

Ed giggled. 'Hah, well. We'll talk about that later, eh?' He offered
her another cigarette. She'd forgotten he was still there.

Shiv began to tune the conversation out as each of the men tried
to grab for her attention, the names dropping faster and faster. Ed disappeared at one point and returned with the bass player from Sleeper,
who he said he simply had to introduce Shiv to; not to be outdone,
Roger took her off to meet Donna from Elastica, who was trying to
play pool and didn't seem interested in either of them.

When they returned to the table, Roger's hand steering her gently, one finger picking at the waistband of her skirt, Ed had melted into the background somewhere and Pete and Clio were locked in conversation, neither smiling.

'Yeah well, you know where I am, sweetheart, and you know what I could do for you,' he snapped, chucking a business card on the table in front of her. 'Shiv, it's been a pleasure, and I'll definitely arrange another session next week for the article, all right. All yours, Roger.' He raised his middle finger at his colleague as he left.

'Well, girls, just you and me, eh?' Roger said.

'Shiv could do with another drink, Roger,' said Clio, smoothly, turning a beautiful smile on him. 'Could you oblige? There's a boy.'

They sat there, for a second, as Roger's skinny frame was swallowed by a mass of bodies. Then Clio reached across the table and grabbed her wrist. Up close, Shiv could see her make-up was running into the cracks around her eyes, and her tongue was stained purple and white.

'Listen, doll. I'm clearly cramping your style, so I'm going to head off now. I am. I just want to tell you something first. Don't laugh it off, OK – consider this a wee gift from your fairy godmother, who's been there and done this so you don't have to.'

Shiv was really wishing the whole thing would stop. Ed was waving to get her attention from another table. Clio's chipped fingernails were digging into her palm, pupils bulging like an old witch delivering an ineffectual curse.

'Just give me one minute, OK? Don't fuck them. That's all it is. Don't fuck any of them. Any of the men sitting at this table tonight, any of the men like them. Don't do it unless you want to, and you really fancy them, and you're in control of the situation. Right now, this evening, even though they're trying to make you think you are, you're not in control. You only have power here while you keep your legs closed. It sounds fucking sexist, but that's because this is a fucking sexist shark pool we're swimming in. They'll put your beautiful face on their magazines, but the second they've had you they'll chuck you aside. And they're not discreet, either. OK? Whatever you end up doing this evening, make sure that record-company berk gets you a taxi on expenses back to your hotel. By yourself. Promise me that.'

Shiv breathed in. It was a disappointment. This ranting mad-woman was not the Clio Campbell who had squeezed her hand in Ullapool and promised her she could be whatever she wanted to be.

'Listen, thanks, but I'll be fine. I'm a tough cookie and I can handle myself. Yeah?' She pointed over at Ed's new table. 'I'd probably better go.'

'Gotcha. Good luck out there, wee Siobhan. Stay safe.'

Shiv tried to shrug the experience off, but it had soured the whole night. She couldn't look at Roger from the *NME* without blushing, and without seeing how unattractive he was, really. No, she didn't fancy him, so why should he be allowed to slip his hand up her skirt and trace his fingers across her tights? She wriggled away and away from him, eventually going off to hide in the cubicle for a while, flick-ing a full wrap between her fingers. He'd gone when she came back. As the music got louder, she watched the shifting faces around the table, mostly from bands she'd admired or at least read about before she'd arrived here, and couldn't be bothered trying to work out what they were saying. They all seemed to have the same accent, sliding posher and posher the louder they got. She tapped Ed on the arm.

'Listen, pal, I think I'd probably like to go home now. Been a long week. Could you get me a taxi? I don't really know where I'm going, and I don't want to get lost.'

Never quite off the job, Ed snapped to attention.

'Absolutely. Absolutely, sweetheart. Just let me get my jacket. Back in a sec, folks. Here we go.'

Stepping out into frozen air was refreshing after the Marlboro fug of the pub, even if Shiv's denim jacket wasn't anywhere near warm enough for the weather. Ed noticed her shivering and insisted on throwing his mint-new parka round her shoulders. They walked round the side of the bar towards the high street, the air full of late-night yowling and the same songs drifting out of other doorways. As they reached the bottle bins from the pub, a sharp smell of something human and rotten rising from them, Shiv heard a sort of rhythmic groaning. Ed chuckled, nervously.

'Someone's having fun, eh? Ha ha. Heh.'

Behind the biggest bin, thanks to a nearby street light, Shiv could just make out a man's face, his mouth open and his eyes closed. It took her a second to realize it was Pete, and that his fingers were tangled into a mass of red curly hair moving up and down at his waist. Shiv turned her face away and felt very very far from home indeed.

Glasgow, 2017

Up on the little stage, as she plugged in the guitar and strummed a few notes, and the drunks at the front whooped, she took stock of the room through her fringe. There were fewer people than she'd thought at first, really, and it wasn't what she'd call a beautiful crowd. Clio was flitting between groups, barely settling, and Siobhan wondered how many of these dear, dear friends she was really at her ease with.

'Hello everyone. I'm Siobhan.'

'We know!' bellowed Clio, from the middle of the room.

Siobhan stuck her tongue out.

'Now, Clio asked me to perform a particular song, and while I hate to disappoint the birthday girl, there's something else I think I need to sing tonight. This song is called "Seraphim" . . .'

As expected, the crowd started cheering. Siobhan waited for the noise to fade slightly and leaned back into the microphone.

'And I've not really said this in public, but I actually wrote this song when I was about twenty, a very long time ago now, and I was just a wee lass beginning to negotiate my way through the big bad world of the music industry. There was a musician, a female musician, who'd been through all that a few years before me, and she might not remember it, but one night she appeared in a bar like my fairy godmother, and gave me some very good advice that would see me through some of the rougher times. This is a song about sister-hood, about women looking out for each other, and it feels right that I'm singing it in tribute to the woman who inspired it. Happy birth-day, Clio.'

'Seraphim' was usually a harder, driving number, benefiting a lot from a heavy bassline and a violent beat. She'd never really done it acoustic, and she stumbled a few times slowing it down. Not her finest performance by a long shot, but Clio, pushing through the crowd and hugging her, didn't seem to mind.

'Is that true? Is that true? You bad bitch. Is that true?'

Siobhan nodded, breathed in perfume and felt a bit fraudulent. She hadn't thought of the origins of that song in years until tonight; it had become its own thing completely separate from Clio. It reminded her of that perfect sunset performance at Glastonbury, feeling Daisy kick inside her to the thrum as the crowd screamed; she almost wished she'd kept it for herself now.

Clio was restless, snatched or distracted away from her side almost immediately. As she tried to cut her way back across to the people she knew, a small man tapped her on the shoulder.

'Great set, Shiv. Really.'

'Och, it was just the one song.'

'I mean it. Really interesting to hear the origins of that one, too.'

He had a soft voice and his balding scalp was damp with the heat, the hair brushed over it sweaty. She wondered why he didn't take his leather jacket off.

'So, is there anything else in the pipeline?'

'I'm sorry? Do I—?'

'Um. Neil Munro? From the *Standard*? We've met. I've interviewed you quite a few times over the years?'

Nothing, but she let her eyes do slow recognition.

'Of course! I'm so sorry. I'm actually slightly face-blind; do you know that? Well, you do now!'

'Not to worry, not to worry. Listen, can I buy you a drink?'

He'd already placed a hand on her back and steered her towards the bar, she noticed.

'Oh no, no, please—'

'Go on.' He winked, and it was awful. 'Glass of wine? G&T? The first time we met you were drinking pints of lager, but I suspect your tastes have changed.'

As she waited, helpless and stuck by obligation at the side of the bar, she noticed a young woman trying to work up the nerve to approach. Usually Siobhan tried to avoid these sorts of encounters, as her fans tended to be painfully earnest, but she could use a buffer right now, so she smiled in what she hoped was an encouraging way. The woman simpered, blushed, then began to move forward, arriving just as Neil made his way back from the bar with her drink.

'I just wanted to say that that was amazing,' the woman said. She was probably in her late twenties, heavy, with frizzy hair dyed badly purple and a nose ring. She spoke in almost a monotone.

'That song is everything to me. Everything. I can't tell you. You wouldn't believe it. And then to find out that one of my favourite songs is actually about one of my favourite people. It means – you have no idea. I mean, I think you've literally changed my life tonight.'

Well, you brought this on yourself, Siobhan thought, as Neil inserted himself into the conversation.

'Gin and tonic. It's Harris gin. Nice bottle. I don't know anything about gin, me.'

Siobhan smiled her thanks at him, and then patted the woman on the arm.

'I'm so glad you told me that. It means a lot to me too. Neil, this is – oh! I haven't asked your name.'

'Verity. I'm a very big fan of – actually, no, I don't think the word fan really covers it. I don't want you to think I'm one of those silly girls who scream nonsense at the concerts. I'm not. I'm more than – I mean, when I was growing up, you were basically my idol.'

Neil had raised an eyebrow at her, but Siobhan was in full Princess Diana mode, gracious and smiling, gently adjusting the weight on her feet to ease herself away from him.

'Did I get the order right?' he asked, pointing at the drink, as though Verity wasn't there.

'It's always good to hear that what we do has reached some-one, Verity. Thank you. Tell me about yourself – how do you know Clio?'

'I started following her on Twitter after she was talking about her depression because I also suffer from depression –' ('No kidding,' Neil muttered, in Siobhan's ear) '– and I found her very inspiring. And she took the time to respond to me, and we got into conversation, and she's been just a huge part of my life this last year. I've never met her before tonight, though, so I felt a bit nervous about coming. I've come all the way from Manchester for tonight, you know. But it's been amazing, there are loads of people I've spoken to on Twitter here and it's a very supportive environment. And I can't believe I'm actually talking to you.'

'Yeah, it's always great to meet your heroes,' said Neil, looking at her for the first time. 'I felt like this when I got to interview Bowie, you know?'

'David Bowie was really a problematic person,' said Verity. 'There are a lot of issues relating to his treatment of teenage groupies, his flirtation with fascist iconography, and his appropriation of queer identity.'

'David Bowie was a fucking genius.' Neil's face got redder.

'Of course you would think that. Old white men love other old white men.' The girl was so fabulously blunt Siobhan thought she might kiss her. Instead, she grabbed each of their hands in turn for a quick squeeze.

'Listen, guys, I'm just going to pop to the loo, OK? I'll leave you two to fight this one out.' She had never moved faster in heels.

About an hour later, as the conversation she was in drifted to a natural halt – there was only so much you could say to people you didn't really know that well – Siobhan began to gather her things. Coat on, guitar picked up from behind the tiny sound booth, and she scanned the room for Clio, who was leaning against the bar, looking tired.

'You're not going? No no no, you're not going. We're going to TALK. I never see you. We're going to talk.'

The words slurred; the insistence of a melancholy drunk. Siobhan found herself shunted into a booth and they crashed their stiletto-weary limbs down together on a sticky leather seat.

'So, how you doing, birthday girl?'

'Taking stock, Shiv. I'm taking stock. You will too when it comes for you, this one. The big five-oh. I've been in forward motion, Shiv. All my life. I've seen other people fall down along the way and just kept pushing on. I mean, I'm not saying it's led to the success you've had, but I can see it. A long clear line through my life, push push push, don't stop. Like, what are those things they put on horses, to make them focus?'

'Blinkers.'

'Blinkers. It's not that I've had some brilliant career or that this line has even been a straight one, you know? Just that I've never lost that focus. I've never settled for anything I didn't feel was right. Maybe I should have. Maybe I should have.'

Siobhan looked at the clock above the bar, committed herself to missing the last train home.

'But you didn't, and that makes you you.'

Clio was in full surge now, words vomiting from her almost before she could shape them.

'I dunno, Shiv. I kind of feel like you and me, we didn't pay attention when they were trying to beat us down. You watch women trying to go through their lives and there's always some sort of fucking thing that chucks them off eventually, like, they're bred without ambition, or they have it all knocked out of them? Internalized repression. You hear me? And, God knows, it wasn't that I had a stable or even supportive childhood, fuck no, so I don't know where I got it from. It strikes me that it's a very male trait, this thing we have. Not saying, like, that the desire to push yourself forward is all to do with whichever chromosome you have. I think it's there at the beginning in all of us, and most little girls are ground right down by it. I've seen brilliant women drop out of the race because there wasn't enough security or because they faced too much misogyny and couldn't get any higher, or they got pregnant, or they were worried about their biological clocks . . . they always give up, like it's been pre-programmed inside them. Built-in obsolescence, making way for a younger model. But not us, babe.'

Siobhan had had many conversations like this with Clio over the years. Drunk, in bars, at the ends of nights. She was trying to remember if they'd ever actually spoken sober, but she'd concluded that this was probably how Clio conducted most of her conversations – after all, it had been how Siobhan herself had conversed for most of her adult life, long, rambling monologues where the other participant could nod along emphatically or shout against the flow, trying to change its direction. She prepared to wade in.

'I don't know. I feel it. I feel that little voice trying to whisper me down most days. A lot more now, since the kids. It's been a constant fight against it, to do anything.'

'No, you're wrong. I don't see that for you—'

'And yeah, when you're nineteen or twenty-one and the whole fucking world is telling you you're great and sexy, of course you believe them, you take it as read. But all of those people had agendas. I mean, that skinny little body I used to have, those perky wee tits, they were other people's currency. I might not have shagged anyone for work, but I changed hands a lot more than I'm comfortable admitting, and when there weren't enough drugs to block it out, it took its toll. I mean, they sold that whole first album on a picture of my crotch, babe. Your single cover, the one with the tight T-shirt for "Rise Up"? And you're telling me you've never faced it? Come on, Clio. Your whole career has been marked by blokes shouting you down.'

'And I've never listened to them. That's the point I'm making. Neither have you. This is why – I'm trying to pass on my wisdom here, you know. Woman artist to woman artist. You and me, we have something deep inside us that drives us that other women have lost, I think.'

There was an image nudging away in Siobhan's head. Some bins, a street light.

'Clio. I'm forty-two, with over twenty years in the music business behind me. I'm not that much younger than you and I'm not a wee lassie any more. Don't tell me how I'm supposed to feel now. I'm bloody exhausted, is how I feel. I told myself this shit for years, too; that I'd managed to make it through the machine, the way it grinds you up, because I was in some way hardier or smarter than the other girls. Then I got to forty and the interest started drying up because fewer people want to fuck a pudgy wee woman who can't shift the baby weight—'

'It's not *shit*,' Clio was saying, her voice getting louder, as a pair of hands planted themselves on the sides of the booth, fencing them in to a tiny space together.

'Ladies. What are we drinking?'

He just wouldn't go away, would he? Siobhan glared at him. Clio gave him a quick look.

'Gin and white wine, Neil. Thanks.'

'Not all together, I hope?'

Neither of them laughed and he backed away towards the empty bar, nodding, looking for purpose.

'So you're telling me,' Siobhan said, enjoying the space between her words but speaking quickly enough that Clio couldn't start in again, 'that you've never found yourself subjugated or disadvantaged by being a woman?'

'Not in here, no.' She tapped the coiled, pinned arrangement of hair. 'The outside world can say what it wants; I can rest easy knowing that I've stayed true to me. I've never had to compromise my sense of self for a sniff at fame or anything. It's made me hard and good, and I'm fucking proud of that is all I'm trying to say.'

Siobhan remembered the noise that journalist guy had made in that alleyway, all those years ago. That groaning that men did. It wasn't even a very logical argument, when she thought about it, but it was obvious that Clio needed to tell herself this story, had needed to rewrite her past to get herself to this moment. Maybe she genuinely didn't remember? Maybe it didn't suit her to remember. Who knows, Siobhan thought, what bits of my history are hiding from me? Let her have it. On her birthday. Let her be.

Three glasses were plonked down on the table, an announcement of presence.

'So. Ladies. Having a good night?' he said.

IDA
Euston–Oxenholme, 2011

Just before the train pulled out and north, a woman shoved herself down into the seat opposite. Arms and legs flustered, big showy movements to take off her jacket, cram her bag under the table. She looked about herself irritably, hard face, trampy make-up, thin lips drawn. A bad light coming off her and the iron-rich smell of blood between them in the hot carriage; time of the month and wants everyone to know it, Ida thought, raising her magazine up higher, a feeble barrier between them. She'd bought the magazine for this very purpose. Peeping over, Ida saw the woman had taken out a book and wasn't reading it, a notepad and wasn't writing in it. She fiddled with a phone and stared out the window, all of her gestures screaming for attention.

Ida knew this type. Her own sister, God rest her, had been this type. The sort of person who sucked in all the light, recast everyone else as the spear carriers in her own personal drama. May had given nothing and nothing and nothing for seventy-two years; at her funeral people had whispered that Ida was an unfeeling bitch, or just in shock, sitting up there in the front row and not crying a drop. It was relief, that's what it was, and it was none of their business what else.

This woman wanted Ida. She had some long story to tell, fat with indignation, full of people who had done her wrong, and she needed

Ida to sit there, clucking and patting her shoulder, agreeing that every outrage was terrible, terrible. Then they'd get to Oxenholme and Ida would get off the train and the woman would have forgotten her face before the doors had even closed. Ida didn't need this story. She didn't need anything from this woman at all, and she was old and ugly enough now to know that you could resist these people, when they clamoured for you, even in emotional distress, and not feel guilty afterwards. Ida had her smart new suitcase packed and her hair done, and she was off for a spa weekend she'd got a great deal on in the back of the *Express*. She would get off the train, and she would not think of the woman again, even if it meant rereading the same gruesome stories of incest, celebrity divorce and freakish cysts the size of footballs for the whole three-hour journey. That magazine was not coming down.

It worked well enough, for the first half hour or so. The woman tutted loudly, tried to buffet her way in with interjections in a surprisingly lovely, soft Scottish accent. 'That's the ticket inspector coming.' 'Don't suppose you have change of a fiver, do you?' Ida grunted upward and downward in turn from behind her shield. You've mistaken me for a nice old lady, my girl, she thought. Should have caught me when I was a nice young lady.

They were just pulling out of Crewe when the woman's phone rang, a little burst of classical music or something that Ida knew from somewhere. It wasn't unpleasant. She almost broke cover to point out that this was the *quiet* carriage, but caught herself just in time.

'It is. Um, two-two-sixty-seven-two-five-four-four. Yes. Right. OK. Please.'

. . .

'No.'

. . .

'So there's no chance it could—'

. . .

'I'm here, I'm here. I just – just taking it in.'

'No, I'm on my way up north just now. It's my mother's birthday. Do you need me to—'

. . .

'I just. Can you – is there. Is there. Absolutely no way it could turn around or still still still still continue?'

. . .

'Yeah I can do yeah no OK I will—'

. . .

'Yes. Thank you. OK. Thank you. Yes. Thank you.'

The woman didn't seem to be moving. She'd put her own invisible shield up, didn't want Ida any more. Wasn't aware of Ida.

Ida risked lowering the magazine. The woman was looking down in the direction of the table. Her left hand was there, open, palm up, no ring, but she wasn't really looking at it. Moving gently and quickly, Ida extracted herself from the seat, careful not to nudge the woman's legs. She'd always loved the feeling of walking down a train carriage, against the direction of travel, the pull on her body as it fought the risk of stumbling. People saw the nice old lady coming, hauling herself from handle to handle on the edges of seats, and moved themselves in without meeting her eye. In what it had pleased the train guard to call 'the dining carriage', although 'grimy coffee stand with three sandwiches and a beer fridge' might have been closer to the truth, a uniformed man with a sagging face groaned at her as he scooshed hot water over teabags.

'You would not believe the day that I'm having, my love.'

'No,' she said, handing him the exact money and closing her face to him. 'I probably wouldn't.'

Back at the seat, she nudged the second cup across the table to the woman, who was still in exactly the same position, and readied herself for a conversation she'd had twice before and would have once more in her life.

'It's got sugar in it,' she said. 'For the shock.'

The woman nodded slowly, and curled her hands around the card-board slip cover.

'I've lost my baby,' she said.

'I thought it might have been that,' Ida said.

It broke the seal, and the tears began.

'The tea'll help,' said Ida. 'Well, nothing will help. Not now. And not for a good few months, my duck, I'm going to be honest with you. But take a sip of tea. The heat and the sugar will just bring you back to yourself again.'

The woman nodded.

'How long?' Ida asked.

'Eight weeks,' said the woman. 'I only found out a month ago.'

'Was it a planned one?'

'No. God no. I thought I'd managed to avoi— Well. I'm not exactly in the first flush of youth, am I.'

'Mm. "Youth" is a relative thing,' said Ida. The woman almost smiled.

'Is it your first?'

The woman nodded, then remembered something, shook her head.

'I'm bleeding. I've been bleeding for a while. That's how I found out. They did tests – but they thought it was holding steady. The numbers were going up, but they've dropped now. Too much. They've dropped too much.'

'And they're telling you – what? Just to wait it out?'

'Just to let this thing carry on dying. I'm just to go about my day, and it will keep dying, and eventually the numbers will tell me that it's properly dead. I might need antibiotics, to f—. To fight it. Make my body flush it out. Like an infection. I didn't even know if I wanted it. I was thinking about getting rid of it. And then I was thinking, if it could push its way through my old ovaries and a con-dom, it must have some force behind it, you know, like maybe it was meant to be. But no. But no. Little – *fucking* – quitter, eh? Scuse my language.'

Ida waved a hand to brush away the word, brought it down on the table to rest near the woman's wrist.

'My last one was at forty-six. I thought it was the change. A nasty little postscript on the end of twenty years.'

'Your last one?'

'There were five.' The woman gulped air. 'I'm telling you this because in the next few months you're going to realize that nobody will talk about it with you. At all. It happens to so many women and they all keep it to themselves, buttoned all the way up. Oh, I don't know why. Maybe we just don't want to bother people with it. Because it's about blood, death and, you know, our parts, and nobody wants to think about those. It's not nice for people. Anyway, you're going to find the silence around it very hard, my duck. Very hard indeed. At least this way you're prepared for it.'

'I can't imagine coping with five. I can't imagine coping with this one.'

'It didn't get easier; I changed to accommodate it. We changed, my husband and me.'

The woman flinched a little, and Ida thought she wouldn't ask. She carried on. 'He wanted it more than me, at first, anyway. He gave up hoping round about the third one, but I was determined to prove I could do it. Needed to have a victory over my body, or God, or fate or something. Silly young fool I was. Should have just accepted it, I told myself later. Adopted, something. The last one broke him.'

She left the space between them, a courtesy. The woman finished her tea and set the cup down.

'My boyfriend doesn't know.'

Boyfriend, then.

'He's – we had all these conversations about, oh, aren't we lucky, neither of us want kids, they would just, like, stop us from doing what we want to. Don't we have this good life. And we do. We do. But I think – I don't really want to think about this, but if I'm honest, it's always been there – he's fourteen years younger than me, you see. And we keep it quiet, because of his family and his fans and all that, load of bullshit. But I think, if it came to it, I think nothing would scare him off faster than a baby shackling him to this. This mess. It doesn't seem to matter how many times he tells me otherwise, and I'm *not* asking him for it. I'm not. I'm not one of those needy fucking arscholes – sorry – always nipping away at their men, tell me you love me, tell me you love me. It's there, though.'

Ida nodded, squeezed her hand quickly, put it back under the table again. The woman turned away and put her face on the window for a while, shuddering out the occasional sob.

'The other thing you need to be prepared for is the way it will come back on you,' Ida said, after a pause. 'Some months away, maybe even years, you can think it's fine. You might have stopped remembering it every day, you might have moved on. And then you'll see something on telly, or maybe your body will do something, and it can hit you all over again. Often in the worst places. When you're at work. When you're waiting in the queue at the post office. Whenever your brain is running low on energy and has nothing to distract itself. Now that, that does get better over the years. It's the sort of thing a silly old woman *would* say, but time really is a great healer in this case. I want you to know that too.'

'But I need to get over it. I never wanted them. I never did. I actually got divorced because I never wanted them – did me a favour there, right enough. But still. I'm not the mothering kind. I'm just not. This doesn't make any sense.'

'Never mind all that. This is a physical trauma. It's happening to your body, which is flooding you with hormones, and they're unleashing all these emotions. You just need to let it happen for now. Get yourself somewhere safe for tonight – I overheard you say you're going to visit your mother?'

The woman snorted. 'She'll be no use. She's possibly the last person anyone would ever want to turn to in this situation. Ha! With such a fucking – sorry – shining example of glorious motherhood it's no wonder I didnay want kids, eh. It's not even her actual birthday – that was last week. She doesn't let me take her out on her actual birthday because she's always got plans with her husband and his people. And we have to meet in a big town away from where she actually lives because she's ashamed of me. She tells me as much. Every time. Yeah, that's going to be a real balm for the soul.'

Ida thought for a second.

'Do you know what I would do? Put her off for a night. Sometimes, I like to check myself into a hotel. One of the big ones, run by a big company. Maybe one with a spa. Somewhere where nobody knows you, and there are people on call to bring you what you want and call you Miss whatever-your-name-is. They give you a clean, lovely room with a door that locks behind you and a big dressing gown to put on. And you make that room yours, for a night, make it into whatever you want it to be. You'd need to spend a bit of money, mind you.'

The woman followed her eyeline, over the ripped jeans, shabby rucksack, chipped nail polish, and managed a bit more of a smile.

'I've never really agreed with that sort of place.'

'You've never been to one, then. You pick up a phone – it'll probably be someone from Poland or some place like that, because nobody British works in hotels any more it seems – and you tell them that you want steak and chips, maybe, and a glass of sherry. Whatever you fancy. And it comes to your door. And you can eat it on a big bed, or in a bubble bath. The whole point about these places is that they're anonymous and nobody asks any questions. These people are actually paid to serve you – you don't even have to thank them.' You could probably even swear at them if you like, seeing as it comes so naturally to you, she thought and didn't say.

'That's what I'm doing just now. Spa weekend in the Lakes. I just buried my sister – no, don't say you're sorry. You're not and I'm not, and that's fine. Organizing a funeral is a lot of work, so I'm going somewhere nice and far away to pay someone young and foreign to cover me in deep sea mud or whatever they call it and bring me a glass of champagne. Have you ever done anything like that? No? Well, you're missing out. There's a whole world out there designed to take your money and spoil you in return. It's not going to fix any of this, duck, but it will help you begin to get past it. If you ask a silly old lady.'

They drifted into silence until the announcement – ladies and gentlemen, we will shortly be approaching Oxenholme. The woman looked up as Ida began to gather her things. Huge, lost eyes. Ida pulled her coat on and bent down.

'Not here – this one's mine – but why don't you get off at the next stop. Penrith or Carlisle or something. Go to the taxi rank, ask the driver to take you to the most expensive hotel in the area.'

The woman shrugged a bit.

'Oh, for goodness' sake,' Ida said. She grabbed her purse and took out five twenties, pushed them across the table. 'You'll need more, but that's a good start.'

'I can't –'

'Well, I'm not taking it back, so it's either you or a big fat tip for that rude little ticket inspector. Go on.'

'Why are you –?'

'Because of the silence, duck. Because I know the silence.'

The woman blinked.

'Thank you. Thank you so much. I don't think you're a silly old lady, by the way.'

'Good,' said Ida. She pulled up the little handle of her smart new suitcase and stepped off the train. She thought of that woman running herself a big, deep bath, of the feeling of muscles unclenching in hot water. Perhaps this was the person she was going to be now, after May, after Reg, for the next twenty years or however long it pleased God to give her. It didn't feel half bad.

Scotland on Sunday, September 2013

Telling It Like It Is

Your week in politics with Brian McConn

Another day, another bona fide Scottish sleb zooms up the M24 and crashes into the independence debate.

This week's dose of low-wattage star power comes courtesy of Clio Campbell, who you might remember from her 1990s one-hit wonder . . . no?

Well how about that literal crime-scene of an album she came out with a few years ago, where she encouraged a bunch of East London thugs to urinate – I'm sorry, 'rap' – all over the work of our great bard Robert Burns while she trilled an off-key lesbian take on 'Highland Mary'? Forgotten that too? Lucky old you. Some of us haven't yet managed to scrub it from our brains.

Anyway, unlike her luvvie brethren in the cause (Alan Cumming and Brian Cox, to name but two), Miss Campbell has had the good grace to actually gift us her presence and (one presumes) tax monies before she began pronouncing on our constitutional question.

'I just felt a pull to come home again,' she said, loftily, in an interview granted to a pro-Nat website famed for its disregard for the spellchecker. 'I've travelled all across Europe to protest injustice, only to discover a really inspiring fight right here on my doorstep. I was taking a break from London to support the amazing work of the anti-austerity movement in Greece, and talking to the people there, seeing their passion for bringing about change to their own home, I suddenly knew that Glasgow, not London, was the place for me to be.'

While it's still unclear what exactly is so 'inspiring' to a so-called freedom fighter about supporting Big Eck's sleazy wee power-grab, at least we can count on this seasoned political campaigner to bring a much-needed touch of gravitas to the Yes campaign, eh?

Well, not exactly.

Miss Campbell made her entrance into the political arena with an appearance on BBC Scotland's *Big Debate* programme, hosted at Glasgow University with an all-student audience. Joining her on the panel were a couple of Nat wannabes from organizations with names like 'Business for Scotland' and 'English Scots for Yes' (all suspiciously Scottish-accented and un-business-suited, but they'll doubtlessly pop up on an SNP selection list near you soon), against the Right Honourable Gordon Duke MP, the well-spoken if quiet Lib Dem Mary Jackson, and the economist and voice of reason Jack Heughan. Really, though, it doesn't matter who else was there, as the event descended into a shouting match between Miss Campbell and Mr Duke, who, a source informs me, may have been romantically involved, back in the day. Easy to see why that's no longer the case. Screaming and shouting from the first moment Mr Duke dared to challenge one of her florid and sentimental assertions about the essentially left-wing nature of the Scottish psyche (which, as a Labour politician who has represented Glasgow constituencies for twenty-five years while she's been travelling London and Europe, one might assume he knows something about), anything melodic about the so-called singer's voice was lost in a banshee-like screech, which brought to mind the hysterical pitch of a maiden aunt lecturing boys in the street for running too quickly.

'Judas!' she whined at him, standing up and pointing a witchy fingernail, while the students in the audience, apparently unfamiliar with Miss Campbell's 'cool' former career as a pop star several years before their birth, sniggered openly.

Judging from a recent Yes Campaign press release, we can look forward to further interventions on the subject from Miss Campbell. They seem somewhat proud of their newest recruit, and good on them. What this debate was really missing was some authentic fishwife sensibility.

SAMMI

2009–11

In the end, Clio's newspaper contact – young, hungry, barely able to contain himself over the magnitude of the story that had fallen into his lap – had done all the sleuthing for them. They were helped by a whistleblower: another former police spy who had been embedded in the anti-fascist movement, who came forward after the first allegations broke. He'd been one of Mark's – Michael's – colleagues. Through this man's transcript, she learned that the undercover cops referred to them all, all the people they were spying on, as 'wearies'. An under-race, dreadlocked and earnest, unwashed and stupid; a different class of person. Maybe not a person at all. That will occur to Sam at nights, when she's lying there by herself, while Dale's big body sweats and farts beside her and there's no one at all to get her out of this. Maybe he didn't see her as a person. A body, right enough. A sexy body, and a passport into all this. She provided him with legitimacy; a young black girlfriend with impeccable radical credentials. Her nineteen-year-old body gave him cover and pleasure, and the rest didn't matter, because she wasn't a person. Not like the people he knew.

She flashes on to his face, again and again, the face of someone who did not exist. He had only ever been a performance, a sleight of hand and costume. She will imagine this man, this stranger, Michael Carrington, this Oxford-educated former public schoolboy, sneering at them all as he makes his monthly reports, sneering and despising the people he eats and sleeps and builds things with, the people he says he loves.

"'My hope is that by coming forward I'll be able to shine a spotlight on this gross abuse of police power,' Campbell said. "By being honest about what's been done to me here, in the United Kingdom, not in a so-called police state – and, let's be clear, what I experienced was nothing less than state-sanctioned rape—" Are you all right, love?' Dale put the paper down, stopped reading.

'I don't want to hear any more just now, OK?'

Sam turned up the volume on the telly. It amazed her that it all just seemed to happen, while she sat on the sofa with three days of baby sick on her tracky bottoms, seeing nobody but medical professionals. She'd been unable to produce any milk to feed Elliot. It felt like it had solidified in there, mastitis hitting her like flu. The community midwife put her cold hands on Sam's concrete-hard breasts, trying to milk her like a cow, but nothing came.

'Not to worry, Mummy. He's taking the bottle like a lickle champ, isn't he. Now. Shall we just pop your pants off and see how your perineum's doing?'

As she had promised, Clio took most of the press on herself, coming forward as the only witness willing to be named and using the shreds of her old faded fame to draw the headlines around her. The papers let her shine, allowed her to ascend to Madonna-like status; Clio required no contextualizing second name. She saw in newsprint Clio reincarnated as one of the policeman's 'many lovers' in a 'free love commune'; read a pseudonymed Fran ('Cecilia') describing how 'Officer 1' had pressured her into experimenting with her sexuality even though she'd protested she was a lesbian.

It got so bad Sam couldn't sleep in the same bed as Dale any more. Any tiny noise he made, she started, jumped, spent hours staring at him with her eyes watering onto the pillows, trying to see if his sleeping face gave anything away. She would wait till the baby woke and carry him downstairs for his bottle, lay him in the basket by the sofa and stare at the living-room ceiling. On a good night, she managed three hours' sleep. The bad nights felt like they were killing her.

One day she came home, and Dale and her brother were in the living room, a map of Surrey spread out on the coffee table.

'What you doing?' she asked. They didn't reply for a bit, and then her brother muttered, you know what we're doing, Sam.

'We're going to make that cunt pay, Sam. We're going to sort this for you.' Oh Dale, her man, always her man, shaking with the anger of it.

'You won't do that, love,' she said. 'How you going to do that? You're not a hard man.'

Sam herself gave testimony only three times. The first was to the lawyer her friend Kevin had found for them when she'd asked him, painting on a glib face – 'I've got these mates who need legal advice. Potentially huge case, ramifications across the entire justice system, but they've no money.' The second time was to Clio's excited young journalist, who came round to her house when the baby was two weeks old and stayed for hours, through naps and changes, not taking any hints. He phoned her again and again through-out the following months, checking her story, clarifying words and turns of phrase until Dale told him not to bloody call again and hung up.

The third time was in the small room where the hearing happened, Clio and Spider sitting outside sipping water in plastic cups, waiting for their turns, Avril walking Elliot round and round the corridors, bent over and moving at his toddler snail-pace till her back spasmed. Clio grabbed for her hand as she walked in. Sam did not return the grip.

*

It wasn't how she'd imagined telling her story. She'd hoped to take the stand, put her hand on the Bible and swear to tell the whole truth, clock a girl with Debbie's high cheekbones, about ten years younger than her in the courtroom, lean and golden and worried. Sammi had wanted to look right at Chief Inspector Michael Carrington, make him see her, and then move her eyes slowly and carefully over the crowd, so that he knew she was telling it all straight to the golden girl, the acknowledged and admitted daughter.

Instead, she sat at a table, with four other people in the room. The walls were very close; as though they'd been built around the table. Her lawyer, Alex, poured her water from a jug, a stack of glasses awaiting the next four people to file in. It felt like a job interview. The others were all in suits, in grey. One of them told her in official, formal language that the proceedings would be recorded. There were wrapped biscuits, on a plate.

She'd known it would be like this – Alex had told her – but she'd still dressed carefully, as though for court. As though she was going to see him again. She'd put on lipstick, she'd contoured her cheek fat, pulled out an expensive scarf she'd got from work colleagues for her thirtieth and never worn. She'd positioned it with her granny's brooch. She wanted to look like a professional woman. Someone who mattered. Someone who you couldn't sneer at or deny.

She had known he wouldn't be there. But some bit of her thought he would want to come. Knowing it was happening. Knowing she would be testifying that day. Wouldn't he at least want to reason with her, give her some – any – sort of explanation?

No, it seemed, he didn't. But he would hear this testimony, wouldn't he? Mark or Michael, he would need to know every single thing that was being said. That sort of vanity, that wasn't the kind of thing you could fake, shrug on and off for the sake of playing a character. So she spoke to the recorder, to them all, through them all to him, imagining that worried, radiant blonde daughter, sunlight from the window pooling in a halo round her head.

'I remember it was the first night we had a party in the squat,' she said. 'I'd been up on the roof. It must have been about six in the morning. The party had died down – there was a lot of people sleeping in heaps, in the living room, in the bath. There was a party still raging in the free-shop space, but the power had run out so there was no more music. I could hear noises coming from the office, where we ran the magazine from, so I went along to investigate. There was Mark – sorry, there was Chief Inspector Carrington. He was naked, and he'd got this girl bent over the layout desk. He was fucking her in the arsehole – I'm sorry. He was – sodomizing – her? The look on his face, I've always remembered it. This expression of wild joy, like he couldn't believe his life. Like something feral. He was utterly and totally happy. His hands were on the small of her back, pushing her down, and he was staring at his own coc— *penis* going in and out.'

Mark's daughter, she'd imagined, would shudder, cry out, hide her face in her hands at this point.

'In and out. In and out. Fast. I remember thinking it must have hurt her. Anyway, eventually he saw me, and he reached out an arm to me. He called me his Nubian princess and asked me to come and join them. I took a couple of steps into the room, and then I recognized the girl. She was part of this group of schoolgirls who had been hanging around the place. She wasn't an activist, or anything, she wasn't in with us. Fucking this girl wasn't going to get him any more sort of credibility or bolster his position in any way.

'I went over, and he put his hand up my top and kissed me, bent me down beside this girl. I could see her face then – she looked totally out of it, drugs or something. Something. I was speaking to her, saying, here, babe, you OK? I mean, I was just nineteen then, when me and Mark – sorry, Inspector Carrington – were together, but this girl must've been even younger than that. Sixteen, maybe? Younger? I was worried. Mark didn't seem to care, he was busy pulling my skirt up. I said, Mark, you've got to stop, this girl needs her bed, man. And he was like, no, she's fine, aren't you? And she said yeah, yeah, I'm fine.

Fuck off. So I thought, fair enough, if the girl's consented. But I didn't want anything to do with that scene after that, so I left them to it. He got straight back into her, sawing away. And I think about that now, knowing what I know, and I think, he must have been really dedicated to his role, Chief Inspector Carrington must have been, to go that deep under cover. I imagine it was a real hardship for him, having to have anal sex with drugged-up teenage girls at parties when he'd much rather have been home with his wife and children.'

She had planned saying this for weeks, lying awake in the dark on the sofa while Elliot murmured in his sleep. The golden daughter would have been crying now, and she would have looked from her to Chief Inspector Michael Carrington, whose face would have turned a chalky grey. She would have looked him right in the eye. A ripple would have gone around the courtroom as she paused for effect.

Instead, the questioning continued, soberly, none of the people in the room seeming to feel the impact of what she'd said. He'd hear it, though, wouldn't he? He'd read the transcripts. He'd demand to. He'd hear his actions read back to him and he'd have to admit – even to himself. Surely.

Forty minutes later she was back outside, the door shut behind her and the dank smell of the squat in her mouth. There was red hair rising all around her and a sharp blast of perfume as Clio pulled her in for a hug.

'You brave girl. You brave, brave girl. How are you feeling? You've done so well. Honestly. You've done the right thing.'

'Your mum had to take the little fella out, matey,' said Spider, standing up and endeavouring to support the hug without touching either of them. ''E was kicking off something chronic. Got some lungs on him, eh? Well, you'll have heard that.'

No, she hadn't. She hadn't heard anything at all.

*

They were planning Elliot's second birthday when the offer came in. Well, Dale was planning it. Sam was lying in bed in Debbie's old room with her phone in her hand and Dale was sitting outside the door calling options through to her.

'A bouncy castle, love. I know a bloke who can get us one for thirty quid, for the whole afternoon. And if we're doing it in your mum's church? Well, more to spend on the boy, int there?'

Beautiful Dale. It's not you, he had kept telling her. This is just a thing you're going through. Because of the bad stuff that's been done to you. It will pass, love. For better and worse, eh? He'd still say that even as she packed her suitcase, even as the taxi pulled up.

But on this day, she was lying on Debbie's sweat-stained bed, having refused to change the sheets in the five months since Debbie had gone to stay with her grandmother. The phone in her hand rang, loudly, and she looked at it for a few seconds, in surprise, before pressing the button.

'Samantha,' said Alex the lawyer. 'They've offered a settlement.'

'What is all this supposed to be about? Settling? Settling?'

Clio dispensed with all pleasantries, any preamble, and marched past her into the house. Sam stood there on the doorstep, tea-splashed dressing gown to the world, muttering to the street, 'No, please do come inside won't you?'

'You can't settle, Sammi. What are you doing to us?'

Clio stood in the living room, poised and incongruous between the pile of Duplo and the overflowing ironing basket, hair on fire in the blind-slatted sunlight. The angel of death, the angel of something awful, anyway, always returning to toss her out of any crappy little Eden she managed to scrape together.

'Kitchen, please,' she found the strength to say, gesturing to Elliot, his round eyes popping at the visitor from another planet. On her way out of the room she pushed the volume control on the remote hard.

In the kitchen, she put the kettle on, a reflex that came as naturally to her as breathing, found herself thankful for the few seconds of time it had bought her.

'I'm not going to ask how you got my address. But I am going to say that I've already made it perfectly clear that I do not like these kind of surprise visits.'

'Well, if you won't respond to my messages, what am I supposed to do?'

'I don't have to reply to you, Clio. You are not my bank, my kid's school, the emergency services or my mother.'

'No. I'm just the co-defendant in a case you've decided to throw. A case we had agreed was one of the most important political actions of the day, probably the most important thing we'd ever do.'

'I don't remember agreeing to that. Don't go putting even more words in my mouth, woman. I'm bout having enough of it already.'

'What do you mean?'

'The interviews. The speaking over me in meetings, and with the lawyers. You you you all over the papers.'

'We talked about that. As a group. I went public to get us noticed and to protect you. Draw the heat.'

'Protect me?' Sam wheeled round on her, holding onto the worktop to stop herself from flying across the lino, claws outstretched. 'Protect me. Well, a right bloody good job you've done there, Clio Campbell. Gold fucking star to you. Do you even see me? Look at me. Really, really look at me. I can't work because I have a nervous fucking breakdown half the time I leave this house. I ain't got dressed in about a week, I don't reckon. That little boy through there – him's two year old and this is all the mamma he's ever known, this fucking useless husk of a thing who sits around crying and shaking, because this fucking carry-on of yours has been going on for longer than he's even been alive – and my little girl won't even talk to me, don't even live here no more, because she don't understand why her mum just emotionally fucking disappeared on her and can't look her in the eye.

I got trauma flashbacks every night, my marriage has fallen to pieces and ain't going back together any way that I can see, and every morning I have to force myself to go downstairs, make a cup of tea and not just open my fucking wrists in a bath. So yes. Nice protection you gave me there.'

The kettle screamed, that tinny electronic whistle Dale had thought was classy, and she turned away to sort it out.

'Sammi. Sammi.' There was a hand on her back, the accent thick, glossy Scottish honey. 'I had no idea. That's so shit. That's so, so shit. What he's done to you. What they've done to you. But this is exactly why we've got to keep fighting. They destroyed your life; you're clearly suffering PTSD and they fart out that insulting wee offer to wash their hands of you – we can get psychological evidence, really shame them—'

'NO.' It was the biggest, loudest word she'd ever put into the air. It reverberated. They were both silent, as a new episode of *Teletubbies* cued itself up on the DVD player, all birdsong and sweetness.

'Mumma?' yelled Elliot.

'You stay here,' Sam muttered, clenched fists at Clio as she pushed past her.

Elliot was standing near the kitchen door, tiny and lost. She picked him up and took him back through to the calm, glowing telly, held him tight on the sofa for a second, his little face warm and wet in her neck.

'Mumma crying.'

'Yes, darlin. Yes, my baby love. Mumma's always crying, int she? Just being silly. Do you want to watch *Teletubbies*? Just for a little minute more? Look, here's your blankie, and here's Boss Teddy. Yeah? Mumma be back soon, eh?'

Clio was stirring a spoon around a mug. Even the clinking of it made Sam want to break something.

'You are going to go now. You are too much. You've been too much in my life. We was fine. We was proper and honest happy before you turned up, tipped everything in the air and dragged me off on your fucking stupid crusade.'

'My what?'

'I mean it.'

'My crusade? Sammi, this was a thing done to you. A giant, terrible wrong. We have been working to right it. Don't blame me for the corrupt, horrendous actions of the state. We're taking action for every woman in the country – for every citizen of this country – to stop them living in fear of surveillance culture . . .'

She'll say 'state-sanctioned rape' next, thought Sam.

'. . . of state-sanctioned rape. Listen, my sister. My girl. I canny pretend to know what this has been like for you, just like I canny take this burden from you, much as I want to. But I can be here with you, eh? I can walk beside you. I can hold your hand. It's you and me, Sammi. We've got to stick together. We've got to stand up, working-class girls, to this obscenity being done to us by this upper-class, patriarchal—'

'Oh stop. Stop trying to say we're the same. You've always gone on about this and I've always secretly been, like, *what* – because, babe, we blatantly ain't the same. Just because we both grew up poor don't mean a thing. Don't mean that we both had the same life experience. Don't mean that you ain't been able to disappear into a crowd, or put some different clothes on and blend in with power. I'm a black woman in a poor fucking neighbourhood I've almost never left. I always got to be working eight times as hard to prove myself worthy of a job, that I got even half a brain, that I know and understand theory or might have read a book once in a while. You? You fucking float above it, don't you? Poor, sure. But beautiful, white, famous, talking your good fight and singing your lovely folk songs all round the world. This, for you, this is a publicity campaign. This is a hobby you doing just now. Your latest *thing*. Because that's how you stitched yourself together a life out a bunch of floaty fucking scarves or something. None of them touch the ground. It's my life, Clio. My. Fucking. Life. My home, my babies, my husband, my job, the day-to-day boring fucking reality of living in the one place trying to keep the kids fed and watching the telly on the same sofa every night. You got to pick not to do that. And then you try and speak for me. You get the spotlight on you and you use it to put your own words round my story, take more away from me on top of what those police cunts already got. For why? Because you was bored? Lonely? I don't know. But last week I got a phone call offering me money and an end. I'm taking that. I'm getting off. This stops now. And you can go. Out here –' She gestured to the back door, which opened on to the echoey concrete alley that led to the street. 'I don't want him seeing you again. I don't want me seeing you again.'

'Sammi. I – OK. OK, I'm going. But I did this out of principle. I couldn't let you go on living without knowing this. I couldn't. You had to find this out, and it had to be stopped. For the world.'

Two hundred and fifty thousand pounds. Not that much for a life. Not really. Alex wanted to push for more, and she knew through him that Clio and Fran did too, but she couldn't take another second of this. It didn't stop, though. Even knowing the money was coming, even after more months, once her bank statement was swollen with zeros, didn't make anything stop. Dale set up counselling appointments for her and she watched the minutes ticking up to them, unable to leave Debbie's old bed. One day she found herself, each muscle shot through with sheer red anger, picking up a stropping, flailing Elliot and throwing him down onto the sofa. He giggled a little, looked up at her as though the game was going to continue, then he stopped, stared at her face. She locked herself in the bathroom, away from him, texted Avril to come round and get him.

'At least tell me where you're going. Please, babe. Please, my love.'
    'You don't need me around right now, darlin.'

'Yes I do. We all need you. That boy there needs his mummy, don't he?'

'Yeah. I got to go and see if I can get her back.'

She had left the country by air three times before: twice as little Sammi Smith, flying to Jamaica to see her cousins, fighting with her brother till her mother separated them; once as Samantha Burke, a married woman with her new husband and old daughter, off to a resort in Turkey, sitting squashed up on a charter flight twitchy with casual racists. She'd never been this alone. *Get the bus to the ferry port, or a taxi if you'd rather (it'll cost way more!)*, her instructions said. She needed that taxi, though, the air-conditioned space and plush head-rest, tinted windows to watch the tower blocks and balcony washing lines of a foreign country through.

Samantha Burke had never been on a ferry before. She'd never been on a boat of any sort, she realized. Not even the paddle boats on the park pond because Avril had always been terrified of them. She watched her fellow travellers vomiting over the railings, the violence and force the waves slapped the boat's sides with as the sun beat down hard, and couldn't feel anything physical at all.

Xanthe was there, at the shabby little port, a tall column of sense in a yellow sundress and two firm hands on her shoulders.

'You do not need to talk to me at all tonight. You don't even need to talk to me in the car. I am going to get you to your room, show you how to work the shower, then let you lie in some nice clean sheets for as long as you need to. You got me, sis?'

The car smelled of patchouli, of Fran burning oils around the squat to try and ward off the damp, of so many of the things she was trying to get away from that Sam, slumped in the back seat, dug her fingernails deep into her palms and wondered if she was making a huge mistake.

*

She woke to sunlight, white cotton, the white ceiling of her cave room, light purple drapes floating, green leaves peeping round the sides and a great mounting pressure of dread in her chest. Xanthe found her curled on the floor around her suitcase an hour or so later when she looked in to let her know lunch was ready.

'I'm so sorry, Xanthe. I shouldn't be here. I shouldn't have come. I can't cope with it, or with anything, and instead of just removing myself from the whole situation I've gone and landed you with a big bloody problem instead, int I? Maybe – I'm thinking I could go to a hotel or something and just leave you be if you could just get me a taxi or the like I dunno.'

Xanthe said nothing, hugged her.

That first day, she only made it to the terrace outside the house, walked around the circumference, staring down the hill at the road and the cliffs and sea just beyond it.

The air was so clear and warm, the sea a more real colour than anything Sam could think of back home. The stonework had all been painted white, the land was scrubby khaki, disrupted by extraordinary flashes of magenta flowers sprouting from far-off buildings. There was nobody else around, nothing making a noise. Nobody at all here but herself. No one she loved had any idea where she was. She knew this was what she'd wanted, but now, faced with it, she felt everything was wrong.

She was sitting under the trellis, in the shade of what she supposed were vine leaves, her feet tracing the pattern of a mosaic in the stone. The paperback she'd picked up from the tiny shelf in the house sat splayed on her lap. An Agatha Christie, the only book there that didn't have 'mindfulness' in its title. She watched a tall brown figure, sunglasses and shorts, make her way across the road, a big clay pot held across her hip. As she came further up the stairs, Sam realized it wasn't Xanthe.

'Mum thought you might like some of this. Fava beans. She said to tell you that it's got to be made with love. Brought you some bread too, and a pot of olives.'

'Bloody hell. You're never Dido? I ain't seen you since you was a baby! Like, I mean, just learning to walk and stuff. You took your first steps into my hands!'

She heard the words come spilling out of her like the embarrassing old auntie she'd always known she'd turn into, her accent meeting the girl's faint cockney and growing broader in its light.

Dido smiled, awkward, didn't know where to look.

Sam watched her walk back down, crossing the road with all the confidence of someone who knew no cars were ever going to hit her. She must be coming up eighteen years old, Dido, those long legs a physical manifestation of the time passed. An entire adult's worth of space between Sammi Smith and Samantha Burke.

The sun began to set, like no sunset she'd ever encountered in London. The whole dome of sky glowing other-worldly, alien pink. Out on what she'd assumed was a clifftop car parking space by Xanthe's house, three figures unrolled mats, saluted the sea. Xanthe and her daughter were the same height, Sam noted – she couldn't tell which was which at this distance. The third was shorter, long hair, but still recognizably male – must be the boyfriend.

Fran had done yoga occasionally in the squat, had tried to get the rest of them into it. Sam remembered having to contort her legs (sometimes forcibly, using her hands to place them where they wouldn't go), the stiff strain on Fran's face, Spider farting and the whole thing dissolving into giggles. This was something else, something very beautiful to see, the three silhouettes engaged in some sort of primal dance, fluid, worked in harmony with the sky and the water, gradually bringing their bodies lower and lower to the ground as the sun sank behind the sea and the moon got brighter.

There are other ways of being in the world, aren't there, she thought. There is space, standing still for a while, taking it all in. Of course, having the money to buy that space helped.

She watched the two women particularly, noting how closely together they stood, their movements in mirror image. The harmony. On their way back into the house, one of them – she assumed Dido – looped her arm round the other's neck. Sam ached for Debbie.

'Do you want to talk about it at all?'

They were sitting on a beach, just twenty minutes' sweaty, sun-rocked road-walk away from the house. Red cliffs enclosed them from the road and anyone else; their little woven rug was spread on dark red sand, surprisingly soft. Old blood, flowing into that shockingly turquoise sea. It was too much, was what it was.

'Do you know what I can't get over, Xanth? The colours. Colours here are, like, colours with the brightness turned all the way up. Why don't we have colours this bright in the city? We're good at faking shit, ain't we?'

Xanthe nodded, poured them both a glass of wine from the bottle in her shoulder bag, replaced the stopper.

Sam took a sip. 'That wasn't a no, by the way. I just don't know how to start. I don't know what to say.'

'Yeah. I'm not sure I would.'

'Thing is, I need to start talking about it, don't I? Otherwise it's going to eat me up. I can't just be this silent thing in the house, sitting about crying while my husband looks after the little one, saving it all up to scream in Clio Campbell's face every two years. It's going to kill me, innit?'

'Clio? You screamed at Clio?'

'Mate. You have no idea.'

And it unlocked, the resentment spewing out of her throat into the air around them. Words and words and words.

'Steamrollered, Xanthe. I feel like she steamrollered me,' Sam found herself saying in conclusion. 'She took it all down – my life, everything I thought I knew about myself, particularly my relation-ship with Debbie. It's all gone. I'm just here, sitting on a beach with someone I haven't seen in years, wondering if there's even any point in my going back. I used to think at least I'm good for people, you know? My life might not have been the most wonderful –' she flapped a dismissive hand at that sea, its obscenity of hue '– but I was doing the best with it. I was a good mum to Debbie. I helped kids in my job. I could actually hold down a job. I was in love and could love back. And it broke me, the case, the knowledge. I exist in a house with a man of infinite fucking patience who says he loves me and shows it every day and I wake up terrified and sometimes wondering if I should kill him before it's all revealed a second time. I'm poison in that house, now. I'm poison to my kids. I can't separate that from her, and that she didn't even stop to consider for one second what knowing all – *this* – would do to me.'

She stopped. This was too far. Something about being able to say this to a face from the past that had made her relax more than she ought to have done. That face; Xanthe's, familiar, but older, motherly, calm and absent of the thousand quick frustrations Sam realized she'd expected to find there. It occurred to her she didn't know that she could trust it. In fact, given what she'd already found out about her old comrades, why would the one who was hiding out in Greece, the one who'd refused to testify or get involved, but had replied immediately when a post-settlement Sam had asked her if she could come and stay at her retreat, not be in on it? What if Xanthe had bought this place with a payout from the police? What if this was an extended experiment on her, to see how she was reacting psychologically? What if they were watching her in that little sunny room in the house? Sam thought all of these things at lightning speed, registered each one in the time it took Xanthe to open her mouth for a reply, and stood up, dusted the sand from her legs, gestured towards the sea.

'I can go in that, yeah? I mean, there ain't sharks or nothing?'

'No sharks. Not this close to the shore. But take it easy, eh? You've had a big glass of wine on a hot day. Don't go too far out. Make sure your feet can touch the bottom.'

Sam grunted, as though Xanthe were a nagging schoolteacher issuing orders, discarded her wrap and strode out into the water in the pregnancy swimming costume she still fitted, almost three years on. It wasn't cold. She'd been expecting cold. The ocean floor was pebbled, uneven; she must look to Xanthe on the shore like a foal trying to walk, a complete novice. Little city girl in the big sea. She stopped for a second, swore out loud at its uninterrupted hugeness, its cunty beauty, the cheek of it, pressed on shakily. Once she got to waist-height she squatted down, let it all pool about her, not cold but still a shock on the overheated skin of her back. She tried swimming strokes, just with her arms at first, then pushed off with her feet, knees bumping along the rocks below. It was nothing like swimming at the Brockwell Lido. She was aware all the time of everything being much bigger and wilder than herself, the floor untiled, the force of waves and currents. There was nothing and nothing in front of her, and it was blue. The waves blew up, slapped her face, salt water up her nose making her cough and lose her footing. There was nothing underneath and she panicked, choked, wondered if she would sink. It would matter. It would matter if she did.

Turning herself around in the water, she realized she hadn't come very far at all. She could still make out Xanthe's face, a friendly arm extended and waving gently at her. She doggy-paddled her way back to where she could feel rocks under foot again and told herself she was a fucking idiot.

She was surprised at how quickly her skin dried off. Xanthe received her back to their picnic with smiling silence. There were vine leaves and flatbread unwrapped from waxy wrappers waiting for her, and she filled her mouth gratefully.

'Listen, mate. I went too far there. You must be wondering what sort of psychopath you've given houseroom to. Honestly, I'm not – I'm not a risk.'

'I didn't think you were, Sam. I'd be more worried if you seemed absolutely fine about the whole thing.'

'I just don't know how I'm supposed to go about rebuilding myself now. What does a person do?'

Xanthe breathed out, reached into her bag and lit a cigarette.

'It takes time, and it takes a lot of strength. You just need to be sure enough of yourself to have something to hold on to.'

Sam hadn't smoked since she'd had Debbie, but something about the smell, out here in the sunshine, was making her reconsider. She motioned to the packet and Xanthe nodded, exhaled, continued.

'Talking from personal experience, the main thing I found was not to let it bury you. Keeping a good hold of your self, your selfhood. If you've got that you can fight for it.'

'Oh God. I don't know if I have any more.'

'Well, you're here. You did this. I think you still do, Sammi. Honestly. And treat yourself like a pressure valve. You've got to, got to let it out. Got to have some sort of release. Someone to talk to, something to punch. There has to be something. Remember how angry I was in my twenties? I felt all the time like a coiled spring, one wrong touch away from . . . *boom*. No pressure valve.'

They stared at the sea for a second and then Xanthe steered them away.

'I can't say I'm surprised; what you're saying about Clio. She was always a bit of a forceful one. Took no prisoners. I was following the case through the English papers here and I did wonder why there was so much focus on her. I mean, I get it, she's sort of famous, and the rest of you were staying anonymous, but – well, her and Mark—'

'Ha! They didn't like each other. Too fucking similar. Other people were just fucking collateral damage. For both of them.'

'Well. She certainly liked us to be an attentive audience.'

'What does it take, though? To be that focused on one thing, your political ideal, or your fucking undercover mission or whatever, that you just roll over actual other humans? Know what I'm saying?'

'Bearing in mind I haven't seen her for fifteen years, she did always seem a bit, well . . . There was always so much going on, but I don't know if she actually had anyone properly close to her. Did she? She would come and go from us as she pleased, and I envied her freedom at the time, but I don't think she was returning anywhere. I rather got the impression that we were the home she was coming back to. And none of us were really that tight-knit. Not really.'

'Nah, she's strictly short-term, mate. And it's warped her, I reckon. She's, like, physically unable to see that other people might make deeper connections. Might want to put down roots. Belong to something other than a cause.'

Sam left the island four days later, the same route that she'd come. She wasn't cured, she knew that. But she could feel the sea lurch and spin beneath her on the boat. She'd held an aum, chanting at the sun with Dido, Xanthe and Xanthe's gentle boyfriend Nico, found something in that strange harsh sound reverberating through her throat, her chest, her body that had made her feel a bit more like one person, body and mind, one being even, again. For a couple of days there, she'd become the sort of person she would have laughed at at home. The sort of person she hoped she would laugh at again.

Using the Wi-Fi at the airport, she booked herself into a hotel not far from Avril's house. Streets she'd know, but not her house. Just as the cabin crew were doing their safety check, she tapped out a message to her mother, that she'd be back tomorrow, she wouldn't be staying at the house, and she'd like to see Debbie as soon as she could.

'You know what, Xanthe,' she'd said, sitting at the kitchen table the night before as Xanthe sliced fruit. 'I don't think it's that I'm jealous of you exactly. I mean, it's stunning and calm here and everything, but I don't think I could do it, out here all the time. I need a bit of bustle, me. I need a bit of ugly in my day-to-day. That sea would just piss me off, if I had to look at it every morning. What you got with Dido, though. That. I don't know if I'm ever going to have that again, with either of my kids. Specially not with Debbie. Not now.'

Xanthe turned and hugged her from behind, long brown arms looped over the chair and round her shoulders. This was a lot of physical contact for Sam, but she relaxed into it. Her friend smelled of sun cream and oil.

'You just need to let her back in, I reckon. Does she know? About all the . . . stuff?'

'She knows I was involved in a court case. That's all.'

'How old is she now? Sixteen?'

'Fifteen. Near enough sixteen.'

'They know more than you give them credit for at that age. Do you reckon she could take it?'

'I reckon she probably could.'

'That's what you have to do, then.'

In the years that followed, it would be gently suggested to Samantha Burke and Samantha Smith, by psychologists, during marriage counselling sessions, and at various survivors' groups, that she was too focused on Clio Campbell, that she was perhaps using her anger at Clio as a distraction from probing the real issues and how they had affected her.

'You're distancing yourself,' said one of them, one of their voices, and Sam had wanted to say, actually, no, you're wrong. This is when I'm closest to myself. But she nodded and swallowed it and tried to show them progress and healing.

It was easy to avoid her, avoid hearing of her. The anonymity Clio herself had ensured was built into Sam's interactions with the journalists and lawyers made it easy for her to drop back out of sight. Clio, she understood from occasional swipes up onto her Facebook page, at night, when the feelings were strongest, had moved home to Scotland, was involved in some other political campaign up there, posted links to articles with increasingly hysterical capital letters.

Dale woke up one night, glanced over at the glowing screen and sighed.

'Babe. Again? This woman again. You need to stop it. Everyone's said.'

It was one of the last nights they'd spend together, the relation-ship already broken beyond fixing. Dale said no, and he kept on saying no – for better or worse, he said, crying, holding onto her hand – but Sam couldn't stand the nights spent red-eyed and scanning his face, the secret compulsion to check his phone all the time, the very double fact of him in her – that she knew with her conscious brain he was as loyal and honest a man as you could find, but there would always be a second voice whispering secrets and doubts whenever he was in her line of vision.

'I don't know if I'm ever going to be able to be with anyone again, love. I think this is it for me. You need to be with someone with a brain that works right. You're too nice a man for all this.' Get out, get out, get out. Eventually she had had to physically shove him out of the door, both of them in tears. And she sat down on her sofa, no longer anybody's love, anybody's body, just a mother, a daughter, a woman on her own. Debbie came downstairs, sleepy in her big T-shirt.

'He's gone then?'

'He's gone, baby.'

'He was good, Mum. A good man.'

'He'll still be a good man, my love. And a good daddy to your little brother and a good stepdaddy to you if you want him. But I couldn't ask him to stay. Not with this old broken thing your mum. It wasn't fair. You see?'

Debbie curled herself into her mother's side. They didn't touch often any more, and Debbie was a lithe giraffe of a girl, towering over Sam by a good head and a half. Sam marvelled at how small her grown daughter could make herself, how their soft selves still slotted together.

'You ain't that old, Mum. Not really.'

She grinned, her lovely face nobody's but her own in that second.

ADELE
Royal Alexandra Hospital, Paisley, 2015

Something about the way the lights flickered in the foyer of the building always seemed to activate a switch in Adele's head. She'd noticed it over the years, a different way of existing and responding to things when on the ward, as though she processed emotion through a thick protective suit, a layer of blubber or something. The fact was, you needed to keep all the normal, instinctive human reactions at bay to be any good at this job. They had to be superseded by practicality, by logic, by process and knowledge. Years ago, when she was still new to this, a boy with the exact same date of birth as her Jamie had come in. Seventeen. Smashed up. Motorcycle crash. Never regained consciousness. She'd tried to blank out the older nurses muttering that he never would, but couldn't quite hold the tears in, ended up shouting at Pat the charge nurse in the tea-break room. Pat had sat her down and calmly, kindly told her that they couldn't afford to think this way.

'Take ten minutes, my dear. It's all I can give you, I'm afraid. Come back out ready to give that boy the care he needs till he breathes his last, or decide that you can't do it, and look for another job.'

Adele had shuddered, everything crashing over her, and Pat had reached for her shoulders.

'Listen. Every single nurse who comes to ICU has one of these moments. Every single one. All of them out there, and a few who decided they couldn't. I don't judge them that can't, you know. Better to find it out early. Not everyone can do this job. I think you can, though.'

Adele had, in the end, been in the room when the consultant had broken it to the boy's mother, had held her hand tight, tight as they switched the life support off. She'd pushed through three night shifts in a row, making the drive home with the radio on in the dim morning light, poured herself cereal then climbed into bed beside Dougie's warm form, eye mask to block out the sun, wax earplugs to block out the noise of Dougie getting the boys up for school, woken at three, showered, prepared a lasagne for them all, eaten, taken five minutes to curl up with the cat in the silence of the living room before turning the car back on to the motorway, walked swiftly back through that foyer with the change of light on her eyes. Only after the third shift, when she awoke into a free space where nothing was expected of her for two whole days, did she allow it to come out. She took herself out of the house, walked down by the canal, past the bit of the path popular with joggers, and cried, for that boy and her boy and both of their mothers.

'Nobody's asking you to be a robot,' Pat had said. 'It's just a matter of compartmentalizing, isn't it? We just have to work through the things later. I'm not going to say it gets easier, just that you get better at it.'

Eight years on, and she would say that yes, it probably had. And she had. To an extent. Three hours into her shift that day, and they got word of a new patient coming in from A&E.

'Female, probably late forties/early fifties. Suicide attempt. As yet unidentified but they're working on it.'

'Yours, Adele,' the charge nurse had said.

2013–14

Dougie had had on his politics show when she got home. She usually snapped at him to shut it off; her jangled nerves couldn't take the shouting they all did, not after a twelve-hour shift. This time, though, there was a voice, one she hadn't heard for decades, and the voice was in her living room.

Cliodhna Johnstone had always had that silky, twisty way of speaking, so that even when she was just raising her hand to give an answer in class the others would always hush to quiet. It made her a target, just as much as the big head of ginger frizz, the strange golden eyes always darting about, the way her singing rose above the others as they droned out the hymns and Burns in assembly. Just as much as her weird name – Jean, the teachers had called her, and she'd refuse to respond. Cliodhna, she'd said, when pressed. *Clee-oh-nah*, and it sounded like music. 'Jean is my *middle* name.'

That wee pointy chin, aimed at the ceiling to hide the wobbling. At first she'd been skelped for it. What a thing, Adele thought now, whacking tiny, five-year-old palms with a ruler just because their owner asked to be called something else. They got you submissive early in that place. Beat out anything that could maybe even begin to grow into cheek. Jean she became, until high school; until she revealed she'd been wearing that name under her clothes all this time, holding it tight to her. And Adele, sharing the bus with her and the other kids from the village all the way to the big school in the town, admired her for it from behind a magazine.

On the bus, Cliodhna befriended that weird couple of older girls from up the hill, and Adele heard them call her Clio; she seemed to arrive at the big school a newly christened, fully formed person, sloughing off her former primary-school classmates and names. Adele would see her in the corridors sometimes, although they never shared a class, laughing and chatting and shoving into people, hiding cigarettes at break time with a new gang who all stood over on the opposite street corner and wore lots of make-up.

Adele stayed close to the children she'd grown up with; they walked together in a pack around the school, were known as the 'sooties from the village', miners' kids. They looked out for each other as the popular kids faked hacking coughs behind their backs, didn't really mingle.

She remembered sitting in the study hall near the music block once, listening in to the conversation behind her. The girls were all in her class, but they might as well have been a different species.

'I mean it,' Clio was saying. 'Robert Burns was full-on sexy! Have you not seen the pictures? It's right there in the back of the book they give us; just not in the bits they read out to us in class. He just got to go around getting all these girls pregnant – he had about thirty kids – and dropping them, and everyone would say oh, pal, och Rabbie, it's fine because you're so talented and handsome. Typical man thing.'

'Men,' said one of the other girls, knowledgeably.

'So his love, the one like a rose?'

'One of many,' Clio said, wise. 'He shagged about like nobody's business. And I bet it's dirty. I bet he's talking about her nipples or something.'

Clio did 'A Red, Red Rose' at the school Burns Night concert that year. She stepped into the wobbly spotlight, apparently shy and unsure of herself, plucked three frail notes from her school-issued acoustic guitar and cleared her throat before she began to sing. The assembly hall went silent like it never was.

The Clio Johnstone who won the prizes for her singing each year, who was tall and beautiful and famous around the school, faded gradually away into a slump of shoulders during the half-hour bus trip back to the village each afternoon, while the 'sooties' grew back into themselves again as they got home. Clio didn't come down the village cross with the others, never showed up at anyone's house for the party if they had an empty. Adele would see her walking along the street with her two weird pals, or just by herself, would offer her a half-smile if there was nobody else around, would sometimes get one back.

How strange, she thought now, to have grown up side by side with somebody, breathing the same bad air from the run-offs, singing the same songs at school, and not have anything to say to them. But at fourteen, fifteen, most of the village kids knew where their lives were going – the boys were really just kicking their heels, counting the hours till they would join their fathers down the pits; some of them already coupled up with the girls they would marry. Clio Johnstone looked at them, found them wanting, kept herself separate. And Adele resented and envied her for it in equal measure. Then there was the scandal, and Clio disappeared, and they talked about her in whispers for a while, but soon after that the strike failure and pit closure had forced Adele and most of her classmates to leave home anyway, scatter to the bigger towns around in search of apprenticeships, secretarial courses, in order to support suddenly unemployed parents. She'd completely forgotten about Clio Johnstone's disgrace by 1990, the summer that Jamie was a newborn and that voice came drifting back through the radio every time she switched it on, it seemed. Rise up. People got to rise up.

There was that voice now, on the telly, as Dougie watched and Adele didn't snap at him to switch that shit off. That voice, talking about how Scotland had always voted differently from England, how there was a democratic deficit. Saying that this was a fresh chance, a new start – an opportunity to make the kind of country they wanted. Then, she said, we could rescue the NHS. Adele found herself staying, leaning in the doorway, taking it in.

'I went to school with her. She's from the village,' she said.

'Aye?' Dougie muttered, eyes on the box.

The man sitting opposite Clio had a particularly irritating smug chuckle. It farted out of his mouth whenever Clio spoke, announcing that an interjection was coming. 'Jesus,' Adele found herself hissing. 'Just let the lassie get a sentence out.'

Dougie had begun to chuckle right along with the man. 'Aye, he's right enough there. Tell you something, your school pal's talking a fair bit of pish.'

The man on the telly swept a palm through thick silvery hair, spread his arms and legs wide in his chair, leaned forward to the camera and began a monologue. He reminded Adele of that consultant prick she'd had to argue with last month, the way he'd dismissed her with a pat on the shoulder.

'Who is he, that guy?' she asked Dougie.

'Godsake, Adele, you just never know any of the politicians, do you? That's Gordon Duke. An MP. He was the housing minister or something. Naw – he was health! You ought to know that! Pals with Brown and Blair, that lot. He's always on the telly.'

Cliodhna was trying to talk, turn it back into conversation, but the man allowed her no space, using practised tricks to keep ploughing on. As the camera cut back to her face she got more and more agitated, and Adele could understand why. The moderator sitting in between them seemed to have no interest in letting her speak either. Suddenly she jumped up, wheeled round at the man, pointed a beautifully painted green fingernail at him. The cameras followed her quickly.

'What an utter Judas you are, Gordon Duke. You used to actually stand up for the people. You used to actually stand for something. What are you now? An empty suit? Talking over a woman with your practised lines because your friends in Parliament have taught you that you can? Whose interests are you representing here today, Gordon? The people in your constituency? Or your posh pals down in Westminster?'

She was tall and angry and commanding, that girl on the stage at school assemblies again. The man stayed seated. The smirk spread.

'Now now, let's not lose our tempers, Clio.' He was talking to her like she was a child, Adele thought, found her own face getting hot. Dougie wriggled his bum into the sofa cushions in pleasure.

A week or so later, in the break room, Ash had sidled up to Adele holding her phone.

'I was wondering – don't take this the wrong way or anything, and tell me to piss off if you want – but where are you on the whole Scottish independence thing?'

'Eh. I haven't really given it much thought, to be honest. It's more Dougie's thing, politics.'

'Well, I was wondering if you fancied coming along to a meeting in the town hall with me tonight. After we're done here. It'll just be an hour or two. It's for women only, and they're going to talk about the NHS, education, childcare. That sort of thing. How we might be able to change them, with independence. There's some good people talking at it.'

Adele was making her mouth into the shape of a no when Ash handed her phone screen over. Cliodhna's face, spliced into a picture with three other women Adele didn't recognize.

At the town hall, the applause had been loudest for Cliodhna, introduced as 'the woman who got us dancing in our teens and had us cheering last week when she faced down the mansplainers on *Question Time*'. Ash, sitting beside Adele, had actually gone 'Wooooo!'

'I went to school with her, you know,' Adele had said, nudging Ash.

And Cliodhna had spoken. She talked about the ways that men in power had tried to squash the politics out of her, all her life; she talked about the ways that women could do politics differently, by sitting down and talking to each other. She talked about the things a country with women's interests at its heart would prioritize. Then she began to mention the little town she grew up in, how it had been pulled apart by Thatcher, by the contempt – less than that, Cliodhna said – by a deliberate refusal to acknowledge poor working people as human.

'I've seen strike action fail. I've seen governments ride roughshod over the will of the people, from the miners to the anti-Iraq War protesters. And it seemed like we'd all just given up, didn't it? Until recently. Maybe until this. In a smaller country, one that never votes Tory, that will always vote at least a centre-left government in,' she said, 'we could look our politicians in the eye and hold them accountable. Make them do the jobs they promised to do when campaigning.'

Adele thought about the scandal, about how some of the old men back home would feel hearing 'that wee Johnstone hoor' casting up their struggle. And then she thought about all the mistakes she herself had made at sixteen, and the very different person she was at forty-six.

Cliodhna's voice had the same timbre as it had at school, but there were so many other notes in there – at times Adele thought she sounded like she was off *EastEnders*; at times she sounded drawly and foreign. But when she began to speak about the village Adele recognized Eileen Johnstone's tones in her daughter's throat, remembered Eileen hectoring them all in the church hall to keep making sandwiches, keep slopping mayonnaise from that big industrial tub onto endless slices of bread. Eileen had pretty much run the strike, but couldn't seem to make her own daughter turn up for duty.

'Imagine that, though,' Adele's own mother would mutter, just afterwards, when her dad wasn't around. 'Imagine just turning your daughter out. No matter what she'd done. She's still your blood.' Adele's mother had never really liked Eileen; it had always been known and never mentioned in the house.

In the town hall, the women sitting around Adele, maybe about sixty of them, all different ages, a lot of them seeming to be just middle-aged mums, like her, cheered and clapped as Cliodhna finished speaking. Some of them stood up. It was a nice feeling, to be amongst them. Afterwards there were drinks – glasses of wine and chocolate biscuits out on a table, poured by two women about Adele's own age.

'Go on,' Ash said, pushing a glass into Adele's hand. 'Nobody'll mind if you just have one after a long shift.' The four speakers were brought off the stage and ushered to the back of the room by the woman who had introduced them, each of them given a glass, surrounded by a small crowd. Cliodhna particularly.

'Are you going to say hi to her?'

'Och, I don't think I could. Not after all this time. Thirty years and we never really knew each other. It's just nice – nice to see her, who she is now. You know?'

It was that distance, Adele thought. That cordoned-off space Cliodhna had always maintained from the people around her. It was fine for her to talk about the village really – it was something she'd seen first-hand, grown up with, but also something she'd made a point of never belonging to. Maybe even that tiny five-year-old could sense the way that town would have sucked her under if she'd let it, got its clumsy black thumbprints all over her face as it turned her into plain Jean Johnstone, married her off.

Adele watched Cliodhna move around the room, a room full of women who wanted to talk to her, smile at her, celebrate her, because she had always been able to stand up, resist the push to conform. The warm, sharp wine sloshed on her tongue and she walked over to the table where a woman stood with a clipboard and stickers, under a hand-drawn sign that read JOIN US!, wrote down her name, phone number and email address.

Later, she would wonder where she'd found all that extra energy from. The eighteen months after she attended a meeting just because of an old acquaintance's face were the busiest she remembered since the boys were small. She found herself listening to a variety of speakers at nearby village halls, nodding along in agreement at the sheer obviousness and sense they were talking. She who had a bone-chilling fear of drawing attention to herself in public, decorated her car with stickers – BAIRNS NOT BOMBS; SAVE OUR NHYES – until Dougie refused to ride in it any more. She went on marches, holding up banners with the Paisley Women for Independence group that Ash had helped to start.

She and Jamie and Jamie's girlfriend Sarah caught the train through to Edinburgh and climbed a hill, amongst thousands of others, for a huge rally overlooking that old city and its peaks. Cliodhna sang that day, one amongst a line-up of thirty; and Adele's voice got lost in the crowd singing her chorus back to her. People gotta rise up. People gotta rise up.

'Did I ever tell you I went to school with her?' she shouted into Jamie's ear, over the loud guitar noises.

'No! No way, Mum! You should totally go and talk to her afterwards. Maybe you can get us all backstage.'

'Och no. No, no. I don't think so, son. She wouldn't remember me.'

Looking back, Adele wonders who that person was, the one who overcame shyness and stress to knock on doors, handing flyers to strangers and trying to engage them in conversation. The one who drove back to her home town to host a 'listening party' coffee morning attended only by her mum and three of her cronies, who tried in vain to assuage their fears about their pensions. The one who stood on street corners under banners in the weeks running up to the referendum. That person who fitted it all in around her work, around walking the ward, around the deaths of four long-term patients. Where once she would have gone to the canal and cried in silence at the end of a shift, now she channelled the emotional impact into her fight. She'd been fond of saying, as she knocked on the doors, handing out flyers, that she'd never really been one for politics, but that this campaign had changed her mind. People listened to her; they did. She spoke quietly but confidently to them, channelling all those years of difficult conversations with patients and their families to get her messages across softly but well. The first time she changed someone's mind from No to Yes in a ten-minute doorstep conversation she texted Ash in delight and the two of them scampered off down the pub to celebrate.

Dougie would have none of it. The harder into it Adele got, the harder he stood his ground, knuckled down, declared his loyalty to his football club and the Union Jack. Jamie stopped talking to him completely after a huge and heated argument over Sunday lunch; Adele just stopped talking to him about it. She would come in late, pat him on the shoulder as he sat watching television, go to her computer in the boys' old room to check in, tell his warm body 'night night, love', as they faced their separate ways in the bed.

A large group of them had headed through to Glasgow on the day of the referendum, after casting their votes. Ash and Big Meg had walked up and down their carriage on the train painting tiny glittery blue Saltires on all the women's cheeks so they felt like a team; they sang songs, grinned and waved at everyone else they saw wearing a Yes badge; all of them waved back. An old man at the station bent low on one knee and kissed Adele's hand. The atmosphere in George Square – 'Freedom Square! We're crying it Freedom Square now!' roared Ash – was like nothing Adele had ever seen before. Banners waving, more smiling faces than she'd ever seen in one space in Scotland, some earnest boys onstage playing guitar and a beautiful girl, surely no more than twenty, moving through the crowd handing out flowers. Adele put hers behind her ear, a fat pink daisy, felt young again.

They had tickets that evening for a concert, where they'd be able to watch the results come in. Clio Campbell and Friends. Adele had wanted so much to see her again on this day of all days, feel everything coming back full circle, that she'd hustled to organize tickets for a group of seventeen friends, take deposits, make sure the transport routes were sorted out. Onstage, introducing other musicians, talking to the crowd, Cliodhna seemed smooth and certain – what other result could there be? she said. You've seen it out there, on the streets. Glasgow is saying Yes! Adele whooped and clapped with the rest of them, amazed again that this poised, elegant woman could have grown up in the same sooty space as her. Had they, really? Adele tried to place the girl on the adult and only succeeded some of the time.

There was a big screen behind the stage and it would flicker into life every now and again, showing live BBC and STV coverage of the referendum, at a command from Cliodhna to what Adele presumed was her stage manager or something. The faces in the studio Adele had only learned recently, after years of their having been an irritation, one of Dougie's things; the crowd whooped for their favourites and booed and hissed the Better Together spokespeople as though they were at a panto. Cliodhna's set was full of in-jokes that the crowd were drunkenly, happily lapping up; at one point she came onstage eating a bowl of cereal, in reference to an infamous sexist campaign advert, and all the women in the audience burst out laughing and cheering, started calling her name. 'Go on yourself, Clio!'

Ash had bought two little plastic bottles of Prosecco from the bar for the first result coming in. Adele agreed to drink one glass – she was on shift the next morning – and the two of them popped and poured, ready to toast. The first region to announce was Clackmannanshire, a former mining area in Fife. Working class. Exactly the sort of place, everyone had said, that would vote Yes by a landslide. Adele had thought back to her unsuccessful coffee mornings, the scowling faces in her own village, and hadn't been so sure, but everyone else had told her no, no, the pollsters know what they're doing.

The shock hit the room in a harsh vibration. Adele found herself actually shivering with it. On the stage, Cliodhna was frozen beside the screen with her own, much bigger, bottle of Prosecco, a half-daft smile stuck on her face. The stage-manager guy cut the sound from the screen and the room was silent, its lifeblood drained; everybody knowing right then, even though there were so many more results to come in. A wavering spotlight found Cliodhna; she stepped forward into it, her body apparently being sucked in on itself. There she was, Adele realized. There was the girl, the girl being dragged back to the small, sooty village she didn't want to live in by a relentless, clanking old bus and the smell of mayonnaise sandwiches.

2015

The bed was wheeled in, the porter clipped it into place and the anaes-thetist handed over the chart. Unidentified female. Suicide attempt: cuts on both wrists. Blood alcohol levels high. Found in a bath at a hotel after the water had leaked through the floorboards, two rounds of bystander CPR at the scene and a further two in A&E, currently unconscious but stable. Some blood loss, but a haemorrhage pre-vented. The hotel had been unable to confirm her identity as she'd checked in as 'Jean Johnstone' but the reservation had been made under a card with a different name. Adele walked up to the bed to begin her checks, and there she was. Bandage-bound wrists above the covers. Up close, she recognized that same face from the stage, the one scored by defeat. Up close, there were as many wrinkles as she herself had, counting their shared years on the planet. Up close, on the pillow, there were threads of grey running through the mass of red hair. Nobody had washed the smeared make-up off her face yet, grubby grey tear-stains marking her nose and cheeks.

'I can identify this patient,' she told the ward sister. 'I went to school with her.'

'Are you declaring a personal interest?'

'No. Not at all. I haven't spoken to her in decades. But I know exactly who she is.'

Once she was sure the woman was stable, once she'd checked the tubes and lines, hung a new blood bag, put in the catheter and drained her bladder, Adele took a seat by Cliodhna's head, began gently wiping her face with cotton wool. And she whispered to her as she did, quietly, so as not to wake the other patients, so the charge nurse couldn't hear her.

'Well then, Cliodhna. Well then. This wasn't your time, pal. Not this time. I know, I know what it feels like, but you – you've got so much more to do. So many more people waiting to hear from you.

You're going to do big things, my lady. Trust me. When it is your time, you'll make it count. Much more than this.'

It might have been the night, the shadows, her imagination, but Adele was sure her patient's face had changed, just slightly, as she spoke.

NEIL
Glasgow, 25 January 2018

'Neil, pal. Mate. Mate.'

Neil really missed the days before Craig could remember his name. This new whirring and whining at his ear, the reek of after-shave making his head light, a feeling of being craned in on, his space invaded – this was what colleagues who worked on the politics and sports desks (the bits that still got clicks) had been bitching about all year. Craig was a manager with no ability to manage, would swoop down and intimidate to get his results, increasing pressure, making Neil feel as though he couldn't walk across the office floor without issuing a progress report.

Yesterday, it had all started with the feminists. Someone out there on the Internet had taken umbrage at his meek little paragraph of an obituary. Craig had ambled over in that laid-back way he'd cultivated to disguise his excitement, somehow braying out another *maaaate* while simultaneously sucking air in through his teeth.

'Aren't you checking your mentions, pal? Blowing up. Absolutely blowing up. And I mean, yeah, that's great, but it's not a very good look, is it? Not for the paper. You know what these girls are like now, don't you? I get where you're coming from. It's the sort of thing I wouldn't have thought twice about a few years ago myself. You know. You know, mate. But, given the current climate –' he sucked the air back over his teeth again '– bit of contrition probably wouldn't go amiss. We're going to walk back a bit on that feature for the weekend, too – I think we probably need to get a girl in to write a bit of it. But let's see, shall we? Anyway, just keep up with your mentions this afternoon, eh?'

Neil was dizzy from the man's scent, found himself gazing into the tiny pores and clean skin of the nose up at his face.

'On Twitter, pal. On Twitter. Hear me? Have a look, maybe draft a little mea culpa, let me have a squizz before you post? Sorted.'

A few little @s on his Twitter feed bubbled and snapped with righteous anger. He'd no idea how writing that simple, truthful, pared-down version of Clio's life – just the bare bones, in two hundred and fifty words – had caused so much consternation.

> WTF is this? 'Despite her undoubted beauty in her younger years'
> Seriously, @NeilMunroWrites @ScottishStandard, what the hell is
> THAT?

> a woman: is amazing and accomplished, dies.
> @NeilMunroWrites, a man: well, she's not as hot as she used to be

> Never mind the f**king beauty stuff in this @NeilMunroWrites wank.
> Why the need to mention that she didn't have kids? Would you even
> think to mention it if she was a man?

> Good old @ScottishStandard. An extraordinary woman dies
> tragically and your journalist @NeilMunroWrites reduces her down
> to her attractiveness, her ex-husband and her childlessness.

There were about fifteen of them altogether, plus the retweets. A couple more just addressed to the newspaper alone. Not the massive storm Craig had hyped him for. For fuck's sake. He missed the days before the Internet, when only the angriest old men could be bothered to reply, in green ink, a week after the fact. Well, the fact was that she wasn't as beautiful as she had been, and surely even none of these outraged keyboard warriors would deny that her beauty had been an important part in the signing of that record deal. He was proud to call himself a feminist, but that was just how the industry worked. She had been breathtaking in her twenties, but thirty years of smoking and drinking had cost her and there was no pretending around that. He remembered the amount of make-up he'd noticed on her face, when he'd moved in for that rejected kiss at the end of her fiftieth birthday party, peach emulsion rucked up in each crease, as he'd swung dizzily away into the Argyle Street night. Mentioning children, or the lack of them, in the final line was standard obituary format, and it was definitely in the public interest to raise a musician's former marriage to a well-known industry figure. He should not have to apologize for any of this, and he said as much to Craig when the boss buzzed back over to him half an hour later. What he didn't say was that the idea of being forced to apologize by a man who just yesterday had been salivating over a possible celebrity lesbian suicide was making him want to punch something.

'Mate. I hear you. I hear you. Believe me. Let's maybe backtrack a bit – perhaps a little public statement about your friendship with her? You're grieving, aren't you –' Craig began a rhythmic patting of his shoulder and Neil's pulse began beating in time, obediently '– just let them know you need a little space. You would never dream of disrespecting such a dear friend and just wanted to celebrate her life; you hope to make amends in the Saturday magazine special edition. Nice wee trailer. That sort of thing. Brilliant.'

What would be the future if he just walked out? He'd worked here for so long he couldn't imagine himself being anywhere else. It had come to define him, this building, the regular push to hit a deadline, the eight-year-old byline picture with a still-full head of hair that he used online everywhere. Well, he would stay until this thing was put to bed, anyway. He would do his duty and remember her well.

Clio Campbell was a very close friend of mine, someone I'd known
for more than thirty years. I was still in shock when I wrote her
obituary yesterday. Please look out for my article as part of
@ScottishStandard's Weekend Magazine tribute to this extraordinary
woman, this Saturday.

Post.

He'd felt dirty, taken a long lunch break at the Albannach, chewing and chewing a big white-bread cheese sandwich that had come
out of the beer fridge wrapped in cling film. He hadn't really worked
out what to say yet, in this piece, this big piece to heal all ills, this
properly fitting tribute.

The fly was still buzzing about his desk when he got back in.

'Neil! Mate. Mate. Where you been? Breaking news on the Clio
Campbell story – need to get your take on it right away, online.
Pronto. As our arts man. Our music guy.'

Back at his desk, her name typed into the search bar via auto-
complete, he let the updates spill over him. Some rapper in London
had announced he'd been in a six-year relationship with Clio. He was
young, handsome and Indian-looking – it took Neil's whisky-smirred
brain a few minutes to realize it was that guy who'd been up for the
Mercury Prize a few years ago. In fact, he even had the album.

'So. So. Mate. What do we reckon, eh?' Neil wondered whether
Craig was actually doing any work on any other sections of the paper
this week. 'Need a quick story up there right now with your reaction
– his music, in context. I mean, he's a big name, right? This is going
to blow it wide open. I'm thinking for the Saturday feature, maybe
a page on "The Many Loves of Clio Campbell", eh? I mean, this guy,
the MP guy, the music-festival guy, wasn't there a sleazy-cop thing
too?'

'I think the women you made— I apologized to this morning might
have something to say about that, Craig? Shouldn't we be concen-
trating on who she was as a person, after all? Current climate?'

Craig swatted the very idea of it away, hand slicing through the feeble air con.

'Like you said, mate. Public interest. So, quick three hundred or whatever just now, then let's see if we can get a quote from this-guy-what's-his-name in Saturday's. Good lad. Let's get to it – next half hour, yeah?'

Carol, Neil's neighbour across the desk, who kept her head down on the local council beat for the evening paper, had looked round her monitor to smile sympathetically.

'Wouldn't be happening if the powers that be hadn't thought the role of Features Editor was dispensable, would it now. You need a coffee, pet?'

She'd made it strong and it felt like a lifeline, a small gesture of solidarity from an old comrade. As though the paper itself, the institution of it all, still had his back.

Hamza Hassan, or Za Flow, as it pleased him to call himself, had been Clio's 'secret lover' from 2005, it seemed. Not long after Neil and Clio had had their one, drunken night, she had taken this much, much younger man, all muscle tone and eyes and hip-hop fashion, into her bed on the regular. Neil thought of himself at almost forty; he'd been in far better shape than he was now, but he was no 22-year-old rapper. Za Flow at thirty-six was in better shape than Neil had been at twenty-two. A quick search of the reviews of his latest album seemed to suggest he mattered, too; serious music magazines, big-name journalists that Neil had always respected, praising him for melding political sensibilities with humour and intelligence, for well-constructed basslines, an ability to marry a catchy party hook with hard-hitting lyrical content. A young beautiful boyfriend with a brain, who'd shared her two passions. Who she'd actually been able to make music with. Neil should have noticed the *Northern Lass* collaboration himself. This should have been his story to break.

Gogsy Duke. Danny Mansfield. Now this. She had a type. Let's just admit it. Pal. Mate. Clio Campbell wanted alpha males. She hunted them down, their swagger and their pull. Their money. All this time, you've been dreaming you were locked in a love story for the ages, that one day she'd finally down tools and commit. To you? You were a drunken mistake. A puny little accidental shag, a chancer who got lucky one night when she was down. Weren't you?

Remember me well.

None of them made her happy, though, did they? She was too restless, too wild for Gogsy or Mansfield. Who knows what happened with this one, but Neil had a funny feeling it wouldn't have been a fairy tale. Of course, nothing had made her happy, in the end. That was sort of the point, wasn't it?

He filed his word count on the 'hunky grime star' to the online ed like a dutiful little typewriter, then muttered to Carol he was off to finish the Saturday feature at home, left her to deal with Craig's bluster and babble about presenteeism alone. Even back in his flat there was no escaping Clio. The door she'd hovered in all those years ago. That space near the bed where her weird cowboy boots had sat. The CD case for *The Northern Lass* was still sitting out; he scanned the liner notes quickly, and there it was, tacked on at the end – 'For H, always'.

The Twitter notification, turned back on on his phone at Craig's insistence, started chiming again, and he wondered when all this would stop. Three days now, of nothing but Clio, grinding away in his head.

Write the piece. Just write the piece. Neil had never had too much of a problem meeting a word count before; he'd accepted long ago that nobody cared how beautifully constructed your prose was when you were working to a deadline and your primary focus was the conveyance of information. He plonked them out now, words, usually didn't stop to analyse his process as they appeared on the screen, three or four small articles a day, filling the space, creating content. But none of them had mattered. He would usually start a story knowing exactly where he needed the words to take him to get to the end; telling Clio's story, suddenly, he had no idea where it could possibly go. There was so much of her, spilling out in all directions, even after she'd drawn her own full stop. How did you do it? How did you use words, black on white with a finite limit, slotting into a pre-designed space on a page, to describe what a person's life had been? He'd tried sticking to the very bare facts as he saw them, the way he'd usually build a story, and been told he was wrong. All he'd managed to write was her name, and now he wasn't even sure what that meant; the four letters peeling apart from each other, just scratches, lines and dots, a circle.

He was just going to have to get really, really drunk for this one. It proved harder than he'd expected; the ballast of whisky he'd kept topping up over the past three days tilting the scale unfairly. But eventually he felt it. A click, a flow. It came. Clio. Clio Clio Clio.

When had he got to sleep? Three? Four? There had not been enough of it, for sure. Not enough to allow him to deal with the morning lights of the office, with Craig, already advancing. Neil tried to hide behind the sausage roll he'd grabbed from the Greggs round the corner, realized immediately how foolish a plan that was.

'Mate. Maaaate. Have you seen it? Have you? Did she send it to you as well? I'm going to forward it to you just in case, all right? This is going to change everything.'

The email had been sent using software that let organizations hurl out pre-designed communications to mailing lists. There was a corporate logo at the top right-hand corner, incongruous, a little cartoon of a monkey's face. Her name in the Sender file.

Subject: Clio Campbell Suicide Note.

Hello
    My name is Clio Campbell and I'm dead.
    You probably know this by now, as it happened three days ago. I hope you appreciate the timing of this letter. By now, I imagine, obituaries will have been written, tweets will have

been posted by enemies old and new, expressing regret and moving on, and life will have settled back to normal again. I'm under no illusions about what I meant to the world, a shouty former pop singer who never knew her place. I'm not Bowie, or Prince. Nowhere near. You might have shed a tear and watched a video of me in my young and toothy prime on Tuesday, maybe played one of my songs on the radio. One more day and you'll be over it. But today, I suspect, you'll still be listening.

If I know the way you work, oh free press of this noble and just country, certain easy-to-reach-for narratives will have attached themselves to my ageing womanly corpse by now. So let's clear some things up, while we've got the time.

– Despite being female and over fifty, I haven't killed myself because I'm lonely and never found the right man. I found the right man many times, thank you.

– Nor am I dead of heartache over never having had children. I would have been a terrible mother and unlike some had the good sense to realize it early on. Being child-free has enabled me to live the sort of life I wanted.

– I can't claim that the decision I've made is entirely unrelated to the ongoing mental health issues I've experienced throughout the years. Would I still be doing this if I hadn't suffered depression? Who knows. But is this action that I'm taking – killing myself – motivated by that? No, not entirely. Not even mostly.

Here's why I'm doing this: Nobody shuts up a dead woman. Well, you do; you will, you'll trample my memory back into the ground at some point, dust to dust and all that. But when a person is newly dead, let's say three days or so, she's interesting again. I thought this was probably my one chance to set the record straight. No voices butting in, no sarcastic commentary from the gentlemen of the fourth estate, no angry tweets from bitter, socially awkward forty-something boys in their mum's sheds, calling me an overweight past-it old whore as they type one-handed.

Are you going to speak ill of me, now I've gone? You could try, but nobody will really listen. Once I'm dead, I've ascended. You can't touch me, and you can't drown me out. I can't be demoralized, dissuaded or patronized into irrelevance. And I suspect, as well, that your readers might want to hear from me just now. Even if they've just heard my one hit playing on the radio in memoriam this week, I think they might like to know why I Did It.

And you would too, wouldn't you?

Keep reading.

I'm killing myself to draw attention to the fact that you are all sleepwalking into fascism and chaos. I'm killing myself – a white woman, privileged enough to have this tiny posthumous platform – because we are failing. We are all failing each other. The codes that this modern world was built on are breaking down, allowing the worst bits of ourselves to rampage. We're all hardening, dismissing other people's humanity with a wink and a meme and a scroll-on-down. We're too easily distracted, and we're letting the bastards win. We've become desensitized to horrors committed against desperate souls who come here seeking asylum, to the routine demonization of anyone who isn't white and rich and straight and male. I'm killing myself because the world is getting worse and all those rights we fought so hard for are being reversed. I'm killing myself because we are losing our moral compass. It is not moral, the way we exist together. I'm killing myself because the people we elect to govern us do not even pretend to morals, and are applauded for it. Something has gone badly, badly wrong. I'm killing myself because you, the media, are doing nothing to stop any of this; in fact, you're fanning it, trying to prop up your own dwindling sales by outrage, mob war and dissatisfaction. I'm killing myself because I want to shout STOP to each and every one of you, and this is the only way to get you to listen.

I've tried saying it. A middle-aged woman, especially if she used to be famous and beautiful and young, if her politics are anywhere left of centre, isn't posh or anything even approaching middle class, and dares to be passionate about something, is too easily mocked to be worth listening to. I'm gambling on the chance that that same woman dead just might be.

I've taken the decision to end my own life because it seems that only something as big and shocking as this could make this country come to attention. I've tried other methods. I spent years protesting; raising my voice with those of others, massing our bodies together. I wrote songs and wore slogan T-shirts on television. I tried to shout in interviews. I got involved in debates and tried to influence voters. Violence seems like the only remaining option, and it's only death that really stops you all in your tracks, isn't it? I have no desire to murder anyone else, to strap bombs to myself and walk into town, or take a knife to the throat of a politician; I don't have access to any other, more famous, people to kill for my cause (and it's not like any of those acts get their various perpetrators' views a more sympathetic hearing), and I don't want to further the suffering of those poor animals at the

Grand National by throwing myself under a racehorse. My
tiny bit of fame, managed badly and drifting away after all
these years but hopefully still worth something once I'm
dead, is all the resources I have. So, pills, vodka and a strongly
worded letter to every major media outlet in the country it
is. If the forces of darkness, racism, hatred and capitalism
have won, I don't want to be around to see it. If there's still a
chance that any of you could be turned around, made to stop
and think and reconsider how you're treating the planet and
other human beings, then this body is all the bargaining chips
I've got left.

No, it's not subtle. But we're not living in a subtle time.
Today's 'best' politicians, the ones who get the populist
votes, don't do subtle. They do big filthy slogans and instant
gratification and slather their never-kept promises on the
sides of buses. BREXIT MEANS BREXIT. MAKE
AMERICA GREAT AGAIN. They make instant fleeting
hits on people's minds, rouse them up on hatred and other
potent emotions. This feels like the only way of matching
them.

Shrug me off if you like. Most of you would, if you hadn't
already realized that this letter will make such a damn good
story. And you don't know which other publications will be
running with it, do you? You don't want to miss out. Edit it
down if you like; the whole thing will go online anyway, and
you know the sites that publish me uncut will get the most
hits.

That's the final word of St Clio the martyr. Just pre-empting
the jokes there. There are worse things to die for, and I'm
going out happy. You're all winding each other up into a
senseless tangle and it's making this world unliveable. I'm

looking forward to the noise stopping. By the time you read
this it already will have. I bet it's peaceful over here.

Clio Campbell

Neil came back to himself and saw Craig's face, still there, hovering over the monitor, bathed in seraphimic light.

'Well. Well well, eh!'

'You're not thinking about printing this?'

'Got it in one, mate. And as soon as we possibly can. Need you to
signal-boost the tweet and obviously give us some analysis, seeing as
you're our expert in the field here.'

Neil scrabbled about in the workings of his brain to make the
words come.

'Craig, there are press guidelines for reporting suicides. The first
one, right up there, is that you never disclose whether there was a
suicide note, much less report its contents.'

'The lady said it herself, Neil. We don't know who else will be printing this. We've already put it on the website and I want your analysis
in half an hour max. You're not letting me down on this one. This
is tomorrow's editorial. It changes everything. I mean, think about
it – we could really lead the way with some sensitive reporting; I'd be
surprised if she doesn't tap into a real public mood. I mean, we could
be looking at a wave. Brexit suicides. Copycatting.'

'That's exactly why they tell you not to print the notes. Craig,
come on.'

Craig moved so quickly Neil wasn't quite sure what had happened.
Suddenly there was no one leaning over the back of his desk chair, and
his boss stood in front of him, seemingly a foot taller than normal,
staring him down with tiny cold eyes.

'Let's have a deal, going forward, mate. You get on with your job
and I get on with mine. My job is selling papers. Your job, right now,

is writing whatever the fuck I need you to write to sell those papers. All right? Good.'

Carol did not meet his eye this time as that upright spine retreated across the newsroom, and he was grateful for it. He tried to turn his attention back to the mass of words on his screen. The only phrase he could think of for it was political suicide, but that wasn't right, was it? Political suicide was when MPs were caught with hookers, called old ladies bigots, or murmured that Hitler had really been quite a promising artist. It didn't mean actually killing yourself because of politics. Actually killing yourself to try and change people's politics.

Neil couldn't for a second imagine what it would take to be that person. To decide to take that sort of action. Not so much the suicide; that had been understandable when she'd just been a depressed fifty-year-old woman with a failed career. He'd been able to empathize then. He'd thought he'd got it. But this. This whole – stunt. Planning your death out as a public event, intended to impact beyond your immediate circle.

Jesus Christ, the woman had balls. Great big balls, and an ego to match.

So, what did this mean for him? He checked his email; no, he hadn't been copied into the mass suicide note. She had decided to communicate with him privately. Send one thing out to the world, and a last, tiny hope, stretched out to him and him alone.

Remember me well. Please.

It was as though he heard music swelling behind him.

The Pool, **February 2018**

The Long Read:

Clio Campbell, Brexit and the Genoa G8 | 7min

In the wake of Clio Campbell's shocking suicide, novelist and cultural commentator Jess Blake-Hewson looks back at her old comrade-in-arms

We took the children to Genoa last summer. A family holiday used to heal old wounds; in part a pilgrimage. We meandered around ice-cream-coloured clusters of houses, watched girls in off-the-shoulder ruffles direct their boyfriends to Instagram them outside the cathedral and on the Porto Antico rocks at sunset, stuffed our faces with pizza from the street carts and sat on the harbour front with our legs dangling into the water, tanned and happy.

It didn't seem to be the same place. I didn't remember it at all. Was that saffron-coloured wall up an alley the one we were corralled against for hours, maybe a hundred of us hemmed in by police dogs and guns at either end, barely able to move from the pressure of terrified bodies all around? Or was it just another cute little lane with some overpriced tourist shops?

I'd last been there sixteen years earlier, twenty-one years old, unsure about how to maintain my still-new dreadlocks, with a week's worth of clothing stuffed into a lightweight rucksack. Someone from a group at uni had heard there were places going on a bus; we couldn't fly because they'd be watching for us at the gates, the bastards, he said, and we all nodded. We were there to protest the presence of the G8, who had chosen that pleasant old tourist town for their conference. We were anti-globalization, devoted to Naomi Klein. Us and 200,000 others.

That protest is now legendary – it was the first time the world media really paid attention to the anti-globalization movement, because the images of police brutality against protesters were so extreme that they couldn't be ignored, and because of the death of 23-year-old protester Carlo Giuliani, shot in the street then reversed over by a police Land Rover, just to make sure.

On the second night we were there, before the marches began, before our muscles learned to tense for flight at the smallest noise, we attended a gig at the Genoa Social Forum, the centre of the protest for those of us in the Red and Pink Blocks, who advocated peaceful, non-violent resistance. It was a warm evening; the air was still. I was pushing back through the crowd, pockets loaded with cans of cheap Italian lager from a stall, when a new act came on to the stage. It caught my attention because it was the first song in English I'd heard all evening; I then realized I dimly remembered it from my child-hood. She was young, red-headed and her voice soared out across the crowd.

'Who's this?' I asked my friend Simon.

He gave me that look that said *God, Jess, you know nothing about music* as he popped the tab on his beer. 'It's Clio Campbell. Clio Campbell. Don't you remember?'

Two days later, walking with the Pink Block in formation along the Corso Italia, we noticed the crowds swearing at us. Nobody in Genoa seemed to be very pleased to see us. I'm still to this day not sure what it was that flicked, whether the police were waiting for a signal, whether they had something planned. Later, we'd hear rumours that they had undercover agents posing as Black Block agents provocateurs, starting trouble to give them an excuse for a show of force and power to impress the visiting world leaders, exactly as Silvio Berlusconi had intended. From nowhere, there were batons, raining down on us, shouts in Italian from both the riot police and the protesters.

'*Non violenta! Non violenta!*' I shouted, as we'd been taught in the non-violent direct action workshop the day before. I tried to make my body go limp. Remember, the Pink Block believed in non-violent resistance. We were absolutely the least likely people to fight back. That's why we made such a good target, I suppose.

There were limbs all around me. I had no idea which of them belonged to my friends. I was twenty-one, I was far away from home, and a baton had slammed into my shoulder, sending a dull, weird ache juddering through my arm. This was nothing like the demonstrations I'd been on in England, where we'd waved banners and sung songs and had a laugh in a public park then caught the bus back home again with a bag of chips. I'm pretty sure I was crying at this point, but I don't remember. I felt very very young and very afraid.

Then someone grabbed my hand and pulled me towards them. '*Non violenta,*' I muttered. Someone was holding me, had their arms around me, was pulling me out of the scrum and away from the main fight, up an alleyway. They were whispering something in my ear, in English.

'It's OK. Come on now, little darlin. It's OK. Come on now.'

I leaned against the sunny yellow wall, caught my breath, let this woman give me sips of water from a bottle.

'Hey there. You OK now? Can you tell me your name? *Sta bene? Come ti chiami?*'

I held on to her and smiled up at her and I never wanted to let her go again.

As you've all probably guessed now, that was my first proper meeting with Clio Campbell, when she saw a young girl about to fall under the feet of a state-sponsored riot and pulled me out, got me to safety. That yellow alleyway we had hidden ourselves in would later become a site for kettling, a procedure used on the Iraq War demonstrators two years later by a clearly impressed

UK Home Office, but one which we weren't familiar with at the time. I was ready to collapse, but had to stay on my feet as more and more bodies were hounded into our space – to sit would have been to be crushed. This tall Scottish stranger held me up for three hours, fed me water and kept me conscious and talking, muttering jokes and funny commentary, when she could have been attending to her own needs. I think you really learn the truth about people's characters in these sorts of extreme situations. And this was someone I didn't want to let out of my life.

Clio Campbell was, for a time, one of my closest friends, despite our twelve-year age difference. I watched as the aftermath of Genoa (we crushed souls up the alleyway escaped relatively lightly) and its implications set her alight, burning for truth; I watched as the aftermath of the Iraq War demonstrations squashed her into a depressed apathy, only to rise again and again. She got involved with land rights movements in the Scottish Highlands; led a campaign against corrupt undercover cops; I was eventually pulled into a life of baby sensory classes and school postcode lotteries while she kept on doggedly fighting for what she believed in – always justice, always for the oppressed. Those paths intersected less and less; as I grew further away from the person I'd been at twenty-one, there was something almost childlike about Clio that allowed her to keep believing.

Suddenly ten years have passed since Clio brought the congregation to tears singing Joni Mitchell's 'A Case of You' at my wedding, and my husband is waking me with terrible news shining through his phone. Clio's suicide, reported last week, made minor headlines – never a tabloid-friendly celebrity, the impact she had had always been on the fringes. Clio's suicide note, released three days later, however, seems to have split the country wide open. I'm aware that even by writing about that note I'm contravening all the suggested ethics rules around reporting suicides, but the details have been so widely circulated by now that it's impossible not to write about Clio without discussing it.

Clio's note suggested that, after a lifetime of activism, actually killing herself was the only way a woman, especially an older woman, would actually be listened to in this public arena of jeering and opprobrium that exists now instead of civil discourse. It's manifestly not true – one has only to look at the ages of female MPs, mostly Clio's peers, or the happily increasing number of female political journalists making good and salient points about our current political crisis on a daily basis – but that anybody could come to feel that, and actually go forward with their action, suggests a serious crisis in the ways we communicate with each other these days. It's one of the main reasons why I feel that, in this case, the causes Clio claimed for her suicide should be examined. We need to be looking at this.

Then there were the cynics who scoffed at her even in death. To them, I can only say that the person who pulled an injured stranger out of a tangle of bodies and chaos and protected her for five hours is exactly the person who would think to lay down herself as a final protest against what she described as 'a country sleepwalking into fascism'. No, of course you shouldn't kill yourself over Brexit, or the treatment of asylum seekers. Stay alive and keep fighting if it means that much to you. But Clio felt things more intensely and keenly than the rest of us seem to; and that intensity motivated her actions. She managed to hold on to her moral code while all around were losing theirs; never filtered anything through a layer of irony in order to block life out.

We used to talk a lot about 'the movement' as student revolutionaries. A single body of people marching with one aim. I'm not sure there can be such a thing any more; the causes that anger the left seem to be so diverse they create rifts rather than solidarity. It's difficult to imagine a united left-wing movement defeating something like the poll tax, which Clio always referred to as 'the cause that made me', these days. But then perhaps, as a middle-class, commuter-belt *soi-disant* yummy mummy, I'm just not hearing its songs.

In Genoa last year my children skipped along the beachfront Corso Italia. It's a very beautiful street and they were fascinated by its fairy-tale pavement mosaics, leaned over the railings to gaze at the azure sea below. It was so far removed from that dusty scene of overturned cars, gassed air and broken glass I dimly remembered from my youth that it seemed I must have dreamed that second image. But then, I had the luxury of being able to tell myself that.

RUTH
Glasgow, 2014

Watching Clio in arguments on Twitter possessed Ruth like a drawn-out panic attack during the independence referendum. The relentlessness of it, the piranhas swarming for attack at her every statement. Her profile was high enough to attract them; her public statements sufficiently unmodest to keep them fuelled and ready. The debate had racked up nearly two years of increasingly fraught coverage in the time since Clio had moved back to Scotland needing friends and a place in the world; she had found it as an outspoken advocate for Scottish self-determination. The Scottish media had very much enjoyed the spectacle she'd made for them, and Ruth, like the rest of the country, couldn't look away. She'd saved Clio's name as a search, tapped it in automatically every time she clicked on to the app, lost herself in scrolling and scrolling as the second-hand stress began to bubble through her veins. It seemed as though the world, or the very worst subsects of it, was rising up to show Clio her place, each opinion met with a barrage of blokey disdain, an obscene-seeming wet-eyed emoji of laughter. To be fair to her, Clio didn't moderate her behaviour. She didn't tone it down or attempt to pacify them. But she would argue with them relentlessly, into the night, sometimes five or six at a time, lost in long trails of oblique replies and misunderstanding, refusing to let any of her anonymous sparring partners have the last word.

'I'm fit for them, doll. Don't worry.'

Ruth worried. Of course she worried.

On the morning after the independence referendum, Clio had turned up unannounced, leaning down hard on the buzzer to Ruth's old flat in the Southside. She'd entered in an unwashed, boozy cloud, dishevelled, squinting at Ruth already dressed and washed.

'You're not going to work today, are you?'

'I thought I'd try. Not sure I'm not going to burst into tears on the train, though.'

'Fuck that, doll. Let's stay in and drink.'

'I need to go, Clio. I need to get out there and do something. At least just see what it's like.'

'I've been out there. I've been.' The words smeared together on the roof of her mouth. 'I'll save you the bother: s'shite out there. S'a dreich bloody day in a country full of fearful idiots who've jus condemned ussall. It's exactly the bloody same. Everything out there is exactly bloody the same as it ever was.'

As she stepped over the threshold and into the light, Ruth could see her eyes were red, swollen from a night of it.

'Clio, have you even been to bed?'

'Yes. I went to bed. I was supposed to be playing a gig an they were screening the live results on the telly in between acts. Then they went to fucking – fucking Clackanmannannanshire. Fucking mining country, babe. I'm from mining country. I'll tell you this, they've got a warped bloody idea of solidarity, is what they do. Turn on their own in a heartbeat if thass what the bloody Labour Party tells them to do, I'll tell you. And he was all over there with his big face, fucking voice of doom, wassn' he? Gordon Brown. Bomp bomp bomp – thass his theme song. Big sad tuba or something. Bomp bomp bomp—'

She began marching around Ruth's hallway, playing an imaginary trombone.

'Clio. Clio, come on. Let's get you sitting down.'

Ruth steered her into the kitchen.

'Anyway, I was supposed to be playing this big big triumphant set, right, all the hits, ending up with "Rise Up" backed by a fucking choir – I mean, a community choir, but still. An I just sat there thinking how did we not see this. Because I knew. We all knew. Whole fucking auditorium knew just because of that one wee Fife village. It got quiet, and people started to leave. How did we not see this? How did we fucking dare to hope that this wee shithole country could just – for once – for once, zat was all I'd asked, eh, overcome its inner fucking nyaff and actually try for something good and pure and positive? I mean, we planned a fucking choir. How fucking stupid are we? And see them all, all these men, all these men men men who've been dragging me through their shitey newspapers since I dared to come back to Scotland and be a woman with an opinion, they'll all just be so smug. They'll be sitting there, taking their celebratory dumps on their mahogany toilet seats someone cut down a rainforest and sent to B&Q to warm their arses with, tweeting each other their congratulations after they all write their one article again.'

Ruth put the kettle on.

'How much have you had to drink?'

Clio flapped away an imaginary fly.

'It doesn't matter. Tell you why it doesn't matter? Because nothing matters. Nothing I do or you do will ever make the slightest bit of fucking difference. So why not have a drink.'

With some difficulty, she fumbled in the pocket of her coat for her phone.

'Lookit. Lookit. Started already. The tweeting. The relentless little nip-nip-nip away from men men men. I've taken it hard from them for a year. I've let that bloated sack of tatties at the *Scotland on Sunday* and the weirdo at the *Daily Mail* and all their crowing cronies in their mums' fucking sheds on Twitter rip me to shreds and I've taken it, babe. I have not flinched. I have turned the other cheek.'

Ruth kept her own counsel here.

'I just let them get on with it. It was water off a duck's back, jus rolled right off and ignored it. And why? Because I was so sure that what we were doing was going to work, and they'd all come round eventually, when their kids or whatever were getting amazing Scandinavian education and we had an oil fund underpinning a citizen's income and we were tackling poverty properly and putting money into green energy programmes and all those beautiful things we were going to do. That they'd see then.'

She'd slumped forward on to the table, was talking from between her arms. Ruth set the mug of tea down beside her face.

'But they won't. They were never going to. Because they knew this country. They knew that most of the country was just fearty little boys like them, making snidey jokes because they're afraid to believe in anything. That's what it is. It's why anyone from here goes away and does well, we start laughing at them when they come back again. It's why we'll never actually manage to do anything positive that could actually make a meaningful difference in people's lives, is it? There's always some wee Scottish gremlin sitting there on yer shoulder, whispering its mantra. Naw. Naw. Naw.'

She slid slowly down to the floor, looked up at Ruth with huge eyes, terrified.

'I mean, what is this world, pal? Why do these fuckers keep on winning? I need – I need – I need to keep believing that at some point it will stop, and they'll listen, and we'll make everything all right. But every time – every time—'

Ruth had tucked her up in her own bed, the bedside cabinet turned rescue stop, its surface covered with a pint glass of water, a couple of paracetamol, a packet of crisps and a plastic bag for vomit.

Out in the street, everything did look the same, but shot through a slightly different lens. Maybe it had all been shifted a couple of millimetres over? Ruth found her seat on a train where no one spoke, leaned her head against the window and, sure enough, burst into tears, big noisy sobs, her whole body shaking. Sure, she'd cheered and booed at elections as one set of politicians lost and another won, but none of it had ever come quite so close, meant quite so much. She'd never felt the possibility of change for good quite so keenly, never before been quite so partisan that she'd managed to block out dissenting voices if their arguments bothered her.

There was a tap on her shoulder. The conductor was standing there. She fumbled for her ticket and he shook his head, handed her a crumpled fist of toilet paper. He squeezed her arm, a message passed on, and moved slowly up the carriage.

She'd left the office after three hours. Hadn't had the energy for it. Clio was still in her bed when she got back, and Ruth climbed in beside her, fully dressed. Clio passed her the almost-empty bottle of whisky, turned back to her phone, her hands flying over its surface.

'I'm gonna take them down, Ruth. Each and every single fucker who comes at me. This is the best possible response I could have to today, isn't it. Don't say anything. I'm going to end each one of them individually today.'

Glasgow, 25 January 2018

'Why would you do a thing, keep doing it, when it gave you no joy and instead put such a strain on you?' Ruth had tried to ask Alison one night, just after Brexit, having ventured a look at Clio's Twitter stream and almost physically recoiling from the frenzy, the fur flying. Alison had only looked at her knowingly, and Ruth sensed another lecture about standing up for herself, not letting Clio use her, changed the subject loudly and forcefully.

*

On the third day after she'd found the body, her second day of occu-
pation of Alison's sofa, watching the Disney movies of her childhood
under blankets, Ruth decided that she'd had enough. Alison's house
was always too hot, and Ruth had no idea how to work the glowing
remote-control thermostat that mocked her with a blinking, brazen
display of all twenty-two degrees from the centre of the coffee table.
'Try and stay offline,' Alison had warned her this morning. 'It'll all
blow over soon.' There had been pictures of the outside of her cottage,
neighbours from the village interviewed by a couple of the papers.
Her boss had texted, saying that he understood she couldn't really
go home or come in, but asked her to maybe think about working
remotely tomorrow, if she felt up to it.

Alison had been dead against Ruth making the trip to Ayr, to Clio's
never-talked-about mother, but Ruth had been resolute. The nursing-
home staff needed warned, if nothing else, she'd said. She didn't want
some unscrupulous bastard journalist sneaking in and breaking it to
her, taking pictures, getting quotes on the sly. Alison had taken the
day off and insisted on waiting in the car outside Glendale Retire-
ment Home. Inside, Ruth sat there with this shrivelled person, this
Eileen Johnstone who looked nothing like Clio, patted the proffered
hand awkwardly while the old woman's sentences roamed out of the
corners of her mouth, lapsing in and out of years in a single breath.
Finally, Ruth had almost snapped at her.

'She's dead, though. You understand that, don't you? Your daughter Clio. She's dead.'

Alison had wrapped her shaken girlfriend up in her own coat in
the passenger seat and driven her home again.

Ruth had never been any good at sitting still. She was a nurse, not
a patient. Alison's perpetual need to fuss over her had always been her
least favourite part of their relationship and it grew more and more
intense the longer she stayed in that stuffy little house, blankets and
blankets tucked around her. She broke her phone out of its jail cell in
her bag, on top of the wardrobe. 'Try and stay offline,' she said to the

empty house, doing Clio's impression of Alison's nasal tones, feeling bad immediately.

Clio's name was still trending on Twitter. Still! Three days after her death! I mean, my God, she said to the house again, she wasn't *that* famous.

Clio Campbell: suicide was over Brexit

Political suicide: Explosive Clio Campbell Suicide Note Reveals Singer's 'Martyrdom'

Clio Campbell blames Brexit in suicide note

Clio Campbell: THAT suicide note in full!

But there wasn't a suicide note, Ruth thought. She had looked, and Alison had looked, just before they left Ruth's cottage. There had been nothing left for Ruth, just the body, that grimace, the way it changed the air.

And she clicked, and she clicked again.

I'm looking forward to the noise stopping.

That was the first bit she took in. That bit made sense. That had been written by the listless, strained Clio whose unwashed hair had hung down the back of Gran's old armchair. It was the rest of the letter Ruth had a problem with

I'm gambling on the chance that that same woman dead just might be.

Ruth had to read that through a few times. She had to read the whole letter through a few times, hearing Clio's most self-righteous voice, her perpetual inability to ever have a sense of humour at her own expense, bell-clear. Her eyes would have been brimming, Ruth thought, as she wrote this. She would have been extremely moved by her own plight, the way she was crafting it for others.

Gambling.

Gambling.

So, this was all part of a plan, then? Part of a long-drawn-out plan. Ruth thought of Clio's fiftieth birthday party last year and all the work she hadn't minded doing, to help her get set up. It seemed like such a good thing for her to do. But Clio had been driven by a weird desperation as they planned the party; the same mood as she'd been in in the pub the other night. The party to end all parties. Got to be, she'd said.

So had she already planned it then? More than a year ago? The party, the strange staginess of her last depressed period that Ruth had noticed but filed away, the trips she'd mentioned making last autumn to see long-lost friends. The intent of it all. And the intent was what? Always to have Ruth discover her body, report her as depressed, then rise like a ginger lipsticked Jesus three days later with a fucking press release to the national media?

But not even to leave a little scrap of paper. Not even to put something down in writing for the friend of more than a decade who would have to deal with her dead body. Not even a tiny, private acknowledgement. Sorry I left my corpse for you to find! Thanks for everything! Love you!

Ruth felt exposed. Her small, tightly held schoolgirl crush turned into a resource, knowingly exploited over years. The blood rushed to her big already red cheeks, to her head, and she wasn't sure whether it was shame or anger pulsing there, tick tick tick in her temple.

When Alison came home, there were fresh flowers in a jug on the table, and Ruth called to her from the kitchen, sank her face into her neck, poured her a glass of wine. After dinner, with candles flickering, she reached for her girlfriend's hand over the table.

'Ali. You are the one person in my life who has consistently and openly been there for me. I want you to know how much I appreciate you. And I wanted to ask you whether you'd consider marrying me. I want to spend the rest of our lives together.'

Yeah. Take that, Clio. Take that, take that.

DONALD
Achiltibuie, 24 January 2018

When was the last time he had seen her? Four years? Five? They'd been booked on the bill of the same gig in Perth, a Scottish independence thing he'd found himself doing. It had been a surprise to turn up there and see her name on the list, have her run up to him and bury her head in his shoulder like the years hadn't gone by and she was that wee girl again. Their connection wasn't one he thought of often, any more – after the failure of that album she'd drifted away from him, spun out into space, and Morna's family, with a new baby every couple of years or so and a vacant space where a grandfather should be, had reached out to anchor him. This, here, was where he belonged, looking out of the window to the islands beyond as he washed the dishes from the guests' breakfasts, keeping himself active, still playing the fiddle on Sunday nights in the big hotel up the way every couple of months.

There had been a line-up reshuffle at her request, her childlike insistence hanging awkwardly in the air, at odds with the older woman it came from, while the young event organizer looked at his feet. They'd sung together – a couple of their old Burns rejigs, 'A Man's a Man' – him knocking time on his fiddle while her voice cut the air, the audience rising to its feet at the end, but she'd been loud and vocal in the bar area afterwards, surrounded by a crowd, while he hung about awkwardly, eventually drifted back to his B&B.

And then nothing at all until last year, November. Just a few months ago. He'd driven back from a St Andrew's Day gig in Garve in the night – he liked driving at night, liked the blackness, even though Morna wished he wouldn't do it, not at his age – and Morna had still been waiting up for him in the kitchen when he fumbled the latch in the dark.

'You had a visitor. Malcolm's girl. Cliodhna.'

'I – what?'

'She came up with the school bus from Ullapool. I told her you weren't like to be home till now, and so she walked up the road to the hotel, presumably sat in the pub for three hours till the bus came back.'

'You didn't ask her to stay? We've room.'

'Well, of course I did, Donald Bain. No matter what I think of her I'm not going to turn away a visitor, am I now? She wouldn't. She said no, she had somewhere else to be. I told her if she'd just phoned ahead – but she said she wanted to surprise you.'

Donald didn't know what to say. Time had folded in on itself and a teenage girl in bright red stilettos was clacking down the stairs to his old bothy.

'I mean really, though. Who just turns up at someone's house, miles away from anywhere? We're not in the city now. Just that expectation, too, that you would be here, waiting for her.'

She had been crackling with indignation. Donald had imagined the welcome Cliodhna would have received at the guest house, was unsurprised she had decided not to stay.

Now, looking at the newspaper, knowing her gone, he wondered whether that had been a last chance. He'd heard of dying people doing a farewell tour – had she already decided what she was going to do then? Could he have changed her mind, if he'd just been there, if Morna had been a bit more hospitable? If she'd stayed, just for the night. Could he have made her breakfast, reminded her gently of the girl she used to be? Brought her back?

Well, you didn't manage it with her father, did you now, Donald Bain? You would have shat it. Shuffled away. Shiter.

SAMMI
Brixton, 3 April 2018

It must have been well over three years since Sam had checked in on any of Clio's intense, shouty social-media feeds. A while since she'd thought about her, even. She sat there, hunched over her phone in the corner of the café near Elliot's football practice, frying smell in her nose, letting it all pour back in. Obituaries and despairing tweets from fans, articles and discussions, video clips with the sound turned down. She thought about the reality of Clio. That thin, frenzied woman, in her bedsit with beanbags, turning up unannounced to disrupt a working day, pungent, unwashed and urgent, trailing chaos. She looked at the way two months of death had crafted her into something else, a statue of her, built out of words and pictures, a statue that didn't need to be anything like the reality. That wasn't the point.

Suicide as political statement, eh? Well, it was on-brand. She could say that much. She'd read Clio's last letter and was surprised at how un-Clio-like it sounded, how thoughtful. Measured, almost. In her wake, the commentary: analysis, long think pieces. Even Fran had contributed one. Sammi began to zone out the screeds of comments underneath each article, analysing, criticizing, shouting their partisan slogans, cracking jokes. Thousands of pseudonyms, all across the Internet, all round the world, all of them the same. It was exhausting. This was why she couldn't take on politics any more.

People had been shocked, she could see that. The right had chucked scorn from a respectful distance, while a left-wing MP had tried to start a debate in Parliament. But then all the news hits stopped, she noticed, just trailed away about four or five weeks ago. The world had created something huge, enthused and grieved it, debated what it meant, and then moved on, busy, to the next thing.

Sam wondered if there had been anyone inclined to rethink themselves as a result. Had a woman actually killing herself made anyone, anyone real, who wasn't paid to have opinions, stop and say, hold on, she's got a point. I *am* sleepwalking into fascism. I need to be better, to stop, to be more aware, more active. It was the sort of thing that the Internet wouldn't ever be able to tell her.

At least she'd been true to herself, had Clio. She'd gone out in a great big political blaze of publicity.

Sam's work notification pinged and, although she welcomed the distraction, she flinched, like she always did now. The message was from a woman who called herself Carrie and she was properly addicted. She needed a reading every two or three days, to help her think through the most minor of problems, had probably spent upwards of a thousand pounds in the last month alone, money that Sam was not sure she had. Sam's doing. 'Build relationships with them' had been the major directive when she'd got the job. 'Keep them coming back, keep them spending.'

'I mean, of course, you're all here because you've got the gift,' the spivvy young guy who'd done their training had said, smoothing over the nervous wobble that moved the room with an oversized wink, like a Butlin's comedian. 'But here are some tricks of the trade to, well, to help your readings really *flow*.'

Well, she needed the money, and she needed to avoid any obligation to look people in the eye. That was how she justified it. It was easier doing it online, not having to be on the end of a phone, hearing accents, inflection. There didn't always have to be a person behind the words if you just read them as written. She called herself Psychic Samantha. It wasn't a very original name – they had all been encouraged to create new personas for themselves, in the single half-day training workshop in an empty office space above a shop in Fulham – but it worked well enough for her purposes. It meant that she couldn't disassociate herself, wasn't hiding away behind anyone else's identity. That's what she said, to herself. She hadn't told anyone else, anyone in her real life, what she was doing.

'Clio', it occurred to her now, would have been a much better name for a fraudulent psychic.

Well, Carrie was probably a cow, anyway. Her daughter didn't talk to her; she seemed to be in a perpetual chaotic storm, always churning something else up. There was always a next enemy and a next one: the neighbour, the woman at work, the ex-husband's new wife, the local shopkeeper, all of them picking on Carrie, poor Carrie. Poor Carrie who clearly bulldozed her way through life, starting fights, emotionally deaf and blind or just not caring enough to bother reading people. *Today its the bloody pig next door again Samatha and I just can't with my nerves any more she won't stop. Sorry cant handle it meant to say. Those bloody children screaming in the garden every afternoon when they come home, running about quite wild and she had the cheek to actually shout at me this time when I dared to work up the courage to say something if you know what I mean. Anyway please tell me what the cards say I'm not sure how much longer I can bear this!!!*

Her messages almost always started this way, right in the middle of a thought, like they were just carrying on a conversation and she was shouting through from another room. Carrie had clicked on the cards already, and Sam scrolled back over their message history to check her last few readings. She kept the book in a pocket of her bag at all times. It had cost thirty-five pounds and had to be bought as part of the training package – she'd been assured it would normally retail at fifty pounds, though. 'Impossible to do the job without it. Pays for itself within a week.' Somehow it was both 'the foremost reference source for tarot cards by the world's leading authority' and 'not available in shops'.

The Knave of Cups, a reversed Queen of Pentacles, and the bound female figure of the Eight of Swords.

Like clockwork, her fingers began flicking the pages, already knowing roughly where in the book each one would be found. These were all cards that Carrie had drawn before, too – and then there was orange, in the corner of her eye – a flash of red hair on a woman going round the corner, out of the window.

Sam felt as though she'd just been plunged into ice. Acute physical shock as the realization finally sank in, hours after she'd heard it. It wasn't Clio. Clio Campbell was dead. She'd stopped being in the world, removed herself from it. Clio Campbell no longer existed.

She found herself sinking low over the table in the café, as though someone was pressing gently down on her back. There was too much to think about. On her screen, Carrie's message was still flashing, agitated, awaiting instruction. She flicked past it, her fingers reaching out to call him before she'd even thought through what she was doing.

Dale answered on the second ring.

'Sam, Sam – everything all right, love? Has something happened to Elliot?'

'What? No, no, he's fine. Don't worry.'

'I just thought. Because he's at his football. Maybe an injury or something. That's good.'

'He's fine.'

'Yeah. So. What can I do for you?'

She took a second. Why was she calling again? Why was she doing this?

'Dale, she died. That woman. Clio.'

'Yeah, I know, love. I heard it a few months ago.'

'I've just found out.'

'Oh, right. I didn't want to mention it to you just in case – well, you might have been dealing with it in some way. I didn't know—Anyway. How you doing? How you taking it?'

'Doing a lot of thinking, Dale. Suddenly seeing everything kind of – kind of clearly for the first time but kind of, kind of like I'm really really far out from it all now. Does that make sense? That doesn't even make sense, does it. Fucking hell.'

'Nah, you're making sense just fine, Sam. You are.'

'Anyway. I think I might want to change some things. I think I need to take a serious look at some things. In a good way. Definitely in a good way. Listen – would you be up for coming round for dinner tonight? Elliot would love to see you. A treat. Know what I'm saying? I could do with it too.'

She could hear something unspoken in his silence. After what seemed like an hour and was probably only a few seconds, he coughed, made words.

'Ah. Yeah. No, tonight – tonight won't work, Sam. Sorry Me and Melissa was going to have a special dinner.'

Of course. Of course Melissa. She tried to breeze over it, cover herself.

'No worries. No worries at all. Short notice, innit.'

She felt him pulsing, conflicted, down the line. Was she imagining it? Was she?

'But maybe, maybe next week? I could come round one night next week, have dinner with the boy, see you both?'

'Sure! Sure. Great. Yeah. Just send me a text with a couple of good times.'

'Listen. Listen, love. You look after yourself now. Aight? You hearing me? We'll talk, OK? Next week. Soon.'

As the call ended, her phone buzzed anxiously. Three more messages from Carrie.

What do u mean??
Aare you there?!!!
Samatha?!?!

She breathed in. She turned to the screen, her thumbs blurring as she typed. So many of the words came almost automatically. She was regurgitating platitudes that had been served up to her in years of therapy, counselling and survivors' groups. They were words that hadn't ever quite touched her.

Carrie, what I'm seeing here is the cards sending you the same signals over and over again. I think you need to listen to them, to what they're saying. They're saying that you're using them as a crutch and you need to stop relying on them. You have to live for you, in your moment. You need to be able to make your own decisions without spending hundreds of pounds on an online psychic service, but, much bigger than that, you need to let go of your own issues first. You're holding on to a lot of anger, Carrie, and it's poisoning your every interaction with the outside world. It's stopping you from seeing the whole picture. It's time to work towards something else, Carrie. I don't want to see you on here again after today – all this money could be used much better in getting you some counselling. At least look into anger management. But you're free, Carrie. I free you.

Sam tucked five pounds under her saucer and got up. She left the book on the table, and on her way out of the door she deleted the app the tarot service used. She passed Spider and his buddies again as she walked under the arches and raised her fist in solidarity from her side of the road but didn't cross. She looked up, at the old warehouse, where it had all happened to another, younger person she could barely touch. And for a second she felt all the selves she'd been settling around her shoulders. Then she began to run, down the street and round the corner to the park where Elliot was still huffing his pudgy little body about after a ball he'd never catch.

'Come on, my darling!' she yelled, leaning over the fence and waving, half to embarrass him and half because she just wanted him to know that she was there, have someone acknowledge her. 'You can do it!'

NEIL
Edinburgh International Book Festival, August 2019

'The thing about "Rise Up", I've realized, was that it was brilliant because it was so cheerily vague about its message. A twenty-year-old's idea of politics; people gotta rise up, and then they do, and that will solve everything, ba ba doo doo dum.'

He chuckled; the audience chuckled back, a polite ripple under the canopy.

'Had Clio been less scrupulous or more savvy it would have been a perfect soundtrack for advertising jeans, or Pepsi. For all the explosive value her *Top of the Pops* appearance had at the time, the song itself contains nothing that will really challenge anyone's cosily held values.'

'Well, you know – maybe that's what makes it so evergreen,' said the moderator, a youngish, female music journalist he hadn't heard of before today, all red lips and big dark sexy spectacle frames. 'It meets a need for a protest song and people can put their own energy behind it.'

Neil grinned, waved a hand to skim over her seriousness, before it spoiled his punchline. 'Absolutely. So we can stick it to the man by downloading it again from iTunes.'

Again, that gently tickled chuckle across the tent, which was pleasingly full for the size of it. Later on, he knew, he would bring them to the verge of tears. His well-heeled, middle-aged audience, mostly comfortable former lefties, had all paid their £17.50 plus booking fee for his own unique insights into Clio's life. At least half of them would shortly also pay their £19.99 for the hardback with its lovely black and white shot of Clio's young face, only the lipstick coloured in red, his name embossed in gold across her shoulders. They'd happily queue for up to twenty minutes for his signature and their own tiny bit of time with him. This was his third book festival and seventh public read-ing on the tour. He knew the way it worked now. The sections that went down best as performances were always the ones drawn from his own experience; literary audiences tittered, thrilled at Deek's colour-ful language, and nodded knowingly at mentions of 'Gogsy' Duke and the poll tax protests. He heard his own voice slipping in and out of accents, a thickening in his throat as he described life on the scheme or imitated Danny Mansfield's bodyguard. It was a stark contrast to the assured, still-new cadence he used for answering questions, a ver-sion of his mother's phone voice from back in the day, although its confidence flowed from his absolute mastery of the topic rather than a sense of inferiority hastily covered.

His agent had got him a surprisingly good deal ('Given that you don't work for a national paper, this is pretty generous, yeah? I mean, they need it in four months max to cash in; publication on the anniversary of her death or the whole thing's off, so they're paying you to get writing *now*') and he'd been able to walk out of the newsroom having delivered his resignation right into Craig's close-shaven face, tight with the satisfaction of it. Perhaps there wasn't a lifelong career to be had in just being the world's foremost Clio Campbell expert, but it was certainly opening doors – he'd been asked back onto Radio 4 three times since the launch.

As he'd hoped when he'd taken that leap and made his audacious, brilliant pitch, a big-name publisher and the lunches they could buy had proved a far better passport than his previous, half-mumbled call-ing card. Shiv West, Justine Frischmann, Danny Mansfield, Edwyn Collins and both of the Proclaimers answered his emails personally, perhaps impressed, perhaps afraid of being misrepresented on a grand scale if they didn't reply. Even Za Flow, who had refused to make any other comment, gave his one and only interview to Clio's official biographer. Neil had spent time carefully courting him, met twice with him, touting his old-friend credentials, bringing photographs and mementos to prove himself.

'I want to let people understand the real Clio. The one we knew. The woman behind the headlines. There's something meaningful that needs to be said here – about mental health, about the place of women in the music business, about the amount that she suffered. And I want to do it before the bastards of the world get to have the final say on her. Know what I mean, man?'

'Yeah. Yeah, totally,' the rapper had replied, nodding, taking a sip of his drink. 'Nah, I feel you, man. I got a good feeling. I can trust you, innit. OK. I'm in. I'll do it.'

There had been whispers of other books being written, but Neil had already been there and spoken to everyone. He'd cared enough to put in the work, and he'd won the race. The publisher had insisted he call it *Rise Up: Clio Campbell in Public and Private*; his own suggested title (*The Northern Lass*) was far too provincial, they said. He'd felt aggrieved at the time (though in no position to argue with them), but as the book went into its second print run and continued to sell, he had to admit that they knew what they were doing.

His signing queues were often largely men like him. His people, the red lips on that cover summoning half-forgotten youthful lust. Then the women, the forties to sixties, Clio's contemporaries, still seeing themselves in her. Then a smattering of late teens and early twenty-somethings inspired by the tragic story they'd heard last year, by a newly discovered icon for their walls, their martyr, their rebel girl.

'I saw her onstage at the Iraq War protest.'

'Watching her on *Top of the Pops* changed my life.'

'I used to live round the corner from her. We never spoke, though.'

At each he'd smile sadly, check the spelling of their name, nod till they were done. Occasionally, if they were going on too long and the queue was getting restless, he'd cut them off by misting up, pat a hand, say, 'It really means so much to me, you know, to see how much she's still remembered. That what she did meant something to so many. Thank you for telling me this.'

Heard, validated, given her place in Clio Campbell's life story, the woman bustled off, hugging her copy of the book at chest height, beaming. He was aware of the next body shuffling into the space, reached out for the book, pen at the ready. There was no book. He looked up. A large young black woman, dressed too brightly to blend into the shabbily elegant festival crowd, was glaring at him.

'Hello. Don't you want me to sign anything?'

'No I do not, thank you. You not remember me then, Mr Munro?'

He was drawing a blank, and her voice was loud.

'Nancy. Nancy Okonkwo. We met at Clio's once, one of her dinners. You was drunk, though.'

He hadn't been to dinner more than twice at Clio's, but really had no memory of this woman at all.

'Nancy! Of course. Sorry – it's been a long day.'

'So I'm not going to hold these nice people up. But I wanted to come here and tell you myself that I think you should be ashamed of yourself.'

'I'm sorry?'

'Oh, you heard me. You know, when I first hear that someone was writing a book about Clio I thought yes. That's the right thing. Someone needs to tell the world about my girl, her whole life story. I heard you on the radio, I thought, well, he was a friend of hers. Not a very good friend, mind you, but he knows our Clio. Better than a stranger do it. He will tell it right. And then I read this nonsense –' she paused for a second to flick an impatient hand at the beautiful pyramid of books the shop assistant had created on his signing table '– and it make me so angry I almost ripped up a library book. What you thinking you doing here? With this? Really? You take a kind, honest woman who never did nothing in the world if it wasn't to fight for people in a worse situation than herself, and you make her a laughing stock? You hold her up on a stage, all the little private human things every person got going on with them, and you show them to the world? That's when you not making her whole life all about you, you know. Where's all the mention of her work – her real work? All those years of looking out for the little guy, trying to make a difference? No, you just write about all her ex-boyfriends and laugh at her politics with your rich friends.'

Neil was very, very aware of the eyes of the queue on them. He coughed slightly, to buy himself time, thought fast.

'I'm really sorry the book wasn't to your liking. We all have our different memories of Clio, and these are mine, built up over thirty years of friendship – before you were even born, I suspect. Human beings are such multifaceted things, aren't we – two people can have completely different pictures of the same woman very easily. Just because you don't recognize the woman that I knew and loved, please don't invalidate my memories of her. And how could something as small and flimsy as a book manage to encapsulate the whole of a person's life, especially a life like Clio's, lived so big and brightly?'

She was still glaring, but she didn't interrupt him again. He reached out the hand that didn't hold the pen towards her, being careful not to touch.

'We both miss her hugely, don't we. I think that's pretty clear. I do need to give a bit more time to these people now –' he gesticulated at the queue, which had morphed into a goggling mob around her shoulders '– but I would really like it if you and I could meet up and chat about our memories of Clio later on – are you in town for long? Are you based in Glasgow? Here's my number – I'd love to listen to everything you've got to say. I'll take it on board, I promise; perhaps we could find some common ground about such a brilliant woman eventually?'

He wrote down the numbers quickly on a receipt someone had left on the table, substituted a seven for the final eight at the last second. The bookshop assistants he had summoned with his frantic eye signals hovered nearby, walked her gently out without causing any more of a scene. Neil breathed, took a sip from the glass of wine the publicist had put on the table for him, looked up at the man in the leather jacket who was next in the queue.

'Well,' he said. 'She was some woman, and she's still got the power to make passions run high, eh?' He reached for the book, already open at the title page, and the man in the leather jacket echoed his chuckle.

HAMZA
London, 2018–19

He wished, many many times, he'd never told Gemma about the break-up with Clio.

'A curse?' Gemma had said. 'She actually put a curse on you? With her period blood?'

'Nah. Come on, man, I don't believe in all that. It was just fucking weird was what it was.'

'Mm. Dunno, babe. My grandma would believe in all that. S'a Congolese thing.'

'Yeah well, Clio ain't Congolese. She's a pissed-off middle-aged woman from Scotland who just got dumped, that's all.'

He thought that was an end to it. He himself had completely forgotten it all. And then, seven years later, three days after Clio died, he'd been sleeping on Calvin's couch when the phone tucked under the pillow blared at him, startling him into the morning light. It was difficult to make out what Gemma was saying at first, through the tears, the shuddering snotty breath. She'd taken Snoop out at six in the morning for his usual walk, the streets quiet, the same route they always took. Suddenly he'd broken his lead and run across the road ('like he was possessed or something') just at the point a speeding red sports car had rounded the corner.

'And – and – and I was thinking, I was thinking, babe, what if this is Clio? What if it's her curse? Finally happening, now that she's dead?'

He got an Uber straight back home, wrapped his arms round her, told her over and over, there's no curse, there's no such thing as curses. They mourned their dog together, their previous divisions evaporated, any confusion he was feeling over Clio lost under this more immediate, more pressing grief. Gemma had got pregnant almost immediately afterwards, through two different modes of contraception, as though the huge wave of emotion Snoop left behind him had demanded something to fill it. Two weeks after they'd done the test and before they'd been able to let him know, Hamza's father had a sudden heart attack, just sitting there at the breakfast table, unable to get his last words out to his wife.

Gemma kept herself small and quiet during this time, and Hamza tried, awkwardly, when he remembered, not to shutter himself off from her. She was paranoid about the baby from the start, wouldn't let him fuck her even when all he needed was just to stretch out into his woman and roar and sublimate some of this loss into something physical. Nothing seemed calm any more, nothing he knew was the same. The dog's basket still sat there in the hallway, its emptiness eyeing him sadly whenever he tried to leave the house.

Eventually, Gemma broke. He came in from his mum's one afternoon to find her in tears at the table, having just been made redundant.

'They can't do that to a pregnant woman!'

'Yeah, but they don't know I'm pregnant, do they? Wasn't going to tell them for three weeks yet.'

'Fucksake, man. Who the hell is doing this to us?'

'Listen, Za. Bear with me here. What if – what if Clio did curse us? What if there's something in that after all?'

'Gem. Come on. What, she just leaves us alone for seven years then only comes after us once she's dead?'

'She maybe didn't have the power till she became a spirit. I spoke to my grandma, Za. That's what she reckons. Oh God, listen to me. I know, I know it's stupid. I – just – everyone keeps dying, everything keeps going wrong, and I'm so, so scared for my baby.'

This time he didn't feel able to hush her, and comfort her, because he no longer knew which way the world worked. Could it be he'd angered Clio with his tribute, going public, taking away from her death? How would she know? She's dead, man, he told himself. But there was something he just couldn't let go, now.

'Calvin, you believe in ghosts? Like, that they could haunt you?'

Calvin shook his head, slowly, his stoned eyes stretching in his face.

'Never used to, but I knew a gal who was convinced she was being chased by an evil spirit, mate. She said it needed to be appeased, like with sacrifices an stuff. Terrible things happening to her till she did. Not something you want to mess with, innit?'

Appeasement. That's why he'd spoken to that little Scottish journalist guy, when he came knocking. If his name could help an old friend of Clio's get a book telling her true story published, that was a good thing, wasn't it? In the interview he was only complimentary, allowed his own history to be rewritten, on the record, as he nodded along when the journalist suggested that it was Clio who'd made him political, had made him into a better musician. He bit his fingers and let it happen. Anything just to get her off their back.

The baby was small. Had stopped growing. They needed to get her out early. Gemma had been a ball of tension for eight months, constantly knotting her fingers together, skinny and wrecked except for the fucking huge bump, swelling out of her like a parasite, sucking away at everything that had made her her. Locked in a toilet cubicle for two minutes while they readied her for theatre, Hamza pulled the seat down and curled himself up, knees tucked to his chin, his breath between his knees as he spoke.

'Right. Listen, Clee. I can't do this no more. I'm sorry. I'm sorry for everything. Yes, I used you. I strung you along. All that. I understand you would want to take your revenge. And you have. It's worked. The last nine months has been hellish, man. Fucking worst. I was a cocky little shit and I needed to feel all that. But you's dead now, man. You've got to let us be. Please. Let this baby be all right. Let Gemma just have the baby, and I will – I'll write a song about you. I'll never let them forget what you did. I'll be singing your name always.'

Someone else came into the toilets, coughing ostentatiously to warn of his presence. Hamza didn't care.

'Fuck, man. Know what? I could really do with you to talk to right now, like, I mean the real you. Not this witchy ghost thing I'm making up in my head. My proper Clio queen, right here, because you went through this shit all the time, dint you? You knew your brain when it was being paranoid. You'd be able to sort out my head for me. You'd be able to tell me straight, listen mate, here's what you're going through. Here's how much of it is all in your head; ain't no such thing as ghosts if you don't want there to be.'

The other guy finished pissing, fled the room without even washing his hands.

'I miss you, Clee. I've been missing you for years and not realized it. Look, if you're going to curse me, curse me. But don't let it touch a baby. Don't hurt anyone else. That ain't you, to hurt people. That's the opposite of what you was. Please. Begging you.'

He stopped, breathed in. He needed to get back to Gemma. As he uncurled his legs, wincing a bit, there was a shift in the toilet block. A higher-pitched noise in the air. Something electrical, buzzing, but not bad. Probably just a light, or the air con. Probably. But Hamza blew her a kiss anyway.

2019

They started recording 'Warrior Queen' a year and a half after she'd died. To the day, Hamza realized, checking his calendar as he smoked outside the studio, wanting to greet all of the musicians himself as they arrived. There had already been some good buzz online, thanks to Gemma sprinkling a bit of magic from her still-hot contacts book.

Za Flow going back into the studio after three years

Will fatherhood have softened grime's political firecracker?

Za Flow's new album rumoured to contain tribute to ex-girlfriend Clio Campbell

Clio's Uncle Donald wasn't well enough to come down, but he'd hooked Hamza up with all the people he needed to know, and posted a fat parcel of scored notes, a rearrangement of a song by Robert Burns Hamza hadn't heard before, called 'Bonnie Jean'. Hamza used the first three verses, had a couple of the folk-musician guys from Scotland improvise around them, then worked out a bridge to take it to his own lyrics.

Shiv West had come in on the third day, flown down at his own expense for maybe an hour's recording. She'd not spoken much but fuck, man, she'd delivered on that song. Years of pain and smoke in her voice as she sang, almost like having Clio back there herself.

There was a lass and she was fair,
At kirk or market to be seen;
When a' our fairest maids were met,
The fairest maid was bonnie Jean.

And ay she wrought her Mammie's wark,
And ay she sang sae merrilie;

The blythest bird upon the bush
Had ne'er a lighter heart than she.

But hawks will rob the tender joys
That bless the little lintwhite's nest;
And frost will blight the fairest flowers,
And love will break the soundest rest.

RUTH
Glasgow, 2020

The film was one Alison had chosen. It was a documentary, about free-diving, about men who purposefully slowed down their heart rates and repressed the instinct to breathe in order to push themselves deeper and deeper into the ocean; the sort of thing Alison liked to experience voyeuristically but would never dream of doing in real life. Ruth was curled into her shoulder on their new sofa in their new house, picking at her nails, only half-watching at first.

This man, the one they made a film about. He could have been James Bond, played by Alain Delon or a young Richard Burton. He had that reckless loner glamour that men loved in other men. He was committed to the ocean; it was his passion, his one true love. His friends, now old men, their ears full of hair, giggled that he had a girl in every port; the daughter he abandoned blinked back tears as she said she missed her papa growing up but understood that he had a higher calling.

Alison's body tensed obligingly as the tiny silhouetted body plunged down and down and down into the blue, as the strings on the soundtrack tightened.

The man was filmed at Japanese temples, learning meditation in order to better slow his heartbeat, control his fleshliness. The girls came and went. His friends who lived near the ocean said he would come and stay with them for months at a time while planning a dive, that he never contributed to expenses but that was just his way. They seemed honoured to have assisted with his plan. In sexy honey-rust voiceover, the actor who played him in that big-budget movie in the Eighties read out the man's writing. He wanted to be more like a dolphin. He believed human beings were capable of transcending their physical limitations; he also believed nature would have been better off without us.

The man killed himself in his seventies, alone in the house he'd built, on a cliff, on an island. Loneliness, explained his friends, his daughter. Her voice broke. That great noble sacrifice he'd made to the ocean had come at a cost. But his legacy lived on – they had started a school to teach other people his techniques. Young women who'd idolized him as children swam on underwater cameras, mermaid-free with their hair streaming out behind them.

Alison and Ruth both had tears in their eyes at the end, for different reasons. Ruth excused herself to the kitchen, dug her nails into her palms. Because it's different for men, she whispered, as the cat twisted at her feet. It's always, always different for men.

DONALD
Isle of Skye, 2020

'Well. This is the place. Here we are.'

'That must be it up there on the dune, then? Looks new. Here, man, take my arm.'

'Away, Andy, I'll be fine. It's not far. And I'd rather do this by myself. I'll get you at the car – better you stay in there where it's warm, anyway.'

The wind was sharp on the beach today, bleakly crested waves snapping at the shore. In order to get up to the dune from the small car park, Donald needed to ford a rocky stream cutting down the wet sand. He stumbled, almost dropped his stick, turned back to wave to Morna's anxious son to let him know everything was all right. The dune was footery to climb, although he got purchase on a couple of clumps of grass, managed to haul himself up. There it was, the bench, pale wood and its brass plaque. Just as the pictures he'd ordered from the Internet had promised.

IN MEMORY OF
CLIODHNA CAMPBELL,
AND HER FATHER
MALCOLM CAMPBELL.

THEY WERE HAPPY TOGETHER
ON THIS BEACH ONCE.

He turned round to seat himself down on it, was seized by a momentary panic that he'd got the wrong place. Had it been here, after all? Could it have been two or three coves along? He stared out to the horizon point, strained his eyes for America just like they'd done as young men. No, here was the place. He remembered that rocky stream, of course he did. He looked all around him, tried to conjure up the two figures down by the shore, himself running towards them. The skinny naked man drawn to the sea, the slender toddler eating sand, their red hair blowing into the same sunstruck clouds. Yes, yes, here it had been.

The ancient shrugging mountains watched the old man on the new bench, didn't care.

EILEEN
Glendale Retirement Home, Ayr, 2018

I was black affronted, honest I was, though. Naebody told me I'd hae a visitor. I had to leave her sitting while I went to get my hair on. I'd been in my housecoat. My housecoat! See these wans, these ither wans that sit around here the whole day in their housecoats, you know I'm not like them, hen. You know. Nice wummin, anyway. Big. Tall. Great big rosy cheeks like a butcher. Visitor. There was news she came with but I can't mind it. She didnae mind waiting. Not like some of them'll push you and pull you and say Eileen, Eileen and it's Mrs McIvor, actually. Mrs Campbell-that-was before that bad bastard. Mrs Campbell-that-was. A long time ago now. Bad blood, the Campbells. Bad blood will out, that's what they said. Of course ye don't think of that when you're a wee lassie, do you, when he's all charming you. You don't think he's going to be drinking your wage packet and marching you around the islands and you with a baby. No, you sit down, lassie. You work hard. You sit down while I have my tea and don't you mind some of them. Aye, hard workers, that's whit makes it happen. That's why when you find yourself with a man that drinks your wage packet, you get yourself out of there. I was laughing with oor Senga's girl about it. No I'd not met her before, well I might have. Was she oor Senga's lassie, maybe? The height. She could be. Some colour on her. Big rosy cheeks. Oor Senga wasny stocky, though, no like this wan. Whit was I saying, oh that's right, that he was that lazy, her father, that he never, well, my daddy told me not to marry him, right enough. He just wisnae like the men in my family, though, and that was exciting, right enough. When you're twenty-two and stupit.

Here, you! That's my biscuit. No, I've seen you. I've seen you take wan already. That wan's mine. You can git tae is what you can do, ya cheeky besom.

She's all jealous because I had a visitor today. Did I tell you about my visitor, hen? I did. Oh right. Nice to have a visitor. Well, he was a musician so that was his excuse. Had a bonny voice on him. Her father. She was talking to me. That's why I've got my hair on – it's important to put your best face on. Even in this place. I always like to put my best face on. Not like that thing over there just sitting there. Wan of the nurses gets the panstick special for me and it all comes out of my savings. I saved well, I did. I'm not taking anything off the government except my pension and I paid for that. If you start taking things off them they start thinking of you as a drain, that's what my daddy always said. Or he said before. Alec couldny help it when they closed the pits, though, him and my brother. My poor brother. My poor brother.

No, no you sit here and we'll get a nice chat, hen. I think there was something important, somewan told me today, and I think I need to remember it and maybe I'm supposed to tell somewan. That wee bad bitch, so she is. No, not you. That's my girl. My girl. His girl, more and more. Always his girl. Could tell it in the hair. Not a bit of me about her, not really. I'd thought I'd given her principle. I thought I'd taken her away and given her principles and morals, but I took her too late. Took her away too late and he'd spoiled her. Maybe it was always going to be that way. Bad seed. Campbell rottenness. Islander blood. Lazy. You just always want the best for your children, don't you? You always want the best and you work that hard and you can't tell what's going to come of them. But I'd really thought coming home would do it for her. I did think that, hen, I did.

Aye aye, I'm fine. I am fine. Crying? Am I – I am crying! Well, would ye look at that. I don't know why. I'm no a silly old wummin yet, I'm sure I'm no. Have you seen my legs, hen? Look at these legs. These are not the legs of a wummin of fifty-five! Aye, fifty-five. Are ye sure? Wait.

No, I couldnae be fifty-five, you're right. That was the year I was running the union even though they were trying tae get me to retire. No, I wisnae for retiring, me. I didnae retire until sixty-six. I worked all my days till sixty-six. And then it was that thing. What's that thing that I've got? You know the wan.

Oor Senga's lassie was looking nice, though. I thought she'd maybe had trouble with her man, but she says she doesn't have a man, so I don't know where I got that from. She says she never had any weans but oor Senga was aye banging on about her grandkids so I don't think she knew whit she was oan about there. She was visiting me, to tell me. Oh, to tell me something. It probably doesnae matter. The thing that matters is I had a visitor and nane of youse did. My daughter never visits me any more because she's a worthless bitch. Oh she is. She just messed aboot. Oh, she did some singing, she lost that lovely husband – she had such a handsome man, so she did. Mind you, the handsome wans aren't everything, that I know. What's your man like, hen, is he handsome? I had two of them, two husbands, and the first wan was handsome but he couldn't have been more useless. He left me with a bad bitch of a baby and when she got to grow tits she was a slut and a scab, and she brought shame on oor family name. And Alec, that was my second husband, he sent her oot and quite right too. If we'd no, the whole village would've rounded on us. They still wrote it on the hoose, SCAB HOOR, even though they apologized wance we'd got rid of her. And she would tell me in that café – we would meet in a café in Ayr every year for my birthday, because she couldnae come home, of course not. So I got the train into Ayr so Alec didnae know and she got the train in from Glasgow – Glasgow of all places. Whit was my lassie daein in a place like Glasgow. Have you been to Glasgow, hen? It's noisy and it smells. Still, it was the men were her weakness, my girl. Always. Aye. Because she was that braw, don't get me wrong. She took after her daddy. And I took efter mine, that's how I've goat coal miner's arms, eh no? Ha! It's a joke, hen. It's a joke.

Whit was I talking aboot there? Was it oor Senga? Oor Senga never came to that café, so why would I be talking about oor Senga? It was wan of they fancy Italian cafés with a coffee machine, and she'd aye buy me a wee frothy coffee, that was my birthday treat. Oh, she was bonny, my girl. She was a bonny lassie. I mean, when I think aboot it noo, she maybe couldnae help it. I mean, the men were always staring, right from when she got tits, that young, and I'd shout at them in the street tae get tae, I'd take her hand, my girl. But naw. She knew. She knew, that lassie. She knew there were lines you didnae cross, eh, and she went with him anyway. Out of whit? Just out of badness was it maybe? Oh she's a bad bitch, right enough.

And she left me all alone. She left me here and me no husband, no grandweans, no family eftir my poor, poor brother, eftir oor Senga. Just her and she left me here. Ah've never seen her. Just at Christmas, and I told her, I said you're a bad bitch and you never visit me. Was that this Christmas, hen? I know there was a tree. I know that. Dae we have a tree in here? This lassie today, she was tall and I don't remember seeing her before but she must be family, I was thinking. She said something aboot a funeral and I was trying to tell her it's OK, we buried your mammy years ago. It was a nice service we had for oor Senga. Much nicer than the wan for Peter. Oh, poor poor Peter. Did you ever hear whit happened to oor Peter, did I tell you? He just threw himself into the pit. Afore they had time to put the concrete in. Well, he'd no work for years, neither he had, and the weans needed the money. But the church didnae want to give him a burial, so me and his Annie we ended up in this crematorium in Ayr where they wouldn't let us bury him because you had to pay extra and the scandal was just clinging to us then, so Annie didnae know whit to do. She couldnae bury his ashes in the garden because the cooncil might move her on.

Poor Annie. I've not seen Annie in a while. I wonder how she's keepin. Oh now, wait. Did Annie not top herself too? No, who was it, then?

What am I thinking of suicides for, what was I sayin? No no, hen, there's something important, I'm sure of it. You need to sit here. You hold my hand. She's fine here, sister. She's just keeping me company which is more than my bad-bitch girl would do. Ooh do you not just hate that wan? Sister. Does she not just strike you as somewan who thinks her shit doesnae stink, eh? She's no that young, sister isnae. Wantae watch yourself, sister, or you might end up in here with only oor Senga's lassie to visit you.

I tried to call the girl after my mam. Wee Jean, she was supposed to be. Her father said it was a boring name, and I was that knocked out after the birth I didnae argue. He gied her the name Cliodhna, if you please! There's a name that thinks its shit doesnae stink, eh? Stupit. When we got back home I cried her Jean. Jeannie Johnstone, my family name. She wouldnae take poor Alec's name even though he was a better father to that ungrateful besom than she deserved. Och, the men. They're easy enough to work, if you know how. I knew how, and that girl of mine she sure did, oh, I'll tell you that. But she never got the measure of them, eh. She was always letting them get away, take it too far.

He was a handsome wan, right enough. That wan she went with. We watched them all coming in in the trucks, all of us women, and we had the vegetables ready to throw, and I have to say all of us noticed it. It was like sunlight was shining off of him, that boy, that English boy with the blond hair. You get a feeling – oh aye, you know whit Ah mean, hen! You know whit! How could a boy be that beautiful, a boy? I didnae want to let on, didnae want them to guess, so I worked up a big greener in the back of my throat, hit him right in that beautiful face. I watched it dripping off him, off his cheekbone, my spit. Bloody scab. Bloody damn scab.

It was that feeling got me intae trouble in the first place, with her father. They were the same type. Nae moral fibre, nae nothing there.

Oh, it's fine to be able to turn a lovely tune, so it is, to make people dance, but no when it's your wife's wages are putting dinner on the table and you're drinking yourself stupit with your beardy pals, with a baby crying, with a rich American woman winding her fingers in your hair. Oh aye. They just mince about daein whit they fancy, and it's left to the likes of you and me to feed them. There were the clues that my lassie was goingty turn oot like her daddy but I didnae mind them like I should've. She didnae get a job, she wantit to stay on at the school, she would go into the toon on a weekend and spend poor Alec's and my money on lipsticks, do you know, money she lifted from the savings jar. Lipsticks and records and fancy coffees, the bad bitch. It was boys bought her fancy coffees, probably. I'd like a bitty more tea, this wan's gone cold. Aye, there we go. I will drink it. I am drinking it.

Oh aye, there'll be naebody smiling on oor Senga's lassie, right enough. Nice lassie but no braw. Still, you take pride in the beauties, you tease oot their hair before you send them off to school, you buy them ribbons and then what happens, eh? You've raised a wee hoor with no morals. If I had my time over again I would've spoiled those looks of hers somehow. She had brains, my girl did. She could've done something. Because she's a woman grown now and what has she got tae show? No man, no job, no hoose, no weans. Too late for aw of that now. I said that to her, I did, we were sitting beside the Christmas tree because those lights kept flashing on and off – see, I still remember things, hen. That's just the same as what happened to her daddy, I told her, drank himself to death eftir all his fine girls left him, eftir that American bitch sent him packing. And there he was, fifty and nothing. Just like my girl. It was near Christmas. It's her birthday just eftir. She was fifty, she'll be fifty-one. Naw, how old is she now? That canny be right. That wee thing fifty. She never looks her age. She got that from me because her daddy was ruined at the end. I've never looked my age either. Folk aye thought I was a teenager when I was thirty! Somewan thought I was Alec's daughter wance, in a bar! Me! No a bad wee trick to have up your sleeve, because sometimes it's harder to keep yourself looking nice, you know? When you haven't got the money for it. Mind you, I'd always keep us respectable, me and her. Not like her father wearing holes in all his elbows. It was when we would meet in that wee Italian café where the waiters were all a bit racy, you know, and I'd sometimes just ask her right out, what on earth are you wearing? Rags? I raised you to have self-respect, I'd tell her. I mean, I was always proud that she kept her lipstick up. Aye, she got that from me. She was always bonny, my girl. But och, no, I couldny be doing with her clothes. I was affronted somewan might see us together – well, it was all right eftir Alec died, I suppose. Naebody left to care then. But she never came home. I suppose she won't now, that's what oor Senga's lassie says.

That's what.

That's what.

Naw, that can't be right either. That's no right.

Naw.

Oor Senga's lassie would look so much better with a wee doddy lipstick, really. There's all that colour in her face, she needs to pull it somewhere. A nice red lipstick like my girl wears, maybe a wee bit more to the purple to even oot they big red cheeks. I told her that. She said she'd wear some at the funeral.

Well.

All alone, I told her. You've left me all alone. I told her that I'm telling everyone – I tell the doctor, when he comes in here. I tell him my daughter never comes to visit me. Aye well, she should hear it, so she should. She was quiet on her birthday – usually she'd shout back at me. Ach well, whit wummin wants to turn fifty, eh? Funny to think of my girl fifty. Getting the flushes. Not a chance of a baby now, eh no. I gave up on that a long time ago. All the time others spent messing aboot wi grandchildren they're too auld to care for, I wis general sec-retary of the local Labour Party! Aye. I kept the whole thing ticking. Elected three cooncillors. Ye might as well be putting something back into the community. Do you know, they took a vote as to whether they were goingty throw me and Alec oot, eftir what she did? They did. Oh, there's no shame like it, there really isn't. Because they're all looking at you, too. Every time you're down the shops. I couldn't show my face at the picket any more because they'd all turn their backs on me. We stopped drinking at the Labour Club for a while. That's whit she never got, that bad bitch. She never worked oot the way her actions hurt her mammy. Thoughtless, the pair of them. He never realized that if you drink that money, we cannae buy food for the baby. If you run off with some American tart, you dinnae get to see your daughter. Aye. Consequences. Aye, dinnae love a dreamer, hen. You take my advice. And it just goes to show you, doesn't it? I thought I'd got her away from his nonsense early enough, but it was in that blood. Changing her name, didn't matter. Teaching her whit's right, didn't matter. Bringing her up in a community with values, and she'd just turn her back on all that and betray them. It had all just died down, although I don't think my poor Alec's heart ever recovered, and then she got herself on the telly, and it was all happening again. And nobody had the work by then so they just blamed my girl for it. Poll tax! Who was she to go on the telly singing aboot the poll tax? She was on the telly singing aboot solidarity. The hoor. Somewan left a burning jobbie on oor doorstep, and the front windae got broken.

I thought you'd be pleased, she says to me, when we were in that wee café in Ayr. She was aye saying that. She'd tell me all these things that she was doing, always something different every year, could never settle down, that wan. And she aye said it like she was back at school, showing me a shitey picture, you know the sort of thing that weans do, bless them, like she was wanting me to be proud of her. Proud! Of whit? Of her in that big bloody rabble that were on the telly marching in London, with tattoos and those scaffy black boots? I saw them. We had a word for folk like that when I was growing up, hen. Naw, she never got that it wisnae aboot the action you took. It wis aboot why ye did it. We did it because we were a community and they were ripping oot oor heart, and we had tae fight them. We did it because

ordinary working folk aw over the country were being put oot their
jobs they'd had all their lives, their hooses. Her, she just floated. I told
her that, under that Christmas tree, I said you just drift aboot, don't
you? She meant nothing more than a wee bitty thistledown, my girl
did, at the end of the day. Oh, she would always have these causes,
she'd tell me, these issues, these things that had to be fought, but I
would be trying to say to her, what do they mean to you, eh hen,
really? I'm doing what's right, Mum, she'd say. And do you know whit,
oan her last birthday I'd finally had enough of it. This nonsense. I said,
aye, could have done with you daein whit wis right when you were sixteen, missy. Bit late noo, noo you've wasted your life, is it not? Because
I could see she was trying. The lassie wis trying. But we couldny have
her in the house again. No eftir.

Oh ho ho, it wis a fine procession, let me tell you, hen. Dod Mackay
and his bony-necked wife heading it up, all the wee nosy buggers from
around the street. Wummin I'd stood with on the picket just the day
before, hissing at me. Because it was me they blamed. All of them.
Because I'd lived away, because I'd opened my legs and brought this
bad blood back home. And Dod clears his throat and he calls me Mrs
McIvor, no Eileen like he'd cried me every day of oor lives, Mrs McIvor.
We have reason to believe your daughter is fraternizing with the scabs
at the barracks. Talking like he's a police officer or something. And oor
Alec comes to the door and he's saying, Dod man, whit are ye talking
aboot? And Dod's bitch of a wife opens her mooth and screams at me,
looking that pleased with herself, aye, she's away up there just noo.
I saw her. Walking up the road kissing that big blond yin. Probably
letting them all get it up her, so she is.

Here's whit I said that would cost me, really. I said, don't you dare
talk aboot my daughter like that, you common bitch. I said, don't you
dare. And I would've went for her but for Alec holding my arms back.
Aye, that bit of loyalty, that's what did it for me. Funny, eh. And Dod's
saying to Alec, you need to sort this oot, pal. You need that girl telt or
the whole town'll tell her.

Dod loaned us his car so we could drive up there and get her before the rest of them did. He was always all right wis Dod, shame aboot that arse ay a wife ay his. The barracks wis aboot half an hour away, so who knows what Brenda Mackay was doing up that way, oh wait, did her brother not work the farm up there? Aye, that was maybe it, hen, that was maybe it. Alec walks right up and bangs on the door and marches in. They were all English, all young boys, I remember that. Probably no that much older than her. They'd have to be, really, to come up there. All away from their own mammies. They'd have to be young to not understand why they shouldn't. Alec was shouting which of you scab bastards has got my daughter here, and that wis the last time he'd call her that, right enough. And one of them goes to him, calm down mate, in that funny flat accent they've got, and he wheels on him, he says I am not and will never be your mate.

They were in a barn oot the back, like a pair ay animals. Alec hauled him off, the blond one, off the top of her. I minded my spit running doon his cheek and I felt glad. I hoped it wis hot when it hit him. She wis naked apart from her slip, round her waist, and I marched up and got her by the ear. I told her to cover herself and we got her into the back of Dod's car still barefoot, covered her with the tartan rug in there to get her back into the hoose. Scab hoor, I wis muttering, and when we got there, that's what they'd painted on the wall. Aye, I said those things to my own daughter, hen, and I don't regret it. She wis. She did that. They were chucking things at her as we walked her back into the hoose, they were swearing. My ain folk, folk I'd known aw my life.

Alec couldnae even look at her. I want her oot ma hoose, he said, and he went away and locked himself in the toilet. Me and her, we went up to her room. I brought her a binbag because it was aw we had, and I told her she'd better put her things in it. She was crying, breathing like an asthma attack, and she looked like wan of her daddy's Highland Marys under that rug. Mammy, she says to me. Mammy please.

I'm no made of stone, hen. I'm no. That wis still my girl there, in front of me. But whit could I dae? She couldny stay with us, no now. And who in the town would take her in? Nobody. What aboot ma Highers, she's saying, whit aboot the school? And I'm saying, you'd no get through a day alive at the school eftir this, baby. She went to get into my arms for a bit cuddle there but I couldny do it. I stepped back. Why did you dae it, my girl? I asked her. She says, because I felt sorry for him, Mammy. They're all so lonely. They're all so scared. Load a shite if you ask me. She saw something she fancied so she went for it. Didnae think. That's what. That's what.

What will I do, Mammy? she's asking me. I said at first why don't you see if your fine boyfriend will take you down tae England? They might have you there! But she needed my help, still, despite whit she'd done. So I took her to the train station – it was hard getting her oot the door, right enough, some of the younger wans started pushing the car about while I was trying to start it. The girl was crying oot their names – she was at school with some of them. Charlie, she was crying. Davy. Dinnae. Dinnae.

When we got to the train station she was calmer. She was holding the neck of her binbag tight. I never liked that place, she told me. Aye, I said, well it knows that noo, doesn't it? There'll be trains to Ayr coming, my girl. Your best bet is to get as far as possible, then choose a town, look for work in a hotel. You'll need to scrub floors now. And I pulled the jar out of my bag, the savings jar. That's yours and Alec's money, she said. Aye, I said, but you're going to need it more than us, hen. Well, I was wrong there. Oor Alec never got another job eftir the mines and I ended up with another wan living off me, although at least it wisnae his fault. The cough finished him off in the end, so it did. It got most of them that way, no compensation either. Oh, I've seen a lotty people die, hen, and I bet I'm no as old as most of them in here. No as old as that wan, anyway. State of her. You've got dribble on your face, dear! Dribble! Goan wipe her mouth, hen, it's making me sick to look at her.

I took a wee bit of her hair in my finger, but I didnae touch her, and she got oot the car and went to the platform. She didnae wave, and I didnae see my girl again till she was – whit, twenty-five? Twenty-seven? She wrote me a letter. Alec found it but he didnae say anything. I couldny talk aboot her again, in the hoose, or in the town. I wis allowed to stay as long as I didnae mention my girl. And where else would I have gone? Back up to Inverness? Back to the islands, to her father's snooty Wee Free sister? Naw, I wasn't having that thrawn wee besom take my life away from me. No my home.

Where's your home, hen? Is it far from here? Is it bonny? My home's no bonny. I don't know that I'll ever see it again, anyway. Not unless my girl takes me away. She might be all right, to go back there noo. Those wans she was at school with, they might still remember though, aye, maybe we should just leave it. It's better if she doesny exist, so it is. No, no, you need to stay here till I mind of it, what it is, the thing. I'll need to get my nails done, I know that much. I'll maybe need the hairdresser in. I've got the money, you just ask sister. It's a big thing, hen, a big thing I've got coming up. Did you see I had a visitor earlier? She knows all aboot it. She had something she had to tell me, but it couldny be right. She's going to come and pick me up, though – that was it, hen, I've minded now. She's going to come and pick me up in a week. We're goingty go out then for the funeral and it'll be fine, so I'll need my hair done. I'll need my hair done for that.

ACKNOWLEDGEMENTS

A novel is a group effort, as one of my favourite people always says. This one wouldn't have been possible without the effort of a pretty wonderful group, all of whom deserve thanks:

- Bekah Mackenzie, Caitrin Armstrong and Ellie Shaw, for decades of friendship in general and support and encouragement on this book in particular
- Simon Sylvester, Rachel McCrum and Lisa Brideau, for very useful early feedback
- Catriona Duffy, for politicizing Clio's lipstick
- Jen Dolan, for organizing Adele's ward
- Gemma Cossins and Rhiannon Handslip, who found a home for Hamza
- Gillian Steel and Rowena Goalby, for lending me space to write in
- Charlene Boyd, Kate Robertson, Outi Smith, Irene Bissett and Bridget Innes, for childcare, without which writing would and could not have happened
- Sarah-Jane Forder, for a thorough and thoughtful copy-edit
- Jordan Mulligan at 4th Estate, for being the most passionate advocate a long and unwieldy political novel with multiple narrators could ever hope for
- Charlie Brotherstone, for continuing to believe in me over many years
- and Alan Bissett, for understanding, loving, fact-checking my knowledge of 1980s blue-eyed soul, letting me bounce ideas off him, and working so very, very hard to earn money for both of us so that I could finish this book in time before our second baby was born. This one's always for you, fella.